RIPTIDE RUMORS

Center Point
Large Print

Also by Melody Carlson and available from
Center Point Large Print:

I'll Be Seeing You
As Time Goes By
We'll Meet Again
Harbor Secrets

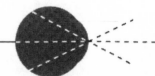

**This Large Print Book carries the
Seal of Approval of N.A.V.H.**

THE LEGACY OF SUNSET COVE

RIPTIDE RUMORS

BOOK TWO

MELODY CARLSON

CENTER POINT LARGE PRINT
THORNDIKE, MAINE

This Center Point Large Print edition
is published in the year 2020 by arrangement with
WhiteFire Publishing.

This is a work of fiction. All characters and events
portrayed in this novel are either fictitious
or used fictitiously.

The text of this Large Print edition is unabridged.
In other aspects, this book may vary
from the original edition.
Printed in the United States of America
on permanent paper.
Set in 16-point Times New Roman type.

ISBN: 978-1-64358-601-4

The Library of Congress has cataloged this record under
Library of Congress Control Number: 2020930501

CHAPTER 1

Mid-September 1916

Anna McDowell felt slightly sickened as she hung up the telephone. For the past few weeks, life had grown relatively peaceful in Sunset Cove. Most folks in town had begun to breathe easier, and as editor in chief of the *Sunset Times*, Anna had focused most of the news stories on the upcoming election. But everything changed in the course of one phone call.

"What's wrong?" Virginia, the longtime receptionist, looked over the tops of her glasses, studying Anna curiously. "What did Chief Rollins have to say?"

"Bad news." Anna glumly shook her head. "Albert Krauss broke out of the county jail early this morning. Rather, he was *broken* out. Apparently he had help."

"Oh dear." The older receptionist frowned as she set the morning mail on Anna's desk. "Mrs. Krauss must be on pins and needles."

"He's already informed Clara and sent police protection. He feels it's possible that Albert could return to Sunset Cove."

"Poor Mrs. Krauss." Virginia's brows arched. "What about the Krauss boy? Did he escape with his no-account father?"

"No, thank goodness. That would've been disastrous. AJ's trial is next month, and he's been cooperating with his legal counsel. And Randall feels hopeful he can get a reduced sentence. But not if AJ escapes."

"Who do you think helped Mr. Krauss?"

"The chief suspects some of the rumrunners are behind it."

"That seems pretty risky, busting him out like that. You'd think they'd be worried about getting caught themselves."

"That might've been their motivation." Anna picked up a pencil and spun it between her fingers as her mind started to spin a story. "I suspect Albert's buddies were worried he might talk. Might turn over state's evidence against them."

"Aha." Virginia nodded.

"Not just about the rum-running, but possibly about Wesley Kempton's murder too." Anna sighed. She still ached to think of the reporter's tragic death. Poor Mac had been devastated by the news. Even though they'd all observed Wesley's running with the wrong crowd, Anna's father still partially blamed himself. Mac had tried so hard to mentor Wesley over the years . . . practically treating him as a son. But, as Anna had pointed out more than once this past summer, Wesley made his own choices. He'd refused to heed their warnings.

"So perhaps Mr. Krauss wasn't the murderer after all," Virginia mused. "And maybe someone out there didn't want him revealing who was truly responsible."

"That's exactly what I'm thinking." Anna slid a paper into her typewriter. "Please send Jim in here on your way back to the reception desk. I want him to cover the jailbreak story in time for tomorrow's edition."

"Will do." Virginia nodded, and, as she slipped out, Anna began to type a new editorial piece to go into the Saturday paper. She glanced at the clock, realizing she was cutting it close to make these changes in time for press. She was just starting her second paragraph when Jim came in.

"I just heard the news," he said. "Want me to handle it?"

"Yes." She looked up. "Definitely front-page stuff. Get everything you can, and if you need any help, let me know. I just want to finish this editorial first." She quickly told him about her speculation regarding the motivation behind the jailbreak. "That's partially what I'm writing about now. But see what you can find out at city hall and around town as well as the county jail. And let the typesetters know we're going to make some changes before the end of the day." She pursed her lips. "In fact, tell them to move the current front page back. We'll fill the new front page with this and related stories."

"I'm on it." Jim clapped his hands together. "Might make for a long day."

"I know." She forced a sad smile. "But I feel like we're doing part of this for Wesley's sake. I know he made his mistakes, but he didn't deserve to be murdered. Anything we can do to figure out who's behind it is time well spent."

"Couldn't agree more." He reached for the doorknob. "I'll check in with you in a couple hours, let you know how it's going."

After Jim left, she returned to her typewriter. The last time she'd written an opinion piece about the consequences for prohibition breakers was right after Wesley's murder. She'd gone after it pretty hard then, but for the past couple of weeks, she'd tried to editorialize on less disturbing topics, as well as some uplifting ones. Now it was time to remind the good citizens of Sunset Cove of the dangers of lawbreaking. Oh, she knew there were varied opinions on prohibition, and as editor in chief, she tried to honor those voices by allowing them space in the "Letters to the Editor" section. But tomorrow's editorial would express the position of the newspaper in general. Her father would approve.

Anna had just finished her piece when her daughter burst into the office. "I just heard about Mr. Krauss's escape from jail," Katy said with wide eyes. "A policeman came by the school to check on Ellen. She's pretty shaken up and scared."

"Poor Ellen . . . and Clara too." Anna looked at the clock. "What are you doing out of school at this hour?"

"Lunchtime."

"Oh, yes. Of course."

"I told Ellen that she and her mom should move back to Grandmother's house. And I even called Grandmother from the school office to let her know they might need a safe place again."

"I expressed similar concerns to Chief Rollins." Anna laid her piece aside. "He assured me that he's aware. He already sent Collins down there to keep an eye on things with Clara." Anna didn't admit that she didn't fully trust Clint Collins. Sure, he could be quite charming and everyone knew he was next in line to replace the chief when Harvey retired next year. But the more she'd become acquainted with Collins, the more she suspected his character. Yet, the chief appeared to trust him. Perhaps she was too judgmental.

"The policeman escorted Ellen home so she could check on her mom," Katy said. "I suggested they both gather up their things and get over to Grandmother's as soon as possible."

"Good thinking." Anna smiled at her daughter. Katy would be seventeen soon, but she'd always seemed older than her years. "So, how's school going?" Anna knew that Katy was disappointed in the academics of the small-town school. They'd discussed it at length over dinner last night, but Katy had remained firm. She did not want to return to Portland to finish her high school education.

"Funny that you mention that, Mother." Katy's blue eyes twinkled. "The principal, Mr. Johnson, took me aside this morning. He suggested that I might want to take an equivalency test. He said it's pretty difficult, but that I could get my high school diploma early if I pass it."

"Would you really want to do that?"

"I'm thinking about it."

Anna frowned. "Would that sort of degree meet college requirements?"

Katy looked away. "I don't know."

"Well, that is an interesting idea." Anna didn't want to sound impatient with her daughter, but she was eager to check on Jim and turn in her editorial.

"Of course, Ellen doesn't want me to do it."

"That's understandable. But as much as you love Ellen, you can't plan your life around her, Katy."

"I know that." Katy scooped her napkin from her lap and put it on the table by her plate.

"And speaking of Ellen, I promised to meet her at Grandmother's house. I better get over there."

Anna nodded. She was still slightly amazed that her mother had not only reentered their lives, but appeared to have been welcomed by almost everyone in town. Including Anna . . . but only after Lucille managed to prove herself by helping Clara and Ellen. Still, Anna was not as won over by her flamboyant mother as Katy and Mac. But at least they were on cordial speaking terms now. To be honest, Lucille was steadily growing on her. It was rather nice to have a mother . . . even if she was a bit eccentric.

Anna was about to take her opinion piece to the typesetters when Jim entered her office. "I'm afraid I agreed to too many tasks." He quickly explained his dilemma. "I scheduled an interview with the jailer who was on duty when the break occurred. He lives just outside of town, and his wife told me to come by at two. But then I got an appointment to speak with Albert's cellmate at the county jail. But the visiting hour is at two as well."

"Which one do you want me to take?"

He rubbed his chin. "Well, I'm not sure a woman would be very welcome inside the jail. So you probably should talk to the jail-keeper. His name's Tom Gardner. He works the night shift. According to his wife, he doesn't usually get up until around three, but she was willing to wake him earlier for me." He handed her a slip of paper. "Here's the address. It'll take you about forty minutes to get there."

"I'll go home and get the Runabout and a quick bite of lunch, then I'll be on my way." Anna reached for her hat and satchel.

"Be careful out there."

"Why?"

"The chief is concerned that Albert could be hiding out in town."

"I know. I've been wondering if he might try to get supplies or money or even a boat from his business."

"Police are posted around the docks. But if Albert sees them, he'll probably lay low or look for another opportunity. And you know that he's not very fond of you."

"That's putting it mildly." She grimly shook her head. She knew better than anyone how much Clara's husband despised Anna's "interference."

"So watch out."

She nodded. So much for breathing easy in Sunset Cove now. But she didn't really mind. Excitement was always a part of a reporter's life, and, although she didn't like taking unnecessary risks, she did like the adventurous side of her work. She would hate to imagine Sunset Cove returning to a sleepy little coastal town with nothing beyond the grange meetings and bridge club to report on. Apparently that was not going to be a problem just yet.

CHAPTER 2

Lucille immediately set her live-in house-keeper to work after Katy's phone call. But with so much to do in preparation for the return of her houseguests, she decided to roll up her sleeves as well. While Sally was at work in the kitchen, Lucille prepared the guest rooms by opening the windows, setting out fresh linens, and even putting small bouquets of autumnal flowers in pretty crystal vases.

Clara and Ellen had returned to their house near the docks shortly after Albert's arrest. Lucille understood their desire to move back home, but she'd instantly missed their company. She'd enjoyed the hustle-bustle activities that her houseguests had brought with them, including numerous visits from her daughter and grand-daughter. It had been fun—and their absence had made her large home feel rather quiet and lonely. Although Lucille wasn't exactly glad that Clara's good-for-nothing husband was on the loose again, she couldn't help but be happy to have her houseguests returning.

"Grandmother!"

"I'm up here," Lucille called down the stairs.

"Thank you for opening your home again." Katy embraced Lucille. "Ellen was so happy to hear you didn't mind."

"I'm delighted to have them." Lucille set the last towels on the bureau, looking around with satisfaction.

"I thought they'd be here by now, but I suppose it takes time to pack."

"Should I send my car for them?"

"No. Ellen said she'll drive their truck back to town."

"Any news on the whereabouts of that nasty Albert Krauss?"

"Nothing more than I already told you. And I was just at the newspaper office, and Mother didn't mention anything." Katy looked at the vase of flowers. "Pretty!"

"Thank you." Lucille beamed at her. "I do want Clara and Ellen to feel welcome."

"I'm sure they will. Ellen sounded very grateful." Katy's face turned serious. "Grandmother, I'd like your opinion on something."

"Well, as you know, I've never been one to keep my opinions to myself. What is it?"

Katy began to describe her discontent with Sunset Cove High School. "It's so small. Only twelve students in my class." She rolled her eyes. "Do you know that I had nearly two hundred in my old school?"

Lucille felt alarmed. "Do you want to go back to Portland for your schooling?"

Katy waved a hand. "No, no. Not at all." Now she explained her teacher's suggestion that she take a test to acquire her diploma early. "But the problem is college. It might make it difficult to get into a college." She looked at Lucille with a slightly desperate expression. "But that is exactly the issue, Grandmother. I'm not sure I want to go to college."

Lucille smiled. "Then why should you?"

"Grandpa and Mother both want me to go."

"Oh . . . I see." She nodded knowingly. Mac and Anna could be awfully stubborn about some things.

"The things I most want to do don't require a college education."

"You mean things related to art?"

"Yes, I suppose. Art and film both interest me. But not as much as dress design. You know how much I love fashion, Grandmother."

"Yes." She nodded. "I know. That's why I offered to help Ellen and you to start a dress shop—after you're done with your schooling." Lucille had not forgotten the rather terse warning she'd received from Anna about this. Neither Anna nor Mac wanted anything to interrupt or derail Katy's education.

"But what if I was done with my schooling now?" Katy asked eagerly.

17

"I, uh, I don't know."

"Do you know what my dream is?" Her eyes sparkled with hope.

"What's that, dear?" More than anything, Lucille would love to help her granddaughter's dreams to come true. "What is your dream?"

"To study under someone like *Jeanne Paquin.*" Katy let out a long wistful sigh.

"Who is Jeanne Paquin?"

"Oh, she's this amazing French woman. One of the first world-renowned female dress designers. A truly amazing artist. I first read about her in *Vogue* magazine. She's won some prestigious awards and runs the House of Paquin in Paris. And she designs for theater too. Her designs have been shown all over the world. She even toured the United States a few years ago. Oh, I would give anything to go and work for someone like Jeanne Paquin."

"You'd go to France?" Lucille concealed her shock.

"Well, I know it's impossible right now. Not with the war over there."

Lucille felt calmer. "So . . . how did this Jeanne Paquin get *her* start?"

"As a dressmaker. She started as a very young woman."

"Why couldn't you do something like that? You're so talented, Katy. Such an artist. I see no reason why you couldn't become an American

Jeanne Paquin, with time and work. And perhaps when the war is over . . . Well, perhaps I could take you to France."

Katy grabbed Lucille's hands. "Oh, Grandmother, that would be a dream come true! Would you really take me there?"

"Why not? In the meantime, until the European war is over, you could be getting plenty of experience right here—in your own little dress shop."

"That's exactly what I want! I could take that test and be done with high school and start designing dresses. But there's Mother and Grandpa and . . . Well, you know what they'll say."

"Yes, I do know. But perhaps if we work together on them. Maybe we can persuade them . . . encourage them to see your side."

"Will you help me?" Katy peered hopefully into Lucille's eyes.

"Of course I will." Lucille heard the front doorbell. "I do believe our guests have arrived. Please go let them in while I finish up in here. I still need to put some soaps out."

Katy kissed Lucille on the cheek. "Thank you. I knew you'd understand."

Lucille did understand. A young girl should not be deprived of her dreams. As Lucille unwrapped a bar of rose-scented soap, she remembered when she was about Katy's age . . . meeting

Mac down in San Francisco and being swept off her feet by the charming young newspaperman. After marrying him in haste, with high hopes in her heart, they returned to Sunset Cove to live happily ever after. And they might've too. If only Mac's mother hadn't insisted on running their household in her own way. Lucille set the soap in the dish. How her mother-in-law disapproved of such luxuries. Never mind that they could afford such things. "It's a waste of money," she would chide young Lucille. Day by day, she would rule and reign over Lucille, squashing all her hopes and dreams until Lucille felt like a prisoner in her home. Was it any wonder she'd left her husband and child? It had seemed the only answer at the time.

Hearing excited voices downstairs, Lucille fluffed the last pillow, then went down to greet her guests. "I'm sorry for the circumstances." She placed a hand on Clara's shoulder. "But I'm very glad to have my houseguests back." She turned to Ellen. "Your rooms are ready for you to get settled in."

"We better get back to school." Katy grabbed Ellen by the hand. "I promised Mr. Johnson we wouldn't be too late."

"Yes, you girls grab something from the kitchen and hurry along," Lucille told them. "I'll get Sally to help get your things upstairs."

"You be careful," Clara warned Ellen.

"Keep your eyes open as you go through town. Remember what Lieutenant Collins said."

"Don't worry about her," Katy assured Clara. "I won't let her out of my sight."

After they were gone, Clara deflated. "I thought the worst of this was over." She let Lucille lead her to the sofa to sit. "And now this. It's so upsetting to know that Albert is out there . . . *somewhere*. Who knows what he might do next. I honestly believe he may be crazy."

"I'll bet you haven't had lunch." Lucille called out to Sally, asking her to bring some tea and sandwiches. "And when you're done, Sally, I'd like you to help unload the ladies' bags from their vehicle." Now Lucille sat down next to Clara. "I know this must be difficult, but remember you have friends to help you. And everyone in town will be on the lookout for Albert. If he's anywhere nearby, I'm sure he will be picked up soon. In the meantime, why not enjoy your stay here?" She smiled. "I know I'm looking forward to it."

"You're so kind." Clara seemed to relax. "I don't know what we'd do without you and the rest of your family. These friendships make me realize how terribly isolated and lonely I was . . . before. I never want to go back to that."

Lucille understood. Before returning to Sunset Cove last spring, she had felt lonely too. In fact, she'd felt lonelier than ever when she'd first arrived. It had seemed that the whole town—most of all, her only daughter—were intent on shunning her. But time and persistence had paid off. She felt more at home than ever now. And it was wonderful being able to help someone else.

CHAPTER 3

A nna's motoring skills had improved considerably in the last few weeks, but truth
be told, her daughter was a far superior driver.
Still, that did not deter Anna from continuing
to practice. Really, once she got going, it was
not that difficult. As she drove down the rutted
coastal road toward the Gardner home, she tried
to line up some questions in her head for the
jail-keeper. She wasn't sure how helpful this
interview would prove, but hopefully it would
provide enough information for a small article to
fill in some space on the new front page.

When she got to what appeared to be the right
house, she noticed that the property looked rather
neglected. But the address on the mailbox was
correct, so she parked the Runabout and got out.
She was barely on the porch steps when an angry-
looking man came out in wrinkled trousers and
an undershirt. "What d'ya want?" he demanded.

She smiled and stuck out her hand. "I'm Anna
McDowell, editor in chief of the *Sunset Times*,
and I—"

"My wife said a man was coming," he growled.
"Not that it makes any difference. I didn't plan

to talk to him either. So you can just be on your way."

"I only want to ask you a few questions," she persisted. "It's such exciting news to hear about a jailbreak and—"

"Listen, lady, I'm not talking to you." He folded his arms across his burly chest, glaring.

"But your story must be very interesting, Mr. Gardner." Anna gave what she hoped was an expression of admiration. "And your job must be very exciting too. I assume you have to be very brave and strong and capable to do what you do. I thought you'd want people to know about it."

His brow creased as if he were considering her words. "You telling me you're not gonna write a story about how I slacked on the job? And that's why the prisoner escaped? Isn't that your angle?"

"I don't have an angle, Mr. Gardner. I only came to hear *your* side of the story. I would think you'd want it told. Especially if you don't want people thinking you were sleeping on the job."

"I was not sleeping!"

"Exactly. For the record, I never considered that you were in any way to blame, sir. I'm sure being a prison guard is a difficult job. Not many men would be able to do such a challenging task."

"You got that right."

She removed her notebook and pencil, as if she were beginning her interview. "I'd like to know more about the jail. How old it is and in what sort of condition . . . and what sort of measures are used to keep prisoners secured."

He scratched his head. "The jail was built about twenty years ago. It's a two-story brick structure with the usual locking cells. One to two men per cell, depending on how full we are."

"How full are you?"

"Near to capacity. Thirty-seven inmates." He frowned. "Well, thirty-six now."

"I've heard that prison facilities are filling up as a result of prohibition."

He made a harrumph sound as he sat down on a worn wooden rocker, indicating she could sit on the other one. "Well, you're right about that. And you're right that guarding the jail is a tough job. And a thankless one too." He began to ramble a bit now, telling about how some people treated him badly. "Both on the inside and the outside. Don't get no respect from nobody."

"That must be difficult." She shook her head. "So what time did the jailbreak occur?"

"It was pretty early. Before daybreak. I estimated it to be about five thirty. About the time I put on a fresh pot of coffee."

"Everything must've been very quiet then. How did you discover a prisoner had escaped?"

"The explosion."

"Explosion?" Anna hadn't heard about this.

"Yeah. They used dynamite to blast out the wall."

"The exterior wall in Albert Krauss's cell?"

"That's right."

"How do you think they knew where to set the dynamite? Was there a way to tell it was Krauss's cell? Is it possible they were actually trying to free someone else?"

"They was there for Krauss." He rubbed his unshaved chin. "Not hard to find out which cell was his. Folks talk. Both on the inside and the outside."

"Yes, I can imagine." She studied him closely. Something about this man did not sit right with her, and she felt fairly certain she could smell alcohol on his breath. But she kept her expression even, determined not to show any suspicions. "So you heard the explosion. I'm sure you must've been taken by surprise. What did you do?"

"Well . . ." He glanced over his shoulder and then back at her. Was he trying to make up an answer? "At first I thought it was the boiler. It's pretty worn out and makes clunky noises sometimes. I thought maybe it'd blown up."

"So you went to check on it?"

He nodded with an interesting glint in his eyes. Almost as if she'd just fed him an answer. "Yeah, as a matter of fact, I did go check it out. I was surprised to see it was just fine. Then I heard the yelling."

"Yelling?"

"Yeah. Krauss's cellmate was screaming like a

banshee. He got hit by some of the debris from the explosion, and he was in pain."

"Was he seriously hurt?"

"Nah. Nothing we couldn't handle, but he claimed his ears were ringing pretty bad."

"What about Krauss?"

"Oh, he was long gone by the time I got there."

"I wonder that he didn't get hurt by flying debris." She looked up from her notes.

"According to his cellmate, Krauss was hunkered down behind the bunk, shielding himself with his mattress."

"So he obviously was expecting the explosion."

He shrugged again, but something in his eyes still seemed to suggest he was keeping some information to himself.

"How do you think Krauss knew there was going to be a jailbreak just then? Who clued him in on it?"

"Like I said. Folks talk . . . inside and outside."

"Right." She nodded firmly. "How many guards were on duty last night?"

"Just the two of us."

"Just two guards? Is that normal?"

"Normally we have three, but Bud went home sick."

"I see. And the other guard? What's his name?"

"Harry Bower."

"What was Harry doing when the explosion occurred?"

"He was on the other side of the jail." He chuckled. "For all I know, he was probably sleeping."

"Sleeping on the job?"

He shrugged again. "It happens."

"But you weren't sleeping?"

He scowled darkly. "I told you I was awake."

She smiled. "Doing your job."

"That's right."

"So Harry. Do you really think he was sleeping? I mean, if he was, wouldn't that be a problem?"

"For him, it would."

"Do you think there's any chance that Harry was the one who tipped off the guys behind the jailbreak? Could he have told them the location of Krauss's cell? Or done anything else to help them?"

He rubbed his chin again. "Hmm . . . interesting question. I suppose he might've. You'd have to ask him."

She made a note of this. "How long has he been employed as a guard?"

"I dunno. Ten years, maybe."

"And you?"

"Me?"

"How long have you worked for the county jail?"

He shrugged again. "About a year."

"Had you been a prison guard somewhere else?"

28

"No, but I worked as a policeman for a couple years."

"That makes sense." She made note of this. "What about the Krauss boy? Isn't he incarcerated there too?" She already knew that AJ was there but wanted to see if Mr. Gardner had a reaction.

"Yeah, he's an inmate."

"But there were no attempts to break him out too?"

"Not so far."

She tried not to respond to what seemed an odd answer. Did Mr. Gardner know something? "Do you *expect* an attempt?"

"I didn't expect last night's breakout," he growled.

"No, of course, not. But can we assume the Krauss boy will be kept in an extra-secure place now? Perhaps on the second floor?"

"That'd be up to the warden." He stood with a hardened look. "That's all I'm gonna say. I haven't even had my breakfast yet."

"And do you work tonight?"

"That's right."

She smiled brightly. "Well, thank you for your time, sir. And thank you for your good work at the county jail."

He narrowed his eyes. "Yeah right. You thanking me after a jailbreak?"

She weighed her words carefully. "Well, it's not

as if you were responsible for it, Mr. Gardner."

"You got that right." He turned away and stomped back into the house.

Anna heard a noise behind her and turned to see a scraggly cat coming around a stack of crates in the corner of the porch. Behind the crates, she spotted what definitely looked like an empty whiskey bottle. Not homemade either. Of course, it might've been there previous to the prohibition act, but she doubted it. And not eager to have Tom Gardner see her spying on his porch, she tucked away her notebook and pencil and scurried down the steps.

But she felt slightly shaky as she got into the car. Partly with excitement and partly with concern. She had a bad feeling about Tom Gardner. She could be wrong, but she had a strong suspicion that he was involved in Albert Krauss's escape. He could easily have been the information source on the inside. It wouldn't surprise her. Not that she could write about that.

Yes, she felt certain she'd uncovered a story but knew she couldn't print it. Not yet anyway. But they would do some more investigating. For now, she would write a story with the "facts" Tom Gardner had supplied her with. And she'd be sure to quote him about his belief that both "insiders and outsiders" were involved. The question would be, who were they? Somehow she would write the article in such a way that the reader could draw their own conclusions . . . or at least ask the questions. How convenient it would be to have someone related to the criminal elements on the inside. And it wouldn't be the first time.

As she turned the Runabout around, she couldn't help but observe how his out-of-the-way house was so handily located near the beach—and not far from the main road. And judging by the piles of boxes and debris around the ramshackle house, it would be an easy place to stash cases of prohibited substances. She doubted that anyone would even notice them. Of course, she couldn't write about that. Not yet anyway. But she would assign Jim to do some more investigative reporting. As she drove back to town, she began to make a list of people—starting with the other two night guards—for Jim to interview for a follow-up article in Tuesday's paper. For right now, she needed to get back to the office and get the front page worked up for tomorrow's paper. And she was eager to compare notes with Jim. What had he found out at the jail?

CHAPTER 4

Mac had been determined to stay up until Anna came home from the newspaper, but after falling asleep in his chair, Mickey persuaded him to retire for the evening. Seeing it was past ten and Mickey looked worn out, Mac had given in. But he watched with dismay as Mickey patiently worked the confounded buttons. How could such a simple, childish task prove so impossible for Mac? Despite his daily therapy exercises, both to improve his speech as well as physical coordination, he was still partially impaired by his stroke.

According to Dr. Daniel Hollister, it would take about a year to know how much he would recover, but, when pressed, the doctor's honest prognosis was that Mac probably wouldn't regain the use of his right arm. And Mac could live with that. At least his walking had gotten better. Now if only his speech would return to normal.

Mac had always been considered well-spoken if not downright loquacious, and he was weary of communicating like a five-year-old. Of course, that was an improvement from recent months when he'd babbled like an infant. Maybe Mac should do as Katy kept telling him: "Just count your blessings." So as Mac lay in his bed fighting back his stroke-related frustrations, he attempted to count his blessings. As usual, he always started with the recent reunion with his daughter and granddaughter . . . and then with his ex-wife, Lucille. And he knew that he never would've reconnected with these three women if not for his stroke. So perhaps that was a blessing too . . . a blessing in disguise.

Mac woke with the sun the next morning. According to his alarm clock, it was a bit past six, which meant Mickey should be up and ready to help him prepare for the day. Impatient to wait a minute longer than necessary, Mac went ahead and rang his brass bell. It wasn't long until Mickey shuffled in and began assisting Mac with his usual morning routine.

"Is Anna up yet?" Mac asked in his stilted voice as Mickey finished with his morning shave. Despite his ability to use his left hand for many daily tasks, he still didn't trust himself with the sharp straight-edged razor.

"I haven't seen her yet. But Miss Katy is. She and Miss Ellen went down to the beach to look for shells. There was a rough sea last night and a minus tide this morning. Good time for beachcombing."

"The girls better be careful out there." Mac wiped his face with a towel.

"You mean because of the riptides?" Mickey reached for Mac's clean shirt.

"Riptide is one thing. That and rumrunners." Mac waited as Mickey did the buttons. "Both are dangerous."

"Yes, but the runners like the high tide . . . and nighttime."

"That's true." Mac nodded. Mickey was right about that. Rumrunners would definitely prefer high tides and darkness. That was a comfort. Still, he didn't like the idea of those girls down on the beach alone. Not when everyone knew that notorious Albert Krauss was on the loose again. If only Mac's right leg was stronger, he'd go down and join them. But with his unreliable leg and cane, he'd be sure to topple down the beach stairs. And then he'd really be up a creek without a paddle.

"Want a tie?" Mickey opened the closet, waiting.

"Nah. It's Saturday. Just my blue sweater."

As Mickey helped him into the wool cardigan, Mac informed him he preferred to take breakfast in his sitting room. "Unless Anna is up."

"Yes, sir. I'll check on that for you." Mickey waited as Mac slowly made his way to the sitting room that connected with the master bedroom.

"And bring the paper."

Mickey nodded as he pulled open the heavy drapes, exposing the view Mac loved, overlooking a clear blue ocean. "I'll bring the paper with your coffee."

"Thank you." Mac eased himself into his favorite chair.

Before long, he was settled with his coffee and newspaper, eagerly reading the first page. Anna had done a good job of throwing it all together in the eleventh hour. He'd envied her last night, imagining his staff scrambling in the newspaper office, the lights burning brightly after dark, everyone working hard to implement the changes necessitated by yesterday's excitement.

The jailbreak story was the headliner—and well done. But the other stories—about the jail being nearly full to capacity and the comments from guards and prisoners and police force—made for good reading too. Mac honestly didn't think he could've done a better job himself, before his stroke. In his present condition, he never could've pulled it off. Not only that but Anna's editorial was top-notch too.

Anna was proving herself to be an impressively capable newspaperwoman. Not that he planned to admit as much to her. No need to give her a swollen head. Not that she was that sort. But, besides that, Mac still liked to think that there might be a thing or two he could teach his daughter. He hoped so.

"Good morning, Mac." Anna came into his room looking surprisingly fresh considering

36

yesterday's long day at the newspaper office. She'd brought her coffee with her.

"Morning." He gave her his lopsided smile. "You look pretty."

"Well, thank you very much." She sat down, setting her coffee on the table between them. "I told Bernice I'd have my breakfast in here with you, if you don't mind."

He beamed at her. "You know I don't." Anna always seemed younger on Saturdays. Probably because she wasn't wearing one of those severe suits she claimed earned her more respect at the newspaper office. Today she had on a pastel-print cotton dress, and her auburn curls were loosely tied back with a blue satin ribbon. No one would believe Anna was old enough to be the mother of a sixteen-year-old daughter. Remembering Katy, Mac explained that the girls were beach-combing.

"Just the two of them?" Anna's brow creased with concern as she stood up. "Down there on the beach *alone?*"

"Yeah." Mac shared Mickey's reassurance with her, but Anna still went close to the window to peer down below.

"Ah, there they are." She sounded relieved. "Looks like they're heading for the stairs now." She turned away from the window. "It was so nice not to feel worried these past few weeks. Life had settled down. But finding out that Albert is on the lam again . . . Well, it's disconcerting to say the least."

"I heard Clara and Ellen moved back with Lucille."

"It's so good of her to open her home to them again." Anna pointed to the newspaper still in his lap. "What did you think of that?"

"Good job." Mac nodded his approval.

"Thanks." She sighed as she sat back down. "It was a long night for everyone but worth it, I think."

"You bet." He tapped the article she'd written about the situation at the county jail and her interview with Tom Gardner. "Interesting."

Her brows arched. "How so?"

"You have some . . . suspicions?"

She leaned forward with wide eyes. "Was it that obvious?"

"No . . . not obvious. Reading between the lines." He grinned. "That what you wanted?"

Her smile looked slightly sly. "Maybe so."

"Tell me what you think, Anna."

She waited as Mickey and Bernice brought in their breakfast trays. "This looks lovely," she told Bernice. "Thank you. I always look forward to leisurely weekend breakfasts. No need to rush."

Bernice pointed to the little jar of jam. "I just put up those blackberry preserves yesterday. Not bad, if I do say so myself."

After Mickey and Bernice left, Anna began

to tell Mac about her visit with the jail guard yesterday. "I really hate being so distrustful, but everything just seemed to add up to trouble." She described the disarray, the crates, the smell on Tom Gardner's breath, even what she suspected was a whiskey bottle. "And he was so defensive—almost as if he bore some guilt."

Mac just nodded. "You quoted him. 'On the inside.' "

"Exactly. It certainly wouldn't be the first time there was corruption in the system." Now she told him what she'd learned from Jim last night. "He said that Gardner isn't very well liked by the other guards. And that Albert's cellmate sounded like he was afraid of Gardner, as if he were afraid to say too much for fear of retaliation."

"Understandable."

"I've already tipped off Chief Rollins."

"Good. I'm sure Harvey will look into it."

"And I've assigned Jim a follow-up article for Tuesday's paper. I want him to interview the other night guards. According to Gardner, one of them might've been asleep and the other went home sick."

"Convenient."

"That's what I thought." She spread jam on her toast. "It sure would be fun to blow this thing wide open. I mean, if we're right about the insider connection. I wouldn't mind seeing Mr. Gardner being caught . . . if he's guilty."

"Don't forget those are big ifs, Anna."

"Don't worry, Mac. I don't plan to get the newspaper accused of libel."

"I know."

"Just the facts." She grinned. "Good investigative reporting means asking the hard questions."

"I'm glad Jim is handling that."

She set down her fork with a frown. "Because I'm a woman? You don't think I can handle it, Mac?"

"Not that." He slowly shook his head. "I *know* you can handle it, Anna. But don't make more enemies. You're editor in chief."

"Oh." She sipped her coffee. "I see your point. Diplomacy."

Now Katy came into the room, sharing treasures she'd gathered from the beach. "Ellen found seven sand dollars. I only found three."

"Good for Ellen," Anna said. "She needed the encouragement."

Katy nodded as she replaced her shells in the basket. "Yes, I suppose that's right. She and Mrs. Krauss are feeling pretty uneasy."

"I felt a bit uneasy knowing you girls were down on the beach by yourselves." Anna sent Katy a pointed look. "Under the circumstances—"

"You shouldn't worry, Mother. There's a plain-clothes policeman posted at Grandmother's house. He said he would be keeping an eye on us."

"Well, that's a relief."

Katy smiled. "Ellen and I are going to work on campaign buttons this afternoon. Grandmother said we can make them at her house. My order for supplies arrived at the mercantile yesterday. I used some campaign funds to get ribbon and lace for the buttons—"

"Ribbons and lace?" Mac frowned.

"That does sound rather feminine," Anna agreed. She knew how much her daughter loved working with those sorts of materials. But for Wally Morris's campaign buttons?

"I want the buttons to be beautiful," Katy exclaimed.

"But lace?" Mac asked.

"I want every voting-age woman in Sunset Cove to be wearing one," Katy explained.

Anna's brows arched. "I see."

"Yes," Mac agreed. "I see too."

"Mrs. Morris is very pleased with this plan," Katy informed them.

"I'm sure Wally will be pleased too." Anna refilled her coffee cup. "But I wonder that all this effort is even necessary now. Everyone in town knows that Mayor Snyder was associated with some rather unsavory characters. I really can't imagine he has much chance of being reelected in light of the recent arrests and developments."

"Don't be too sure about that," Mac warned. "What about Snyder's known connections to

Krauss? Everyone is aware of that. And now with Krauss on the run, they'll be reminded again."

"Don't forget that a lot of voters still oppose prohibition," Mac reminded her.

"Don't forget that women have the vote now." Anna winked at her daughter.

Mac grinned. "That's true enough. But don't underestimate Snyder. He's a wily opponent."

"Do you think Snyder could do something to upset the election?" Katy asked Mac with wide-eyed concern.

"Still more'n a month to go yet," he told her. "Anything can happen."

"That's why I will campaign harder than ever," Katy declared as she headed for the door. "Wally Morris is going to be Sunset Cove's next mayor, or my name is not Kathleen Rebecca McDowell! I will not give in to defeat!" She shook a defiant fist in the air, then exited with aplomb.

As soon as she was out of earshot, both Anna and Mac chuckled.

"That is one determined young woman," Mac said slowly.

"Stubborn is more like it." Yet Anna's eyes glinted with pride. "Wonder where she gets *that* from."

Mac grinned. "I wonder . . . ."

"What you said about Calvin Snyder, Mac. Do you really think he'd have a chance of getting reelected? I just can't fathom what a blow that would be for the morale of Sunset Cove. I don't want to make any accusations, but I feel certain that Mayor Snyder is a criminal. One of those 'insiders' like Tom Gardner was talking about. I'm sure he's used his position to hide his crooked connections."

"Yeah, I think you're right."

"So how could he possibly win at the polls?"

"Calvin won't play fair." Mac rubbed his chin. "You keep your eye on him, Anna."

"Do some investigating?"

Mac nodded. "Keep your cards close to your chest."

Her brow creased. "Then how do we expose him?"

"Timing . . . not too soon. People forget."

"Yes," she said eagerly. "We'll start gathering anything we can on Snyder. And I'll be sure to confirm it so there's no chance of his calling foul play or accusing us of slander."

"Make use of Randall for counsel," Mac advised. Besides the fact that he respected the young attorney for his expertise, he suspected that Anna might have feelings for her childhood friend. However, Mac knew there were a couple of other fellows in the running as well—including Dr. Hollister and Jim Stafford. His pretty daughter had experienced no shortage of potential beaus since moving back home. Still, Mac wasn't eager to see her married off. He liked having Anna and Katy in the house. He didn't want anything or anyone to change that.

"Yes, I'll be sure to run everything by Randall before printing a word against Snyder. I'm so glad we decided to put him on retainer. He's got a level head."

"Sensible young man."

"So, we'll get our information gathered and stories lined up." She leaned back in the chair with a thoughtful expression. "Then, a week or so before the election, we'll make it known to the good people of Sunset Cove."

"Shout it from the rooftops."

Anna's mouth twisted to one side. "One question, Mac."

"What's that?"

"Should we keep this plan under wraps in the meantime? I don't want to say I don't trust all your staff, but I do know some of your writers like to talk. And you know how folks can gossip in this town. I'd hate for the word to get out that we're working on this. I'd like for Snyder to assume that no one's paying much attention to his less-than-honorable schemes."

Mac considered this. "Don't ignore him altogether, Anna. Too suspicious."

"Yes, that's true. But what if I just let Jim in on this plan? He and I can collect what we need."

Mac nodded eagerly. "Good plan. You can trust Jim."

"I know." Her smile seemed to suggest an interest in something beyond a work relationship with Jim, but Mac concealed his curiosity. Was Anna romantically interested in Jim Stafford? Jim was a good man, no doubt, but Anna needed to remember she was editor in chief. Getting romantically involved with a staffer could be problematic. Mac considered mentioning his concern to her but remembered how he'd interfered once before. That had not gone well. No, this time he would keep his big mouth shut. And hope for the best.

CHAPTER 5

On Monday morning, Anna invited Jim into her office for a private meeting. Since she'd appointed him managing editor a while back, she knew there was nothing unusual about meeting with him like this.

"I'll keep it short," she told him. "I know we have work to do for tomorrow's paper, but I wanted you to know what our pre-election plan is going to be."

"A pre-election plan?" he asked with interest.

She quickly explained the idea that she and Mac had conceived over the weekend, and Jim was in full agreement. "Mac is right. We can't assume that Wally Morris is a sure winner for mayor. I've only lived here a few years but long enough to know that our sleepy little town is still divided on the prohibition issue. I'm sure that's the main reason Snyder won the previous election."

"You mean because women didn't have the vote yet?"

He nodded. "From what I've heard, he slipped right into office because of his statement of opposition. And unless the majority of voting

47

females—and all the other prohibitionists—get out to vote, he might slip in again."

Anna glumly shook her head. "That makes me glad that Katy is doing what she's doing."

"What is she doing?"

She told him about the lacy buttons Katy and Ellen had constructed over the weekend. "At first I was worried they'd be too frilly, but now I understand."

"Katy is a smart girl."

They went over some preliminary plans for gathering information that could later be used to expose Snyder's true colors, then agreed to meet again on Wednesday.

As Anna went back to work, she felt grateful the Tuesday edition was always much lighter than Saturday's. On Tuesdays, they focused on what Mac used to call the three Ss: society, school, and sports. Even so, she didn't want to slack on it. Fortunately, her writers already had most of their stories either in the works or ready to go.

In the afternoon, Anna paid a visit to Chief Rollins. Her primary purpose was to discover if any progress had been made in discovering the whereabouts of Albert Krauss.

"I'm not asking as the editor of the paper," she said, "but as a friend to Clara and Ellen. And out of concern for my own daughter. Katy spends so much time with them. I want to know just how dangerous you think this situation could be."

"Quite frankly, I would be more concerned for *your* welfare, Anna."

"More concerned for me?" She blinked. "Why?"

"Albert Krauss probably sees you as the enemy. Compared to you, I'd think his wife and daughter should be relatively safe."

"Then why do you have plainclothes policemen watching them? I've assumed you were worried about their safety. I'd even wondered about kidnapping."

"I've considered that. With a desperate man, that's always a possibility. But I'm mostly hoping Krauss will approach his wife. Then we'll snag him."

"Do you think that's likely—that he'd try to contact Clara?"

He fiddled with a brass button on his uniform. "Not terribly. But you never know. Krauss is an odd one. No one ever expected he'd be able to break out of jail."

"But he had help."

"Yes . . . I know."

"But back to the safety of Clara and Ellen and anyone else. I want to know exactly what I should be concerned about."

"Well, it's occurred to me that he might try to use Clara to get money or food or clothes. And if he knows she's living with Lucille, he might assume he could extract some cash from her."

She nodded. "Yes, I've wondered about the same thing. In fact, I haven't been very comfortable having Katy over there so much. Except that you have your policeman posted there. So I tell myself she's probably safer there than anywhere else. But you hear of kidnapping stories . . . and, well, I can't help but feel uneasy. Although, I've reminded both Katy and Ellen to be very cautious. And I've told Lucille to keep her house locked tight and let no one she doesn't know inside. She's assured me she's taking no chances."

"That's good. We've told her the same. But, honestly, Anna, I think if Krauss wanted to harm or kidnap someone, you would be a prime candidate. And I'm not saying this lightly. As editor in chief of a newspaper that's printed some tough articles about him, not to mention your friendship with his wife . . . Well, I'm sure your welfare is not of great concern to him."

"You're probably right."

"Just so you know, the policemen guarding Lucille's house have been told to keep an eye on Mac's house as well. Convenient that they're so close to each other." He chuckled. "I can only assume that wasn't a coincidence."

"What do you mean?"

"The town gossip is that Lucille and Mac will be back together by Christmas."

Anna stifled the urge to scoff. "I would be genuinely surprised at that. But you've been good friends with Mac for years. I suppose your guess is as good as any."

Chief Rollins shrugged. "Frankly, I'd be surprised too. But I suppose stranger things have happened."

Anna wasn't even sure why this assumption made her bristle, but for some reason, the mere idea of her parents reuniting filled her with apprehension. She supposed there were several concerns. For one thing, she was just getting reacquainted with Mac and didn't like the idea of his full-time attention going to Lucille. Yes, it was childish, but—she would never admit this to anyone—she suspected it was true. But her primary concern was that if Lucille and Mac got back together, it could all blow up again. And then what? She didn't want to think about that. Not for either of them. And certainly not for Katy and herself.

"Well, thank you for your time, Chief." Anna gathered her gloves and satchel. "I hope you'll keep me informed as to any new developments in regard to Krauss. Feel free to call any time—day or night."

"I would say the same to you." His brow furrowed. "And assure me that you'll be careful. If you get a lead on a story, don't forget to keep me in the loop, Anna."

"Most definitely."

"And . . ." He paused with a furrowed brow. "I didn't really plan to mention this, because it came from an unreliable source."

"Yes?"

"Strictly confidential?"

"Absolutely," she eagerly agreed.

"Someone reportedly spotted Krauss near the old chowder house."

"Charlie's?"

"Yes. You know that Mayor Snyder owns it now."

"Yes." She narrowed her eyes. "And some people believe he's using it to cover his illegal activities."

"Believe me, I've heard those rumors. But we've already run several raids this past year— and nothing. Not a single thing. Not even an old pre-prohibition bottle of ale. Very discouraging. And Calvin's been pretty hot around the collar about it. He threatened to sue the force for harassment, and I'm sure he would happily do so. Unfortunately, without real evidence to validate a search warrant, my hands are tied. I have to go very carefully now."

"Right. I understand. But if someone believes they saw Albert up there, isn't that enough to issue a warrant?"

"It would be if I could be certain. But, like I said, my source isn't too trustworthy, and I'm treading on thin ice here. You can be sure I've got my guys watching Charlie's, though."

She nodded. "Well, that's all you can do."

"The only reason I'm telling you this is so you'll be extra careful, Anna. And I'm warning you—don't go poking around up there." His dark scowl told her he meant business.

"Don't worry, I don't plan to." She smiled slyly. "But I might put my most trusted reporter on alert. You know, just in case he hears or sees something."

"You mean Jim?"

She nodded.

"Well, be sure to tell him that if he observes anything, he better report directly to me—or else!"

"I'll do that, Chief. And thank you for letting me know about Albert."

"Like I said, it did not come from a reliable source. Take it with a grain of salt. And I actually feel that Albert would've gotten out of town by now. Just the same, I want you to be careful."

"I promise I will."

But as Anna walked back to the office, she wasn't certain she could be completely careful. What kind of journalist was overly cautious? Of course, she knew Mac would remind her that she was not acting as a reporter now—she was editor in chief, and that came with responsibilities. For that reason she would be cautious, but she couldn't control what other people did . . . or if she wound up at the wrong place at the wrong time. But she wouldn't do it intentionally.

CHAPTER 6

Toward the end of the week, Anna scheduled a meeting with her attorney friend, Randall Douglas, asking him to come to the newspaper office to meet with her. It was her way of maintaining control in the relationship, a reminder to Randall that this was about business. She knew that her old school chum still carried a torch for her and that he was eager to take their friendship to a higher level. He hadn't bothered to conceal the fact that he felt somewhat jealous of both Daniel and Jim. Although she couldn't deny she enjoyed the attention, she also knew it could be problematic.

"You're looking lovely today," Randall said pleasantly as he sat across from her.

"Thank you." Anna smiled with amusement as she twirled a pencil between her fingers. How lovely could she possibly look in her brown wool suit, severe white shirt, and black silk tie? Just this morning, Katy had told her that if she drew a mustache on her upper lip, she could probably pass for a man. Of course, Anna had simply laughed. It wouldn't have been the first time she'd masqueraded as a fellow. But Katy's fashion leanings were very feminine, not something Anna could ever feel comfortable wearing in a male-dominated workplace. But if Randall thought she looked lovely, why argue?

"I asked you here to advise me on our pre-election coverage," she began. "Specifically the mayoral candidates."

"And for this you need legal counsel?"

She quickly described the plan to print some exposé articles on Calvin Snyder during the week before the election. "Mac asked me to speak to you about the legal issues that might arise. Naturally, I don't plan to print anything libelous, but I suspect that no matter how carefully we research the facts, Mayor Snyder will probably accuse us of slander."

He nodded. "That sounds about right."

"So we need you to be in the know up front, Randall. I know we have you on retainer, and I don't want to tie up too much of your time, but I'd appreciate it if you could read the articles about Snyder in advance of publication."

"That's not a problem."

"And only Jim and I will be involved in this. We feel the need to keep it quiet."

"That's wise. I hate to say it, but it's not always easy to tell who you can trust in this town."

Anna frowned. "That's one thing I really hate about prohibition—the way it divides people. Feelings run so strongly."

"But it does make for good news stories."

Her frown faded. "That's true. Controversy is like that."

They discussed the practical aspects of the pre-election campaign and then Randall turned the conversation in a different direction. "My mother has been pestering me to invite you to dinner, Anna. I promised her that I would do so the next chance I got. She wants you and Katy to join us. And Mac too, if he felt like it."

"That's very kind of her. I'd enjoy that. I'm sure Katy and Mac would too."

His eyes lit up. "How about Saturday night?"

"I'll have to check with them, but I haven't heard of any other plans."

"Great. Let me know, and I'll tell my mother."

As Anna told Randall good-bye, she was already having second thoughts. Oh, certainly, she knew she was simply agreeing to a social visit. After all, Rand was their attorney and his mother was an old friend. But Anna needed to keep in mind—and remind Mac and Katy—that Marjorie had a reputation for gossip. Oh, maybe it wasn't exactly gossip, but the store owner did have a knack for passing stories along. Many people visited the mercantile regularly to hear the latest "news," because everyone knew that Marjorie Douglas usually knew it. Unfortunately, she wasn't always the most accurate news source. It was a wonder she'd never suffered from a libel suit. But at least she had a lawyer for a son.

Anna was just getting ready to go home on Friday when Jim knocked on the door to her office. He stuck in his head with an eager expression. "Got a minute?"

"Sure." She waved him in.

"I just meandered up to Charlie's Chowder House," he told her as he closed the door. "Looked like Snyder was getting a big delivery."

"A big delivery?"

"Yes. And everyone knows the place has been barely open since he took ownership. So why does he need a lot of supplies?"

"Did you see any police around? Chief Rollins told me earlier this week that his guys are watching the place."

"I know. But, as you've probably noticed, things seem to have settled down. Everyone is assuming that Albert Krauss is long gone. Rumor has it that he's probably in Mexico by now."

"I'm not buying that."

Jim shrugged. "Anyway, I got an idea."

"Yes?"

"How about writing a business piece on the chowder house? We could interview Snyder and see what his plans are."

"That is a good idea. Except that Ed's in charge

of the business section. So he should be the one to write an article on that."

"Exactly. And Ed wouldn't be too suspicious. Especially if Snyder thought a business piece would be good publicity for his mayoral campaign."

"That's true. But do you think Ed would really uncover anything? I mean, it's not like we want to tip our hand, Jim. We don't want it to get out that we're looking for dirt on Snyder." She pursed her lips. It wasn't that she didn't trust Ed. In fact, Mac had assured her that Ed was a good reporter—well, other than the fact that he didn't respect newspaperwomen. Especially one at the helm.

"Ed is not a Snyder supporter, if that's what you mean."

"That's reassuring. I haven't had the chance to get very well acquainted with Ed."

Jim grinned. "I'm sure Ed has made sure of that. But I think he's slowly coming around to you. Give him time."

"Well, how about if you assign the story to him? He'd probably take it better from you. And let's not run it until next Saturday." She drummed her fingers on the desk, thinking. "And how about asking Ed to write it from the angle that folks in town have been missing the *old* Charlie's Chowder House? Ask Snyder to explain why it's taking him so long to get it running again. How can he make any profits if he never seems to have it open? Never seems to have customers? He needs to ask the hard questions, but make sure he does so in a friendly way. Gets Snyder to trust him."

"Right." Jim nodded as he scribbled on his notepad. "All good ideas, Anna. This could prove interesting."

"Hopefully." She glanced at the clock. "Well, I promised not to be late for dinner tonight. Did you finish the final proofs yet?"

"Almost done. I'll lock up the front office after you leave."

"Thanks." She turned off the desk lamp.

"Unless you want me to escort you home again?"

"I really appreciate your security measures, but I think I'll be just fine, Jim."

He looked disappointed. "You know I'm not only walking you home to ensure your safety, Anna. I enjoy your company too."

Anna wasn't sure how to respond. The truth was she had felt safer with Jim by her side on her short walk home. Especially on evenings when she worked late. She looked out the window to see that the fog had rolled in again. "You know, I wouldn't mind being walked home again. But why don't I wait for you to finish the proofing for tomorrow's edition? Then we can both lock up."

"Great. I won't be long."

After Jim left, Anna called home and, when Bernice answered, asked about inviting Jim to join them for dinner. "He's a bachelor, you know, and he's been so good to escort me home each evening. It seems a nice way to thank him."

"That's just fine," Bernice assured her. "I'm already cooking for a small crowd."

"A small crowd?"

"It started with Katy. After school, she invited her grandmother and the Krauss women to join us. Then, after his weekly examination, Mac invited his doctor to dine as well." Bernice counted out loud. "That'll make eight."

"What time do you plan to serve?"

"Seven—if that works for you."

"Perfect."

As Jim walked Anna home, she explained the impromptu dinner party. "We'd love for you to join us."

"But I'm not dressed for dinner."

Anna glanced at his gray suit. "I think you look just fine, Jim, but if you want to run home first, you've plenty of time. Dinner isn't until seven."

"Well, knowing how your daughter and mother enjoy dressing for dinner, I think I'd like to spruce up a bit."

"I understand. And Katy will probably insist I do the same."

"She's such a fashionable young woman."

"That's true. And I can honestly say she didn't get that from me."

"Perhaps her grandmother?"

Anna laughed. "I'm sure you're right. Lucille definitely has a very strong sense of style." She almost added that her mother's style certainly wasn't Anna's, but she knew that sounded rather catty.

"You know that our newspaper doesn't have a fashion column, Anna. Most of the larger newspapers cover that topic. Women readers probably appreciate it."

"A fashion column?" she mused. "That's not a bad idea. Especially in light of trying to appeal to our female readers in the upcoming election."

"Katy could probably write a good fashion column."

"Katy?" Anna considered this.

"She's artistic and well spoken, and she certainly knows a lot about fashion. Assuming she can write, I think it would be worth talking to her about."

"But she's still in school."

"Oh?" He sounded doubtful.

She turned to look at him, noticing he had a funny expression. "What have you heard?"

"Oh . . . nothing."

"You must've heard something, Jim."

"Well, Katy was chatting with me the other day. She was waiting for you to finish a phone call.

Anyway, she casually mentioned her boredom in school . . . and her interest in taking some sort of test to earn her diploma early and her hopes to start a dress shop with her grandmother's help."

"She actually *told* you that?" Anna felt slightly indignant. Katy wasn't even seventeen yet—and she was bragging about her plans to finish her schooling early and start a dress shop? Goodness!

"Maybe she just said she was *thinking* about it," he backpedaled. "Sort of like a dream."

"Hmm. Maybe." Anna paused in front of the house. "And, of course, it's fine to have dreams. But Mac and I have been hoping to send her to the university. Many young women are pursuing college degrees nowadays." She scowled. "I often scold myself for not having the good sense to do so when I was Katy's age. That was what Mac had wanted for me."

"I suppose our dreams don't often match our parents'."

"Yes, I suppose you're right." She brightened. "Well, thank you for getting me home safely. I'll let you be on your way."

He nodded. "I'll be back soon."

Anna tried not to feel too aggravated at her daughter's enthusiasm as she went inside. She knew that Katy considered Jim a friend. She had probably just been chattering to him like she would do with Ellen. Hopefully she wasn't still

63

serious about the idea of giving up her schooling to sew dresses. Whatever the case, Anna was determined not to mention it tonight. They could discuss it privately later on.

"Mother!" Katy exclaimed as soon as Anna was upstairs. "You're late."

"Not very late." Anna removed her hat. "Bernice said dinner isn't until seven."

"I know, but you need to get ready."

Anna looked at Katy's blue silk dress. "Is that new?"

Katy spun around. "I've been working on it all week. Ellen and Grandmother helped me some. Do you like it?"

Anna suppressed the urge to say what she really felt. The sophisticated style made Katy look too old—and her hair pinned up like that didn't help. "That color is lovely on you, Katy. And the dress is beautiful."

"Thank you." Katy followed Anna into her room. "I was going to insist that you wear it, but I tried it on and just couldn't take it off. I guess I'm selfish."

Anna smiled. "You're just young. And, naturally, you like looking pretty."

Katy pointed to a pale-pink dress lying on Anna's bed. "I thought you might want to wear this tonight."

Anna almost had to bite her tongue. Katy had chosen a dress that felt too young for Anna—

and here she was wearing one that made herself look older. Still, Anna couldn't help but feel amused.

Katy picked up the dress. "This will look lovely on you."

"It feels a little youthful."

"But you're young, Mother. Anyway, you look young. At least you do when you're not wearing those old, dowdy work suits."

"You know why I do that."

"Yes. But you're not at work tonight. So why not look pretty?"

"Why not?" Anna gave in—and Katy began helping her to get ready, chattering happily as she did the buttons in back. Anna was tempted to ask her about what Jim had just said but determined to stick to her plan—to wait until later. Finally, Katy was done and satisfied with her results.

"There," Katy declared, turning Anna toward the bureau mirror and standing beside her. "How do we look?"

Anna smiled. "We look just fine . . . thanks to you."

"I think we could pass as sisters." Katy looped her arm around Anna's. "And it's nearly seven now."

As they went downstairs, Anna couldn't help but wonder if this was part of Katy's clever plan. By making herself appear older and her mother

younger, did she think she could convince everyone that she was a mature adult . . . ready to finish
her schooling and take up her career running a
dress shop? Anna hoped not.

CHAPTER 7

Sometimes Mac resented entertaining dinner guests in his own home, but not tonight. He hadn't even complained when Mickey had helped him to dress for dinner. Because this evening he was surrounded by trusted loved ones and close friends. No need to feel apologetic or embarrassed when his clumsy left hand dropped the salad fork or when he responded with stilted language skills. Everyone sitting around his table was kind and understanding. And it was enjoyable to just listen to their lively conversation, contributing when he could but doing so without pressure.

"It's always such a delight to dine here." Daniel said as the meal wound down. "The food is great and the company even better. Far superior to eating my sorry cooking alone in my kitchen. And I get tired of eating at the hotel."

"I know just what you mean," Jim agreed. "Bachelor homemaking leaves a lot to be desired."

"I've considered hiring a cook, but it seems extravagant for just one person. Now, if I could get someone like Bernice just a few times a week . . ." Daniel winked at Mac.

"Not on your life." Mac shook a finger at the doctor.

"What if you two bachelors shared a cook?" Anna suggested.

"My mother is a very good cook," Ellen told them.

"That's true." Lucille offered a bright smile. "Clara has taken over my kitchen, and, although my housekeeper complains a bit—from jealousy—you'll hear no complaints from me."

"Say, that's not a bad idea." Daniel looked hopefully at Clara. "If you ever decide you need a job, let me know."

"But Clara is such a fine seamstress," Katy said. "I think her skills could be useful in other ways."

Sensing that Clara was uncomfortable with the focus on her, Mac attempted to change the subject. "Did you get the paper put to bed all right?"

"Yes," Anna assured him. "Nothing too sensational, thank goodness."

"Not yet." Jim's eyes twinkled.

"Meaning you're expecting some more big stories?" Daniel looked from one of them to the other.

"With the upcoming election, I'm sure there will be some interesting developments." Anna gave a vague smile.

"Speaking of the election, I've noticed a lot of

Wally Morris buttons around town," Daniel said. "Almost every woman I see is wearing one."

"I had lots of help." Katy beamed. "I never would've gotten them done without Grandmother and Clara and Ellen. I just wish I had more time to organize teas. Lots of women are interested in chatting with Wally." She glanced at Anna. "It's difficult being a campaign manager and going to school."

The table got quiet for a moment, and Mac noticed a slight crease in Anna's forehead. "You should get help," he suggested. "Gladys Rollins could help."

"That's a great idea." Anna nodded. "Gladys knows everyone in town. She could easily organize teas."

Katy looked slightly disappointed but agreed. "And being the police chief's wife, she probably has a good influence."

"Yes, she could have her husband lock up anyone who refuses to come," Jim teased.

Although everyone laughed, Mac felt bad for Clara and Ellen. That joke was probably not that funny to them.

"Bernice made blackberry cobbler for dessert," Mac said slowly. "I know because I snuck a bite." He grinned. "I recommend."

"I wish I hadn't eaten so much dinner." Lucille pressed a hand to her stomach. "I adore a good cobbler."

As dessert was served, the conversation grew livelier, and Mac used the opportunity to observe. He was well aware that Daniel, the good doctor, was interested in Anna. But it seemed that Jim was also eagerly vying for her attention. But both Katy and Ellen were engaging in the banter too. As they argued over whether or not President Wilson would be reelected, Mac knew he couldn't keep up. So he let Bernice know he wanted to take coffee in the front room, and Lucille and Clara opted to join him.

"Leave the young'uns to argue their politics," Lucille said jokingly as they exited the dining room where the conversation had just shifted to the war in Europe. Her brows arched high. "I'm sorry, Clara." They sat down. "I didn't mean to infer you were old." She chuckled. "I suppose you're just more mature than the others."

Clara simply smiled. "That's all right. I sometimes feel that I'm much older."

"You've lived through a lot," Lucille told her. "But that's behind you now."

"Not everything," Clara said glumly.

"Have you spoken with AJ?" Mac asked. "Since Albert escaped?"

She nodded. "I visited him on Wednesday. Chief Rollins drove me to the jail."

"How is he?" Mac asked.

"He's all right . . . considering. Although he was upset about his father breaking out of jail."

70

"Upset?" Mac hoped he wasn't being too nosy, but the newspaperman in him was rising up. This was a story he wanted to hear.

"He was worried about his father." She shook her head. "I told him that Albert didn't deserve his concern."

"Why was he worried?" Mac asked.

"He has a theory." Clara looked uneasy. "I haven't mentioned this to anyone."

"What did AJ say?" Mac persisted, eager to get to the bottom of it.

"It would actually be a relief to tell someone," she admitted. "I know I can trust both of you. AJ feels sure that the men who helped Albert to escape have a reason."

"What reason?" Mac said quietly.

"To shut him up. AJ said that could be the only reason they would go to such measures to get Albert out of jail. They want to keep him from talking to the law—they don't want him naming names."

Mac slowly nodded. "Makes sense."

"What about AJ?" Lucille put her hand on Clara's. "Will he be safe? Won't they be worried that he'll talk too?"

"He's in a cell by himself on the second floor," Clara explained. "But I do think he's worried as well. He doesn't trust all of the jailers."

Mac remembered Anna's concerns. "That's good. He shouldn't."

Clara looked slightly alarmed. "Is he in danger?"

"Hard to say." Mac rubbed his chin. "But you should tell Chief Rollins. You can trust Harvey."

"If you say so." She let out a slow breath. "I will. I don't want anything to happen to AJ. He told me that he's had time to think about everything. He realizes how wrong he was to do what he did. He wishes he could undo it. I told him that his father is partly to blame. What sort of man leads his son into a mess like that?" She reached for her handkerchief and dabbed at an escaped tear.

"It's not too late for AJ," Mac assured her. "He can change his path."

"Yes, I believe that." Clara gripped the handkerchief. "He wants to enlist in the army. And even though the thought of him in a battle worries me, I would much rather he was in the army than in jail . . . or under the influence of his father and his friends."

"The army will make a man out of him," Lucille declared. "That's what my mother said the army did for my father—he was an officer for the Union during the Civil War. And he survived that war just fine. It was the gold mine that did him in, back when I was just a little girl."

"I didn't know that," Mac said with surprise.

Lucille's eyes gleamed. "There's a lot you don't know."

But before Mac could ask her more questions, the others were joining them, and the conversation moved to a debate over whether motion pictures were a form of informative art or useless entertainment. And Mac knew he'd have to wait until later to learn more about the woman he'd married as a youth.

Saturday passed without an opportunity for Anna to question Katy about her plans for the future. But Anna couldn't fault her daughter since she knew that Katy and Ellen were busy at Lucille's house, making more buttons and posters for Wally's campaign. By the time Anna saw Katy, they had to hurry to go to dinner at the Douglas home. Rand had driven over to pick them up since it was raining and Mac's Roundabout only seated two under cover.

"We've certainly had fun lately," Katy said brightly as Randall helped Anna and her into the back seat of his car and Mac into the front seat. "I feel just like a social butterfly."

"I remember when you were so worried that Sunset Cove would be boring," Anna teased her daughter. "Didn't you call it a one-horse town?"

"You have to admit it's not the same as Portland," Katy said. "But I really do think I like Sunset Cove better. It's easier to get to know people here."

"I know my mother is looking forward to having all of you tonight." Randall got behind the wheel. "I'm so glad you could come. How are you getting along, Mac?"

"Much better. Better every day."

"As long as you keep doing your therapy," Katy reminded him.

"Katy is the boss." Mac chuckled.

"Yes," Anna agreed. "She is a formidable task-master."

"Oh, Mother, you make me sound horrible."

"Not horrible. Just rather strong-willed." Anna refrained from calling her stubborn. "But we need strong women in today's society."

"My mother is one to appreciate strong women," Randall said.

"How long has she been running the mercantile?" Katy asked.

"Since my dad died. That was about twelve years ago."

"Mrs. Douglas helped with women's suffrage in Oregon," Anna told Katy.

"Along with your great-grandmother," Mac added.

Katy's brows lifted. "Were they friends?"

"Yes," Randall said. "Mac's mother took mine under her wing."

Mac sighed. "My mother never saw women get the vote."

"But she was part of it." Anna leaned forward

to pat his shoulder. "She and Marjorie both helped."

"You did too, Mother," Katy reminded her. "You worked for it in Portland."

Anna nodded. "That's true."

"We'll be outnumbered by the strong women tonight," Randall said as he parked in front of his family home. It wasn't a large house and not nearly as grand as Mac's, but it was one of the nicer homes in Sunset Cove.

"Hope we don't have to vote on anything," Mac teased as they got out.

They hurried through the rain, went into the house, and removed their wet outer garments as they were greeted by Marjorie Douglas.

"Welcome, welcome!" After hanging their coats, she led them into a somewhat fussy-looking parlor, where a fire was glowing warmly in the fireplace. Marjorie grasped Mac's good hand, leading him to a settee near the hearth. "It's so good to see you're out and about and well again."

"Thank you." He sat down with her help, and she sat next to him.

"You look just as good as ever," she told Mac, still grasping his hand.

"Looks can be deceiving." He gave them a slow grin.

"Oh, Mac, you've still got your sense of humor. I certainly enjoy a man who can share a good laugh. Especially at our age." She released his hand and turned to the others, inviting them to sit.

Anna tried to conceal her surprise as she sat on a padded rocker—was Marjorie actually flirting with Mac? Was that the purpose of this little gathering? And what would Mac think if it were? Anna smiled at Marjorie. "On our way over here, Mac was telling us that you and my grandmother worked together for women's suffrage in Oregon. You must've been so pleased and proud when women got the vote."

"You better believe it," Marjorie said. "And I'm champing at the bit to cast my first vote in a major election. It's long overdue, if you ask me. I can't wait to walk into those polls with my head held high."

"I know just what you mean." Anna rocked in time to her nod. "I plan to write a special piece on it for the newspaper that week. Maybe I should interview you."

"Speaking of the upcoming election, I've just made new posters for Wally Morris's mayoral campaign." Katy turned her smile on their hostess. "Would you be willing to post one in your store? They're quite nice looking, if I do say so myself."

Marjorie's frown looked uncertain. "I might need to think about that, Katy. I like to remain nonpartisan when it comes to the mercantile.

You see, I don't want to alienate any of my customers."

"But, Mom," Randall protested, "you were just saying—"

"My store is my business, Randall."

"But it's all right for a business to express a political opinion," Randall argued. "Lots of folks are putting up campaign signs."

"I think that's for me to determine," she said a bit sharply. "I have the right to vote and choose as I please. No one can tell me what to do."

The room grew uncomfortably quiet, and Anna tried to think of another subject to introduce, except that felt like ignoring the elephant in the room. "As you probably know, we're supporting Wally Morris," she calmly told Marjorie. "But a newspaper is expected to endorse a candidate. I can understand your wanting to give careful consideration with the mercantile. And, of course, that is your right."

"Thank you for respecting that." Marjorie nodded, but everyone else remained awkwardly quiet.

Although Anna could partially understand Marjorie's position, another part of her was curious. Was it possible that Marjorie liked their present mayor? Or that she opposed prohibition? Simply because she was a woman didn't mean she was a prohibitionist. After all, Lucille certainly was not. And everyone knew that Marjorie Douglas was a woman with strong opinions. It was possible she liked Calvin Snyder and equally possible that she opposed prohibition.

"May I ask you a question, Mrs. Douglas?" Katy said politely.

"Certainly." Marjorie's lips twitched. "Everyone knows I have no trouble expressing my opinions."

"And I like that," Katy said. "But I am curious if you hope to see Mayor Snyder reelected? And, naturally, you're entitled to your opinion. But most of the women in this town don't like him. So, unless you are supportive of Calvin Snyder, I would think you wouldn't be worried about offending your customers, especially since I'm sure that most of your shoppers are women. At least, when I've been there, they have been."

Anna didn't know whether to shush her daughter or clap her hands in approval.

"Well, that's a fair question, Katy." Marjorie pursed her lips. "Truth be told, I do not care for Calvin Snyder."

"So you don't want him reelected?" Katy looked relieved.

"Not particularly."

"Then that raises another question," Katy continued. "Are you in favor of prohibition, Mrs. Douglas?"

Anna did want to shush her inquisitive daughter now, but what could she do?

To Anna's relief, Marjorie simply smiled. "How old are you, Katy?"

"Almost seventeen."

"You ask rather adult questions for a girl your age. But I admire you for that." Marjorie took a deep breath. "And in answer to your adult question, I'll give you an adult answer. I worry that prohibition brings with it . . . a whole new set of problems. Some that we've already been experiencing. Rum-running and bootleggers who make illegal alcohol that might be dangerous. I'm concerned that the problems of prohibition will outweigh the advantages. Does that make sense to you?"

Katy seemed to be considering this. "I'm not sure I agree with you, but I think it's worthy of discussion."

"I know what Marjorie means," Mac said solemnly. "I've had similar thoughts."

"Maybe so," Rand added, "but as a lawyer, I support the law of the land. The constituents voted for it; the law-abiding citizens need to uphold it or answer to the law."

"*I* didn't vote for it," Marjorie declared. "And based on what our little town has been through these past few months, I feel even more convinced I voted right."

"I suppose time will tell." Anna tried to sound

light. "And I must agree, Marjorie. Prohibition laws have taken their toll on Sunset Cove recently. But I can only blame the criminal elements for that. Hopefully this whole thing will smooth out in time."

"Don't forget that the criminal element you mentioned wasn't quite so prevalent *before* prohibition."

Anna knew she couldn't argue with this. She didn't even want to.

"Well, I must say that this criminal activity does provide more work for lawyers," Randall said brightly. "Can't complain about that."

"And it sells more newspapers," Mac put in wryly.

Marjorie just shook her head.

"Thank you for being so honest," Katy told Marjorie. "You've given me food for thought."

"Speaking of food." Marjorie stood. "Let's move into the dining room. My roast must be done by now."

To Anna's relief, their conversation shifted from prohibition to other less controversial topics while they ate dinner. But she couldn't help but think about Marjorie's position. She'd had no idea that Randall's mother had this other side to her. She always seemed somewhat flippant and chatty in the mercantile. But her argument against prohibition seemed surprisingly well thought out. Perhaps even more surprising to Anna was her daughter's intelligent questions. Suddenly Katy really did seem more adult than child. But Anna wasn't sure she was ready for her little girl to grow up . . . not just yet.

CHAPTER 8

Anna felt a bit stunned after reading Ed's article for the business section. His interview with Mayor Snyder had produced some rather interesting quotes, and, although she liked Ed's angle, this piece had turned out to be somewhat controversial and possibly inflammatory. For that reason, she called Ed into her office for a brief meeting on Friday morning. She wished that Jim could join them, but he was at the county jail getting some final interviews for the piece they wanted to run in tomorrow's paper.

"You wanted to speak to me, Miss McDowell?" Ed waited outside her partially opened door.

"Yes, please come in. And, please, call me Anna." Since her decision to remain in Sunset Cove as editor in chief, Anna had requested that her writing staff and Virginia call her by her first name. It was the way Mac had run the paper, and Anna felt it might help to warm things up a bit. However, Ed was rather old-fashioned and had persisted in using her surname. "Have a seat, Ed." She intentionally used his first name as a reminder.

After he sat down, with a somewhat dubious

expression, Anna cleared her throat and picked up his article. "This is very good," she began, watching as Ed's expression brightened slightly. "I like it very, very much."

"Why . . . thank you." He blinked in surprise.

She laid down the page and looked directly into his eyes. "I take it you're not a fan of our illustrious mayor."

Ed's lips twitched to one side. "Is that a problem?"

"No, of course not. As you know, our paper is endorsing Wally Morris. And I'm sure that Jim told you my purpose in requesting a story on our mayor's business dealings with the chowder house was *twofold*."

"Meaning you want to expose Snyder for the snake he is in the form of an innocent-looking business article?" The corners of Ed's mouth tipped slightly upward, and Anna realized it was the first time she'd witnessed anything close to a smile on the older gentleman.

Anna couldn't help but smile back. "Yes, but I had no idea you'd do such an excellent job."

"You wanted me to do less than my best?"

"No, not at all." She leaned forward slightly. "Can I trust you, Ed?"

He looked uncertain. "I like to think of myself as generally trustworthy, Miss—I mean, Anna. To what regard are you referring?"

And so Anna tipped her hand about her plan for

Snyder. "But we planned to hold off most of it until the week before the election."

Ed just nodded. "I figured that was what you were going to do. Mac used to do the same thing before an election. We called it bringing out all the big guns."

She picked up his article. "This isn't exactly a big gun, but it does feel a bit loaded."

He shrugged. "Election's only about a month off. I figured it was about time to start reminding our readers of Calvin Snyder's true nature."

She tapped a finger on her desk as she considered. "That does make sense, but just to be safe, I'd like to run this piece by our legal counsel."

Ed looked surprised. "If you think that's really necessary."

"Well, as I'm sure you realize, this article doesn't paint Snyder in a very positive light."

"It's all true. Those were the man's own words."

She glanced down at the page. "He really said that he bought the chowder house with the intent to turn it into a roadhouse that serves alcohol? Even though everyone knows he bought it *after* the prohibition act?"

"That's what he said."

"And he also said that he still planned to transform it into a private social club? In other words, a speakeasy?"

Ed frowned. *"Speakeasy?"*

"It's a New Yorker phrase for an unlicensed saloon. I did an article on one in Portland last spring. It got raided by the police, but from what I've read in the *Oregonian*, it seems several others have popped up since then. A real challenge for law enforcement."

"Well, Snyder didn't call it a speakeasy. And, although he said it doesn't *currently* serve alcohol, he did mention that intent. He described it as a place for members to gather for social activities like cards and music. And, naturally, he claimed it would be legal. He said he didn't expect any trouble with the law."

"I wonder how he plans to work that."

"I suspect he's looking forward to the chief's retirement. Everyone expects Clint Collins to step into his shoes."

Anna grimaced. She'd heard that rumor too. But something about Lieutenant Collins still didn't sit well with her. "And Snyder actually said that in time he plans to turn his social club into a tavern that will serve alcohol?"

"I swear those were his words. You can check my notes if you like."

"That's rather brazen, don't you think?"

"Snyder has never been one to mince words. He feels certain that prohibition will be struck down before long. He claims he's been talking to people in high places who feel the same. And he blames the whole thing on women getting the vote."

"He actually said that?" Anna felt both irritated and jubilant. "And he was fully aware you were interviewing him for the newspaper when he made these statements?"

"Of course."

"And he didn't seem the least bit worried about how he might appear?"

"Here's what I think . . . Snyder knows that a good part of this town opposes prohibition. He's simply laying his cards on the table. He didn't say anything that could get him into any real legal trouble. After all, a man is entitled to his opinions."

"That's true." Anna remembered Marjorie Douglas's proclamation last week.

"So, it's really in his best interest—when it comes to reelection—to just call a spade a spade. He's hoping he'll get full support from his like-minded constituents."

Anna nodded. "Yes, I suppose so."

"And, as far as anyone can see, at least on the surface, he's not breaking the law. He might fraternize with some thugs, but he's never been caught red-handed. Of course, that could change—especially if the police ever get lucky."

"All right." Anna grinned. "I'm running this article in Saturday's paper, Ed. Good work."

"I've got an idea for a follow-up piece," he

said. "I thought I could interview merchants in town, find out how businesses have fared under our mayor's leadership, as well as since prohibition."

"That's a great idea. I just hope we don't discover that businesses approve the mayor . . . that could be tricky." She sighed. "Although, it would be an eye-opener."

"We don't have to print it if the results are disappointing."

She shrugged. "The truth is the truth. It's not like I want to shield our readers from it—even if we don't like how it sounds." Once again, Anna realized this election was not as cut-and-dried as she'd imagined last summer. Snyder was slippery, and he knew how to work the system to his advantage. Still, she couldn't imagine Sunset Cove under his leadership for another term. Somehow they had to fight this. "Well, let's bring out the big guns. And I think you're right; it's not too soon."

He gave her a mock solute and a grin. "Sounds like a solid plan."

"Just the same, I'll run this by our attorney. And don't throw away your notes, Ed. Just in case Snyder recants."

"They're already in a file."

After Ed left, Anna called Randall and described the article. "I'd like you to take a look, if you have time. We'd like to run it in tomorrow's paper, which means I'd need your approval by this afternoon."

"I can do it during my lunch hour," he said in a slightly sly tone. "But only if you join me."

Anna narrowed her eyes at the telephone. "Is this a setup to—"

"Take it or leave it, Anna."

"Fine. I guess I have to eat."

"Hotel at high noon?"

"I'll be there." As she hung up, she felt a mixture of aggravation and amusement. As payback, she would let him pay for lunch.

As Anna walked to the hotel, she paid close attention to the shops and businesses. Many of them had campaign posters for Wally Morris. But not all of them—including, but not surprisingly, the mercantile. Anna couldn't help but wonder if the businesses without signs were in agreement with Marjorie. But at least they weren't displaying posters for Snyder. So far, she'd only seen a few Snyder signs. But she supposed that could simply be the mayor's way of showing his confidence in regard to his campaign.

"Hello, Anna." Daniel fell into step with her, tipping his hat.

"Good day, good doctor." She smiled up at him.

"Are you on your lunch hour?"

"I am. But it's a business lunch."

He looked disappointed. "It's such a nice day that I'd imagined taking some lunch down to the beach, and I was about to invite you to join me for an impromptu picnic."

She frowned. "That sounds lovely, but I really need to get an article approved by our legal counsel." She patted her satchel. "I want it in tomorrow's paper."

"Meeting Randall?"

"Yes." She paused by the hotel entrance. "But it's a perfect day for a picnic." She glanced at the blue sky overhead. "I wonder if this grand weather will stick around for the weekend."

Daniel brightened. "Perhaps you could give me a rain check. Or I should say a *sun* check. How about having a beach picnic with me tomorrow— weather permitting?"

"That sounds delightful. I'd love it. Weather permitting."

"May I pick you up around noon?"

"Perfect. How about if I get Bernice to fix us a basket?"

His eyes lit up. "That would be wonderful. Until then." He tipped his hat again and continued on his way.

As Anna went inside the rather stuffy hotel, she realized she would've much rather been going on a picnic with Daniel. But business was business, and she had no intentions of running Ed's piece without Randall's approval. Before long, they were seated and, after exchanging pleasantries, lunch was ordered.

"Here's the piece." Anna slid it from her satchel. "Ed did a fine job, he assured me that every quote is true, and he still has his interview notes as proof, but, as you can see, it might be considered, well, somewhat seditious."

"Seditious you say?" His brows lifted as she handed him the paper.

"Well, it could turn some voters against our mayor."

"As long as it's not slanderous." As he began to read, Anna sipped her tea, watching his reaction to certain parts. Finally, he laid it down and looked at her. "Ed swears this is all true?"

"Absolutely."

"Ed has a good reputation in this town. I doubt many would question him on this. But I'm surprised that Snyder was so forthcoming."

She told him Ed's theory, and Randall simply nodded. "Yes, I suppose that makes sense."

"So your professional opinion?"

"I don't see any problem with it." He handed it back to her. "But I can understand your concern, Anna. Quite frankly, I wondered if it could've been a setup. You should be on your guard for that. Snyder could attempt to set the newspaper up with something—perhaps from an unreliable source—that he could claim was slanderous. You know from past experiences with the man, he wouldn't mind taking down the paper."

She nodded as she tucked the article safely

back into her satchel. "I'm well aware of that. And I do plan to be careful—and to run anything questionable through you."

He smiled. "So we can have more business lunches?"

"Are you honestly saying that you're so busy with work that your lunch hour is your only time to meet with me?"

"It's a most favorable time to meet . . . don't you think?"

She made a demure shrug. As much as she liked Randall as a friend—and he was a good friend—she wasn't sure she wanted to get romantically involved with him. And, although she tried to tell herself otherwise, she was fairly certain that was what he had in mind. Still, this wasn't the time or place to discuss such things.

"I wanted to talk to you, Anna," he said in a more serious tone.

"Oh?" She set down her teacup, giving him her full attention.

"I've been concerned about things my mother said on Saturday night. I had no idea she would espouse her political views like that. I hope she didn't offend you or your family."

Anna waved a hand. "Not at all. In fact, I found it quite informative. And it prompted a rather interesting conversation with Katy and Mac the next morning."

"I didn't know she was so anti-prohibition. It's

not something we've really discussed before. But then I remembered how my parents used to make blackberry wine every autumn. Right around this time of year. It was one of the things they enjoyed doing together, and I suspect she was thinking of that . . . and of him . . . and perhaps her nostalgia prompted her political views."

"I can imagine that. But, really, you don't need to apologize for her."

"It's just that I know Mom can be a bit outspoken at the mercantile. And some people consider her to be abrasive . . . and something of a busybody. But I'd hoped that we'd have a nice evening and become better acquainted and that you'd see the other side of her."

Anna couldn't help but chuckle. "I did see the other side of her, Randall. And don't worry, I liked it. There's more to your mother than I realized."

Randall looked relieved, but their orders were being served, so no more was said about Saturday night. Still, Anna felt uncomfortable. It concerned her that Randall was worried about the impression his mother had made on her, that he wanted to be sure Anna liked Marjorie. What did that mean? Was Randall hinting that he felt their relationship was progressing beyond just friends? And if so, what could she do about it?

As a result, Anna kept their conversation focused on the newspaper business and asked him questions about the legal issues surrounding libel and slander and how difficult it was to prove or defend a lawsuit. By the time they finished eating, not only had she managed to keep this strictly business, she had also gleaned some valuable legal information.

"Thank you for your time," she told Randall as they stood outside of the hotel. "I feel that I learned a lot just now. I can see you really are an expert at law."

His grin was slightly sheepish. "To be honest, I've been brushing up on cases regarding publishing law . . . just in case."

"Well, I certainly do appreciate it." She politely shook his hand. "Now, if you'll excuse me, I have a paper to get out." As Anna hurried away, she hoped that her professionalism had made the right impression on him. She had tried not to be too chilly, but she didn't want to do anything to foster false hope.

Because the more she thought about it, the more certain she felt that she would never have true romantic feelings toward Randall. As much as she liked him, she had no interest in becoming his wife. And if she'd done anything to encourage that line of thinking, she regretted it. No doubt, it had been flattering to have his attention . . . along with her other male friends. But she suddenly felt determined to do whatever needed to be done to put the brakes on this thing with Randall.

She just hoped it wouldn't damage the relationship they had. Randall had proved a valuable friend. And one could never have too many of those.

CHAPTER 9

Anna was glad to wake up to nothing but blue sky and sunshine on Saturday morning. Her picnic with Daniel would not be called off for rain. And, although she'd told Bernice not to go to any special trouble, the sweet woman had promised to make fried chicken, potato salad, and a couple of blackberry tarts. "If Doctor Dan and you are going for a picnic, it should be a very nice picnic," Bernice had told her. Of course, Anna knew that Bernice was quite fond of 'Doctor Dan.' Partially because of his conscientious treatment of Mac and partly because Daniel always complimented Bernice on her fine cooking skills.

As Anna admired the sparkling view from her bedroom, she remembered how the Oregon Coast was renowned for its beautiful autumn weather. Often much better than the summers, which could be foggy and cool. A fall picnic on the beach would be a real treat.

And catching up with Daniel—just the two of them—would be a treat too. Anna wasn't absolutely certain of her feelings toward Daniel . . . except to admit—if only to herself—that they were stronger than her feelings toward Randall. Still, she'd never spent enough time with Daniel to be absolutely sure. And the truth was that Anna was not convinced she *wanted* to be sure. Not yet anyway. She simply wanted to enjoy a fun picnic with an interesting friend. If that led to something more substantial . . . Well, she would just have to cross that bridge when she got there.

Anna searched her closet until she found what she hoped would be a feminine yet picnic-appropriate ensemble. An ecru linen dress with lace trim, a broad-brimmed straw hat, cotton gloves, and her brown oxford shoes. Oh, Katy would not approve of the mannish shoes, but they would be practical for the beach and the dunes.

Despite her sturdy shoes, Anna's heart felt light as she went downstairs to breakfast, where Katy and Mac were already eating.

"Good morning," Mac greeted her.

"Is that what you're wearing today for your picnic with Dr. Hollister?" Katy asked with a concerned tone.

Anna simply smiled. "You disapprove?"

"It's all right, I suppose, but not very festive. I thought you'd want to wear something more feminine, Mother. Perhaps with a few ruffles? Or a dress that goes nicely with a parasol? I could loan you my—"

"I appreciate your kind offers, Katy." Anna sat down, placing a napkin in her lap. "But I'm perfectly comfortable in this outfit. And it's only a picnic, dear. Not a garden party." She chuckled as she poured a cup of coffee.

"A picnic with Daniel?" Mac's brows arched. "This is the first I've heard of it."

"Bernice was the only one I mentioned this to." Anna glanced at Katy. "How did you find out?"

"I asked Bernice about the basket in the kitchen," Katy admitted. "Why? Was this picnic meant to be a secret tryst?"

"No, of course not." Anna suppressed irritation as she removed a hotcake from the platter.

"So does this mean you and my doctor are—"

"Daniel and I are simply good friends," Anna told her father. "I enjoy his company, and that is all."

Mac's smile was crookedly charming. "I just wonder sometimes . . . It seems my daughter has many suitors. I can't keep up."

"Did you know that Mother never had suitors in Portland?" Katy looked at Mac, acting almost as if Anna weren't there. "Not a single one. She always claimed she was too busy for men. If I questioned her about it, she would act as if romance was just a silly notion. I never dreamed she'd have a suitor. But it seems there's no end to them here in Sunset Cove." Katy giggled.

"Oh, *please.*" Anna shook her head with disapproval.

"You know it's true, Mother."

Turning from her precocious daughter, Anna pointed to the newspaper at Mac's elbow. "Did you read that yet?"

"I did." His expression grew grim. "That piece . . . by Ed . . . that could mean trouble, Anna. I'm surprised Ed wrote it . . . and that you ran it."

"You're worried about a libel suit?"

He just nodded.

Meanwhile, Katy snatched up the paper and began reading the article.

"I was concerned too." Anna explained yesterday's meeting with Ed and her business lunch with their attorney. "After hearing the facts, Randall gave the article his seal of approval."

"I don't know, Anna." Mac shook his head.

"Ed is convinced that Snyder actually wants voters to know he opposes prohibition. It's as if he's making that a significant part of his reelection platform. He disagrees with the law and doesn't care who knows it."

"That's ridiculous." Katy set down the newspaper. "Who wants to vote for a criminal?"

"No one has proven him a criminal . . . yet." Mac refilled his coffee cup, only sloshing a little into the saucer. His hands were getting steadier.

"And remember what Marjorie Douglas said last Saturday," Anna reminded Katy. "People are still divided on the prohibition issue."

"I still think it's crazy," Katy argued. "If Snyder thinks that admitting he's a mayor who's above the law will win him the election, he's in for a big surprise."

Anna wished she felt as confident as her daughter. But, unfortunately, the more she considered Snyder's tactics for winning votes, the more concerned she felt.

After breakfast, Katy challenged Mac to a chess game, and Anna carried their dishes into the kitchen and found Bernice putting the fried chicken into the icebox to chill. "That looks yummy," Anna said over her shoulder.

"Oh, Anna." Bernice jumped in surprise. "I've told you not to pick up the dishes. I do that."

"Old habits die hard." Anna peeked at the potato salad that was half-finished. "Need any help?"

"No, it's all under control."

"But I didn't expect you to do everything yourself."

Bernice put her hands on her hips. "I told you I would, didn't I?"

"Yes, but—"

"Is there anything wrong with what I've fixed for you and Doctor Dan?"

"No, of course not. It's far superior to anything I could've put together. And I know Daniel will be thrilled."

Bernice smiled. "Then why don't you leave me to it?"

Anna nodded. "All right, I will." Realizing she

had a couple of hours to spend as she liked, she returned to her room and got out the James Joyce book that she'd been wanting to read. Caught up in the short stories in *Dubliners*, Anna lost track of time and was surprised to see that it was past eleven when Katy announced that she was wanted on the telephone.

To Anna's dismay, it was Daniel calling to tell her he would have to cancel their picnic lunch date. "Mrs. Preston has gone into labor, and since her last delivery was slow and difficult, I need to be there for this one, otherwise I'd leave her in the midwife's hands for a while. I'm sorry."

"That's all right." Anna inserted cheer into her voice. "I understand. Give Mrs. Preston my best."

"Instead of a rain check, I suppose I should ask for a baby check."

Anna laughed. "Yes, I will hold you to that, Daniel." As she hung up the phone, Anna vaguely mused what it would feel like to be a doctor's wife. It probably took a fairly independent sort of woman. Someone who was used to being on her own. Someone like Anna. Not that she was actually thinking about marriage . . . was she?

She was interrupted from giving this too much thought by the ringing of the front doorbell. Assuming that Mickey was occupied in the yard, Anna went to get it. Mindful that Albert Krauss was still on the loose, she cautiously approached the door and peeked through the side window. To her surprise, it was Jim Stafford.

She opened the door. "Hello, Jim. What are you doing here?"

"I was just getting some coffee at the café, and I overheard an interesting conversation. I thought you'd like to know."

"Come in." She led him into the front room and invited him to sit.

"Well, I was sitting in the back corner by myself, just minding my own business and working on that book I've been writing. The place was pretty empty, and I heard someone come in but didn't look up. Then I heard Calvin Snyder's voice, and I decided to do some eavesdropping. You know how it's a little dark in that back corner; I doubt that Snyder even realized I was there. Anyway, he was talking with Clint Collins. Clint was questioning Snyder about that article Ed wrote, and he was clearly not pleased. Snyder was trying to reassure him that it was okay and part of his plan. Then Snyder lowered his voice, which really made my ears prick up, and asked Clint if he'd been found yet."

"*Who'd* been found?"

"He didn't say. He just said, 'Has he been found yet?' Those were his exact words."

"Who do you think he was referring to?"

"Well, Albert Krauss seems like the obvious choice."

"Yes, that's what I thought." Anna nodded. "But what's so special about that? Everyone is on the lookout for Krauss."

"It's what was said next that was worth noting. Collin's answer was that no one had found him yet, but he said, 'It's about time.' "

"Well, I agree. It *is* about time. We'll all sleep better when he's securely locked up again."

"Then Snyder told Collins he should *do something* to make sure he's found *soon*."

Anna still didn't really understand why Jim thought this was such big news. "I'd have to agree with Snyder again. Lieutenant Collins and the rest of the force should *do something*. The sooner the better."

"That's when Collins told Snyder he was on it, and he promised him that he would be found by tomorrow morning."

"Really?"

"That's what he said."

"I wonder how he could be so certain."

"Sounds to me as if he knows where Krauss is hiding out. As if maybe he planned to bring him in."

"Interesting."

"So, here's my plan, Anna. I'm going to trail Collins tomorrow. I want to see what's going on."

"But that could be dangerous."

"I'll be careful—and I'll make sure he doesn't know I'm trailing him."

"Exciting." She sighed. "Makes me wish I could help you."

He grinned. "Ready to don your newsboy disguise again?"

"Newsboy?" She frowned.

"That's what you looked like in that getup. Like a twelve-year-old newsboy."

She chuckled. "Thanks a lot. And here I thought I was intimidating."

"Intimidating who?" Katy asked as she entered the front room.

"Never mind," Anna told her.

"Hello, Mr. Stafford," Katy said politely. "How are you doing on this beautiful, sunny day?"

"I'm fine, thank you. How about you, Katy? Working on Wally's campaign?"

"Not today." She glanced at the mantel clock. "Mother, I thought you were going on a picnic—"

"That's been cancelled," Anna said.

"But what about that lovely basket in the kitchen? Are you going to let it go to waste?" She grinned at Jim. "You should see what Bernice packed."

"A picnic?" His brows rose hopefully. "Sounds like fun."

"I know," Katy exclaimed. "Why don't we three go? I'm sure Bernice packed more than enough food."

"That's a great idea," Anna agreed. "How about it, Jim? We've got fried chicken and potato salad and—"

"You don't need to ask me twice." He eagerly stood. "What can I carry?"

Before long, they were traipsing down the beach, looking for the perfect spot to set up their picnic. It wasn't exactly how Anna had hoped to spend the day, but it turned out to be surprisingly fun. And Katy and Jim got along so well that it made for a very pleasant afternoon. But a bank of fog was starting to roll in and the wind was picking up, so they gathered their things and headed back to the house.

"Be careful tomorrow," Anna told Jim again as they said good-bye in front of the house.

"Careful about what?" Katy asked.

"Oh, nothing," Anna told her. "He's just following a story."

"Must be an interesting one." Katy's eyes widened with interest.

"Speaking of stories," Jim said to Katy. "Did your mother tell you my idea for getting you to write for the newspaper?"

"What idea?" Katy turned to Anna.

Slightly aggravated by Jim's mentioning this, but glad to change the subject, Anna briefly explained Jim's suggestion that Katy could be a fashion writer.

"A fashion column in the *Sunset Times*?" Katy

nodded. "That's a brilliant idea. Do you really think I could do it?"

"You seem to be a fashion expert," Jim told her. "Can you write?"

"Katy is a very good writer," Anna said with pride. "And what she doesn't know about newspaper writing, she could easily learn."

"I'd *love* to be your fashion columnist," Katy told Anna. "That's a fabulous idea."

"Well, let's see how it goes." Anna still questioned whether Katy was old enough for this much responsibility.

"I can't wait to tell Ellen the news." Katy took the picnic basket from Jim, told them both goodbye, and hurried into the house.

"I meant what I said, Jim," Anna quietly warned him. "You be careful tomorrow. And let me know what happens."

"Will do, boss." He grinned. "And thanks for including me on your picnic. I can't think of a better way to while away a Saturday afternoon than spending time with the lovely McDowell girls."

Anna thanked him and went into the house. As much as she enjoyed Jim's company, she was growing increasingly concerned about the relationship. Jim Stafford was a good guy, but he was still her employee. She was his boss. And they both needed to remember that. Otherwise, it could get extremely awkward . . . for everyone.

Not for the first time, Anna wished she was a man. Oh, not really—she did enjoy being a woman. However, she did not enjoy the limitations of her feminine sex. If she were a man, she could pal around with Jim. She could go with him to trail after Collins tomorrow. And no one would question their relationship at all. But she was a woman, and even though times were changing—they were not changing fast enough!

CHAPTER 10

O n Sunday morning, Katy, Mac, and Anna were just getting into the car to go to church when Anna noticed Jim walking up to the house. Remembering his plan to follow Lieutenant Collins this morning, she was eager to hear how it had gone. "Go on without me," she told Katy and Mac. "I'll walk to church—after I talk to Jim about something." Without giving them a chance to question this, Anna hurried over to Jim.

"Have you heard the news?" he asked.

"No. I've heard nothing." She waved as Katy backed the Roundabout out of the driveway, then headed down the street.

"Albert Krauss has been found."

"Oh." She sighed with relief. "That's good news."

"No, no . . . not exactly."

"What do you mean?"

Jim glanced down the street toward Lucille's house. "Are Ellen and Clara home?"

"I'm not sure. They might've left for church by now."

"Albert was found . . . *dead*."

A chill ran through her. Although she didn't

like Albert Krauss, she had never wished him dead. "How? What happened? When?"

"Too soon to say, but I think it—"

"Let's not talk out here." Anna turned back to the house, but her hands were shaking slightly as she unlocked the front door and led him inside. How would Clara and Ellen react to this news? "Let me call Lucille's house," she said. "I want to stop them before they leave. I'd hate for them to hear about this at church." She hurried to the phone to place the call, but before Lucille answered, Anna realized she needed to be careful of what she said. It was no secret that some of the switchboard operators liked to eavesdrop . . . and they also liked to share items of interest. News like this would spread like wildfire.

"Lucille," Anna said in relief. "You're still home."

"We were about to leave for church," Lucille said pleasantly.

"Please, don't go. Not today."

"What? What's wrong, Anna?"

"I'll be over to explain everything in a few minutes," Anna promised. "Just keep Clara and Ellen home—please—it's important."

"Yes, of course. If you say so."

"I'll be down there shortly."

After she hung up the phone, Jim described how he'd followed Lieutenant Collins from his house. "He wasn't in uniform, and it looked like he planned to do some fishing, because he had a pole and tackle box. He went down to the docks, but instead of fishing, he started chatting with some fisherman, acting like he wanted to rent a dinghy. So they started poking around the boats, and Collins pointed out the one he wanted. But when the guy pulled the tarp off . . . Well, it wasn't good."

Jim grimly shook his head. "The expression on the old fisherman's face told me something was seriously wrong. So I went on down to see. A body was in the boat. The first thing I noticed was what appeared to be a prison uniform, although it was so dirty you could barely see the stripes. But it was obviously Krauss. And, without going into detail, I'll just say he appeared to have been there a few days."

Anna felt slightly sick, but she reminded herself she was a newspaperwoman. "Do you know how he died?"

"Collins was talking like it was suicide, but I'm not convinced."

"Why?"

"Mostly because Collins was so quick to jump to that conclusion."

"Do you know how he died?"

"Gunshot wound to the head."

"So possibly murder?"

"Seems worth considering. Collins flashed his badge then and warned everyone not to touch a thing while he went up to the bait shop to call the chief. I stuck around questioning the fishermen to see if they'd noticed or heard anything in the past few days. Naturally, everyone had something to say. But nothing very definitive. And it's hard to say when Krauss was put there, or how long since he'd died. Chief Rollins and a few officers arrived and took over the scene. The chief told me that he couldn't rule out murder and said he planned to ask Daniel to do an autopsy report."

"Oh my." Anna thought of Clara and Ellen again . . . and AJ.

"Looks like we've got the lead story for Tuesday's paper. Of course, everyone will have heard most of the news by then, although I plan to do some sleuthing around in the meantime. Hopefully Daniel can pin down the cause of death."

"Do you think it was possibly suicide?"

"Anything's possible. I just didn't like how eager Collins was to call it."

"I know, but what if Krauss felt regret for what he'd done . . . what he'd put his family through?"

"Yeah, that crossed my mind. But don't forget AJ's concern that someone wanted to shut his dad up, and that could've been the motive for the jailbreak."

"That's true." She nodded solemnly. "I sure hope they're keeping AJ safe."

"I asked the chief about that. He plans to get AJ transferred to a more secure prison."

"I need to tell Clara and Ellen." She shook her head. This wouldn't be easy.

"That was my main reason for stopping by just now. I thought it would be easier for them to hear it from you."

"Easier for them . . . not for me."

"Do you want me to go with you?"

"Would you?"

He agreed, but it was a somber walk to Lucille's house. All three women, dressed for church, eagerly waited for Anna to explain. "We have some difficult news," she began as they stood huddled in the foyer. "Jim just told me about it, and I thought you should know."

"Is it about Albert?" Clara had a slight tremor in her voice.

Anna nodded. "Yes. He was found this morning. I'm sorry to tell you he has, uh, Albert has passed on."

"He's dead?" Ellen asked with wide eyes.

"Yes. I'm so sorry."

Clara's eyes filled with tears, and as she began to quietly sob, Ellen wrapped her arms around her. "We'll be okay. Please don't cry. Just think, Mama, it's all over now. He can't hurt you any-more."

"I know . . . I know," Clara muttered. "Still . . . it's hard to think . . . he's dead."

"Let's go sit down." Lucille led them to the parlor. "This is most distressing—most distressing."

After they were seated and Clara began to recover, she asked questions. Much like what Anna had just asked Jim. They kept their answers brief but honest, admitting it was too soon to really know. Finally, Clara inquired as to her son's welfare. "What about AJ? If Albert was murdered to keep him quiet, would they want to kill AJ too? He must've associated with the same men as Albert. He must know things . . . information that could put him in danger."

Jim told her about talking to the chief about those very concerns. "He assured me he will do all he can to keep AJ safe."

"But maybe Lieutenant Collins is right," Ellen said solemnly. "Maybe he killed himself."

"I don't know." Clara shook her head. "That doesn't sound like Albert."

"Then who do you think killed him?" Ellen demanded. "What did he know that was so threatening? A lot of men are involved in rum-running. Why would anyone care enough to commit murder?"

"Albert could probably name names," Anna told Ellen. "Perhaps he knew who murdered my newsman, Wesley Kempton. That would be worth shutting him up."

"So you really believe it's related?" Clara

wiped her eyes with her handkerchief. "The rum-running and Wesley's murder?"

"It all adds up," Jim said quietly. "I don't think anyone can assume it was suicide."

"That could mean we might still have a murderer in the area," Anna said glumly. "Although I don't think we should be overly concerned, we should continue to be cautious." She considered mentioning her uncertainties about Lieutenant Collins but felt like Clara and Ellen already had enough to distress them at the moment. Even though Albert hadn't been a good husband or father, Anna understood—only too well—how mixed their emotions could be running right now.

"You've heard my story," she murmured to Clara. "I've told you how my husband, Katy's father, got involved with the wrong people when Katy was a baby and that he died in prison." Refraining from sharing her suspicion that Darrell had been murdered too, she grasped Clara's hand. "So you know that I understand what you're going through and how your feelings will be conflicted and upsetting. In one moment I'd be relieved that Darrell was gone. But the next moment I'd feel guilty for my relief. Then I'd question myself—if I'd only done something differently, could it have turned out better? Or ask myself why I ever married him in the first place. Except then I wouldn't have Katy. I'd go round and round over the whole thing. It took me years to get past it. But that might be because I didn't have anyone to talk to about it."

Lucille placed a hand on Anna's shoulder. "I wish I'd been there with you, Anna. I'm so sorry I wasn't a better mother. I hope I can make up for it."

Anna thanked her, then turned back to Clara and Ellen. "So if either of you ever need to talk, I am more than willing. Because I really do understand."

"I know you do." Clara let out a shaky sigh. "Thank you, Anna."

"I'm sure the news of this will travel fast," Jim told them. "And there will probably be various theories. You know how people gossip. Try not to listen."

"And, naturally, we'll report on it in Tuesday's edition, but we'll cover the story with respect . . . and honesty," Anna assured them. "No sensationalism."

"I think the big question will be—*how did it happen?* And if it turns out to be murder—*who did it?*" Jim stood. "Now, if you ladies will excuse me, I plan to do some more investigation. I have some leads to follow up."

After Jim left, Lucille asked Sally to serve them tea, and the four women talked for a while longer. Anna's heart went out to both Clara and Ellen, but she felt especially concerned that Ellen had not shed a single tear. And she seemed to be clinging to the belief that her father had killed himself—as if that gave her some satisfaction. But she was keeping her emotions completely in check. Even though Anna knew Albert had failed Ellen as a father, she would've felt better if his daughter cried just a little. Because Anna knew from experience that crying truly was good for the soul.

CHAPTER 11

The week passed without any new developments or discoveries about Albert Krauss's demise. According to the chief, Daniel's autopsy report had only confirmed that a handgun had been used at very close range. It could be murder or suicide. However, Lieutenant Collins was convinced it had been self-inflicted, and that is what he told anyone who wanted to listen. And it seemed that both Clara and Ellen were adhering to his theory. Anna supposed it reassured Clara in regard to AJ—he seemed in less danger if Albert had killed himself. But at least the chief had moved AJ to a safer place. An undisclosed location where, the chief reassured Clara, her boy would be safe. AJ's testimony was too valuable to allow him to be at risk.

"How has your investigation been going?" Anna asked Jim on the following Monday morning. "Are you still convinced Krauss was murdered?"

"I am. And I'm still working on it." His tone lacked enthusiasm as he sat down in her office.

"But you still suspect that Lieutenant Collins and Mayor Snyder are involved somehow?"

"I can't seem to uncover anything rock-solid, but I believe they're connected."

"When I questioned the chief about Collins, he almost seemed offended. Mac told me it's because the chief sees Clint like family."

"Sort of like how Mac felt toward Wesley." Jim shook his head. "Sometimes people can be blinded when the heart's involved."

"Or maybe we're wrong about Clint Collins," Anna mused.

"What about his involvement with Snyder?"

"Maybe he's doing the same thing we are." Anna flipped through the morning mail. "Trying to get information . . . to get to the bottom of this."

"You honestly think Collins is cozying up to Snyder in order to solve this case?"

"It's an interesting theory." She smiled.

"What about Collins discovering Krauss's body?" Jim asked. "Right after he promised Snyder he'd do so? Pretty convenient."

"I'll admit that's a little strange. But when you interviewed Clint, he sure spun the whole thing in his direction. Like he solved the mystery of the escaped prisoner. Some folks in town are heralding him a hero."

Jim scowled. "Never mind that his story sounds completely contrived."

"Well, anyway, I am glad you're still keeping an eye on him."

"And Snyder too."

"Speaking of Snyder, have you noticed how he seems to be suddenly quite interested in campaigning?"

He nodded. "I've seen his posters here and there."

"And how about the meetings he's hosting at the chowder house? Which he's just calling *Charlie's* now. So we can assume they won't be serving chowder." She couldn't keep the sarcasm out of her voice.

"And you're aware they're *private* meetings. By invitation only." Jim drummed his fingers on the chair's armrest. "Wish I could finagle an invite. I've even considered counterfeiting one and wearing a disguise so I can sneak in."

"Except you might need a secret password. Hey, I wonder if Clint Collins will be allowed in."

Jim perked up. "Great idea, Anna."

"What?"

"I'll trail Collins on the night of the next meeting. Be interesting to see if he's part of that."

"I wonder what the chief would think if Clint's there." Anna frowned. "Well, unless this is all just part of their plan. Clint's way of being incognito." She pointed to the clock. "Well, we've both got work to do."

Jim stood. "I meant to ask if you've heard the latest rumor circulating town."

"Which one?"

"That Wally Morris is having some health problems."

"Oh my." She feigned surprise. "I wonder who could've started that one?"

"Well, some folks are buying into it. They're saying Wally has a heart problem, that he's not well enough to serve a full term as mayor."

"Maybe it's time to do an in-depth interview with Wally." She made a note. "I'll take care of this. We'll run it on Saturday."

Jim paused in the doorway. "What if the rumor turns out to be true?"

She just shook her head. "We'll cross that bridge when we get there."

After Jim left, Anna called the Morris house. Wally's wife, Thelma, answered, and Anna inquired as to Thelma's health and was assured she was "fit as a fiddle." "And how's Wally doing? Is he healthy too?"

"Well, he had a little cold earlier this week. But my chicken soup got him right back on his feet again."

"Is he home now?"

"No, he's having coffee with some of his buddies in town."

"Well, that's good to know. So have you heard people discussing Wally's health?"

"You mean because of his cold?"

"No, there are rumors going around town that

Wally's got heart trouble, Thelma. Is there any truth to it?"

Thelma laughed. "You obviously haven't walked the beach with Wally lately. Goodness gracious, that man can go and go. No, no, he doesn't have any heart troubles. Not that I've heard about."

"Has he been examined by the doctor recently?"

"Gracious, no. The last time Wally saw a doctor was when he got thrown from a horse and broke his arm. That was nearly fifty years ago."

"Well, I'd like to squelch that rumor." Anna twirled a pencil between her fingers. "What would Wally say to an examination by Dr. Hollister? You know Mac is quite fond of the doctor. And a clean bill of health from a qualified physician would go a long way to reassure voters."

"I don't know, but I could ask him about it. Was that the main reason you called, Anna?"

"That and I'd like to do an in-depth interview with Wally. But I'd prefer to do it after he gets his clean bill of health from Dr. Hollister. That would really help put an end to the gossip."

"I'll let Wally know. And I think that's a real good idea. I'll have Wally call you back about it."

Anna thanked Thelma, but after she hung up, she decided to give Daniel a call. It wouldn't hurt to get his approval of this idea. But he was with a patient, so she simply left a message with his nurse. However, she didn't completely trust Norma Barrows to deliver the message. For one thing, Norma didn't much like Anna, and for another thing, Norma still seemed to hold out hope that the handsome, widowed doctor might one day fall for his nurse. Based on what Daniel had told her and what she'd seen, Anna felt that was unlikely. Just the same, she decided to stroll over to Daniel's office to see if she could have a word with him.

Anna got there just as the patient was leaving the office, but Norma was clearly not pleased to see her. "Do you have an appointment?" the nurse asked in a slightly uppity tone.

"No, but I just wanted a few minutes of Daniel's time," Anna said politely.

"Is this in regard to your father?" Norma demanded.

"Is Daniel available?" Anna asked.

"Anna McDowell," Daniel said as he came into the reception area. "What are you doing here?" His brow creased. "Everyone well?"

She smiled. "Yes, I just wanted to ask you about something."

He glanced at the clock on the wall. "I believe I owe you a baby check."

Norma's brows shot up, but she didn't say anything.

"Oh, you mean for our cancelled picnic?" Anna remembered.

"I don't have time for a picnic today, but how about I take you to lunch at the hotel? We can talk there."

"Perfect," she agreed.

As they walked through town, Anna told him about the rumors circulating. "But I just spoke to Thelma, and she says other than a little cold earlier this week, Wally is just fine." She explained her idea for Wally to be examined and an article to run in Saturday's edition, and Daniel agreed it was an excellent idea.

"I think citizens should know that their elected officials are in good health. In fact, I might even give Wally a call."

"Maybe Calvin Snyder should undergo an examination too," she said with a tinge of sarcasm.

"Well, let's focus on Wally for starters."

At the hotel's restaurant, their conversation switched from politics to more pleasant topics, and Anna suddenly realized how she had missed Daniel these past couple of weeks. "It sounds like you've been quite busy," she said after he'd filled her in on his recent schedule.

"Much busier than just a year ago. It was so slow when I first started my practice here . . . I wasn't sure I'd be able to make it."

"It looks like you've won people's trust." She sighed. "I wonder if I'll feel like that after I've been running the newspaper for a year."

"Oh, I'm sure you're winning trust, Anna. You're doing an excellent job with the paper. Even your father is impressed."

"Really? Did he tell you that?"

"Not in so many words, but I can tell."

"Sometimes I worry that he resents my taking his place. Oh, not me personally, but just the fact that he's unable to return to work." She set her napkin next to her plate to show the waiter she was finished. "Do you think he'll ever be able?"

"Anything is possible."

"But your honest prognosis?"

He shook his head. "But he's of a retirement age anyway. And I know nothing could've made him happier than having you and Katy in his life." He chuckled. "Lucille too. Do you think your parents will ever remarry?"

"Goodness, I hope not."

Daniel's brows lifted. "Why's that?"

"I don't know. I suppose I'm just worried it could blow up again. The stakes seem high. And Mac seems content as he is. So many years of being a bachelor. I'm afraid it would be like trying to teach an old dog new tricks."

He set his napkin aside with a contemplative expression. "You could be right. I often feel like that myself."

Anna tried not to act surprised. Was this Daniel's way of saying he never intended to marry again? And, really, why should she care? It wasn't as if she ever planned to remarry. And yet . . . "Well, I thank you for this baby check luncheon," she said with a bright smile. "You missed out on a rather nice picnic that day. Bernice's lunch was outstanding, and the weather was gorgeous." She pulled on her gloves and started to stand.

He hurried around to help with her chair. "So you took your picnic without me?"

"Yes." She gave him a teasing smile. "Jim Stafford and Katy and I thoroughly enjoyed the fried chicken that Bernice had prepared especially for you."

"Oh, and now you're rubbing it in."

"I'm sorry." Her smile turned sincere as they went through the lobby. "What you did was so much nobler, Daniel. Who would've guessed Mrs. Preston was having twins?"

"I had my own suspicions." He opened the door for her. "But I didn't want to worry her."

"Well, I called her a few days ago, because I wanted to put a little human interest piece in the paper. It sounds as if the baby boys are doing just fine, and she was very grateful for your professional assistance."

"Yes, I just gave them an examination yesterday. Very healthy little fellows. I suppose you heard she named the firstborn for me."

"I thought that was very nice."

They continued to chat pleasantly as they walked down Main Street, but Anna didn't feel that same spring in her step . . . not like she'd had before lunch. Daniel had given her what seemed a distinct hint . . . her relationship with him was probably only about friendship. Unless she'd misheard him, Daniel Hollister had no plans to remarry. He'd told her once before about his deceased wife. He'd loved her so dearly that her death had nearly killed him. It made sense that he wouldn't want to put himself in that position of vulnerability again. And how many times had she told herself that very thing? Truly, they were much better off being single.

Now if she could just convince her heart.

As Katy sketched a gown she wanted to sew in time for the holidays, she felt distracted. She laid her pencil down and stared out the window that overlooked the ocean. It was a stormy Sunday afternoon, and Katy was holing up in her grandmother's spare bedroom. Her reason for spending time here was twofold. First of all, she knew Grandmother was missing Clara and Ellen after they'd moved back to their own house down by the wharf. But the second reason was that Katy was trying to avoid her mother and grandfather.

She wasn't sure how or exactly when it had

happened, but her life seemed to have grown complicated of late. Perhaps she was making a mountain out of a molehill, but she felt she had some rather prickly problems. For starters, there was Wally's mayoral campaign. It had been so fun at first. And she'd been working hard in the hopes of securing a glorious victory, but lately she'd realized it was much harder than she'd expected. Mayor Snyder seemed to pull out all the stops the past few weeks. Not only was the current mayor slippery and sneaky, he was also an expert at manipulating the constituents. It seemed like every other day a new false rumor would begin circulating town.

The newspaper attempted to disprove the scandal about Wally's "poor" health. But then it was Wally's age. He was older, for sure, but some- one claimed he was in his late eighties when he was only seventy-five! Then the gossips started repeating that Wally had embezzled money from the newspaper, back when he worked for Mac, and that was the reason he could afford to purchase his relatively new automobile. But Katy had gotten Thelma to come forward, telling how she'd inherited money from her family back East and bought the car for them. And so it went. As soon as they extinguished one of these little fires, another one was quickly ignited. Very frustrating. And Katy just knew that Mayor Snyder was behind it. So much so that she'd been tempted to start some stories flying about against Snyder—and for all she knew, they were probably true. But she'd controlled herself.

Her next problem was related to Ellen. Katy had felt Ellen was her closest friend here in Sunset Cove. But lately Ellen had turned rather chilly and distant. Katy was no stranger to girls being mean or acting catty. But usually it was due to jealousy or something equally petty and juvenile. As far as Katy could see, there was nothing like that between Ellen and her. Finally, after talking to Mother, Katy realized that Ellen was cutting herself off from everyone. Mother suspected it was related to Albert Krauss's death, that Ellen was conflicted over the loss of her father. Katy could understand that. Yet Ellen refused to talk about it. Katy was determined to get Ellen to open up. She just wasn't sure how. In the meantime, Katy missed her.

But perhaps Katy's most worrisome problem was her compulsion to take that diploma test, quit her schooling, and start a dress shop. She'd just turned seventeen, and even though she reminded Mother that she'd been only seventeen when she'd left home to get married—against her father's wishes—it hadn't seemed to help Katy's case. Mother was still opposed to this plan.

Katy had decided to bide her time until after the election, but now she was worried. It seemed her mother and grandfather were more determined than ever that Katy attend the university in Eugene. They both seemed to assume—by her silence on the subject—that she'd given up her plan to become a famous dress designer. But she had not. If anything, her desire to make beautiful garments was only growing stronger and stronger. Her one beam of hope was Grandmother. As a result, Katy had been spending more and more time at Lucille's.

"How's it going?" Lucille asked as she poked her head into the spare room.

"Oh, I don't know." Katy shoved the sketch pad off her lap. "I think I'm distracted."

"You've been working so hard on the election lately. Maybe you need to take a break." Lucille came over to peek at Katy's current creation. "Oh, honey, that's perfectly lovely." She patted Katy on the shoulder. "You are a true marvel, dear. I am convinced that someday you are going to be quite famous."

Katy sighed. "Not if Mother and Grandpa have their way."

"They're still pushing you toward the university?"

"Not exactly pushing. But they seem to take it for granted that I'll be enrolled there by fall of 1917 and graduate with the class of 1921. Never mind that Mother didn't attend college, and she seems to have found herself a good career."

"Yes, but perhaps she has regrets."

"Maybe. But is it fair to push her missed opportunities on me? Besides that, I'm well aware that Mother doesn't think I'm ready to test for my high school diploma yet."

"*Are* you ready?"

"I don't like to disparage Sunset Cove High School, but compared to where I went in Portland, well . . . there's no comparison."

"I wish that war in Europe would end." Lucille sat next to Katy on the bed. "Then I would ask to take you to Paris. We could get an apartment together, and you could continue your studies *there.*"

"That would be a dream come true. But according to Jim Stafford—he was our dinner guest last night—the war is only growing bigger. He said that Germany has resumed U-boat attacks and is coming out with new armored vehicles that will make it easier for them to invade even more countries, which will only make the war worse. I don't know why those Germans are such bullies . . . so determined to beat down and take over Europe. But they sound unstoppable to me. Mr. Stafford feels certain that the US will soon be involved. He even spoke of his interest of going over there as a reporter when that happens."

"Well, Europe may have its troubles, but that's no reason for you to put your dreams on hold,

Katy." Lucille picked up the notebook and flipped through some of the other sketches. "You're so talented. I would love to see you pursue this."

"But Mother feels fashion is unimportant foolishness—a senseless, self-centered folly that I will eventually outgrow." Katy rolled her eyes dramatically. "Not nearly as useful and valuable as journalism, which I have no interest in pursuing, thank you very much."

"But I thought she was going to let you write a fashion column for the newspaper."

"Not until *after* the election," Katy informed her. "She said there'll be more space in the paper, but I wouldn't be surprised if she changes her mind by then."

"Well, your dear mother may have no interest in fashion, but, believe me, there are plenty of other women who feel differently. And not just big-city women either." Lucille handed the sketchbook back to Katy. "I wonder if there could be a way to compromise."

Katy frowned. The only college she'd ever been interested in was the Museum Art School in Portland, but now that they didn't live there, her mother felt it was both impractical and expensive. Besides that, Katy knew what she wanted to do—and it wouldn't require a college education. She simply wanted to design dresses.

"There's nothing wrong with more education."

Lucille sighed. "Truth be told, I always felt like I would've fared better if I'd had more schooling. Although, it wasn't an option in my day. Still, I've tried to make myself a student of life. I try to read and learn as I go along."

"That's what I want to do, Grandmother. Just because I stop my formal schooling wouldn't mean I would stop learning. It's just that, more than anything, I want to be creative."

"Well, you know I am ready to back you in your own design business, Katy. I believe you have the talent. And you also know that Clara would gladly work with you. In fact, she's talking about selling the fish company and all her assets. She might be able to invest as well."

"My only obstacle is Mother. Well, Grandpa too. He tends to side with her in regard to education."

"I have an idea . . . . As you know, the election will be over with by Tuesday. After that, life should slow down for everyone. How about if you take your diploma test? And if you pass it, perhaps you could start writing that fashion column. That might help people to see that you're becoming an adult. And then I'll start to work on your grandfather. If we can get him to see our side, it will be easier to persuade your mother."

"Do you think it will work?" Katy felt hopeful.

"All we can do is try." Lucille squeezed her hand. "And hope for the best."

"I'll speak to Mr. Johnson tomorrow about scheduling my test." Katy hugged her grandmother. "Thank you for believing in me."

CHAPTER 12

Because of Election Day, Anna postponed Tuesday's newspaper to Wednesday. "I wonder why we don't always publish our mid-week paper on Wednesday," she mused to Mac over breakfast.

"My father published on Wednesdays and Saturdays," Mac told her.

"Why did you change it?"

He scratched his head. "I can't remember."

"Is there any reason we can't change it back?"

"You are editor in chief." He made a lopsided smile.

"Then I say we change. It always feels rushed to get Tuesday's edition out."

"You will have less time for Saturday," he pointed out. "It's a bigger paper."

"I think it'll work." She hurried to finish her coffee. "It'll be a busy day today, so I'm getting an early start. Don't forget to vote, Mac."

"Don't worry."

"I wish I could vote," Katy said sadly. "I'm afraid Wally is going to need every vote he can get."

"You've done a fantastic job with his

campaign," Anna reassured her dismal daughter. "It's up to the voters to decide now."

"I know." Katy still looked discouraged. "But if Wally loses, I'll have lost too—and I'll blame myself for not having done more."

"You've done plenty." Mac stretched a hand out to pat hers. "Wally and Thelma think you're a wonder."

"But what if I bit off more than I could chew? I was so hopeful last summer when I took on Wally's campaign. But that Mayor Snyder . . . he's a sly one. It makes me sick to think he could win." Katy shook an angry fist. "And he could! What if he's reelected? It will be so horrible!"

"I'll tell you this, Katy." Anna looked her squarely in the eyes. "If Snyder does win, the newspaper will not back off from investigating his involvement in criminal activities. Even if he's not directly to blame, he could be incriminated when AJ goes to trial."

"Why hasn't that happened yet?" Katy demanded.

"Rand is convinced Snyder pulled some strings to delay the court date. It's possible Snyder's worried AJ will expose him. That wouldn't help him get reelected."

"It's just not fair. Sunset Cove could wind up with a crook for a mayor."

"Well, if Snyder gets in hot water with the law, he can be removed from office. So remember that even if he appears to win at the end of the day—and that could happen—it isn't over."

"That's right," Mac confirmed. "It isn't over."

"But what about the victory party I've planned here at the house?" Katy looked close to tears. "It will be so miserable if Wally loses. What will we say or do?"

"We'll cross that bridge when we get there." Anna kissed Katy on the cheek. "Don't worry so much. I'll see you later."

Town seemed extra quiet as Anna walked to work. Because of Election Day, many businesses, as well as the schools, were closed. But it felt like more than just an absence of people. It was as if the fog creeping in from the ocean hadn't only blotted out the morning sunshine but was blotting out hope as well. Sunset Cove did not deserve another term of Mayor Snyder. Katy had good reason for being worried. Anna was worried too.

Anna had been so happy to be back in Sunset Cove and had such high hopes for their small but growing town . . . but it would be a huge disappointment to discover the majority of voters were supportive of a corrupt mayor. And she felt certain Snyder was a crook. She didn't understand why he hadn't been pinned down by the law yet. Sure, he was slippery, but someday he would get caught. Or maybe, like she'd just told Katy, AJ would deliver the evidence. It wouldn't help matters to lose hope.

As Anna turned onto Main Street, she was surprised to see some new signage posted on the outside of various businesses. The words on the hastily-made signs simply read: *Is Wally Morris a Member of the Prohibition Party?* Of course, the word *Is* and the question mark at the end were both nearly illegible. Someone's transparent attempt to avoid a libel lawsuit. Even so, the insinuation was blatantly clear. Snyder wanted to make it appear as if Wally belonged to what was considered a fairly extreme political party. A party that was not popular in this town. And having interviewed Wally several times, Anna knew the allegation wasn't true.

She felt her blood start to boil when she saw that someone had posted a sign on the newspaper office building. Anna tore it off, and, instead of going into the office, she marched straight for Randall's law office. It was next door to the mercantile. But seeing the lights were off and doors locked, she went to the store, and, although it was closed too, she spied Marjorie behind the counter. Anna pounded on the door to get her attention.

"What's wrong?" Marjorie's eyes grew wide as she opened the door. "Is there a fire?"

"I'd like to burn this." Anna waved the sign. "I need to talk to Randall. Calvin Snyder has gone too far this time."

"What's this?" Marjorie frowned at the flyer.

"This is a bold-faced lie. Outright deceit," Anna

told her. "Where is Randall? If he's not available, I'll go to the police. Snyder could be prosecuted for doing this."

"So it's not true? Wally isn't a member of this party?"

"Of course not," Anna declared. "And, for your information, you've got several of these slanderous signs hanging outside your store right now, Marjorie. You might want to talk to your son about the legal implications of being charged with libel."

"I'll take them down right now."

As Marjorie went outside, Randall emerged from the back room. "What's going on? What's all the commotion?"

Anna quickly explained the dilemma, and Randall went out to peer up and down Main Street. "You're right," he told Anna as he came back inside, going straight for the telephone on the wall. "This could definitely be considered slander. And, unless I'm mistaken, some of those signs—including the one closest to the polling place—are a violation of city ordinance. Whether they're slanderous or not."

Before long, he was speaking to Chief Rollins, expressing his legal concerns. He turned to Anna after he hung up. "The chief is sending his men out to remove the signs, which they'll save for evidence. And he plans to round up Snyder for questioning."

"I want to see this for myself." Anna headed outside and watched as a couple of uniformed officers emerged from city hall. "But I'm guessing that Snyder will claim ignorance and innocence when they take him in. He'll say he doesn't know who put up the signs—that it's not his fault."

"Probably so." Randall went with her, both of them watching as the police went to work tearing down the offensive signs. Although most businesses were closed, a number of pedestrians had gathered along the sidewalks, probably on their way to vote, but they'd stopped to discuss the last-minute signage. To Anna's relief, they sounded concerned too. Perhaps Snyder's diabolical plan had backfired. She could only hope.

By the time Anna took her place at the end of a long line, waiting to place her vote, she observed a police car pulling up to city hall. She resisted the urge to cheer as she witnessed a couple of officers remove Calvin Snyder from the back like a common criminal.

"What's going on?" the owner of the lumberyard asked her.

"I believe he's being taken in for questioning," she said loudly enough for others to hear, "for this morning's illegal campaign signage."

Watching with wide eyes, Anna wished that Katy could see the spectacle too. Snyder looked embarrassed and angry as he was escorted into the police station. Naturally, the people waiting to vote began to murmur amongst themselves about the unexpected show. And thanks to the town's usual rumor mill, the word of Snyder's being taken into custody spread quickly. Some folks got the story straight, some speculated, but the general consensus was that it wasn't good.

As the polls in Sunset Cove closed, the national returns were starting to come in over the wire at the newspaper. Ed and Jim were taking turns watching it, but it seemed the presidential race was still too close to call. Although, according to Ed, Wilson was winning. The typesetters had already prepared the headline to reflect Wilson's victory, but Anna had warned them to be ready to change, if necessary. It wasn't that she disapproved of their president being reelected, she just hoped it wasn't forecasting the results for their town's future. More than ever, she wanted Calvin Snyder to lose—and sincerely prayed Wally would win.

By now Anna was well aware that Snyder had talked his way out of any responsibility for the slanderous signs, saying one of his supporters must've gotten carried away but that there'd been no authorization. But at least the chief had kept him at the station for a while, questioning him for a couple of hours before allowing him to leave—while another line of voters watched.

Anna and Jim had written twin sets of election

143

coverage, planning to run whichever ones matched the outcome of the mayoral election. Naturally, the one Anna had written for Wally's victory was longer and more optimistic. The one Jim had written for Snyder was rather brief and terse, but they would pad the page with a secondary article that Anna had written about how the town had been plastered with libelous signage this morning and how Snyder had been detained for questioning. Not such an illustrious start for their notorious elected official. She even left a hint that some citizens might wish to launch a recall campaign . . . in time. She didn't mention that she would gladly lead it.

It was nearly ten o'clock when they heard the firehouse siren, alerting everyone that the results for the Sunset Cove election had been tallied. Anna, along with her staff, grabbed coats and hats and hurried over to city hall to hear the news. A large crowd was already gathered, and Anna spotted Katy across the street. Her face looked clearly worried. Anna tried to press through the crowd toward her daughter, but before she got there, the precinct election officer was making his announcement.

"Wally Morris has been elected as the next mayor of Sunset Cove," he shouted, then repeated himself to make sure everyone heard. After the cheers and applause quieted, the officer quoted the numbers, and, to Anna's pleased surprise, it wasn't very close. She rushed over to Katy, and they embraced.

"We won!" Katy exclaimed, her eyes filled with tears. "We really, really won!"

"Congratulations," Anna told her. "You did a great job, Katy."

"We've got to get home to tell Wally the news." Katy pointed to Mac's Runabout parked nearby. Before long, they were joyfully entering Mac's overflowing and well-lit house as Katy shouted out the good news. "Wally won! Wally is our next mayor!"

Everyone was jubilant as they celebrated the victory, but Anna could only remain long enough to congratulate Wally. She had to get back to the newspaper office to help send it to press. But she didn't mind working late tonight. All in all, it had turned out to be a very good day.

CHAPTER 13

Life in Sunset Cove seemed to settle down after the election, but Anna had the feeling it was only on the surface. Still, she enjoyed returning to a routine that didn't include late nights at the newspaper office. To her relief, Mayor Snyder, who would be replaced by Wally in the New Year, was keeping a low profile. She suspected he was more interested in developing his private "social club" than in being mayor. And that was fine with her. She knew Chief Rollins was keeping an eye on things. Jim was still watching Lieutenant Collins whenever he got the chance, though without making any seriously incriminating discoveries. But Anna was growing hopeful that Collins was simply doing his own secretive work.

The biggest controversy of late, at least at the newspaper office, seemed to be the question of whether the United States should join the Allied forces trying to knock down the German aggressors in Europe. Anna felt it was inevitable, and the more she read of wartime atrocities going on over in Europe, the more she felt the US could no longer play the ostrich with its head in the sand.

"It's just a matter of time," she told Jim after he'd described an informative article he was working on for the next paper. It was their weekly editors' meeting, and, although they hadn't finished going over their agenda, the debate regarding the war pressed on.

"Not with Wilson in office," Reginald declared with confidence. "Everyone knows he opposes US involvement."

"And his reelection proves the voters agree," Ed said without enthusiasm. "So even if he changed his mind, his hands might be tied."

"He better not change his mind," Reginald said sharply. "It's *not* our war."

"Not our war?" Anna countered the outspoken society writer. "How can you say that?"

"Because I'm a US citizen." He folded his arms over his chest. "What happens over in Europe is not our business. I agree with President Wilson— we should stay out of it."

"What country did your ancestors hail from?" she demanded.

"Well, most were from England. Some from Wales." Reginald frowned. "Why?"

"Do you realize how many British casualties occurred the first day of the Somme Offensive?" she asked him. "Nearly sixty thousand. That was just one day, and that battle went on for months."

"That's right," Jim agreed. "And now that the Battle of the Somme has finally ended, do you realize they estimate that one million men have been injured or killed?" He waved the article he was working on. "I just read that number on the United Press wire."

"Do you not think some of those men, ones who were wounded or gave up their lives . . . Might they possibly be related to you, Reginald?" Anna lifted a brow.

"I suppose that's a possibility. But would it make things better if we sent our own young men over there? What good is it to sacrifice American soldiers?"

"What if it made the war end sooner?" Ed said.

"And less loss of life for everyone," Anna added.

"I honestly do not see how President Wilson can keep sitting on his hands," Jim said hotly. "Doesn't he realize that if Germany defeats the Allied Powers, the world will not be safe for anyone? Not even in the United States."

"Are you actually suggesting that Germany will invade American turf and take American lives?" Reginald narrowed his eyes at Jim.

"Don't forget that they sank the Lusitania with Americans aboard." Ed punctuated this with a raised finger. "They didn't seem too sorry about that."

And on they went . . . until Anna finally reminded them the purpose of today's meeting was to plan for this week's editions. "Being that it's Thanksgiving week, I think we should keep the news fairly light and optimistic," she told them. Now they took turns going around the table, each editor reporting on the stories they planned to write for the two editions.

Frank planned to cover the annual turkey shoot and the high school's forthcoming football game, which didn't look encouraging. Jim had the front page, covering the recently ended Battle of the Somme. But when it came to Ed's turn to share his story, Anna nearly fell out of her chair.

"What did you just say?" Her slack-jawed gaze focused on the slightly cocky business reporter.

"I'm reporting on the town's latest new business, Kathleen McDowell's Dress Shop." Ed looked irritatingly amused. "I figured you already knew about it, *Miss McDowell.*"

"Not exactly." Anna didn't care to admit she was completely in the dark. Nor did she remind him to call her by her first name.

"Haven't you seen the sign?" Reginald's frown seemed to be covering a grin too. "Painted right on the front window."

"No, I haven't seen the sign." She tried to regain her composure.

"Well, I poked around a little," Ed told her. "I hear your mother purchased the old hardware store and that she plans to turn it into a very nice dress shop. My wife is over the moon."

"Why is she calling it Kathleen McDowell's?" Reginald asked Anna.

"That's my daughter's name." Anna's tone was terse. "She goes by Katy."

"Oh?" Reginald looked impressed. "Well, I'm sure my wife will be thrilled about this. Rachel's always complaining about the lack of selection at the mercantile."

"Do you know when they plan to open?" Ed asked Anna.

"No, but I plan to find out." Anna felt like someone had slapped her. It was one thing if Lucille wanted to run a dress shop by herself— but to name it after Katy . . . Anna did not like the implication. "Well, I suppose that wraps this up." She pushed to her feet. "I'm sure we all have work to do. Thank you."

Instead of going to her office, Anna got her hat and coat and headed down Main Street, stopping in front of the building that used to be occupied by the hardware store. She knew Mr. Sherman had built a bigger structure on the other end of town. She looked up at the two-story brick building. She had to admit it looked solid and was well located for a dress shop, just a few doors down from the mercantile and across the street from the hotel, but if Lucille thought that Katy was going to participate in this little business venture, she was about to be in for a big surprise.

The windows of the old hardware store were covered with brown paper, but there it was, right on the glass, painted in purple paint with curly letters: Coming Soon – Kathleen McDowell's Dress Shop. Anna squared her shoulders and knocked on the front door, so firmly that the glass in the door rattled.

"Hello?" she called loudly. "Anyone in there?"

To her surprise, Clara opened the door. Her blonde hair was wrapped in a blue scarf, and a dusty apron covered her dress, with guards to protect her sleeves. "Oh, Anna. It's you. Come in."

"What are you doing here?" Anna remained fixed on the sidewalk.

"Working. We have a lot to do to get this place ready." She brushed her hands on the apron and stepped aside. "Please, come inside. See how it's going. The progress is very exciting. We hope to open in December. In time for Christmas shoppers."

Anna went inside to see the walls had been painted a fresh, clean white. The wood floors were gleaming from a recent polishing, and a workman in back appeared to be installing some sort of shelving units. "Where is Lucille?" Anna asked.

"Didn't you know? She went down to San Francisco. A buying trip. She should be back in a couple of days. Before Thanksgiving."

"Right. I suppose I knew she'd gone, but I hadn't heard *why.*" Anna took a deep breath, inhaling the sharp mixed aroma of paint, wood oil, and cleaning agents. She slowly exhaled, determined not to lose her temper, despite the fact that her family had to have been *trying* to hide this from her, for her to have missed it all so long. "In fact, I haven't heard about any of this. And I was taken quite by surprise to learn this shop has been named after my daughter. Do you know why that is?"

Clara's pale brows arched. "I, uh, I thought Katy had told you."

"Told me what?" Anna kept her voice calm.

"About this shop." Clara grimaced. "Lucille bought the building after the election. I guess it's been a couple of weeks now. Apparently, she ran into Mr. Sherman and struck up a deal that they both liked. Don't you think it's an excellent location?" Clara waved her hand. "And already the shop looks so much better. I'm supervising the workmen while Lucille is away. I will be working here too. Sewing and selling. And I'll be a partner as soon as the fish business is sold and I can invest my own funds." She smiled. "This will be such a nice place to work. Even the paint and everything smells much better than dead fish."

"I'm sure that's true."

"And Ellen can work here too," Clara continued with a smile. "And after my house down at the docks is sold, Lucille said that Ellen and I can take the apartment above the store to live in. It's a very roomy space with two bedrooms and a cute little kitchen. And you can actually see the ocean from the living room. It will be so handy to live in town. I still can hardly believe all of this. It's just so wonderful!"

"I'm very pleased for you." And it truly was encouraging to see Clara looking so happy. She'd been through so much these last few months. "But I'm curious as to what Katy's role will be in this, uh, this new business."

"Well, my understanding is that she'll be our designer. She is very talented for one so young. You must be so proud of her."

"But Katy has school."

"Yes, well, so does Ellen. But they have time after school and on weekends. And it won't be long until they're graduated. And then they can—"

"But Katy is going to college," Anna declared. "We expect her to get her degree. That will take time. Four years, in fact. And she'll be living too far away to help here in this shop. Lucille must know that this plan is impossible."

Clara slipped her hands into her apron pockets and, with her lips pressed together, stared down at the floor.

"I'm sorry." Anna placed her hand on Clara's shoulder. "I shouldn't burden you with all this.

But, as I'm sure you've guessed, I'm a bit vexed at my impetuous mother right now. I feel she's stepped over a line."

Clara looked up. "Lucille's intentions are good, Anna."

"I have no doubt. But Katy is my daughter. I don't appreciate Lucille mapping out her future like this."

"I understand. I suppose you'll have to talk to Lucille about that. And Katy too. I'm sure you all will work it out." Clara twisted one of her sleeve guards.

"Yes, I'm sure we will get it all figured out." Anna glanced around the building again. "It's not that I think it's a bad idea to create a dress shop in town. In fact, I'm sure it will be most welcome. But for my mother to assume that Katy will work here—and leaving me out of the plan. Well, it's frustrating. But I won't take any more of your time, Clara. You probably have much to do."

"Yes, that's true. I'm cleaning up in the back. I'm getting it all set up for sewing. Would you like to see it?"

"Not today." Anna tugged at a glove. "I need to get back to the paper."

"Have a good day." Clara smiled brightly.

"You too." Anna attempted a weak smile.

As she walked back to the office, Anna still felt annoyed. Oh, she did like that Lucille was looking out for Clara and Ellen. And a quality dress shop would be an asset to Sunset Cove. But Lucille was not Katy's mother. She had no right to interfere like this. And for Katy to say nothing . . . Well, that just felt downright sneaky.

Even though it wasn't lunchtime yet, Anna decided to go home. She needed to release some steam over this dilemma and knew Mac would be a sympathetic listener. He was as determined to send Katy to college as she. After calling out for him as she went inside, Anna discovered him in his sitting room. But to her dismay, Daniel Hollister was there too.

"What is it?" Mac looked at her with alarm as Daniel stepped back with his stethoscope. "Anna, what's the matter?"

"I'm sorry to interrupt," she spoke quickly. "I forgot about your examination, Mac. I just wanted to talk to you."

"We're done here." Daniel tucked the instrument into his doctor's bag. "Mac is doing just fine. But you sound upset, Anna. Is something wrong?"

She didn't know what to say.

"Is it something at the paper?" Mac studied her with a furrowed brow.

"No, no, that's not it."

"If this is a private conversation, I—"

"No, Daniel," she told him. "You're sort of like family."

"That's right." Mac nodded. "But tell us, Anna, what is troubling you?"

Anna sank down onto one of the club chairs, blowing out a long sigh. "It's that new business in town." She looked at both of them. "Have either of you heard about Kathleen McDowell's Dress Shop?"

"I just saw that this morning," Daniel told her. "I wondered about the name. Is Kathleen for Katy?"

"Yes." Anna glanced at Mac. "Have you heard about this dress shop?"

Mac nodded with a surprisingly knowing look, and, unless she imagined it, his expression seemed somewhat guilty. How long had he known about this?

"So I guess I'm the last one to know." She shook her head, then explained what she'd just uncovered about Lucille's new venture. "Don't get me wrong, it's not that I disapprove of a dress shop, but I am very irked that Lucille has pulled Katy into it—without breathing a word of it to me." She turned to Mac. "We planned for Katy to go to college."

"Is that what Katy wants too?" Daniel asked her.

Anna didn't answer him. Suddenly, she regretted involving him in this conversation. What if he sided with Katy and Lucille?

"Katy is not eager to go to college," Mac

sullenly told Daniel. "She's made no secret of this."

"But she's young. She doesn't always know what's best."

"She's an intelligent young woman," Daniel said quietly. "Quite mature for her age."

"That's my point—she *is* intelligent," Anna argued. "She'd be a fool to throw away her opportunity to get a college degree. This country needs more educated women."

Daniel nodded. "Can't disagree with you there, Anna. But what does Katy want?"

Ignoring him, Anna turned to Mac. "I can't believe you knew all about this."

"What?" Mac had an innocent expression, but she was not buying it.

"*The dress shop.* How long have you known about it?"

"Well . . . Lucille did mention it to me. I suppose it was a week or two ago."

"But you didn't tell me?" Anna felt her temper rising. "So I'm the only one left in the dark?"

Daniel snapped his doctor's case shut. "Maybe I should excuse myself and—"

"No, Daniel." Mac held up his good hand. "I might need you."

"Do you expect your blood pressure to rise?" Daniel sounded like he was joking, but Anna wasn't so sure.

Mac looked back at Anna. "Katy said she

wanted to be the one to tell you. She was waiting for the right time."

"The *right* time?" Anna frowned.

"She wanted the shop all set up. To surprise you."

"Well, she surprised me all right." She shook her finger at Mac. "Are you saying you approve of this craziness? I thought you agreed with me that Katy should continue her schooling. That's what you've been saying."

"I do agree with you." Mac nodded. "But Katy has a say too."

"Has she been confiding to you about all this?" Anna asked. "Persuading you to take her side?"

"Lucille has been talking to me. She told me Katy was unhappy with our plans."

Anna couldn't believe it. Had they all turned against her? "Why didn't Katy tell me that herself?" Come to think of it, Katy hadn't been talking much at all lately. She'd claimed she was absorbed by her studies, which Anna took as a good sign that she wanted to attend college.

"Katy said she'd tried to talk to you. She said you didn't listen." Mac sighed. "I guess I didn't either."

"So she tells Lucille all these things." Anna shook her head in confusion. "But I'm her mother. We've always been close. She's always told me everything."

"She's growing up, Anna." Daniel's words

were gentle. "It's only natural that she should have her own opinions about her future. You've done a wonderful job of raising her. You should be proud of her."

"I am proud of her," Anna conceded. "But she's only seventeen. She hasn't even finished high school, and she—"

"She's taking the test on Wednesday," Mac said quietly. "For her diploma."

"She told *you* that? But not me?"

"Lucille told me. Right before she left for Frisco. She said Katy's been studying hard."

"Of course . . . Lucille told you." Anna pursed her lips, trying not to resent her mother's intrusion. She knew Lucille loved Katy, but did that give her the right to influence Katy like this? It was fine if Lucille wanted to go around in fancy finery. After all, she was sort of a flibbertigibbet. But to entice Katy to that sort of frivolity? It was just plain wrong.

"Some young people grow up faster than others," Daniel said quietly. "Katy has already proven herself to be mature for her age. Consider how she handled Wally's campaign. I remember when she got the idea to be his manager last summer. I don't think any of us truly believed she would follow through all the way to Election Day. But she did."

"She sure did." Mac nodded vigorously. "She did a first-rate job too."

"So you're both telling me to step aside? To let my seventeen-year-old daughter simply do as she pleases? Even if I feel she's making a big mistake?"

"What choice do you really have?" Mac sighed. "Remember when you were seventeen?"

Anna figured it would eventually come down to this. "That was a long time ago, Mac. And I'm not proud of the mistakes I made back then. Are you suggesting I should let my daughter make similar bad decisions? Let history repeat itself? Or can my daughter learn from my choices and make better ones for herself?"

"Maybe what we perceive as mistakes are not always so," Daniel suggested.

"What are you saying?" Anna demanded.

"I think I know what you mean," Mac said with a twinkle in his eye. "My mother said it was a mistake to marry Lucille. But, looking back, I don't believe it was a mistake after all."

"But your marriage failed," Anna reminded him.

Mac just shrugged. "It did then . . . but it's not over. Not yet."

"Besides, they got you out of it." Daniel smiled at Anna. "And even though you married against Mac's wishes when you were seventeen—and despite your calling it a mistake—you got Katy out of it. I know you don't regret that."

"Obviously." She glared at him.

"And I suspect you became a strong, independent woman because of what you call a bad decision." A gleam in Daniel's eye joined his smile.

"And a darn good newspaperwoman too," Mac added.

"So was it a mistake?" Daniel asked.

"Oh, I don't know." Anna pounded the arm of the chair in frustration.

"We never know what's around the corner, yet we all must make our own choices in life," Daniel said. "And then we have to live with them."

"What about listening to advice from our elders?" she challenged.

"Are our elders always right? Lucille is your elder."

She grimaced.

"What I'm trying to say, Anna, is even when we make what we think is a wrong decision, I believe that God can make it right . . . if we let Him. God can bring good out of our bad choices."

Anna didn't disagree with him, but she wasn't ready to give in just yet.

"Forgive me if I said too much." Daniel picked up his doctor's bag and moved toward the door. "I didn't mean to wax so philosophical." He reached for his hat.

"No . . ." Anna stood, forcing a weak smile. "I suspect you're right. It's just that it's hard for me to let go of my dream of Katy's graduating college. I know, I know." She glumly shook her head. "To be honest, a big part of my drive for Katy to attend college probably stems from my not having gone. Mac wanted to send me to college, but I refused. I suppose I thought if Katy went, it would somehow make up for my mistake."

"Mistake?" Daniel asked. "You seem to like that word, Anna."

"Yes, yes . . . I see your point, Daniel." She felt a tiny smile sneak onto her lips. "You're right. God used my mistake to make something good. My daughter."

"That's right," Mac declared.

"Now, if you'll excuse me, I need to get back to the office." Daniel reached for his coat.

"Still joining us for Thanksgiving dinner?"

"I wouldn't miss it." Daniel winked at Mac. "Besides, I want to hear how this all turns out." He turned to Anna. "But, for the record, I'd put my money on Katy. She's got the McDowell strong-willed disposition." He told them both good-bye, then made his exit.

"The McDowell strong-willed disposition?" Anna echoed wryly. "Or just plain old stubborn-ness?"

"Both." Mac chuckled. "Be thankful for it, Anna."

As Anna walked back to the newspaper office, she did feel thankful for her own stubbornness.

It had stood her well while working in a man's world. But to exert her own stubborn will over her daughter's . . . Well, she was beginning to understand that wasn't going to work. She and Katy were similar in some ways yet very different in others. Anna had seen it early on. Katy loved art and clothes and music. Anna loved words and literature and journalism.

Anna had attributed their differences to the fact that Katy had grown up watching her mother fight for career advances while working for the newspaper in Portland. Katy had seen the hardships of a woman competing against male employees. Who could blame her for wanting to take a different, more feminine route? And even if Anna's pride took a blow to accept that her daughter didn't want to "use her pen to change the world," she knew she couldn't stand in Katy's way. She couldn't force her to be someone she wasn't.

By the time she got to the office, Anna had made up her mind. It wouldn't be easy, but she was determined to allow Katy to go her own way . . . and love her just the same. And, hopefully . . . in time . . . Anna would forgive Lucille too. In the meantime, she would simply try to avoid her.

CHAPTER 14

Katy's big plan to surprise her mother with the new dress shop seemed to have been derailed. Grandpa tipped her off shortly after she got home from school on Monday, apologetically informing her that the cat was out of the bag.

"How did she find out?" Katy asked. "Did you tell her?"

"The writing was on the wall," he said mysteriously. "Rather, on the window." He explained about the sign painted on the front window of the shop, then admitted he'd given her mother a full confession.

Katy was relieved when Bernice announced that Anna would miss dinner in order to work late on Monday, allowing Katy to go to bed before her mother got home. And on Tuesday morning, Katy left early to meet up with Ellen to go over some schoolwork. Of course, it was simply an excuse not to have to face Mother at breakfast. Then, later the same day, Katy got home to discover Mother had gone somewhere with Randall Douglas and wouldn't be home until quite late.

As she stood at Grandpa's sitting room

window, watching as clouds rolled in over the horizon, Katy was well aware that her mother and Mr. Douglas were very good friends, but she suddenly wondered if there was something more to their relationship. It had been clear from her first meeting of Mr. Douglas that he was more than a little interested in his old school chum. But what if this friendship had taken a serious turn— and Katy had been too self-absorbed to notice? This reminded her of how little time she'd spent with her mother lately. Perhaps for a month or more. First, there'd been Wally's campaign, and then Katy had really dug into the books, hoping to ace her test. Or else she'd been spending time at Lucille's, making plans for the most wonderful dress shop.

Katy turned around to look at her grandfather. "So . . . where did Mother and Mr. Douglas go?" She tried to appear less curious than she felt. But what if they'd gone off to elope? Wouldn't that be nuts! Katy wasn't quite sure how she'd feel about her mother getting married. Not that she didn't want her to find romance, but it certainly would change everything. Perhaps for the best.

"I'm not supposed to say." Grandpa set aside the book he was reading.

"You weren't supposed to say anything about the dress shop either," Katy reminded him. "Please tell me, where did Mother go? And what is going on between her and Mr. Douglas? I won't back down until you spill the beans, Grandpa, so you might as well get it over with, if you intend to keep reading your book in peace."

"Well, I can't tell you exactly *where* they went. That's a secret they didn't even share with me. But I'll tell you this much—she and Randall went by train to visit AJ. They left around nine this morning and hope to make it home late tonight."

"Oh?" Katy sat on the arm of his chair. "Tell me more."

"As you know, AJ is in a secure, undisclosed place."

"Yes, yes—but why did Mother go with Mr. Randall to see him? Is she doing a piece about AJ for the newspaper?"

He firmly shook his head. "This has nothing to do with the paper, Katy. It's to encourage AJ to talk more openly to Randall."

"Why does Mr. Douglas need her help?"

"AJ has clammed up. And, after his transfer, he's refused to see his own mother."

"Clara mentioned that she's missing AJ. I thought it was because he was too far away, or it was for security reasons."

Grandpa shrugged. "I wondered about that too, but Rand says it's AJ's choice. He can refuse to see anyone." He smiled at Katy. "Although, I'm sure he wouldn't refuse to see you, Katy."

"Maybe someone should've invited *me* to go see him."

"You have to be an adult to visit."

"Okay, but I still don't understand why Mother went. She doesn't even like AJ. Well, she didn't used to like him. Now she probably feels sorry for him."

"Randall thinks AJ will soften up with Anna there. He thinks AJ respects your mother." Grandpa pointed at Katy. "Perhaps he sees her as a link to you."

"Who knows? Hopefully Mother can talk some sense into that boy." Katy stood. "Anyway, I'm relieved she won't get home until late."

"You still haven't talked to her about the dress shop?"

She shook her head. "I'm trying to think of the best way to do it. Originally, I'd wanted to have my diploma in hand and the shop nearly ready to open. Grandmother is supposed to get back tomorrow with loads of wonderful garments and fabrics and goodies that she purchased down in San Francisco. I can't wait! It'll feel like Christmas." She sighed happily.

"Are you ready for your test tomorrow?"

"I think so, but I still plan to study tonight."

"How long is the test?"

"Mr. Johnson said it'll take all morning."

"When will you get the results?"

"He'll grade the test when I'm done. He promised to tell me by the end of the school day tomorrow." She sighed. "That way I don't have to go through Thanksgiving and the weekend before I find out."

Grandpa reached up to pat her head. "Good luck, Katy-girl. I'm sure you'll do fine. And, even if you don't pass it, I give you credit for trying."

"Mother will probably be glad if I don't pass." She scowled. "She thinks I'm too young to chase after my own dreams."

"You're never too young to chase a dream, but you might have to take more time in getting them. Sometimes it takes a lifetime."

"Goodness, I can't wait that long." She leaned over to kiss him on the cheek. "Well, thanks for getting me updated on my mother's mysterious life." She grinned as she grabbed up her schoolbag and coat. Then, humming to herself, she traipsed up the stairs to bury her nose in her geography and science textbooks. These were the subjects she felt weakest in. As she studied a chart with the chemical elements, knowing this was information she'd never utilize, one part of her wanted to forget the whole thing. Wouldn't it make everyone happy if she just gave up? Well, except for Grandmother . . . and Clara . . . and Ellen too. She was excited by the prospects of working for the dress shop, even if it was only part-time until she finished school. It had given her something fresh and new to hope for.

But even if it would please Mother and Grandpa if Katy gave up her dream, she couldn't keep pretending that Sunset Cove High wasn't redundant to her. It was like being held back a grade . . . or two . . . or three. They didn't even teach French. Not that she needed another year of French, since she'd already taken three, but it was just a reminder that Sunset Cove was backward. And, even though they did teach Latin, Katy was already ahead in that subject too. She closed the science book and picked up the geography one. These were the subjects that could put an end to her plans. Not because her previous school hadn't covered these subjects, but because they'd never held much interest for her. Although, she supposed geography could come in handy. If she ever got to visit Europe with Grandmother, it would be helpful to know the general lay of the land.

Despite Mother's lack of support, Katy suddenly felt determined to do her best tomorrow. If that wasn't good enough, she'd just have to accept the consequences. But, like Grandmother had pointed out, Katy and Ellen could still work after school and on weekends in the dress shop. And being stuck in Sunset Cove High would give Katy nearly a year to talk Mother out of her silly college plans. Well, unless Mother wanted to send her to art school in Portland. And perhaps that would be the best way to go.

AJ looked surprised and not overly pleased to see Anna on the other side of the visiting booth. Anna had already heard the guard telling Randall that AJ had declined today's visitors. But then Randall asked the guard to tell him that Miss McDowell was his first visitor, and, after a brief wait, they were informed AJ would cooperate.

"What are you doing here?" he asked sullenly as he sat down across from her, with only vertical metal bars to separate them. "Where's my lawyer?"

"Mr. Douglas is in the waiting room. You can only have one visitor at a time."

"Then why are you here?" He narrowed his eyes with suspicion.

"Because I'm your friend. Remember, it was Katy and I who rescued you that night."

"Yeah, I know." He nodded with downcast eyes. "I thought maybe it was Katy out here—when the guard said *Miss McDowell.*"

"Katy is too young to visit here," she informed him. "But I know she cares about you, AJ. So do I."

He looked up with narrowed eyes. "So did you come to get something for your newspaper? Because if that's your plan, you can just forget it!"

"I give you my word, this has nothing to do with the newspaper. In fact, I already swore to your lawyer that our conversation will remain completely confidential. Otherwise, Randall would never have let me come."

"I don't know," he growled back at her. "I've learned to question everyone about everything. No matter what they say, people can't be trusted."

"Well, there's no harm in being extra careful." Anna offered a bolstering smile. "I'm afraid there are many people who don't deserve your trust. But, I assure you, you can trust me. I am only here as a friend." Anna had anticipated AJ's cool reception and, during the long drive, had contrived a plan to warm up today's conversation. And the subject she'd finally landed upon was actually quite genuine. "I'd like your advice on something," she said with a serious expression. "It has to do with Katy."

His eyes lit up ever so slightly but just as quickly grew dark with suspicion. "Yeah, I'll bet you want my advice. I'm such an expert on life."

"I mean it," she insisted. "I'm having difficulty with my daughter. I honestly don't know what to do."

"Is something wrong with her?" His expression looked concerned enough to convince Anna he was still sweet on Katy.

"I'm not sure if something is wrong with her or with me." Anna sighed. "But something is definitely wrong." She explained about Katy's wanting to be finished with high school and how they didn't agree on it. "She's actually going behind my back to take her diploma test tomorrow. I'd like to put my foot down and force her to finish her final year of high school, but—"

"Don't make her do that," he said suddenly. "That high school is so juvenile. I'm not the smartest kid in town—I'm sure lots of folks would agree to that—but that school felt like they should be teaching ten-year-olds. It's no wonder so many kids quit school before they graduate."

"Really?" Anna slowly nodded. "So it's not just Katy, then?"

"Well, I don't know. I mean, Ellen seems to like school all right. But I sometimes think she just liked getting away from working at the fish shop and being around her friends. Because she's not a great student. She's not as smart as Katy." He shook his head. "But I never met a girl as smart as Katy." He looked directly into Anna's eyes. "I guess she gets that from you, ma'am."

"Thank you, AJ. But she also gets her stubbornness from me, which is probably why we've locked horns over this education problem." Anna told him about the dress shop now. "I really want Katy go to college, but she feels certain she wants to design dresses." She mentioned how Ellen and Clara were involved in the dress shop too. "And I'm glad for them. Your mother and sister get along well with Lucille, and sewing and selling dresses is nice, clean work. They could even live above the dress shop in time."

AJ frowned. "What about our house and the fish company?"

"Oh, I don't know their plans—I simply meant if they *wanted* to." Anna realized it would be a mistake to reveal too much. "You'll have to ask your mother about those things. Has she been here to see you recently?"

He just shook his head.

"She misses you, AJ."

"I know."

"And, despite everything that's happened, she loves you. The way only a mother can do. And I'm sure she would like to come visit."

"Yeah, I know."

"Your mother never gave up on you, you know. She still believes in you . . . that you could have a bright future. It's not too late. I hope you can believe that."

"I don't know. This hoosegow feels like a dead end to me."

"Incarceration shouldn't feel like a day at the beach. But, according to Mr. Douglas, you won't be here for long—that is, if you cooperate."

"I know . . . and I probably will." He pushed a lock of pale hair away from his forehead. "I wish the trial could happen sooner. Do you know why it's taking so long?"

"I've heard various excuses, but Mr. Douglas

is pushing to get you before a judge. In the meantime, be thankful you haven't gone up yet. You're not ready, AJ."

"But it's rough . . . just rotting away in here."

"Then do what you can to cooperate with your attorney. Let him help you. Maybe you'll be out sooner than you think." In an effort to change the topic and possibly give him hope, Anna began sharing the recent news about the war in Europe. "We're always arguing about this at the newspaper," she told him, "but most of us are convinced the United States will soon join forces with the Allies. And that means they'll need a lot of young men to enlist in the military. A lot of fellows have already been signing up."

He brightened. "Mr. Douglas said that the judge might pardon me from a long prison sentence if I enlist in the army."

"That's a good goal. And I know a couple of newspapermen, from where I worked at the *Oregonian* in Portland, who joined the army last spring. I just heard they're stationed in New York—in Fort Slocum, I think—and it sounded like they've already gotten promoted."

"I wish I was somewhere else . . . training for something besides pounding a pickax." He scowled. "Even a battlefield would be better than this."

"I'm sure if you cooperate with your attorney and the court, you'll be released . . . in time. But

Mr. Douglas told me you barely spoke to him the last time he visited. He's worried that you could end up stuck in prison for a long time."

AJ looked into her eyes. "You know what happened to my dad."

"Yes. I'm sorry for your loss, AJ. It's no secret that I wasn't on friendly terms with your father, but I never ever would've wished that for him."

"He didn't kill himself," AJ said quietly.

"I didn't think so." Anna controlled herself from glancing about. Although she wanted to be sure no one was eavesdropping, she didn't want to make AJ uneasy.

"My dad was murdered. I don't know who pulled the trigger, but I could make some pretty good guesses about who gave the command."

She nodded. "Believe me, at the newspaper, we're trying to get to the bottom of this too. I never bought that suicide story. And I have my own suspicions."

"But here's the deal." AJ's eyes darted back and forth—perhaps he was also worried someone could listen in. But the other inmates and visitors looked preoccupied, and the guard near the door was too far away. In a very low voice, AJ continued. "If I speak out on this, there's a chance I'll be killed too. Mr. Douglas and Chief Rollins think I'm safe here, but there's always someone willing to turn on you . . . if the price is right. That's why I'm keeping my mouth shut."

"I'm sure that's true, but that could happen even if you don't talk. If someone believes you're a threat, wouldn't they try to silence you before you had a chance to speak?"

His eyes grew wider as he solemnly nodded.

"I hope you're not living on borrowed time." Anna didn't want to frighten him, but she hoped he'd see the urgency.

"What'll I do?"

"Listen to your legal counsel," she eagerly told him. "Mr. Douglas has your best interests at heart. He wants to help you. But for him to help you, he needs you to tell the court the truth. If you tell all you know, the real criminals can be arrested and prosecuted and locked up. And you can get out of here and on your way. If you join the army, you might wind up on the other side of the country. Maybe we could request Fort Slocum, where my reporter friends are stationed. I'd be happy to write to them, to ask them to help you over there."

For the first time today, AJ looked almost hopeful. "You'd do that? For me?"

"Of course. You know I'm good friends with your mother and sister. So is Katy. We all care about you, AJ. Not everyone is untrustworthy. You need to think about who your real friends are these days. The ones who really love you and want to help you . . . the ones who want to see you have a good future."

"Yeah . . . thanks." The words sounded choked in his throat, and his eyes glistened with tears.

Anna wished she could give the boy a hug, but she'd been warned not to even reach through the bars to touch his hand. She suddenly remembered the arrogant young man she'd met last summer. So cocky and sure and full of himself, acting like he was on top of the world with nothing to fear . . . and now this. Such a sad way to fall, so humiliating. But Anna believed this could be the making of him too. This was one of those *mistakes* Daniel had been talking about . . . something bad that God could use for good. She hoped and prayed that would happen with AJ and that he'd live long enough to turn his life around.

CHAPTER 15

Katy got up early on Wednesday. Too nervous to eat a big breakfast, she left the house with an apple and biscuit and slowly ate as she walked toward town. Mr. Johnson had said to be there around seven and ready to begin the test at seven thirty sharp, and she'd given herself plenty of time. As she walked, she silently prayed, asking God to help her through this day.

She paused on Main Street, looking wistfully at the brick building her grandmother had purchased a few weeks ago. Busy with studying for the test, Katy hadn't been inside the shop for more than a week. She wanted to peek in on the progress, but the windows were still completely covered, and she knew it was too early for Clara to be there. Later this afternoon, after the test, Katy would stop by. Hopefully Grandmother would be back from her buying trip by then. And hopefully Katy would have good news to share with them. Hopefully.

The high school looked quiet and sleepy and small as Katy went up the front steps. The other students weren't here yet, but the front doors were unlocked. As she went inside, she smelled the familiar scents of wood polish and blackboard dust . . . and something else that was pungent and hard to identify. Not a smell she would miss.

She went directly to the main office. One other student was taking the test with her today, and he was already there. Looking as nervous as Katy felt, Caleb Wilt sat outside of Mr. Johnson's office with several sharpened pencils in one hand and a tweed cap in the other.

"Morning, Katy." Caleb tipped his head, then looked down at his boots, which were well worn and dusty. Katy knew he was shy. This was the first time he'd ever addressed her by name.

"Good morning." She smiled. After taking the chair next to him, she smoothed her dark-blue skirt over knees, holding her head high. She didn't know Caleb very well, but he seemed like a nice guy. She knew he was a good student, and, like her, he wanted to get his diploma and get on with his life. She'd heard his family ran a dairy farm on the outskirts of town, and she suspected that Caleb wanted to finish his schooling early in order to help them.

"Are you ready for this?" he asked quietly.

"I'm not sure, but I hope so." Katy had always hated tests of any kind. She would much rather be free to paint and draw and create. Why didn't they give tests for artists? "Are you ready?"

"I guess I'll find out." Caleb cleared his throat.

"I'll bet you'll do just fine. Anyway, I hope you do. Good luck."

"Thank you. I wish you luck too."

After a few minutes, Mr. Johnson and his secretary came out and greeted them. "You'll take the test in my office," he explained. "You must be supervised the entire time. Either Mrs. Mills or I will remain in there."

"You can leave your coats, hats, and bags out here." Mrs. Mills pointed to the coatrack near her desk. "The only thing you can take into Mr. Johnson's office is your pencils."

Caleb and Katy put their items away and then followed Mr. Johnson into his office, where he directed them to a pair of small, separate desks on opposite sides of the room. After they were seated, he went over the instructions and rules, then gave them a chance to ask questions.

"As you know, the test must be completed in four hours," he continued. "At exactly noon, we will remove your tests, and Mrs. Mills and I will check them. You can remain here at school to wait for the results or leave, if you'd prefer, and return around two o'clock. We'll be done checking your answers by then." He looked at the wall clock and nodded. "All right, you can begin. Good luck."

Katy felt dampness on her palms as she stared at the first page. But, taking a deep breath and praying another silent prayer, she picked up her pencil and began. To her relief, most of the questions weren't difficult. But there were others that made her uncertain. Maybe it was nerves, or maybe she wasn't as smart as she'd imagined. All she could do was push forward, one question after the next . . . and hope for the best.

Four hours later, Katy's stomach felt like she'd swallowed a brick, but Mr. Johnson was telling them to put their pencils down, and collecting their test papers.

"I'm sure you both did your very best." He smiled at them. "Now I encourage you to go out and get some fresh air and lunch. And don't worry. You either passed it or you didn't. Whatever will be will be."

Caleb and Katy thanked him, then went out to gather their coats and hats and bags. Katy had no desire to get any lunch, but she did want some fresh air. She told Caleb good-bye, then hurried outside to where the wind was blowing right off the ocean. She breathed deeply and repeated to herself what Mr. Johnson had just said. "Whatever will be will be."

Not eager to go home—or cross paths with her mother—Katy went directly to the dress shop. At the very least, Clara should be there. And she was always a sympathetic listener. It didn't hurt that Clara felt that Katy was artistic and talented. And right now, Katy wanted to be around someone who believed in her. She wasn't sure she even believed in herself anymore. There was only one thing she felt sure about—she did not want to continue her schooling beyond high school. Even if it meant a big fight with her mother, Katy was determined to stand up for herself. If Mother was such a strong believer in a college education, she should go herself!

As Katy walked down Main Street, she vaguely wondered if there were any rules prohibiting middle-aged women from attending university. The idea of her thirty-four-year-old mother attending classes with young coeds and taking nerve-racking tests actually made Katy chuckle as she knocked on the front door to the dress shop.

Clara opened the door wide. "Hello. You look happy—does that mean you passed your test?"

"I wish!" Katy glumly shook her head. "I won't know until two o'clock." She looked around the shop. "Oh my, it looks wonderful in here!"

"Come in, come in," Clara urged. "You have to see everything, Katy. It's all so exciting! Lucille just arrived an hour ago. And we're putting away the beautiful things she found in San Francisco. Oh my, I've never seen such finery!"

Katy set down her bag, peeled off her outerwear, and hurried back to greet her grandmother. It was a happy reunion, and Katy began helping them unpack crates and trunks and boxes, and, just like Katy had imagined, it felt almost like Christmas. As she inspected the yardage and notions, asking about various items she'd requested, Katy felt like this was where she belonged. As she unrolled a bolt of rose-colored silk, she made a decision.

"I have an announcement," she declared.

Grandmother and Clara both turned to look at her.

"I have decided that even if I failed the test today, I am *not* going back to that high school."

"Oh, Katy." Lucille looked worried. "Your mother will not approve."

"I don't care. It's my life."

Clara frowned but said nothing.

"I understand," Lucille said calmly. "But we had an agreement, Katy. I expect you to keep your end of the bargain."

Katy set down the bolt and sighed. "Fine. We won't talk about this until I hear the results of the test." Even so, Katy knew she was done. Already she had more education than either of these women. Oh, she knew that had to do with opportunity. Women hadn't been encouraged to higher education in their day. But Katy also knew plenty of young women who ended their schooling by eighth grade. Boys too, for that matter.

"I spoke to Mac after I got home," Lucille said as they continued to organize and sort in the back room. "He mentioned that Anna went to see AJ yesterday."

"What?" Clara looked both shocked and dismayed. "Why?"

"Randall took her along in the hopes that she could get AJ to open up," Lucille informed them.

"Yes, I knew about that," Katy admitted. She turned to her grandmother. "Did you hear how the visit went?"

"Yes. Although Anna had already gone to work when I stopped in, she'd told Mac that the visit had proven successful. It sounds as if AJ has decided to cooperate with Randall and the court."

"Oh, that's good to hear." Clara blinked rapidly and pulled out her handkerchief. "I've been writing him letters, urging him to do this, but he never writes me back. For all I knew, he never saw my letters. And, after his father died, AJ told Randall that he didn't want me to visit him."

"Well, it sounds like AJ wants to see you now." Lucille grasped Clara's hand. "I believe he's turned a corner. But I'm sure Anna can fill you in on all the details later. Mac said it was after midnight when she got home, but she had to go to work to get the paper out today. I'm sure the poor thing must be worn out."

As Katy sorted buttons and lace and ribbons, her feelings toward her mother softened. It was kind of her to go with Mr. Douglas to help AJ yesterday. Even though Katy no longer entertained any feelings for AJ—well, other than pity—she did care about him. Mostly for Ellen's and Clara's sake. By now, Katy was aware that for AJ's entire life, he'd been under his father's influence. And that had not been a good influence. AJ deserved a second chance, and she hoped he'd finally get one.

"Oh my, it's past two o'clock," Clara said suddenly. "Don't you need to go to school, Katy? To find out about your test?"

Katy almost didn't care about the results anymore. She couldn't admit it to these women, but she felt fairly certain that no matter what, she was done with school. Her grandmother would have to understand. The only problem was Mother . . . Convincing her wouldn't be simple. "Yes." Katy set down the wooden box of ribbons she'd been organizing by color. "I'll go find out now."

Lucille came over to hug her. "Whatever the results, I still think you're a brilliant and creative girl, Kathleen Rebecca. You are a brave and strong young woman. So go find out and hurry back here to let us know."

As Katy walked back to school, she felt in no hurry. More than ever, she was convinced that she'd failed the test. How many times had she looked up to see Caleb writing furiously while she was temporarily stumped? Oh well, better to just get this over with. She marched into the main office to see Mrs. Mills talking on the telephone. But she nodded toward Mr. Johnson's office, and Katy knocked on the door.

"Come in." He smiled as he opened the door wide.

"Thank you," she said meekly. "Do you have the results?"

"I do." He nodded as he picked up a folder. "Congratulations, Miss McDowell." He handed her a certificate that was signed and dated by him. "You are officially a high school graduate."

Katy was shocked speechless.

"And I wish you the best in your future." He firmly shook her hand.

"Are you sure?" Katy asked.

He chuckled. "Why? Don't you think you deserve it?"

Katy felt uncertain—what if the tests had gotten mixed up? What if they had thought Caleb's test was hers . . . and hers was his? "May I ask how Caleb did?"

"He passed as well." Mr. Johnson nodded.

"Oh, thank you!" Katy controlled herself from hugging him. "Thank you so very, very much!"

He wished her well, and she excused herself. "I have to go tell my family the good news." And then she took off. But instead of returning directly to the dress shop, she went home to tell Mac.

"I want you to come see our progress at the dress shop," she told him after showing him her certificate. "I can drive you there."

"I'll get my coat and hat," he said as he reached for his cane.

"And I'd like to pick up Mother too," Katy said as they went out to the car.

She wasn't sure how her mother would react to being abducted from the newspaper office, but Katy was determined to try. As she parked in front of the office, she got an idea. She hurried inside, stopping at Virginia's desk.

"Well, hello, Katy. How are you doing?"

"Can you please give my mother a message?" Katy asked eagerly. "Grandpa is out in the car, and we need Mother to come with us—at once."

"Is this an emergency?"

"Not exactly. But it is urgent. I really need her to come. I'll be out in the car."

Virginia was already on her feet, hurrying back toward Mother's office.

Crossing her fingers, Katy hurried back to the Runabout to open the rumble seat. Hopefully her mother wouldn't mind sitting in back. Katy threw the car robe back there just in case.

"What's going on?" Anna asked as she came outside. "Is someone hurt?"

"Just get in back," Mac told her. "We'll explain when we get there."

To Katy's relief, her mother complied. "I hope she doesn't get too angry," Katy muttered as she drove down Main Street toward the dress shop.

She had barely parked when her mother had hopped out of the rumble seat, demanding to know what was going on.

"What are we doing here?"

"You'll see, Mother." Katy pounded on the door, and soon they were all standing in the front part of the dress shop. Even Ellen was there.

"I have an announcement to make." Katy pulled out her diploma and held it up so everyone could see. "I have officially graduated high school today. Since I won't be going through the graduation ceremony next June, I am inviting you all to celebrate with me today." Katy hugged her mother. "I hope you're pleased."

Anna peered curiously at the diploma. "Well, of course I'm pleased, Katy." Her tone sounded a bit stiff. "And surprised by . . . by all this." She looked around the shop with a slight frown. "It's a lot to take in."

Katy turned to Lucille. "Now that I've kept my part of the agreement, does that mean I'm officially a partner in our business?"

"I won't go back on my promise." Lucille patted Katy's cheek. "Congratulations, honey. I just knew you could do it."

"You must be so proud of Katy." Clara smiled at Anna. "For earning her diploma like that. I know I'll be very proud of my girl when she graduates." She gave Ellen a squeeze. "She's always had a harder time with school, but I think it's because she's left-handed."

"Really, Mother." Ellen scowled at her mother. "You always act like being left-handed is such a curse. *Please!*"

"Well, your father was left- . . . ." Clara's voice trailed off.

To distract them from what could easily turn unpleasant, Katy linked arms with her mother. "I want you to see everything in our lovely little shop. It's all going to be so wonderful." And, with the others trailing behind her, she led her mother on the full tour of the dress shop. By the end of the tour, Katy hoped that her enthusiasm was infecting her mother. But it was hard to read her expression. Her mother had always been a good card player.

"Well, thank you for sharing your good news with me," Anna politely told Katy. "And for the tour. Now, if you will all excuse me, I need to get back to the newspaper." She waved good-bye and exited.

"What do you think?" Katy asked the others. "Did she seem upset to any of you? Do think my little plan worked?"

"Hard to say." Mac rubbed his chin. "Anna is good at hiding her feelings."

"Believe me, I know." Katy frowned.

"She did seem surprised." Ellen squinted. "But does she even *like* surprises?"

"It depends," Katy admitted, although she knew her mother never particularly liked being caught off guard . . . or tricked.

"Well, I'm sure she'll be happy about it," Lucille declared. "Just give her time."

"In the meantime, I can be happy. No more school for me—whoopee!" Katy did a little spin, but then Ellen's scowl caught her attention. "What's wrong?"

"School won't be as much fun now. Why did you have to go and leave me alone there, Katy?"

"I'm sorry." Katy hugged her. "But we'll see each other here every day after school."

"I guess." Ellen still seemed disgruntled.

"And on weekends," Clara added.

Katy nodded, then turned to Mac. "Well, I should probably get Grandpa back home."

"Not before I invite all of you to join us for Thanksgiving dinner tomorrow," Mac announced. "I already told Bernice to expect a crowd."

"But I already got a small turkey to roast," Lucille said. "And Clara and Ellen planned to join me."

"Then bring your turkey and guests to my house," Mac told her.

Lucille smiled. "I'd be happy to." She turned to Katy. "And don't worry, honey, I think your mother is coming around. You'll see."

As Katy drove Grandpa home, she hoped her grandmother was right . . . because Katy was not looking forward to hearing her mother's unguarded thoughts on today's little surprise. Unless she was imagining things—and she didn't think so—her mother was still not happy about the dress shop and Katy's involvement in it. And having her diploma in hand wasn't going to change that.

CHAPTER 16

As Anna stormed backed to the newspaper office, she was grateful for the brisk sea breeze. Hopefully it would cool her off. Because, at the moment, she was feeling disturbingly vexed at her daughter and mother for plotting against her. And Mac too! In fact, she wasn't any too pleased with Clara and Ellen either. It felt as if everyone had turned against her. Even Virginia! What had she been thinking? Rushing into her office like that, acting as if there were some sort of medical emergency with Mac or Katy? What was wrong with people?

Anna entered the building to see Virginia curiously waiting. "Everything all right?"

Anna resisted the urge to say what she really thought. "Yes, yes, everything is just fine."

"Katy seemed rather excited." Virginia was clearly fishing for information.

"Yes, my daughter does get rather excited sometimes." Anna hung up her coat. "Please send Jim to my office. We need to go over some things for Saturday's paper."

"Will do."

Anna took a deep breath as she went into

her office. No need to bring her ill feelings to work. That wouldn't help anything. But, as she organized the papers on her desk, she couldn't let it go. Even when she reminded herself of what Daniel had said about accepting that people make mistakes and that sometimes mistakes turned into good things, Anna still wasn't ready to accept this. And, despite her earlier resolve to let Katy have her way and follow her dreams, Anna wasn't ready to back off from being a parent. Didn't she have a responsibility to make sure her daughter chose a good path? As a parent, shouldn't she try to guide Katy toward higher education? But, judging by Katy's excitement at the dress shop earlier, her only goal was to sew frilly dresses.

Anna wadded a piece of paper and gave it a hard, angry toss just as Jim came in. It hit him solidly in the forehead.

"What?" He rubbed his forehead. "I thought you wanted to see me."

"Sorry about that." She smiled sheepishly.

"Bad shot." He tossed the wad into the waste-basket and sat down.

"I guess I was letting off steam."

"Steam?" His dark brows lifted. "Something up?"

"Nothing newsworthy." She picked up a letter opener and slapped it across her palm. "Just family troubles."

"Is Mac all right?" Jim looked concerned.

"Yes, yes, he's fine." She frowned. "The old betrayer."

"Betrayer?" Jim leaned forward.

"Sorry, I shouldn't have said that."

"That's true. Unless you plan to explain it. I am, after all, a news reporter. It's my job to ask questions."

Anna rolled her eyes. Knowing it would be simpler to just tell him, she spilled the story of Katy's diploma and the surprise dress shop tour.

"That's great." Jim nodded in approval. "That girl of yours has a lot of spunk. I don't understand why you think it's a problem."

"Because I am her mother," Anna declared hotly. "I have raised Katy on my own for her whole life. Just Katy and me. And now that we've been in Sunset Cove for half a year, it's as if everyone else has taken over. Suddenly I'm shoved aside without a say in anything in regard to my own daughter."

"But you say Katy has her high school diploma and gainful employment—your job is done, Anna. You should be glad."

"But Katy is only seventeen. She's a child."

He shrugged. "She sounds pretty grown up to me. I think it's time to cut those apron strings."

Anna stabbed the letter opener into the desk pad.

Jim blinked. "You really are upset about this, aren't you?"

She blew out a long sigh. "Oh, I know I need to calm down. But I suppose I'm just not ready to let go of my little girl."

"She's not a little girl anymore."

"I know that," she said sharply. "But it's hard to let her go. It's hard to see these others interfering . . . using their influence to sway her their way."

Jim chuckled. "I'm no expert on your daughter, Anna, but I know her well enough to think she's not easily influenced by anyone. I think she takes after her mother in that regard."

Anna knew he was probably right, but she wasn't ready to concede. "Well, you're not here to talk about my family problems, Jim." She picked up the list she'd made for him. "Let's run through this, and then I'm going home. I only got a few hours' sleep last night, and I think it's taking its toll." She forced a weary smile. "Probably why I'm in such a foul mood today."

"How did yesterday go?"

Anna pursed her lips. Jim knew she'd gone to visit AJ, but she wasn't sure how much she wanted to say now. "Strictly off the record?"

He held up his hand. "You have my word."

"I think he's going to talk."

Jim nodded eagerly. "That's great news." Now he told her about what little progress he'd made on his ongoing Snyder and Collins investigation. "I'm keeping careful notes of everything I see and hear, but without someone to corroborate and name some names, well, it'll be hard to prove a thing on those crooks."

"Well, I believe AJ is the key."

"The key it'll take to lock up some dirty rats."

They continued over the list until Anna realized she was too tired to think straight. "Here, you take this." She handed him the list. "I'm going home to get some rest."

"At least you have a holiday tomorrow," he said. "You probably need it."

She reached for her satchel. "That's right. Happy Thanksgiving, Jim."

"Yeah, thanks." He didn't sound enthusiastic.

"Do you have any special plans?"

"Nope." He opened the door.

"Why don't you join us? It sounds like Bernice is putting on quite a spread."

"Really? You have room for one more?"

"Of course." She smiled. "After all, you're like family. And I know Mac would love to see you."

"I'd love to come."

She told him what time to arrive as she reached for the light switch. "By the way, Jim, thanks for listening just now. I didn't mean to rant like that. I think I'm just tired."

"I understand. I know how much you love your daughter."

She nodded. "You're right. I do."

"She's a special girl, Anna. You should be proud."

"Yes, that's what everyone keeps telling me." As she turned off the light, she wondered if pride might be the root of her problem. Which was more important to her—being proud of her daughter for following her own dreams . . . or proud of her for following her mother's dreams? It was a disturbing question.

If anyone had told Mac just one year ago that his life would be this full of friends and family, he never would've believed them. But as he and his guests relaxed and visited around his home following a hearty Thanksgiving meal, he felt exceedingly thankful . . . as well as a little concerned.

Anna had been very quiet all day. He suspected she was still simmering over the unwelcome news that Katy was done with school and now planning to spend all her time working at Lucille's new dress shop. To be honest, Mac was a bit disappointed as well. He'd had high hopes that his granddaughter would be a college graduate someday. But, based on the signals Katy was sending, the headstrong young woman had no intention of going to college. Not that he planned to bring up the subject.

"How about a walk?" Katy cheerfully asked everyone. "The wind's let up, and it looks like we might have a gorgeous sunset in an hour or so."

"I'm game," Jim eagerly agreed.

"Come on, Ellen," Katy urged. "Don't you want some fresh air too?"

"I guess so." Ellen sounded reluctant.

After the three of them left, Lucille and Clara excused themselves to go to Lucille's house to look at some catalogues she had brought with her from San Francisco. Now it was just Anna and Daniel and Mac. But Mac was feeling sleepy. Leaning back in his chair, he closed his eyes. Not to his surprise, Anna and Daniel assumed he was asleep. Mac did not set them straight.

"How are you doing?" Daniel asked Anna.

"I'm fine," she answered quickly.

"You don't seem fine."

"Is that your professional medical opinion?" Anna's tone was a bit sharp.

"Maybe. I happen to believe our physical well-being is greatly impacted by our emotional well-being."

"Are you suggesting that I'm unwell emotionally?"

"You just don't seem like yourself. Is something troubling you?"

Anna let out a deep sigh that suggested Daniel had hit the nail on the head.

Mac's ears perked up, but he kept his eyes shut, listening as Anna described Katy's surprise yesterday and how Anna had felt betrayed.

"So Katy got her high school diploma," Daniel said. "I'd think you'd feel proud."

"Everyone keeps saying that," she declared.

"Meaning you don't?"

"Oh, I don't know. To be honest, I feel like pride is part of my problem." Now she confessed how it hurt her pride to think that Katy wouldn't go to college.

"How do you know she won't go? Katy's only seventeen. Perhaps if she has a year of working in the dress shop, she'll rethink her plans. She might welcome the offer of secondary education. Especially if you don't push her too hard."

"Do you really think so?" Anna's tone was hopeful.

"I think Katy is the kind of girl who likes to make up her own mind."

"Well, that's true enough."

"So why not give her time to see what it's like working in a dress shop day after day?"

"Like giving her enough rope that she'll . . ." Anna frowned. "I don't really like that particular metaphor."

"No. But maybe if you step away a bit, Katy will discover being a dressmaker is not all she'd imagined."

"Yes, I think that's a perfect plan, Daniel. Now, if I can just keep from saying too much or pushing her too hard."

"It's probably good that you have other things

200

to occupy yourself, Anna. A lot of mothers feel completely lost after their children grow up and move on. They don't know what to do with themselves or feel that their lives are over."

"You mean, because I have the newspaper?" Her tone grew more serious, and Mac wondered if she was having second thoughts about her role there. Maybe he expected too much of her. Maybe he'd pushed her the same way she'd been trying to push Katy. After all, the apples really didn't fall far from the trees. Perhaps her troubles with Katy were because of him. He hoped not.

"Well, you do enjoy your work there, don't you?" Daniel said.

"Oh yes, I love working at the newspaper. But I don't particularly like the idea of it being my whole life." She paused, and Mac sensed she was looking his way, but he continued to feign sleep. "I know that seemed to work for my father. At least, that's how I remember it when I was growing up. I used to think the paper should be called the *Sunset Sun* since everything seemed to orbit around it." Anna spoke quietly.

"That's not a bad name for the paper." Daniel chuckled.

"I have a feeling that Mac would agree with me that the newspaper was his life . . . and that it took over his life."

"And possibly impacted his health."

"I do wonder about that, whether it contributed to his stroke. Running the paper is a demanding job. I'm seeing that firsthand. But I'm hoping things are settling down."

"Well, you did take over during a rough time, Anna. But, to be honest, I don't imagine life will quiet down too much in these parts. Did you hear about the Washington rumrunners that were caught up near Portland?"

"Yes, but that's good news."

"Good that they were caught, but it might make it worse around here. The absence of one rum-running operation probably seems like an open door to another one. And I have no doubts there's a thriving operation still going on around here."

"I agree." She told him about her theory that Calvin Snyder and a certain policeman were involved in such an operation. Mac controlled the urge to protest this. His good buddy and police chief would defend Clint Collins, and Mac didn't like hearing Anna pointing the finger at him. "Jim's been keeping an eye on them, but he hasn't got enough to make a case yet."

"Do you think they're involved in Albert Krauss's death?"

"Jim is certain of it. Especially when Collins was so quick to call it suicide." Anna paused. "Do you really think it was suicide?"

"It's possible. Close-range shot to the right side of his head. But it could also have been an execution."

"His son, AJ . . . He's certain it wasn't suicide," she said quietly.

"I wish I knew more about forensic pathology."

"What?"

"It's a relatively new medical science that's being used in Europe. Not widely. I believe Vienna and maybe Scotland Yard have implemented forensic doctors—physicians who are specifically trained to work with detectives to solve crimes."

"That's interesting."

"I can say this, and I told Chief Rollins: Albert Krauss was badly bruised and beat up. But that could've been from the explosion at the jail and being on the run. Hard to pinpoint the exact cause, but like I wrote in the report, I'd call it suspicious."

"Daniel," Anna said suddenly. "Did you say the gunshot wound was on the right side?"

"Yes."

"What if Albert Krauss was left-handed?"

"Left-handed? Do you know this for sure?"

"I'm not positive, but I just remembered something Clara said. She was talking about Ellen's being left-handed and how it made school harder—then she mentioned Albert."

"If Albert was left-handed, it would've been

very awkward—and unlikely—that he would aim the gun at the right side of his head."

"Then it probably was murder? And there could be an investigation."

"That seems reasonable."

Mac sat up, opening his eyes. "Well, what are you two waiting for?"

"What?" Anna looked surprised, as if she'd forgotten Mac was even in the room.

"Call Lucille's house and ask Clara," Mac told her.

"Ask Clara what?" Anna narrowed her eyes at him.

"If Albert was left-handed."

Anna turned to Daniel, and they exchanged similar glances, then she made a dash for the telephone. She stopped. "I don't think I should ask that on the telephone."

"The operators," Daniel agreed with a nod.

"What?" Mac asked.

"They listen in," Anna told him. "You mean you didn't know that?"

Mac frowned.

"It's true," Daniel confirmed. "I've been called to see a patient for something, and before I even get there, all the neighbors will have heard about it."

"I'll walk over to Lucille's." Anna spun for the door.

"Need any company?" Daniel offered.

"Sure." Anna smiled at him. "I'll bet you want to hear this."

As the two of them left, Mac wondered . . . Was there something beyond friendship going on between those two? It might be nice to have a doctor in the family. Maybe Mac could get a discount on his examinations.

CHAPTER 17

Anna wasn't quite sure of the best way to ask Clara about her deceased husband. Clara had been doing so well of late. Anna didn't want to be the one to plunge her back into sadness. "Daniel and I were talking," she began after they were seated in Lucille's parlor. "And we think we may have stumbled upon something that could shine some light on the way Albert died."

"Oh?" Clara looked taken aback.

Lucille set aside the catalogue she and Clara had been perusing and put her arm around Clara's shoulder.

Unable to think of an easy way to ask, Anna simply blurted out her question. "Was Albert left-handed?"

"What?" Clara frowned. "Yes . . . but why do you ask?"

Daniel took over the explanation, gently informing Clara of his findings during the autopsy. "So it seems possible that Albert did not kill himself."

Clara's brow creased. "So he was murdered?"

"We can't know for certain, but that's what we suspect," Anna told her.

"Oh." Clara reached for her handkerchief.

"I thought perhaps you'd feel some relief to know he didn't take his own life." Anna placed a hand on Clara's arm.

"I—I'm not sure how I feel." Clara dabbed a tear.

"It must be difficult to hear this." Daniel sighed. "We certainly didn't want to upset you."

"It's just that when I believed that Albert's death was suicide, it brought a morsel of comfort . . . I imagined him being sorry for all the damage he'd done. Not just recently, but all the years when he treated us poorly. I thought of him as remorseful, regretting how he'd hurt us. I know it sounds cruel to say this, but it was reassuring to think he took his own life. It made me less angry at him."

"I understand." Anna nodded.

"Perhaps he *was* remorseful." Daniel leaned forward, bracing his elbows against his knees. "Being in jail did give him time to think about things. And, based on my observations, he didn't have an easy time of it after his jailbreak. I'm no expert on these things, but I suspect he regretted a lot."

"Do you really believe that?" Clara asked him.

"It seems only human."

She dipped her head. "Yes. And Albert wasn't always a bad person. It's just that he got so caught up in gaining riches. First, it was one boat and then two. But that wasn't enough. He wanted a whole fleet. He wanted everyone in town to look up to him. Nothing mattered as much to him as being wealthy and admired. I told myself it was because he'd grown up poor—he never felt that he had enough. And yet, other people come from impoverished families, and they don't do the same sort of things that Albert did."

"Everyone is different," Anna said. "But I can see what you're saying, Clara. It makes sense. Even when we were in school, I remember Albert having a problem with pride." Anna didn't want to say too much, but she'd never liked Albert. He'd seemed superficial and smug. "I wasn't surprised that he was attracted to you, Clara. You were so pretty and smart and came from an established family. You were quite a prize to him." Anna squeezed Clara's hand. "Don't take this wrong, but I never thought he deserved you."

Clara made a sorrowful smile then shook her head. "I knew early on that I'd made a mistake in marrying him. I thought he would change . . . or that I could change him."

"But your marriage brought you two beautiful children. Ellen is a dear. And I honestly do believe AJ is coming around. I have great hopes for him."

"Thank you." Clara wiped her eyes. "I just feel so tired and worn out sometimes . . . as if my marriage to Albert drained the life out of me."

"Nonsense," Lucille declared. "You are still

a young woman, Clara. Goodness, you're only thirty-four years old. There's lots of life left in you. Just look at what we're doing with our little dress shop. Trust me, honey, there are lots of good times ahead."

"That's right," Daniel agreed. "You're simply entering a new chapter of your life. You should embrace it."

Clara's eyes lit up slightly. "I'd like to think that. I hope it's true."

"Of course it's true." Anna patted her arm. "Who knows what good things lie ahead for you?" She gently nudged her with an elbow. "There might even be romance in your future."

"Oh, go on with you." Clara actually chuckled. "I'm too old for that."

"Well, I know you ladies came over here to talk business." Daniel stood. "So I will leave you to it."

"As will I." Anna stood as well. She had no interest in looking at frilly dresses and hats and the latest fashions but didn't intend to say as much. Instead, they all bade good evening, and Daniel and Anna made their exit.

"Look at that sky," Daniel pointed toward the ocean.

"The sunset Katy predicted."

"Want to get a better look?"

"Yes," Anna said eagerly. "Let's hurry to the bluff over there." Feeling slightly childish for not wanting to miss what promised to be a pretty spectacle, Anna began to actually run toward the open area where they would have the best vantage point.

As they ran, Daniel looped his arm around hers. "Let's make sure no one falls. I don't want to set any broken bones tonight."

On the bluff, Anna realized how much she liked the feeling of Daniel so close to her but reminded herself that they were only friends. Daniel had made it clear that was all he was interested in, and she did not plan on setting herself up for a disappointment. And yet, as they walked over to the bench, Daniel didn't release her arm. And, even as they sat down, Anna made no attempt to get free.

"It's chilly up here." Anna shivered as a cold breeze swept in from the ocean.

"Is this better?" Daniel removed his arm from hers, then slipped it around her shoulders, holding her even closer.

"Thank you," she murmured, suddenly feeling awkward and self-conscious.

"Just look at those colors." Daniel blew out an appreciative whistle.

"Beautiful." Anna looked up at the colorful sky.

"I've seen some spectacular sunsets in my time, but I think this one takes the cake."

"I agree." Anna wasn't sure which was better . . . the sky painted in shades of purple, amber, and red . . . or the feeling of Daniel so close to her. But it was a moment she wished could go on and on, a moment she would treasure forever.

Katy, Ellen, and Jim were watching the sunset from the beach. "I've never seen anything so gorgeous," Katy said happily. "I wish I could paint it."

"Why don't you?" Ellen said without enthusiasm. "You've got the time now."

"And I know you've got the talent," Jim added.

"Why, thank you." Katy studied the colors, trying to imagine how she could recreate it with paint. "If I could just memorize it. I'd like to imprint it onto my mind."

"Or perhaps you should just enjoy it," Jim said.

"Yes!" Katy exclaimed, taking both Ellen and Jim by the hand. "Let's dance to the music of the sunset. Come on, you two, let's rejoice in all its glory." And then she began to sing the chorus to "Pretty Baby" but changing the words to *pretty sunset*. Before long, both Jim and Ellen were singing and dancing with her—or trying. But then they all stumbled over a piece of driftwood and tumbled to the sand, laughing loudly.

"That was my fault," Jim said as he helped Katy and Ellen to stand. "As much as I like to dance, I've been accused of having two left feet."

"You probably just need more practice—or a

couple of good teachers." Katy grinned at Ellen. "How about we teach Jim how to do the turkey trot?" And, with Katy calling out the steps, the three of them attempted a rather clumsy turkey trot until Jim gave up.

"I don't think this soft sand makes for the best dance floor." He pointed to the sky. "And just look at how pretty the sky is now. Maybe we should all sit down and just enjoy it."

"I suppose we've worn you out," Katy said as they all flopped down on the side of the sand dune. "I forgot that you're an old man, *Mr. Stafford*." Katy knew it was acceptable to use his first name but wanted to tease him. "You probably need to catch your breath."

"I just can't keep up with you young'uns anymore." He feigned an old man's voice. "I might need to borrow Mac's cane to make it back up those steep beach stairs."

"Oh, let me run up and get it for you," Katy kidded back. "I wouldn't want you to fall and get hurt."

"How old are you anyway?" Ellen asked Jim.

"How old do you think I am?"

"I don't know." Ellen studied him. "I mean, sometimes, like tonight, you don't seem terribly old. But then I think you must be at least as old as my mom. And that's pretty old."

"So you think I'm past my prime?" he sounded slightly offended.

"Are you suggesting that Ellen's mother is past *her* prime?" Katy responded. "That wouldn't be very nice. Especially since she's exactly the same age as *my* mother. And you don't seem to think *she's* past her prime."

"Really?" he sounded surprised. "They're the same age?"

"Yes. They went to school together. Didn't you know that?" Katy asked.

"Well, I . . . I suppose I thought Anna was younger."

"That's because my mother has been through hard times." Ellen sounded defensive. "It's aged her."

"Yes, but it's getting better for her." Katy patted Ellen's shoulder. "For both of you."

"Maybe. But back to how old he is," Ellen persisted. "What do you think, Katy?"

"Hmm." Katy considered this. "I would estimate that he is about . . . uh, thirty-two?"

"Wrong."

"Thirty-five?" Ellen tried.

"Wrong again." He started to laugh. "You know, there was a time when I wanted people to think I was older than I was, but now I'm not so sure."

"You mean you're younger?" Ellen asked.

He simply nodded.

They continued to guess, going down one, then two years each time, until finally Katy guessed twenty-four. "Bingo!" Jim exclaimed.

"You're only twenty-four?" Ellen demanded. "Are you trying to trick us?"

"That's the honest truth," he declared. "But now I'll have to swear you both to absolute secrecy."

"Only if you tell us *why* it's a secret," Katy said.

"Because when Mac hired me, I claimed I was thirty, and that was more than three years ago."

"Why did you pretend to be older?" Katy persisted.

"Because it sounded like I'd had more experience."

"So you *lied* to get the job?" Ellen sounded either scandalized or intrigued. Katy wasn't sure.

"Were you qualified for the job?" Katy asked him.

"Apparently." He chuckled. "No one's fired me yet."

"And you just got promoted," Katy reminded him. "But, if you're only twenty-four, you are ten years younger than my mother!"

"Your arithmetic is right."

"But I, uh, I thought you liked her." Katy felt confused.

Jim's brows shot up. "Of course I like her."

"That's not what I mean," Katy insisted. "I assumed you liked her in a more, uh, a different way."

"Katy thought you wanted to marry her mother," Ellen declared.

"That's not true," Katy argued. Even if it were partly true, she'd recently given up hope that it would ever happen. Mother acted as if she wished to remain unmarried forever. Just today, Katy had to bite her tongue. Despite that they were having guests for Thanksgiving, Mother came down garbed in the drabbest, dullest garment she owned. A clear signal she didn't care to catch a man's eye.

"Well, I can't deny Anna's an intelligent and attractive woman," Jim confessed. "I could certainly do worse."

"Are you in love with her?" Ellen pressed him.

"Ellen Krauss," Katy said sharply. "You shouldn't be so—"

"It's all right," he assured her. "For the record, I have no romantic intentions toward your mother, Katy. I admire and respect her, but we are merely friends and fellow journalists."

"Oh, that's good." Katy felt relief. "I don't know if I could respect a stepfather who is only . . . *seven years* older than me." She turned to stare at him, but the light was fading so quickly it was hard to see his features. Was he really only *twenty-four?* Suddenly, Jim seemed like a different person to her.

"How long do you plan to keep your secret?" Ellen asked him.

"That's a good question." Jim sighed. "I suppose there's no harm in letting the truth out now."

"I doubt my mother will fire you," Katy said wryly.

"But I bet she'll be surprised," Ellen added.

"My grandfather might take his cane to you," Katy teased. "He probably doesn't like being tricked."

"I think he'll understand." Jim stood and helped the girls to their feet again. "Speaking of Mac, he's probably wondering what happened to us. It's getting dark fast. We should get back."

As they went up the beach stairs, Katy was still ruminating over Jim's revelation. It was rather startling to realize he was closer to Katy's age than to her mother's. Perhaps even more startling was the fact that Ellen seemed to be flirting with him. Even now, she was staying close to him, making small talk, teasing, and acting like she thought he was their age. What on earth was her silly friend up to? Was she entertaining a crush on Jim? Whatever the case, Katy planned to get to the bottom of it before the night was over. And, since Ellen was staying over for the night, she should have plenty of time.

The house was warm and bright, and Bernice had laid out a tempting buffet of leftovers. The other guests had returned and were filling their plates and casually eating in the dining room. But, as Katy made herself a turkey sandwich, she invited Ellen to join her in the basement. "We can play a game of pool." She lowered her voice. "And leave the old folks up here."

"Then Jim should come with us," Ellen grinned impishly. "He doesn't belong with the *old* folks."

Jim chuckled. "As a matter of fact, I wouldn't mind a little billiards."

So the three of them carried their food downstairs and set up a game of pool while they ate. But Katy was becoming more and more convinced that Ellen was getting far too friendly with Jim. If he said something just mildly funny, Ellen laughed too loudly. If he made a pithy comment, Ellen acted like he was brilliant. And it was more than a little concerning. After all, Ellen was only sixteen and still in school. What would her mother say?

"You know what I could use to wash this down?" Jim set his empty plate on a side table. "A nice glass of milk."

"I'll get it for you," Ellen offered quickly.

"What? Do you think I'm too old and decrepit to make it up the stairs?"

Ellen laughed. "I'll be right back."

As soon as she was out of earshot, Katy turned to Jim. "I don't know what's wrong with Ellen tonight," she said with aggravation, "but I hope you're not taking her attentions too seriously."

He shrugged. "Oh, she's just a kid, Katy. You both are." He grinned. "And I'm having fun acting like I'm a kid too. But it's nothing to be concerned about." He chalked his cue. "After all, I have to go back to being a grown-up newspaper reporter tomorrow."

"Speaking of newspaper reporters." Anna came down the stairs, with Ellen right on her heels. "I need to talk to you, Jim. About the newspaper."

"But he's playing pool with us," Ellen protested as she handed him a glass of milk.

"Well, as soon as you're done, then," Anna told them. "Come see me before you go home. I'll be in Mac's den."

"Work, work, work," Katy teased Jim as he drank his milk. "Is that all you grown-ups ever think about?"

"Not while I'm beating you girls at billiards." He set down his glass, then carefully aimed his cue and sank a ball into the side pocket. "How about that?" He made a mock bow, then lined up his next shot, which he missed.

Katy took advantage of the way he'd left the table by putting two balls away with one shot. Eager to sink more balls and get this game over with, she carelessly scratched her next shot.

Ellen put the cue ball back on the table, then turned to Jim with wide eyes. "You're so good at this, how about giving me some tips?" Even though Ellen knew better, she held the cue stick at a weird angle.

"Even your cue stick out," Jim told her. "Keep it almost parallel to the table."

"Like this?" She made it even worse.

"Parallel means it's at the same angle," Katy said a bit sharply.

Jim went over to show Ellen what he meant, patiently explaining some basic skills—that Ellen already knew!

"So I just line the white ball up with the red one?" Ellen asked him.

"But hit the red one on the right side."

Katy rolled her eyes and turned away. Why was Ellen acting like such a goof? And would this stupid pool game never end?

"Oh my goodness!" Ellen exclaimed. "I missed again."

"It was close," Jim told her. "And you left me nicely set up."

"Wasn't that sweet of me," Ellen chirped, staying close to Jim as he sank another ball. "Oh, you're so good at this," she gushed.

On they went until only the eight ball remained, and it was Jim's turn. He called the pocket and shot the ball in. "Well, I think that means I won." He put his cue back in the holder, then grinned. "Excuse me, girls, the grown-ups are calling."

With Jim gone, Ellen lost all interest in playing pool, and Katy lost all interest in being with Ellen. She wished she hadn't invited her to spend the night. It had sounded like a fun idea yesterday, but Ellen was anything but fun now. Katy wondered how rude it would be to un-invite her friend. Was Ellen even her friend? It sure didn't feel like it.

CHAPTER 18

After Lucille and Clara left, Mac excused himself to bed, and Anna asked Daniel to stick around to talk to Jim when he finished his billiards game with the girls. She wanted Jim to hear the news about the autopsy and the fact that Albert Krauss was left-handed.

"He should be up soon," she told Daniel as he set another log on the fire that had been burning all day.

"I don't mind waiting." Daniel sat back down. "This is a comfy spot to spend a wintry evening."

Anna studied Daniel in the big, leather arm chair. In his charcoal tweed suit, with his dark hair curling around his ears, those deep, brown eyes, and a handsomely serious expression, he looked perfectly at home in Mac's den. All he needed was a pipe. She felt her cheeks warm as she looked away. Had he noticed her gazing at him like a starry-eyed schoolgirl?

"Do you feel all right?" He leaned forward with a concerned expression. "You look a little flushed."

She touched her cheek. "Oh, it's probably the heat of the fire after being out in the cold." She felt a happy rush to remember how he'd put his arm around her to keep her warm earlier. Nothing else had happened between them, and she knew she was being silly to obsess over such a small gesture, but it did give her hope. Maybe Daniel wasn't as determined to remain single as he'd made her believe a few weeks ago. Or maybe she was letting her imagination run away with her.

"Here I am," Jim announced as he came into the room. "Cozy in here."

"Yes." Anna smiled. "Thanks for joining us. Have a seat. This won't take long."

"What's up?" Jim sat down and listened as Anna and Daniel took turns explaining about tonight's discovery.

"And I know you've been investigating that," Anna told him. "So I thought you should hear it from us. Naturally, Daniel will tell the chief about it."

"Tomorrow," Daniel said.

"Do we write a story on it?" Jim asked eagerly.

"Yes." Anna nodded. "I think so. Unless you can think of any reason to keep it quiet. That's what I wanted to ask you tonight."

"I think we should blow it wide open," Jim said. "If the murderer is out there—or even accomplices, since we're pretty sure that the jailbreak was done by at least two, and maybe more, men—why not make them uneasy?"

"Exactly what I was thinking."

"Calling Krauss's death a suicide gave people a false sense of security," Jim said. "Time to shake things up."

"And it'll be interesting to see how Clint Collins and Calvin Snyder react to this news," Anna said.

"Might be fun to see them getting nervous." Jim grinned. "I'll be sure to pay close attention when the news gets out."

"Now, as soon as Daniel tells the chief tomorrow, Clint Collins will probably hear about it," Anna said to Jim. "You might want to be nearby to see his reaction."

"Especially since he was so certain it was a suicide." Jim turned to Daniel. "And you feel fairly certain it wasn't suicide."

"I'll look at my notes again in the morning to see the angle of the bullet wound. But just knowing Albert was left-handed is enough to make suicide highly unlikely."

"At least it should be enough to reopen the case," Anna said.

"When do you think you'll spring this on the chief?" Jim lifted a brow toward Daniel.

"How does nine o'clock sound?"

"Perfect. I'll be there to get a quote from the chief, which I can use as an excuse to be close to Collins."

"Sounds like a good plan." Anna thanked both of them.

"Well, this is exciting news." Jim stood. "Unless there's anything else I need to know, I think I'll head home now. Maybe pound out a rough draft so that it'll be nearly ready for Saturday's paper. I assume this goes on the front page."

"You bet." Anna nodded firmly. "With a big headline. And, if you get that draft to me, I can go over it while you're at the police station, and you can have the whole day to sleuth around if you need it."

After Jim left, Daniel lingered. Now it seemed like he was watching her. She pretended not to notice as she gazed at the dancing orange flames in the fireplace, but she suddenly wished she'd taken more care with her appearance today. She looked down at the gray woolen dress she'd put on this morning. She'd chosen it for the warmth, because her room was so chilly, but her plan had been to change into something more festive in time for their dinner. Then she'd gotten busy helping Bernice in the kitchen and had completely forgotten. Of course, she'd observed Katy's look of disapproval, but by then it was too late. Now she wished she'd asked her fashionable daughter for some help.

"You really love your work, don't you?" Daniel said.

"Well, yes. I guess it's sort of in my blood."

"Was that always what you wanted to do? I mean, when you were growing up?"

"I guess so. I spent more waking time at the newspaper office than I did here at home. But so did Mac. I did odd jobs at first, but he had me writing small pieces by the time I was twelve. And then, later on, when I needed to support Katy and myself, the only experience I had was with the newspaper, so, naturally, that's where I looked for work. I wouldn't have known what else to do."

"Watching you talking to Jim just now . . . ." Daniel's expression was hard to read. "I could see how much you love your work. You were all lit up and excited." He smiled. "Very pretty."

"Oh." Anna felt her cheeks growing even warmer but resisted the urge to touch her face. "Well, I suppose I get excited about breaking a big story. And for Sunset Cove, the news of Albert Krauss's having been murdered—not suicide—that's a pretty big story."

"I suppose the way you feel about covering a story is like how I feel when I stitch someone up or deliver a baby." He smiled. "It's good to enjoy one's work."

Anna considered this. It was similar to their earlier conversation, and it was interesting that he'd brought it up again. It seemed almost as if he were fishing for something. Well, perhaps she should bite.

"You know, Daniel, as much as I love my job at the newspaper, like I said before, it's not my whole life. At least, I don't want it to be. I do not want to be married to it." She frowned with realization. "In fact, I'm afraid I've let the paper take over too much of my life these last several months. And I'm getting concerned that it might have hurt my relationship with my daughter. Katy and I don't seem to talk nearly as much as we used to. Anyway, it's just occurring to me that I need to delegate more responsibility at the paper. Jim has certainly been helpful, but perhaps it's time to hire another editor. I'll have to run that by Mac tomorrow." She sighed. "Sorry, I didn't mean to go on like that, but I suppose you got me thinking."

"And I'm sure you're tired after a long day." Daniel stood.

Anna knew she should be tired. It was late, and she'd had a busy week. But the truth was she wasn't a bit sleepy. "It was a very good day." She stood, smiling at him. "Thank you for joining us."

"It always feels like family here," he said as she walked him to the front door. "Thank you for inviting me." He pulled on his overcoat. "Rather, thank Mac, since he's the one who actually invited me." He grinned as he picked up his hat. "I almost had the impression you didn't want me to come, Anna. I hope you didn't mind."

"I'm glad you came," she assured him. "I think I was just worked up at the time. You know, worried about Katy and all that." She smiled. "I'm *very* glad you came. And I hope you'll always feel welcome here." She wanted to say more, but suddenly felt self-conscious. "Anyway, stay warm out there. It sounds like the wind is really starting to blow, and Mac is predicting a storm by the weekend."

"That's when I wish for an ocean view, but my house doesn't have one." He reached for the door. "Nothing like watching a good storm from a nice, warm spot."

"Then you must come back for it. Consider yourself invited for a storm watch."

"Thank you." He opened the door just as a gust blasted in. "Looks like that storm is on its way."

She told him good-bye and then closed and locked the door, leaning against it with a dreamy feeling. Perhaps she'd been too hasty in giving up on Daniel Hollister. Unless she were mistaken, he was still interested. But she suspected he would need considerable encouragement. Perhaps it was time to have a fashion consultation with her stylish young daughter, the joint-proprietress of Sunset Cove's quality dress shop.

Katy decided it was too rude to tell Ellen she didn't want her to stay overnight. But, by the time they were in Katy's room, the air between them had grown thick and heavy. Katy wasn't sure if it was related to the way Ellen had been acting toward Jim Stafford or something else, but she was determined to get to the bottom of it. Once they were in their nightgowns, Katy decided to broach the subject.

"Why are you so enamored with Jim Stafford all of a sudden?" Katy sat down on the foot of her bed, waiting.

"Enamored?" Ellen blinked. "What exactly does that mean?"

"If you'd had any French, you'd know. *Amour* is French for *love. Enamored* is related to love. Like having a feeling of love."

"Oh my, aren't you the smart one." Ellen wrinkled her nose. "But then you're a *high school graduate.* I nearly forgot."

Katy studied her friend. Ellen used to be so sweet. Almost too sweet sometimes. But lately, especially in the last month, she had changed—dramatically. She'd become more outspoken and sarcastic. Sometimes she actually seemed bitter. Katy had tried to overlook these somewhat aggravating characteristics, blaming Ellen's new attitudes on all that she'd gone through with her brother and father. But Katy wasn't sure how much more she could take. Weren't friends supposed to be friendly?

"I just don't understand . . . ." Katy said quietly. "I know you've been through a lot, Ellen, but it seems like it's changing you. And not necessarily for the best. I don't want to offend you, but that's the truth."

"Oh." Ellen looked hurt now.

"I'm sorry." Katy scooted closer to where Ellen stood. "But I just want to understand what's going on. Why you're so different. Maybe you don't like me anymore. Do you still want to be friends?"

"Of course I want to be friends." Ellen folded her arms across her front, slumping down into the arm chair by the window. "I suppose I'm just angry."

"At me?"

Ellen scowled. "Sometimes."

Katy sank onto her bed. "But why? What have I done?"

Ellen shrugged. "Oh, let me think. Maybe because you're so perfect. Everyone loves you. You're smart and pretty and creative—"

"But you're smart and pretty and creative too!"

"Not like you." Ellen narrowed her eyes. "Even my own mother thinks you're a wonder. She's so happy that you've taken me under your wing."

"So that's it? You're angry at me?" Katy had experienced jealousy from friends before. It was usually the reason a friendship ended. But she was disappointed to think that Ellen felt like this. "Does this mean our friendship is over?"

Ellen sighed. "I won't be surprised if you want it to be."

"You've been through so much, Ellen. But you never want to talk about it. If this thing is just about me—if that's the only thing troubling you—well then, perhaps I'm not a very good friend for you. I'll understand if you want to—"

"No!" Ellen's face crumbled and then she began to cry. "It's not just you, Katy. It—it's barely you at all. It's—it's everything. *Everything.*"

Katy went over to Ellen, knelt by the chair, and wrapped her arms around her. "I know. You've been through so much these last few months. I don't know how you've held it all inside. You need to talk to someone. You can talk to me."

"But it's all so ugly. All this ugliness is inside of me."

"I don't mind. You can tell me. I'll listen."

"It's my dad, Katy. *I hate him!* And I know it's wrong to hate your parents. Especially if they're dead. But I *do* hate him. And I hate AJ too. I can't believe he did the things he did. He knew that our dad was bad, but he just blindly followed him. And I'm even mad at my mom—and I hate feeling like that—because I really do love her. But she was so weak all the time. She should've left my dad—taken us kids and left him—a long time ago! She could've followed her parents— my grandma and grandpa—when they moved to Salem. I know they left here to get away from Dad. They didn't like him. He ruined everything for everyone! I'm so angry at him. At all of them.

And at myself for feeling like this. It's all so ugly."

"Oh, Ellen. I'm so sorry. It's no wonder you're angry. I would be too."

"Not like this. I'm so filled with anger and hatred—so much ugliness. I try to hold it inside, but it's seeping out. I know it." She looked at Katy with tear-filled eyes. "You're the best friend I've ever had, and I've been horrible to you. I'm so sorry."

"I'm still your best friend," Katy assured her. "And it's about time you let this stuff out. No wonder you're so unhappy! You can't keep all that inside of you."

Ellen just shook her head.

"I used to get angry about my father too," Katy admitted. "You know what he did, how he broke the law . . . died in prison? It's not so different than what happened to you. Except that I was so small at the time, I never really knew. I didn't know he'd been incarcerated until the train ride to Sunset Cove, actually—and I was shocked, I can tell you. But even before that, I struggled with not having a father around. I was about thirteen when I began to understand it. And I got angry then. Mother and I talked about it a lot. And she encouraged me to pray about it. And eventually, I got over it . . . in time. You will too. But you need to talk to someone about it."

"I know. Your grandmother keeps telling me

that too. She's told me that I can talk to her. And you've tried to get me to talk to you."

"It's because we love you, Ellen. We want you to get past this."

She barely nodded. "I want to get past it too."

They talked some more, and Katy knew that they'd made good progress, but she suspected it would take Ellen awhile to get all these things out. And it was late.

"I'm pretty sleepy," Katy confessed. "Maybe we can talk about this some more tomorrow."

"Yeah." Ellen climbed into bed with a loud sigh.

Katy turned out the light, then got into bed too. "And, I know this might sound trite, but I do believe everything looks better in the light of day."

"I hope so."

"And I'm glad we're still friends." Katy felt her eyelids getting heavy.

"Me too. Thanks for not giving up on me."

"I'll never give up on you." Katy hoped that was a promise she could keep. She meant it.

"You said you prayed about the stuff with your dad," Ellen whispered. "Did you really pray? And do you think God was listening?"

"Yes and yes. I still pray about hard stuff. And good stuff. And I believe God answers my prayers. I really do. Maybe not the answers I always want, but He answers."

"I guess I'll have to try that too."

"Good." Katy felt herself drifting.

"And what you asked me about Jim Stafford . . . I guess you were right. The truth is, I am feeling enamored." She made a deep sigh. "And, really, Jim's not that much older than us. And I do want to get married, Katy. More than anything. I don't care that much about the dress shop . . . not like you do. And I don't particularly want to graduate high school. I don't think I need all that education . . . not to be a wife and a mother. And that's all I really want. Just to have a happy home with someone who loves me . . . someone to love." Ellen yawned. "Good night."

Suddenly, Katy felt wide awake. Had she heard Ellen correctly? Had she really just declared that she wanted to *marry* Jim Stafford? That she wanted to quit school to become a wife and mother? What on earth was wrong with her? Katy turned to stare at Ellen, barely able to see her face in the darkened room, but her eyes were shut, and her even breathing told Katy she'd fallen asleep. It was perfectly maddening!

How dare Ellen drop a bombshell like that, then simply drift off to sleep! Katy was tempted to shake her friend awake and demand to know what was behind this startling confession. Except that would be embarrassingly juvenile. And now that she was a high school graduate, Katy was determined not to be childish.

As she closed her eyes and leaned back into her pillow, Katy asked herself why it even mattered. Why was she feeling so outraged? So what if Jim Stafford liked this idea, if he decided to marry Ellen? It wasn't as if older men didn't marry younger women. It happened all the time. And seven years' difference wasn't all that much. So, really, why was Katy so upset by Ellen's proclamation of love? She should be glad for her friend. Ellen deserved some happiness. But, for some reason, the whole thing made Katy want to scream.

CHAPTER 19

T he news that Albert Krauss hadn't died from suicide but was quite likely a murder victim was big news in their little town, and Anna was anxious to hear how it had gone over at the police station. "Were you there when Daniel told Chief Rollins about our discovery?" Anna asked Jim on Friday.

"Yes, we went in together. But the chief didn't seem too surprised, probably because he'd been having suspicions similar to ours."

"I'm sure he's been holding his cards close to his chest." She shuffled through some papers on her desk. "Was Clint Collins around to hear the news?"

Jim grinned. "As a matter of fact, he was with the chief when we told him."

"And his reaction?"

"I acted like I was taking notes on the chief's comments, but I was watching Collins closely. I don't think I imagined it—he looked uncomfortable. Or maybe someone had put too much starch in his collar. And then he made what I think was a fairly absurd suggestion." Jim chuckled. "Although I plan to use it as a quote in my article."

"What?"

"Collins said that Krauss probably shot himself on the right side of the head to make it appear to be murder—because he wanted to get someone else in hot water."

"Seriously?"

Jim glanced at his open notebook. "Yep. Those were his exact words, Anna. And then he excused himself."

"Did you follow him?"

"You bet. I was quite discreet about it, and I'm sure he didn't see me, but guess where he went?"

"To Snyder?"

"That's right. He hightailed it up to Charlie's, which, of course, wasn't open. But Clint went in through the back door and stayed there for about twenty minutes."

"And then?"

"Then he went back to the station."

"So it really seems like he's in cahoots with Snyder." Anna rolled a pen back and forth over her desk pad. "Did you mention this to the chief yet?"

"He's so certain his right-hand boy is trustworthy, I'm not sure it's worthwhile to try to convince him otherwise just yet. We don't want to turn him against us."

"I don't think he'd do that." Anna thought. "He and Mac have been friends for ages. He's always cooperated with the newspaper in the past."

"Maybe . . . but that was with Mac running things."

"What difference should that make?" she demanded.

"Hey, don't shoot the messenger, Anna. It's just that there are certain folks in town who don't cotton to a woman at the helm."

"Stop mixing your metaphors." She frowned. "Besides, you think I don't know some people resent my running this paper?"

"I doubt you hear about it as much as I do," he said glumly. "I take a lot of heat for working for a woman."

She fought the urge to roll her eyes. "I'm sorry about that, but there's not a lot I can do about it."

"Well, I didn't come in here to pick a fight."

"Right. Back to the chief. You really don't think we should tell him?"

"I just don't know. Are you certain he's on the up and up?"

"I can't imagine he's not. Chief Rollins is a good man. But he is getting old. I know he's eager to retire."

"And hand off the reins to Clint." Jim scowled. "What does Mac have to say?"

"Good question. I'll talk to him about this. But I do agree with you—let's not tell the chief about our suspicions regarding Clint. It's still possible that he's working incognito and that we're simply assuming the worst. That'd be embarrassing to mess up their investigation with our own."

"You're right." Jim stood.

"In the meantime, let's not stop our investigation."

"Count on it."

The newspaper ran the story about Krauss on Saturday, and it was the talk of the town for the next few days. But, as usual, it died down as the week progressed. Anna's interest in continuing their investigation, however, did *not* die down. And her conversation with Mac only confirmed that it was the newspaper's responsibility to keep digging. He agreed with her that Harvey Rollins was a good man but that he was eager to give up his position.

"He's older than me," he told Anna. "And he's been complaining about aches and pains lately. He wants to retire while he's still young enough to do some fishing."

"And he's been grooming Clint Collins to step into his shoes," Anna said glumly.

Mac frowned, and Anna knew this was a sore subject with him. Mac identified with his buddy. The way the chief had taken a younger man under his wing was similar to what Mac had done with Wesley Kempton. And, although he never spoke of it, Anna knew that Mac still felt sad over Wesley's death. She did too. As Wesley's boss,

240

she'd often asked herself if there were something she could have done differently. But, one thing was certain, if Wesley's murder was related to Albert Krauss's, it was well worth her time to keep poking around. She wasn't done yet.

For a follow-up article in next Saturday's edition, Anna decided it was time to do some more investigative reporting on the county jail. She felt certain not every stone had been overturned out there. And she still harbored strong suspicions about a certain jail guard. Something about Tom Gardner did not sit well with her. On Wednesday, she asked Jim to meet with her.

"I don't see what you think can be gained," Jim said as they met in her office that afternoon. "I've already covered it."

"But you never got to talk to the other jail-keeper," Anna reminded him. "The one who'd gone home sick the night of the jailbreak. I think his name was Bud."

"That's right. Bud Jackson. He still wasn't back when I was sniffing out the jail." Jim scratched his head. "What exactly are you thinking, Anna?"

"That I'd like to question Bud about Albert. Find out whether their paths crossed much, how he generally felt about Albert. Were they on good terms? Was Albert a difficult inmate? I'm also curious about how he happened to get sick that night. Pretty convenient timing to skip out right before a jailbreak."

"Interesting." Jim nodded eagerly. "Now that I think about it, I'd like to hear his responses too."

"Why don't you come with me?" Anna suggested. "In fact, why don't you set it up for us? If Bud still works the night shift, we might have to be flexible about the time. Maybe we could go to his home." She remembered how revealing that had been with Tom Gardner, with possible clues lying all about the place. And Tom was still on their suspect list. "But don't tip our hand. Just tell Bud we're doing another article on the jail. Make up something if you have to."

"Got it." Jim stood. "I'll let you know." He paused by the door. "Say, I've been meaning to ask you when you plan to start that fashion column we discussed awhile back. I know you wanted to wait until after the election, but with the grand opening of Sunset Cove's fancy new dress shop next week, it seems timely to get it started. And it would be lighter reading during the holidays."

"You're right." She nodded. "I actually asked Katy about this very thing a couple of days ago. She's still interested." Anna glanced at her to-do list, which was already quite long. "And I'd asked Ed about doing a piece about the shop for the business column, but he's still out with that cold. How about if you handle that and Katy's column, Jim? As managing editor, it should be under your purview anyway."

"Meaning you don't want to be the boss of your daughter?" His tone was slightly teasing.

"Meaning I'm learning to delegate more responsibilities around here." She pulled out a stiff smile. "But, besides that, I do think it would be more professional if Katy were to report to you." Although she and her daughter were on polite speaking terms, something in their relationship had felt different of late, and she had no qualms about sloughing this job off onto Jim.

"Well, I think you're right." Jim nodded. "As soon as I nail something down with Bud Jackson, I'll give Katy a call, see if she can meet with me."

"Thank you." Anna returned to her typewriter as Jim left, but, distracted by this talk of Katy, her concentration for Saturday's editorial piece had drifted away. Anna leaned back in her chair, trying to determine why she felt so unsettled in regard to her only daughter. What was going on with them? Would it eventually get better?

There was no denying that Katy had become increasingly distant these past couple of months. Anna knew it had originally been related to their disagreement over schooling and the dress shop. But it hadn't escaped her notice that Katy was growing quite close to her grandmother. She spent all her time at the dress shop these days. Understandably, since the new enterprise was scheduled to open next week. But, for some reason, Anna found this unsettling. It was hard to see Katy moving steadily away from her. Anna hated to admit it, but, besides feeling left out, she felt jealous of Lucille. And that seemed just plain wrong . . . not to mention selfish.

Katy had eventually managed to put Ellen's talk of marrying Jim Stafford behind her. Thankfully, Ellen hadn't raised the subject again. Of course, most of their interaction occurred while working at the dress shop. And, since Ellen could only work on weekends and after school, and because Clara and Lucille were usually nearby, it wasn't the best place to talk about romantic dreams.

Katy was devoted to the success of their shop, spending long hours each day working on designs, creating patterns, as well as doing a lot of the sewing. Although the plan for operating the dress shop was to construct custom garments for individual customers, they hoped to have a good selection of lovely dresses beautifully displayed in the windows and all about the shop. This would allow customers to actually touch the quality materials, admire the designs, and inspect the workmanship. Naturally, this meant a lot of work. In order to get the garments ready for the grand opening next week, all four women were putting in their full effort.

"Do you think we'll be able to slow down after the grand opening?" Ellen asked as she hemmed a lovely taffeta evening dress.

"I hope we don't slow down too much." Katy paused from measuring a length of moiré satin. "We need to sell our garments if we want to stay in business."

"And hopefully we'll start getting orders of some ready-made pieces when people see the samples—shoes, stockings, lingerie, and such. That will help to fill our shelves too." Lucille held up a piece of lacework for Katy to examine. "Is this how you wanted this to look?"

Katy made an adjustment to the lace. "It needs to be at this angle. It looks more graceful on the bodice like that. See?"

"You have such a gift." Lucille smiled at her.

"When do you expect the order of shoes to arrive?" Katy asked. "I'd love to use some in the window display in time for our grand opening."

"I'd hoped they'd be here by now." Lucille pursed her mouth. "Hopefully by the end of the week."

Katy nodded. "In the meantime, we need to work on some hats."

"That reminds me." Lucille's eyes lit up. "I had an idea for a way to make our shop look fuller. What if I bring some of my own things? For instance, I have several fur pieces that would look very festive for winter."

"What if someone wants to purchase one of your furs?" Clara asked with concern.

"Well, I suppose that would be all right."

245

Lucille chuckled. "But I'll make sure to put very high prices on them."

"And I could bring in some dresses and accessories too," Katy suggested. "I have some that are barely worn. They'd be great samples."

"We want this place to look truly grand." Lucille paused to thread a needle. "For our *grand* opening."

"You should hear the women talking about our shop," Clara said. "I was in the mercantile yesterday, and we were the topic of the day. Although, I'm not sure that Marjorie approved."

"I've assured her that we won't be in competition with her store," Lucille said. "We'll only be catering to the most fashionable women. The mercantile will still sell ready-made clothes and fabric and dry goods for everyday use. But Marjorie doesn't carry anything like what we'll have here."

"It's all so exciting." Katy pinned the wide moiré sash onto a holiday dress. "I can't wait to see the response at our opening."

"I still think we should have tea and cookies," Clara said. "And I'm happy to make them."

"Not this time," Katy insisted. "I like Lucille's idea of hosting some special teas later on, with smaller groups."

"That's how they do it in the city." Lucille told them about some of her favorite dress shops in San Francisco. "House of Rousseau is my favorite. Oh my, I wish you ladies could see it. The original House of Rousseau was destroyed in the fires after the earthquake, but when they rebuilt . . ." She sighed. "Bigger and more beautiful than ever."

"Will our shop be as beautiful?" Ellen asked.

Lucille laughed her big, hearty laugh. "No, dear, I'm afraid not. Sunset Cove couldn't begin to support such a place. House of Rousseau, when they rebuilt it, became four stories of the most beautiful clothes imaginable. I used to believe that only millionaires shopped there."

"Did you ever shop there?" Clara's brows arched.

"Sometimes."

"Are you a millionaire?" Ellen asked.

"No, of course not." Lucille shook her head. "But my husband, bless his soul, left me rather comfortable. That's why I'm able to invest in our little shop. But, unless I want to be impoverished in my old age, our enterprise will have to turn a profit."

"Tell us more about House of Rousseau," Katy urged her. "It sounds dreamy."

"I'll take you there someday," Lucille promised. "It is such a gorgeous place that I sometimes would dress up in my finest and go in there just to look around. Even this last time I was in San Francisco, I stopped in." She described the ornate stone building with its marble floors, carved wood, crystal chandeliers, and stained glass. "Four stories with an elegant elevator. And everything in the entire building is for women only. The first floor is called daywear, although it's not anything a housewife would wear. Cashmere suits and silk dresses . . . all very exquisite and very expensive. On the second floor, you'll find accessories and a lovely millinery. Just fabulous hats. And there's a large section dedicated to French perfumes and toiletries." She frowned. "Of course, that's become much sparser due to the war in Europe."

As the bell at the back door rang and Clara went to answer it, Lucille continued to describe the other floors of House of Rousseau. "Such a selection of formal gowns and furs on the third floor. You can't imagine. And finally you get to the top floor, with lingerie, shoes, and jewelry. And a sweet little tea shop as well."

"It sounds amazing." Katy sighed. "I can't wait to see it."

"Our next buying trip," Lucille assured her. "After Christmas."

"Speaking of Christmas." Clara carried a box into their workroom. "Your shipment has arrived. The men are unloading it in back now." Before long, the ladies were eagerly opening the boxes, oohing and aahing over delicate pieces of lingerie and the latest styles of women's shoes.

Katy was just examining a pair of red velvet

pumps when they heard someone knocking on the door in front. "I'll go get it," she told the others. Wondering who it might be and preparing to shoo them away, she cracked open the door. To her surprise, it was Jim Stafford. Her thoughts immediately went to Ellen—had Jim come here to see her? Katy certainly hoped not. About to bluntly inform him they were not officially open until next week, she prepared to shut the door in his face. And then his eyes lit up in a big smile . . . and she felt her chilly resolve melting.

CHAPTER 20

S orry to interrupt anything here." Jim's smile grew bigger as he peered over Katy's shoulder, obviously curious as to what was behind her. "But I needed to speak to you."

"To me?" Katy blinked.

"Yes. And it seems your phone is not working."

"Our phone?" She frowned, trying to recall whether their phone had even been installed yet.

"Yes. I've tried to call this shop's number several times today, but according to the operator, the phone is disconnected."

"Oh? That's possible. We've been moving a lot of things around. Maybe someone knocked the cord loose." She opened the door a bit wider. "But why do you want to talk to me?"

"I have a couple of reasons. Newspaper related."

"Well, then I should probably ask you inside." She glanced nervously around the shop's show-room. It was in various stages of readiness with partially filled shelves, dress and millinery mannequins waiting for their finery, a few boxes and crates here and there. "But only if you promise not to tell anyone about anything you see in here." She locked eyes with him. "You must swear to utmost secrecy."

He chuckled as she closed and locked the door behind him. "I think you can trust me. Don't forget that I shared my secret with you."

"Oh, that's right. Lying about your age." She shook a finger at him. "Something to use against you, Mr. Stafford."

"Please, call me Jim. And, I give you my word, I won't spill the beans about the mysterious goings-on in here." He glanced curiously around the showroom. "Well now, this is looking rather impressive." He pointed at the gilt-framed cheval glass. "Fancy."

"We're trying hard to keep it all hush-hush— we want everyone to be completely surprised at our grand opening."

"That was one of the reasons I came by. We want to run an article about that for Saturday's paper—"

"Yes. Ed Bartley told Lucille that he planned to stop by this week. We thought he'd have been here by now."

"Well, Ed's out with a cold. And, since I wanted to talk to you anyway, I thought I'd kill two birds with one stone."

"Why else did you want to talk to me?"

"Your mother said you're still interested in contributing to a fashion column in the newspaper. As managing editor, I'd like to talk to you about it."

"Yes, we were just discussing it. I thought it would be good publicity for our shop. And cheaper than advertising. Although, we're doing that too. We've already purchased several ads to announce our grand opening and will continue to run a weekly ad as well."

He nodded. "Yes, I know. Anyway, I'd like to run your column once a week to start with. In our Saturday edition. I doubt that you'll be able to have one ready for this week, but if you—"

"What makes you think that?"

"Well, you're so busy here—I just assumed."

She considered her schedule. Perhaps she could write it at home this evening. "When would you need it?"

"You'd have to turn it in by tomorrow afternoon." He rubbed his chin. "I'd need about a hundred words, and I thought it would be nice to have a sketch to go with each piece. You know, to get more feminine attention. Although, we could get by without one tomorrow if that's expecting too much—"

"I can do that," she assured him. "I already have sketches."

He blinked and then smiled. "I'll bet you do." He stuck out his hand. "Okay then, it's a deal. You are officially our fashion editor, Katy. As I said, you will report directly to me." His brow creased. "And I hope you won't be offended, but, if your piece doesn't work or doesn't fit our newspaper . . . or if it seems you're not ready for this sort of responsibility, I reserve the right to cancel our agreement."

Katy frowned. "I do understand your concerns, but I don't think it'll be a problem. I've been reading fashion magazines for years. My mother thinks I'm a fairly good writer. I think I know how to do this."

"Great. Now, I'd like to ask some questions about your new business."

"Shouldn't I get my grandmother?"

"If you like." He shrugged. "But since Kathleen McDowell's Dress Shop is named after you, I'm guessing you can tell me everything I need to know. And, from what I understand, you and your grandmother are partners."

"That's true. All right, I'll answer your questions." She led him over to the seating area that they'd set up outside of the fitting rooms. Two small chairs covered in rose-colored velveteen and a small, matching divan. "Hopefully this won't take long since we've still got much to do." She nodded to the divan. "Please, have a seat."

"Elegant." He ran his hand over the soft fabric, then sat. "Is this to make your customers comfortable?"

"It's for ladies who are waiting for fittings," she explained. "Or for private showings."

"Very refined." Jim pulled out a notebook and got straight to work asking her questions. Fortunately, they were not difficult ones, and Katy was actually enjoying herself. It was fun to tell him about all they'd done and what they hoped to accomplish. She even shared about how she'd learned to sew several years ago. "I was about thirteen when I decided that I wanted to have clothes that looked like what I saw in magazines. Of course, they weren't readily available, and, even if they were, we couldn't afford such luxuries. And my mother had no time to sew them, because she was busy working at the *Oregonian*. So I decided that the only way to get them was to create them myself."

"According to your mother, you have a real knack for fashion."

"I do enjoy it."

"Oh, there you are, Katy." Ellen emerged from the workroom. "I thought I heard voices out here. Who are you talking—" She stopped mid-sentence when she saw that it was Jim Stafford sitting opposite Katy. "Oh." She smoothed her hair and smiled.

"I'm just doing an interview for the newspaper," Katy told Ellen. "I think we must be nearly done." She glanced at Jim.

"Yes, just a few more questions."

"Well, I want to hear this too." Ellen sat next to Jim on the divan. "Please, don't let me interrupt anything." And then she leaned toward Jim with wide-eyed interest that Katy found slightly disconcerting. What was she doing?

Jim simply nodded, then turned back to Katy. "Let's see, where was I? Yes. How do you expect the women of Sunset Cove will respond to your new business?"

"Well, as my grandmother has pointed out, our shop won't be for everyone." Katy knew it was silly, but she suddenly wanted to appear even more grown up and sophisticated—for Ellen's sake. "It's for the stylish women with discriminating taste. The women who want more than our small town can currently offer. These are the women who might hire a dressmaker or do their shopping through catalogues. But ordering clothes from a faraway place can be disappointing."

"I'll say," Ellen jumped in. "I ordered a party dress once, and it didn't even arrive on time. And, when it did get here, it was two sizes too big."

Katy nodded. "Exactly what I mean."

"Yes, but do you think you'll find that special sort of clientele here in our small town? Are there really enough customers to support a dress shop?" Jim asked Katy.

"I am sure we will." Katy tried to express more confidence than she felt. "As you know, my mother and I came from Portland, which is a much larger city. But, based on what I saw there, I'm convinced that more and more modern women are developing a refined sense of fashion. I think it might be related to the women's rights movement." She giggled. "I'm not suggesting that suffragette women were particularly stylish." She shook her finger at Jim. "So please don't print *that!* What I am saying is that, as women come into their own—getting the vote, earning their places in the workforce—like my mother—they also earn the right to embrace fashion and style with feminine independence."

"Feminine independence?" Jim furiously scribbled in his notebook, then finally looked up. "Well said, Katy. I like that."

"Thank you."

"You've just convinced me that you will have no problem with your column."

"What column?" Ellen asked.

"Katy is going to write a weekly fashion column for the paper." Jim flipped the page in his notebook.

"It'll help promote our shop," Katy explained to Ellen.

"Anything else you'd like to say?" Jim waited.

"Yes." Katy nodded. "I want to add that we hope to attract tourist shoppers as well. As you know, Sunset Cove is an increasingly popular tourist destination. Especially in summer. Women visiting from larger cities might enjoy our shop.

And we will carry a variety of seasonal offerings to appeal to them."

Jim's eyes lit up. "Once again, Katy McDowell, that's very well said. I'd like to quote you verbatim on some of this." He held up his notebook. "Mind if I go over a couple of these lines again, just to be sure I got your words right?"

"Not at all." After a few more minutes, they wrapped up the interview, and Jim thanked her for her time. "Tell your grandmother that you handled this perfectly."

She thanked him and was about to walk him to the door when Ellen hopped in front of her. "I'll let him out," Ellen said. "And, don't worry, I'll lock up too."

"Thanks." Katy nodded, backing away.

"Don't forget your fashion column," Jim called to her. "I'll need your article at the paper no later than four tomorrow afternoon."

"I'll get it to you," she promised as she opened the door to the workroom. Lingering there a moment, she could hear Ellen chattering at Jim, pointing out parts of the shop, obviously trying to detain him from leaving too quickly— and shamelessly flirting! Once again, Katy felt aggravated. She'd been telling herself that Ellen's interest in Jim Stafford had been simply a passing fancy. Apparently, she was wrong. But, honestly, why should she care so much?

CHAPTER 21

They were both quiet as Jim drove Anna to their appointment with the county jail-keeper on Friday morning. "It's getting pretty nasty." Jim leaned forward, trying to peer through the windscreen as rain splattered against it. Anna had been driving Mac's Runabout but felt uneasy due to the bad weather and the fact that it wasn't quite light outside. Jim had offered to take over, and she'd gladly agreed.

"Maybe this is the storm we were supposed to get last weekend," she said nervously. "The one that never really blew in." She'd been disappointed when last Saturday had turned out to be sunny and clear. She'd hoped that Daniel would come over to storm watch with her . . . but that had never happened. "I wonder if this is supposed to get worse." She tried not to get worried over the water collecting on the rutted road. Would they be able to get safely back to town?

"I'm sorry we had to go so early." Jim slowed down a bit. "It was the only time Bud Jackson could meet with us."

"I understand," she assured him. "At least we'll

have the whole day left. Well, as long as this road doesn't wash out."

Jim gave an unconvincing laugh. "I think we'll be fine." He braked at what appeared to be a crossroads. "Can you read that sign?"

She peered out to see and read it to him.

"That's the road," he declared. "Just another couple of miles."

The sky was just starting to lighten up a bit when Jim parked the Runabout in front of a white two-story house. "At least the lights are on inside," she said as they got out and ran through the rain up to the porch.

A woman still wearing her housecoat let them in, and they quickly introduced themselves. "I was just putting on some coffee. Would you like a cup?"

"That'd be wonderful," Anna said gratefully as she peeled off her damp coat.

"Bud will be right out. He just got home and needed to get out of his wet clothes. We live a couple miles from the jail, and he walks back and forth. Goodness, what a storm we're getting today."

"Yes. It was quite a drive," Jim said to her as she filled coffee cups.

"Here you go." Mrs. Jackson set them down on the kitchen table. "Make yourself at home. And, if you'll excuse me, I need to get my children up and ready for school."

They thanked her for the coffee, and, as Mrs. Jackson went upstairs, Anna took a quick inventory of their home. The front room was rather sparse but tidy. And the kitchen was small but clean. "She seems nice," Anna murmured.

He nodded, but his eyes were on something else. Anna turned to see a very large man entering the kitchen.

He quickly introduced himself as Bud Jackson, got himself a cup of coffee, and sat down at the table with them.

Jim introduced Anna as editor in chief, and she thanked Bud for meeting with them. "We don't want to take too much of your time. So I'll get right to my questions, if you don't mind."

"First, I have a question." He had a puzzled expression on his face. "A woman is an editor in chief?"

Anna quickly explained about her father's health. "But I was an editor for the *Oregonian* before I moved back to Sunset Cove."

"Never met a newspaperwoman before," he told her.

She made a polite smile, then began asking questions. She started with the usual preliminary ones, how long had he worked at the jail and such. Then, hoping that she'd gained his confidence, she went for the tougher questions.

"I interviewed your coworker right after the Albert Krauss jailbreak," she began. "Mr.

Gardner told me that you'd gone home sick that same night. I'd been curious to speak to you, but time got away from me. What do you remember from that night—I mean, before you became ill? Was there anything unusual going on?"

He rubbed his chin, which was in need of a shave. "Nothing stood out as unusual at the time."

"But does anything stand out in hindsight?" she pressed. "And, if you don't mind, may I ask how you got sick?" She smiled. "You look like a big, strong, healthy fellow to me."

He nodded. "I usually am."

"So was it some sort of influenza? Had anything been going around at the jail?" She didn't really believe it was the flu but wanted to hear this from his own lips.

"Nothing that I know of, but I suppose that's what I thought . . . at first."

"And then later you thought it was something else?"

"Well, I felt just fine when I went to work. It came on real sudden. Not long after lunch break."

"So do you think you ate something that made you sick?" she asked.

He frowned. "Well, Betty always packs my lunch, and she's a darn good cook, so I don't see how that could make me sick. Not like that. I was sick as a dog. Barely made it home that night, because I just wanted to lie down alongside the road and die."

"My goodness. You must've been very ill."

"Sure was. Took me two days before I could get around. Missed four days of work altogether."

"I see. So you probably missed all the excitement surrounding the jailbreak."

"Pretty much. They were already fixing the blasted-out wall by the time I got back to work."

"Right. So Mr. Gardner mentioned that the other guard—I don't recall his name off-hand—"

"That's Harry Bower," Bud said. "He was there that night."

"Right. Anyway, Mr. Gardner told me that Mr. Bower had fallen asleep. Is that very typical? Do night guards normally fall asleep?"

"Nope. I never have." He firmly shook his head. "And I don't know for sure, but I really don't think Harry usually sleeps on the job."

"So did that seem unusual to you?" Anna persisted. "That you got sick and Mr. Bower fell asleep? And then the jail was broken into?"

He slowly nodded. "To be honest, it never occurred to me at first. Not back then. But in hindsight, like you said, I've wondered."

"Have you mentioned it to anyone that you wondered?"

"Just my wife."

"I see. And how well do you know Mr. Gardner?" Anna asked.

"Well, he hasn't been at the jail all that long."

He shrugged. "He seems like a regular guy, but then he keeps mostly to himself."

"Do you think he was a drinking man?"

Bud jutted his jaw out as if unsure how to answer. Or perhaps he didn't want to rat out a fellow guard for breaking the law.

"I meant *before* prohibition laws," she said to help him. "Was he a drinker then?"

"Sure, you could say Tom was a drinking man. It's no secret. A lot of the guards used to imbibe on occasion."

"Did you ever notice Tom Gardner to be on friendly terms with any inmates? I mean, anything out of the ordinary?"

"Not particularly."

"Did you ever observe him in conversation with Albert Krauss?"

"Not that I recall." His tone was slightly suspicious.

"How about you? Did you have much conversation with Albert Krauss?"

"Nothing outside of the ordinary."

"Was Krauss a quiet inmate? Did you ever notice him chatting with other inmates or the jail guards?"

"Not that I remember. Nothing stands out. Oh, he seemed good-natured enough. But kind of nervous too. I guess he was high-strung."

No one spoke for a long moment, the only noise the sounds of footsteps overhead. "Did you hear the latest news about Albert Krauss?" Anna asked. "That he probably didn't kill himself after all? That he was most likely murdered?"

"I heard that." He nodded somberly.

"It has made us wonder," Jim put in, "if Albert Krauss might've been murdered by the ones behind his jailbreak."

"Yes, we're curious about that." She studied their host closely. "What do you think? Have you heard any rumors floating around the jail?"

"There's always some kind of gossip in there. You'd be surprised how inmates can talk." He seemed to be thinking.

"Did you observe any inmates or guards talking about Krauss's murder? What was their reaction to the news?"

His eyes narrowed. "Is this all going in your newspaper?"

"It depends. Mostly we're trying to piece together what happened to Krauss."

"Are you going to write my name in your newspaper? Saying that I told you any of this?" He glanced toward the stairs, and Anna suspected he was concerned about his family.

"Do you want your name mentioned?"

"No thanks." He firmly shook his head.

"Then you won't be quoted," she assured him. "You can be our anonymous source."

"That means you won't use my name?"

"That's right," Jim said.

"Okay. Good." He looked slightly relieved.

"Would you be willing to speak to the police about some of these things? If our investigation suggests it's necessary?" Anna asked.

"I, uh, I don't know about that." He looked even more uneasy.

"What about talking to your superiors at the jail?" Jim asked him. "Will you tell them any of these things?"

"I don't know. I answered the warden's questions back when it happened. I mean, after I got back to work."

"Will you tell him about our conversation today?" Anna asked.

"Maybe." Bud turned at the sound of footsteps on the stairs.

His wife and two little boys were coming down, and Anna knew it was time to wrap this up. "We do appreciate your helpfulness, Mr. Jackson." She stood. "It's been very enlightening." She smiled at his wife and sons, then turned back to Bud. "And it's reassuring to know we have such good, law-abiding guards keeping us safe." She shook his hand. "Thank you for your service."

Jim echoed this praise. Feeling they'd worn out their welcome, Anna led the way back outside. Although the sky was still cloudy and gray, the rain had stopped.

"That was interesting," Jim said as he drove

away. For a while, neither of them spoke. The road was still a muddy mess, but it didn't feel as treacherous as it had earlier. And, although it was a bumpy ride, Mac's Runabout seemed to handle it just fine.

"I thought Bud was believable." Anna held on to the dashboard to keep from bouncing off the seat.

"He seems like a good, stand-up sort of guy." Jim swerved off the road to avoid a pond-sized puddle.

"He seemed nervous, but I felt he was forthcoming. As much as he could be."

At the intersection, Jim turned back onto the main road, which was in only slightly better condition than the side road had been. "I'm not surprised that he wants to stay off the record."

"Yes, even though he seems like a big, tough guy . . . There's his family to consider. He seemed concerned for them."

"Understandably so." Jim shook his head. "If Krauss got knocked off because someone thought he was going to talk, Bud has good reason to be worried."

"So we really must protect his anonymity."

"What do we do next?" he asked. "I think we're on the right track. But should we report our findings to Chief Rollins?"

"Good question." Anna felt uncertain. "Except, I wouldn't want to reveal our source to just anyone in city hall. Not until we know for sure who we can trust."

"Meaning Collins?"

She nodded. "What a messy dilemma. It seems like the more we dig, the more we increase our chances of being buried."

"That's a gruesome thought."

"I didn't mean literally, Jim."

"So what do we know for sure?"

"Well, unless I'm mistaken, Tom Gardner was involved in the jailbreak."

"So you think Gardner slipped something into Bud's lunch that night? To make him sick?"

"Don't you? And it must've been something really nasty to make him that sick."

"And then you think he slipped something to the other guard to make him sleep?" Jim continued. "So no one would be around to interrupt the jailbreak."

"I think it was all curiously convenient." Anna wondered that no one had questioned any of this before. "Three guards on duty. One goes home sick. One is asleep. That leaves Gardner alone. Pretty fishy."

"Why do you think he did it?"

"At first, I thought it was because he and Krauss were buddies. Krauss could've warmed him up and offered him money while in jail. Or Gardner could've been helping Krauss run rum. Gardner's house is conveniently located to send or receive illicit goods. If they were partners, Gardner would surely want Krauss to escape. That way he'd be back in business again. But then Krauss gets murdered—possibly by his jail-break accomplices. That doesn't quite add up." Anna realized the road was smoothing out and let go of the dashboard, leaning back in the seat.

"Or if Gardner was associated with Krauss, he could've been worried Krauss might mention his name to the law. In that case, he wouldn't care if Krauss got knocked off. Maybe he'd even help."

"Or maybe someone on the outside paid Gardner off," she suggested, "to ensure the jail-break was successful."

"So Gardner did it for money?"

"Doesn't that make the most sense? Anyway, it needs looking into." She glanced at Jim. "You want to follow it up?"

"You bet I do."

"As far as the follow-up article I wanted you to write . . ." Anna paused to think. "Maybe we should put it on hold. We need to protect Bud and his family."

"Does that mean we don't go to the chief?" Jim asked.

"For the time being." She sighed as the edge of town came into sight. "I hate keeping things like this from him, but until we know where Collins stands, I can't see risking Bud and his family. We need to keep a lid on this until we know more."

"I agree. In the meantime, I'll keep an eye on Collins and keep sniffing around."

"And, if Randall can get AJ in front of a judge to share his testimony . . . that will help." Anna looked up as they went past Daniel's medical office. "Hey, why don't you let me off here? I'll ask Dr. Hollister about what sort of drugs might've been used on the guards at the jail. Maybe we can trace something back to Gardner."

"Good idea." He parked in front of Daniel's office. "Want me to run Mac's car back home for you?"

"That'd be helpful." She thanked him and hopped out. Hopefully Daniel wouldn't mind her popping in. If he wasn't busy, she would invite him to get coffee with her. To her dismay, Nurse Norma was at the front desk, and, as usual, she wasn't pleased to see Anna.

"Do you have an appointment?" she asked with a blank expression.

"No." Anna glanced toward the door to Daniel's office. "Is he busy?"

"He's with a patient," Norma said crisply. "After all, he is a doctor."

Anna forced a smile. "Please tell him I stopped by."

"Of course." Norma's smile looked as genuine as Anna's.

Anna thanked her, but, as she left, she doubted that the contrary nurse would actually relay the message. Did Daniel realize how rude his nurse could be? Or perhaps her cold manners were reserved only for Anna. As she walked to the newspaper office, she thought perhaps that was a good thing. Because Anna knew Norma had more than just a professional interest in her boss. She'd made that clear on many occasions, which suggested she might be feeling jealous. So, if Norma felt threatened by Anna . . . maybe that should give Anna hope.

Now if only that storm would blow up again. It was clear in town, but some dark, heavy clouds were gathered on the horizon. Hopefully they'd create some serious weather and give Anna an excuse to invite Daniel to stop by . . . to do some storm watching together.

CHAPTER 22

It was mid-afternoon when Anna felt fairly sure that Norma had not relayed her message to Daniel. So she wrote the doctor a quick note, sealed it in an envelope, and had Willy, an errand boy for the newspaper, hand-carry it to him. To Anna's pleased surprise, Daniel showed up at her office shortly afterwards.

He held up the note. "You need to talk to me?" His brow was creased with concern as he waited by her still-opened door.

"I hope I didn't interrupt you." She stood. "I just needed some medical information."

"Are you feeling all right?" He stepped inside.

"Yes, yes, I'm fine. It's not about me. And it's not terribly urgent, Daniel. I stopped by your office this morning and asked Norma if you could give me a call."

"Oh?" He frowned. "She didn't mention that."

"It's okay." She waved to the chair. "Do you have time to talk?"

"I do." He smiled as he sat down. "No more patients today."

She shut the office door. "Oh, good. I need to ask you about poisons and sleeping pills."

273

"What?" His brows arched high.

She couldn't help but chuckle as she rounded her desk and sat again. "Sorry. Let me explain." So she told him about her theory regarding the night of the jailbreak. "I think it's suspicious that one guard fell soundly asleep—which he was not known to do—and the other guard got violently ill shortly after eating."

"That does sound suspicious."

"So . . ." She picked up a pencil and rolled it between her palms. "For starters, what are some easy-to-access poisons—not lethal ones, but strong enough to make a good-sized man become so sick that he had to go home and then miss work for several days?"

"That would be a strong poison." He pursed his lips. "Something readily available? Well, a few substances come to mind, but you're suggesting this was something placed in his food, something he couldn't taste?"

"Yes, because his wife packs his lunch. And she seems like a sweet woman, so I don't suspect her. But perhaps someone else tampered with his lunch. Or put something in his coffee. That sort of thing. Mind you, this is just a theory."

"Arsenic comes to mind. It doesn't have much taste, and it's easy to find."

"Really? Where does one get arsenic?"

"Rat poisons. The hardware store probably carries it."

"But wouldn't arsenic kill a person?"

"It can. Back in Boston, I treated a child who ingested arsenic. Someone had put rat poison on a piece of bread, and the child ate some. Nasty case."

She cringed. "Did he survive?"

"Barely. Fortunately, the mother figured it out quickly and brought him in. But the poor tyke was in the hospital for several weeks. Thankfully, he made a complete recovery."

"Oh, that's good to know. But this man, the one who got sick, I don't think he got medical treatment. But he seemed to be all right."

"You say this was a large man? Perhaps he only ingested enough to make him violently ill. I'm surprised he didn't call his doctor."

"He didn't mention it."

"Do you think he'd be willing to speak to me?"

"I'm not sure." She explained Bud's concern for anonymity—without revealing his name to Daniel, of course.

"I understand, but he could trust me. I'd just want to ask him questions about his symptoms, the duration . . . information that would help me to make a hypothesis as to what might've been used. That could be valuable information if your hunch is right."

"I'll find out if he'll see you." She made a note of this. "Now what about something to make someone fall asleep? Any thoughts on that?"

"That could be a number of things. Substances that are commonly available would include alcohol or ether or a number of herbs like valerian, lavender, and magnolia bark. But those probably aren't strong enough to knock someone out cold. Of course, there's the bromide family. And morphine isn't too difficult to get ahold of. Then there are barbiturates." He paused. "Is this helpful?"

She shrugged. "I'm not sure."

"Once again, I'd suggest I speak to the person who mysteriously fell asleep. A few questions could help me narrow it down. But, even then, I'm only guess—" He paused as someone knocked on the door.

Jim stuck his head in, then apologized for interrupting. "Didn't know you were with someone. Sorry to—"

"It's okay, Jim. Why don't you come hear what Daniel has to say?"

Jim closed the door behind him and waited as Daniel went over the lists of drugs and herbs again. "But, like I just told Anna, without seeing these guards, asking a few questions, it's difficult to say. Even then, it's just an educated guess."

"If I could get these two guards to talk to you, would you be willing to go with me to meet them?" Jim asked eagerly.

"If it could help solve some of these recent crimes, I'm happy to help."

"Let me see what I can arrange." Jim checked his watch. "They work the graveyard shift, so I'm guessing they'll be awake by now. Are you free?"

"Sure."

"I'll make some phone calls and let you know."

After Jim left, Anna thanked Daniel for his cooperation, explaining how she and Jim were conducting their own investigation, independent of the police. "It's not that I don't trust the chief," she confided. "But we're not sure about Clint Collins. And we're concerned about the welfare of these jail guards. We really appreciate their help and don't want it publicly known they're talking to us."

"That seems prudent."

"If we could be relatively sure that the guards really were drugged or poisoned, it would be much easier to indicate someone. We need to proceed carefully."

"And, with two unsolved murders related to your investigation, I would advise you to be extremely cautious." His eyes were concerned, but, before he could say anything else, Jim returned.

"I got hold of both of the guards. And they agreed to talk to us again." Jim looked at Anna. "Think Mac will let me borrow his Runabout again?"

"Of course." She reached for the phone. "I'll call home right now."

"And, if we want to be back before dark," Jim glanced out her window, "and beat that new storm that looks to be rolling in, we should be on our way. Does that work for you, Daniel?"

As the men settled the details, Anna explained to Bernice that Jim was coming for the car, then she inquired about having a couple of guests for dinner. "Bernice will tell Mickey you're coming." Anna told Jim. "When you fellows return Mac's car, you're both invited to join us for dinner."

"Sounds like a good deal to me." Daniel smiled.

"Count me in." Jim grinned too.

"Maybe we'll do some storm watching too," Anna said. "And I can hear how your meeting with the guards went."

The men had barely left her office when someone knocked on her door again. "Come in," she called, looking up from the article she'd been checking. To her surprise, it was Katy. As usual, her stylish daughter looked ready to pose for a cover of one of those magazines that she kept strewn about her bedroom.

"Hello, Mother." Katy looked uneasy.

"What are you doing here?" Anna's brows knit. "Is something wrong?"

"Not exactly. And I apologize if I'm—"

"Katy, dear, you are always welcome here." Anna smiled. "And it's good to see you. You look lovely as always." She pointed to the chair. "Time to sit?"

"I'm sorry to bother you, Mother." Katy held up a folder with a nervous expression. "I was supposed to give this to Jim Stafford, but he was on his way out, and it sounded like he was in a hurry. So he asked me to give it to you."

"What is it?"

"The fashion column. Jim seemed confident I could handle this, and I suppose I was too. At first. But now that I've done it, I'm not so sure." She frowned down at her lap. "Maybe we should just forget it."

"Let me see." Anna reached for the folder, and Katy reluctantly handed it over. The top page was a very nice pen and ink drawing of a woman wearing a stylish ensemble. "Lovely." Anna nodded. "We should get this to Leroy right away."

"Not until you read my column."

"Right." Anna set the sketch aside, then began to read. "Great opening line," she said as she continued to read. About midway through, Anna could see what was wrong, but she kept on reading to the end, then looked up. "Katy, this is quite good. But you've made what I would simply call a beginner's mistake."

Katy frowned. "What is it?"

"You're simply trying to say too much." She carried the paper over for Katy to see, pointing to a paragraph. "This is interesting, dear, but you don't have enough space to adequately cover it.

Save it for your next column." She pointed to the previous paragraph. "All you need to do is expand a bit on what you're saying here. Make a transition sentence to move the reader to the next paragraph, and you're done."

Katy's eyes lit up. "That's it?"

"Yes." Anna looked at the clock. "Since Jim's gone, can you take the sketch to Leroy and let him know your column will be ready soon? Then, use Jim's desk to make the changes to your piece and bring it back to me for a final proof, and you're set."

"Really? That's all?"

"It's a good column, Katy." Anna patted her on the back. "I felt certain you could do this. Just remember your word count and don't try to say more than you have room for. Next week is another opportunity."

Katy beamed. "Thanks, Mother. You really are good at this, aren't you?"

"What's that?"

"Being editor in chief. You know what you're doing."

Anna chuckled. "Well, that's what I want everyone to think. Truth is, I'm still learning. But we don't have to tell everyone that. We should all be learning . . . no matter where we are in life. Now, get that sketch to Leroy and go make those changes and bring it back to me. The clock is ticking."

Katy thanked her again and hurried out.

Anna sighed happily. Perhaps it wasn't too late for her and Katy to reconnect. Maybe having Katy writing this column for the paper would be what linked them back together. And maybe, if Anna just tried a little harder . . . if she showed how much she cared . . . maybe they could rebuild that bridge.

It was past five when Katy returned with her revised column, but it wasn't unusual for Anna to still be in the office this late on a Friday. "Take a seat while I give this a good proofing." Anna reached for her red pencil and went to work. She didn't want to make the paper look like a bloodied mess, but she didn't want her daughter's debut column to have any mistakes either. "This is very good," Anna said as she handed the page back to Katy.

"I made that many mistakes?" Katy asked with dismay.

"Let's not call them mistakes. Just places that needed a bit of improvement. If we had time, I'd explain it now, but Leroy needs it typeset."

"I'll take it to him." Katy stood. "Then are you going home, Mother?"

"I'm almost ready." Anna held up another page she'd just proofed. "Can you take this to Leroy too? Then maybe we can walk home together."

Katy nodded. "I'll be right back."

Anna finished up her last task just as her

daughter returned. "All done," she proclaimed. "What a day."

"Are you tired?" Katy asked as Anna buttoned her overcoat.

"A bit. It's been a long day."

"Bernice told me that you and Jim went somewhere really early this morning."

"Yes. It was still dark when we left." She tugged on her gloves.

"Mother, do you still wear those old things?" Katy pointed to the worn, kid leather gloves.

"They're warm," Anna told her. "And I like them. I've had them for years."

"Believe me, I know." Katy giggled. "I suppose it will give people something to talk about. Your daughter writes the fashion column and runs the sophisticated dress shop. Meanwhile, you dress like, well, like you don't give a whit about style."

Anna stifled the urge to defend herself as she pinned on her brown felt hat.

"I'm sorry, Mother. I shouldn't have said that."

Anna forced a smile. "Except that it's true."

"And that's fine," Katy linked her arm with Anna's. "I love you just the way you are."

Anna blinked. "And I love you too, Katy." They walked together through the office, Anna calling out to various people still at work, but they paused by Virginia's desk by the front door. "You're still here?"

"Just barely." Virginia set a stack of papers aside, then smiled at Katy. "I am looking forward to your grand opening next week."

"I'm so glad to hear that." Katy beamed at her. "I think it'll be quite a surprise for everyone."

"Well, to be honest, I probably won't be your best customer, but as smart and elegant as you always look, Katy, I'm sure you'll have plenty of others."

Katy thanked her and then they stepped outside to where the wind was beginning to blow again. "I hear we've got another storm on the way," Katy said as she held on to her wide-brimmed hat. "I sure hope it's not like this on the day of our grand opening."

"You never know," Anna said. "That's life on the coast."

"Well, I still love it here."

"Speaking of storms, I invited Daniel to join us for dinner. He's been wanting to come over for a storm watch. And Jim is coming too. They're doing an errand together, and I don't expect them back until close to seven."

"That will give us time to clean up and dress."

Anna couldn't help but laugh. "You must mean me, since you already look absolutely perfect."

"Thank you. I've tried to maintain my image— even more so since the shop will open in a few days."

"And your fashion column will run tomorrow."

Anna glanced at her as they hurried against the wind. "Are you excited about that?"

"Yes, of course."

"But it's not as exciting as opening your own dress shop?" Anna ventured, picking up the pace still more when rain began pelting them.

"Well, not quite. Maybe in time it will be."

Anna remembered the first time she'd had her own writing published in the *Oregonian*. Katy had been a little girl and probably oblivious to her mother's jubilation. Of course, Anna had only been ghosting for another editor and had no byline, but, just the same, it had been exhilarating.

"So, Mother, will you dress for dinner tonight?" Katy asked as they went into the house.

Anna began to unbutton her damp wool coat. "Do you think I should?"

Katy just laughed. "You *know* what I think."

"Well, perhaps I need some help." Anna shook off her rather shapeless, soggy hat. "Last summer, you gave me a lot of assistance with my wardrobe. But then you got so busy." She held up her hands in a helpless gesture. "Left to my own devices . . . Well, *this* is what you get." She grimaced.

"All you needed to say was *help*, Mother. I'm more than willing to lend a hand. I just assumed you didn't want me to intervene."

"Help," Anna said. "Please, Katy, intervene."

"Come with me." Katy led her up the stairs. "The fun is about to begin."

Anna had mixed feelings as her daughter began issuing orders. On one hand, Anna was somewhat content with her usual appearance. Sure, it wasn't fashionable, but it was practical as well as useful in the workplace. On the other hand, she had enjoyed dressing and feeling more feminine this past summer. It had been fun. And perhaps she needed a bit more fun in her life. At the very least, it seemed to be reconnecting her with Katy. That alone made it all worthwhile.

CHAPTER 23

Katy wasn't sure what had come over her mother, but she didn't particularly care. Instead of trying to figure it all out—or teasing her mother for her lack of fashion sensibilities— Katy simply kept a pleasant chatter going between them as she helped her dress for dinner. "This shade of dark lilac looks exceptionally well with your coloring, Mother."

"Are you sure this dress isn't too youthful for me?"

"Not at all." Katy stepped back to survey her work. The silk evening dress was one that she'd recently sewn to use as a sample in the shop. "And aren't we fortunate to be nearly the same size? Grandmother suggested the sample gowns be created to fit me. That way I can model ensembles if customers request it."

Anna's brows arched. "And you wouldn't mind doing that?"

"Goodness, no. Why wouldn't I want to show off our pretty dresses? Grandmother says that many big-city shops use live models these days."

"But Sunset Cove isn't a big city, Katy."

"That doesn't mean we can't have big-city

style." Katy picked up a hairbrush and began to style her mother's auburn hair.

"It's just so unlike anything I've been wearing lately."

"You let me dress you in beautiful dresses this past summer, Mother. Remember?"

"But nothing quite this grand." Anna looked doubtful.

"Don't you like it?" Katy frowned.

"Oh, it's absolutely beautiful, dear. I can hardly believe you made it with your own two hands." Anna touched the top layer of the skirt. "So delicate and light. I hope I don't spill anything."

Katy grimaced to think of the gorgeous sample gown being spoiled. "Well, at least we have Clara. Ellen says she's an expert at removing spots."

"Just the same, I'll be careful." Anna fingered the trim around the neckline. "How did you find lace that matched the fabric so perfectly?"

"I dyed it to match."

Anna blinked. "You truly are an artist, Katy."

"Why, thank you." Katy paused. "I think I hear voices downstairs. Do you think that's Dr. Hollister and Jim Stafford?"

Anna went to the hallway to listen, then nodded. "Yes, that's them. I'm sure Mac will keep them company. He was thrilled that they were coming."

"I'm afraid Grandpa has been lonely lately."

Katy got the last tendril in place. "We've both been working long hours the past several weeks."

"I'm hoping to shorten my work hours some," Anna told her. "Especially with the holidays coming. I'm determined to delegate more responsibility to Jim."

"Well, he is your managing editor." Katy set the decorative comb in her mother's hair. "Why not let him manage?"

Anna smiled. "For one so young, you are quite wise, my darling daughter."

Katy sensed her mother was partly teasing, but she didn't mind. "Well, beautiful," she declared, "why don't you go down there and greet our guests while I get myself ready?"

Anna looked carefully at Katy. "You look perfectly ready to me."

"Are you kidding?" Katy gave her mother a gentle nudge toward the door. "I don't even compare to how elegant you look. I'll be down in a few minutes."

"Do you need help?" Anna asked.

"I've become surprisingly adept at getting myself dressed," Katy winked. "And, believe me, it's not always easy doing some of the buttons in back. But I have a few tricks."

"I'm sure you do. Thank you for your assistance." Anna gave her a little hug, then left.

As Katy slipped out of her midnight-blue dress, she agreed with her mother that it would be perfectly acceptable for dinner. Especially if she added a pretty brooch and earrings. But Katy suddenly felt more festive than that tonight. Perhaps it was because she and her mother had turned a corner. It gave her real hope. Certainly, she knew there would likely be more bumps along the way. But it felt like her mother was really trying. Katy wanted to try harder too.

She picked up the shell-pink lace gown. She'd just finished hemming the silk underskirt and hadn't even tried it on yet. It was very elegant and perhaps a bit much for an informal dinner. But, after seeing Mother in the lilac gown, Katy felt this one would look lovely next to it. Besides that, it was her duty as a designer to experience how her creations actually felt when wearing them. It was one thing to look lovely on a stationary mannequin, but what about a living, breathing woman?

Katy did her usual trick of slipping into the dress, turning it around backwards, and buttoning most of the buttons in front. Then, she rotated it around, slid her arms into the elbow-length sleeves, and reached around the back to finish the buttons. This technique wouldn't work for everyone, but, if you were young and limber, it wasn't too challenging.

Next, Katy piled her auburn curls on her head, similar to the way she'd done her mother's hair, securing it with a mother-of-pearl clip. She added a pair of pearl earrings, that her grand-mother had recently given her, and smiled at her reflection. The dress made her seem older. She could probably pass for a woman in her mid-twenties. Appearing more mature was becoming increasingly important to Katy. She suspected that customers would take her more seriously if they felt she were older. For that reason, she'd been working on comportment. Tonight would be good practice for her.

Katy held her head high and moved grace-fully down the stairs, hoping to make an elegant entrance . . . except that, although a fire was cheerfully burning, no one was in the front room. Not surprisingly, she discovered them in Grandpa's sitting room. Although it was dark outside, the drapes were still opened, and she suspected they'd been storm watching.

Their conversation suggested, however, they were now discussing newspaper-related topics. Jim was telling Mac something about some guards who worked at the county jail. But their conversation came to a fast halt as Katy entered the room. Was it because they felt she was too young to listen in on "adult" conversations, or were they simply in awe of her appearance? She hoped it was the latter, but she felt fairly certain it wasn't. Whatever was going on in the county jail was probably not deemed fit conversation for a young lady.

"Please, don't let me interrupt you," she said pleasantly.

"Come in, come in." Grandpa waved to her from his chair. "Now we have two lovely women to admire."

More compliments followed, and Katy felt her cheeks blush as she went over to kiss Grandpa's cheek. But she maintained her demeanor as she greeted the others, then gracefully sat down.

"You must be excited about your soon-to-open dress shop," Dr. Hollister said pleasantly. "I've heard my nurse conversing with a number of female patients about it. They all seem very thrilled with the prospects of such an elegant shop."

"And did you know that Katy is now our fashion columnist?" Jim looked curiously at Katy. "I assume you got your piece ready for the press in time?" He turned to Anna. "I told her you'd help."

"Katy's first column will debut tomorrow." Anna smiled at Katy. "It was very well done. A few simple editorial changes, and it was ready for print."

"Good girl, Katy." Grandpa beamed at her. "Fourth generation. Someday you'll be running that paper."

Katy kept her smile fixed in place. She loved her grandfather too much to tell him that was not her dream. Better to let him enjoy this moment while it was here. Because she only planned to write for the newspaper as long as it was beneficial to the dress shop. And someday—when the war in Europe ended—she planned to take up her grandmother's offer to go to Paris. That was her real dream.

"I hear the dinner bell," Anna told them.

"But Lucille isn't here yet," Grandpa said.

"Grandmother is coming tonight?" Katy asked eagerly.

"Yes." Grandpa nodded as he slowly pushed himself up with the help of his cane. "It was a late invite, but she promised to come."

Katy turned toward the door. "I hear voices out there. It sounds like Grandmother has just arrived."

They went out to see Mickey helping Lucille out of her jacket. "Hello, everyone," she said cheerfully. "Sorry if I'm late. We were having a sewing circle at my house."

"A sewing circle?" Grandpa already had linked her arm around his.

"For the dress shop," she explained. "Clara and Ellen are spending the weekend at my house. We've been putting finishing touches on a few things."

"Oh, we should've asked them to join us," Anna said as Daniel took her arm to escort her into the dining room.

"They've already eaten," Lucille explained.

"May I?" Jim held out his arm to Katy.

"Thank you." Katy smiled demurely at him, acting as if she was accustomed to being escorted to dinner by a handsome, older man.

"I'm glad to hear your column was good," he said quietly as they followed the others. "I knew you could do it."

"I'm not sure how you knew that. To be honest, I was having some doubts about my writing skills. But Mother came to my rescue. She knew exactly what to do to remedy my mess."

"It was not a mess," Anna said over her shoulder. "It just needed a slight adjustment."

"Perhaps . . . but it was an adjustment I was not capable of making on my own." Katy paused as Jim pulled out her chair. "But my mother spotted it immediately."

"That's because Anna is a newspaperwoman." Grandpa took his seat at the head of the table. "We've all got printer's ink running through our veins." He chuckled. Then, with everyone else seated, he bowed his head and said a blessing.

In the past, Katy had felt like the only child at the grown-up table. But not tonight. Tonight she felt that she was earning her place . . . that she was becoming one of them. And, as she participated in their conversation, sometimes with wit and sometimes with insight, she could tell that they were accepting her. And it was lovely.

After dinner, they had just settled in the front

room with their coffee to continue visiting when the doorbell rang. Mickey went to answer it, and, after a minute or two, Ellen stepped into the front room.

"Oh, I'm so sorry to interrupt," she said with a hard-to-read expression. "But I need to speak to Katy."

Katy stood and, excusing herself, went to see Ellen. "Let's go to the den." After she closed the den door, Katy noticed that Ellen looked exceptionally well dressed. "You're wearing a sample dress?"

"Oh, yes. I nearly forgot. I tried it on so that Mama could adjust the hemline. It seemed a bit crooked."

"It looks straight to me." Katy looked curiously at Ellen. "What was it you needed to speak to me about?" She wanted to ask why Ellen hadn't used the telephone but didn't want to sound rude.

"Well, I thought perhaps you wanted to help us with the sewing, Katy. I knew there was a dinner party here tonight, but I didn't realize you'd be part of it." She looked closely at Katy's gown. "Isn't *that* for the shop too?"

"Yes. But I wanted to try it out." Katy bristled slightly at being questioned by Ellen. After all, wasn't the shop named *Kathleen's*?

"Anyway, I thought you would be free to come and—"

"But you could've just called me. You didn't

have to walk over." Katy studied her friend closely. "Or did you come here tonight because you knew Jim was a guest?"

"Of course not!"

Katy wasn't so sure. "Well, as you can see, I am part of the dinner party, and it would be rude to just skip out like that."

Ellen scowled. "You were sitting with Jim just now, Katy. Does that mean anything?"

"It means he's a guest in our home and I was simply conversing with him, and, if you'll excuse me, I should probably get back."

"So you don't want to help with the sewing tonight?"

"I have sewing to do up in my own room." Katy opened the door. "If I'm not too tired, I will probably work on that before going to bed."

"Oh." Ellen followed Katy to the foyer.

Katy forced a smile as she handed Ellen her coat. "Try not to get that dress wet on your way home. I'm afraid that fabric will spot with water."

"I'll be careful." Ellen craned her neck as if trying to peek into the front room.

"I'll see you at the shop tomorrow."

"Yes, I'll see you tomorrow," Ellen said loudly. But instead of putting on her coat, she stepped to where she could see into the front room, obviously trying to catch Jim's eye.

"Good night, Ellen." Katy tried to conceal her exasperation as she moved in front of Ellen, blocking her view of the front room. Why was she acting like such a ninny? Was she really that smitten over Jim Stafford? To put on a sample dress, come over here in the rain, put on this whole show . . . just in the hopes of seeing him? The moment Ellen left, Katy spun back for the dinner party.

"Is Ellen well?" Anna asked after Katy sat back down.

"I'm not sure." Katy immediately regretted her response.

"Is something wrong?" Lucille asked.

"No, nothing is wrong. Ellen simply wanted me to go do some sewing with her."

"But didn't she know we had guests?" Anna asked quietly.

"Yes." Katy nodded. "She knew." Now she turned to Jim with a pleasant smile. "You were just telling me about how you first got interested in journalism. You said it was during college."

As Jim told her about his college days and being the editor of the university's newspaper, Katy felt slightly guilty. Was she being overly interested in Jim simply because it would aggravate Ellen? Or was it because Jim was actually interesting? She wasn't even sure. But she did plan to speak to Ellen about staging these situations. If she wanted to be part of Kathleen's Dress Shop, shouldn't she conduct herself with a bit more decorum as well? Perhaps Grandmother could speak to her about it. Maybe they should have a meeting to discuss manners and etiquette and expectations. Even if Sunset Cove was a small town and their shop was a small shop, they didn't have to be small-minded about it.

CHAPTER 24

A nna still hadn't heard the full story of how Jim and Daniel's visit with the jail guards had gone, so when Jim challenged Katy to a game of billiards, she knew this was her chance. And, since Lucille and Mac were entertained with viewing photos on Mac's old Holmes stereoscope, Anna invited Daniel to the den under the pretense of looking at Mac's Pocket Encyclopedia collection. "It's more than a hundred years old," she explained. "It belonged to Mac's great-grandfather."

"I'd love to see it."

When they were in the den, Anna immediately confessed her real mission. "I'm dying to hear how it went with the jail guards." She sat down on a leather chair near the fireplace. "You and Jim had just started to tell me when Katy came in."

"I assumed you didn't want our findings to become public knowledge." He sat down on the other side of the fireplace. "Not that we can't trust Katy, but I don't think it's something she needs to be involved in."

"That's right." Anna nodded eagerly. "So tell me, how did it go?"

"It sounds to me as if your suspicions are correct. Based on how Bud Jackson answered my questions, he was poisoned, and I wouldn't be surprised if it was arsenic. Obviously, it wasn't enough to kill him. But it was enough to make him seriously ill."

"So maybe rat poison?"

"Maybe."

"What about the other jailer? Mr. Bower?"

"He said he got sleepy before their lunch hour—which is in the middle of their shift. But he'd had some coffee. I asked if he recalled any unusual taste in his coffee, but he said he always has cream and sugar, so it was hard to say. But he got very sleepy afterwards. He didn't wake up until the sound of the explosion. And he said even then he felt groggy, and it took him a while to get his bearings."

"So he might've been slipped something."

"I asked about pharmaceuticals at the jail's dispensary, and it sounds as if there are barbiturates available there."

"So Tom Gardner could've gotten into that?"

"Possibly."

"Well, thank you for going to meet with them. This gives us something more to go on."

"And you still don't plan to tell Chief Rollins about this?"

"Not yet. It feels too risky." She studied him. "Do you mind keeping it quiet?"

"I understand."

"Listen to that wind howling." Anna went over to pull open the drapes, but the glare of the lights on the window kept them from seeing outside.

"That's quite a gale."

"If we dimmed the lights in here, we might be able to see out some."

Daniel turned off the lights, then joined Anna by the window. "It'll take a bit for our eyes to adjust to the dark," he said quietly.

Anna felt a pleasant rush as his arm brushed against hers. "I can see the whitecaps." She pointed out toward the darkened ocean. "They're lit up from lights from the house."

"Those are some mighty big waves."

"Must be high tide—they're breaking on the rocks."

"Not a good night for beach walking."

"And not a good night for fishermen." She shuddered to imagine what it would be like out there.

"Even so, I'll bet some of the larger boats are still out. Some of the best catches are after a storm. But it does make me grateful I'm a doctor and not a fisherman." He sighed. "My grandfather was a fisherman."

"Back in Boston?"

"No. He was a fisherman out of Nantucket. My mother's father. It was my father's side of the family that lived in Boston."

"Did you ever go to Nantucket?"

"I did. My mother and I would take the train there and stay with my grandparents during the heat of summer."

"That must be a happy memory."

"It is."

"Do you ever miss it?" she asked suddenly. "I mean Nantucket or Boston or just being back East?"

"Sometimes I do. Although, Sunset Cove reminds me a bit of Nantucket."

"So is it your family that you miss most?"

"Sometimes I think that's it. Although, my mother passed away nearly ten years ago, and I'm an only child, so I have no siblings back East."

"And your father? Do you miss him?"

"He was always so busy with his work . . . We were never terribly close."

"Didn't you say that your father was a doctor too?"

"He's still a doctor. Even though he's older than Mac, he still practices."

"Was that why you went to medical school? To follow in your father's footsteps?" she asked.

"I suppose that was my initial incentive. I wanted to make him happy."

"But you love being a doctor?"

"Yes. As it turns out, I do love it. I suppose it's like Mac said—you and Katy have printer's ink in your veins, and I suppose there's medicine in mine." He chuckled. "Well, not literally."

"I know what you mean. Do you think your father will ever retire from practicing medicine?"

"I don't know. I've invited him to come out here to visit, but he claims he can't leave his patients for that long."

"So . . . he's married to his work?"

"I suppose so."

Anna stared out into the darkness, watching the white, foamy tips leaping up and pounding against the rocks, and tried to think of something else to say.

"I don't want to be like that."

"Like what?" she asked.

"Married to my work."

Anna was about to respond but heard voices approaching. "Hello?" Katy and Jim were calling. "Anybody there?"

"We're in here." Anna fumbled to turn the desk lamp on. "Just watching the storm."

"We want to play whist," Katy announced. "But we need four players."

"And Mac and Lucille both begged out." Jim held up the deck of cards. "How about it?"

Anna felt a mixture of disappointment and relief as the men set up the card table and chairs. On one hand, she'd been enjoying her time with Daniel, but, on the other hand, she'd realized that her questions had gotten overly personal too quickly.

She didn't like to make him uncomfortable or overwhelm him, but sometimes the news reporter in her forgot to mind its manners. She wanted all the answers, and she wanted them now. She needed to practice patience . . . and pace herself.

On Saturday morning, Katy used the Runabout to take all the various garments she'd been working on at home over to the dress shop. Fortunately, last night's storm had moved on, and, by the time she parked in the alley behind the shop, the sun was shining brightly. Hopefully this good weather would stick around for their grand opening in a few days.

"Need a hand there?"

Katy looked up from where she was unloading the back of the car to see Jim smiling down at her. "I'd love some help." She handed him a hatbox. "You take this, and I'll run ahead and unlock the back door."

She held the door open as he carried in an armful of boxes. "Thanks so much."

"Why don't I unload the rest of the stuff?" he offered.

"That's very gallant of you."

He did a mock bow. "At your service, my lady."

"I'm surprised you're still speaking to me after I caused us to lose at whist last night."

"All is forgiven."

She laughed as she turned on the lights. Jim

was a good sport. And it really had been her fault they'd lost last night. She'd made a silly mistake that had cost them the game. Even so, it had been fun. And, unless she was mistaken, her mother and Dr. Hollister were exchanging some interesting glances—and not just about the cards either.

"I think that's the last of it." Jim laid some garments on the worktable. "All ready for your big opening?"

"Hardly. We'll be burning the midnight oil the next few days."

"Well, let me know if you need any help."

"Do you even know how to thread a needle?" she teased.

"Well, no. To be honest, I don't even know how to properly sew on a button. But I can lift and move things."

"Oh, I see. You're offering us your brawn—not your brain."

"Speaking of brains." He tapped her forehead. "All might be forgiven, but I must say that was a pretty dumb move last night, *partner.*"

"Well, *partner,* I suppose I was getting tired and not thinking clearly." She pursed her lips. "Speaking of last night, I'm curious . . . did you notice anything, well, anything of interest . . . between my mother and the good doctor?"

He grinned. "As a matter of fact, I did."

"So it wasn't just me!"

Now he shrugged. "But let's not jump to conclusions. It might've just been because they were winning."

Katy nodded, but she didn't think so.

"Well, I'll let you get to work." He stopped. "But wait a minute, Katy. Did you see today's paper yet? Your column?"

"No. I left early. Even before Bernice had started breakfast. I don't think it had been delivered yet."

"Would you like to see it?"

She nodded eagerly.

"I have an idea. I was just on my way to get a donut and coffee. What if I bring some to you—along with a newspaper?"

"That'd be great. Thank you!"

"I'll be right back."

As Katy went to work putting things away and getting ready for the day ahead, she wondered. Was Jim being nice to her simply because she was his boss's daughter . . . . Or could it be something more? And if it was something more, how did she feel about it? Honestly, she wasn't sure. At the moment, the only thing on her mind was getting all the dresses finished and the shop looking like perfection . . . and having a successful grand opening. All her thoughts and energy had been focused on this one goal lately.

As she put the shell-pink lace dress on a mannequin, she decided that Jim was being helpful and kind because of her mother and grandfather. He'd said before that the McDowells were like family to him. That meant she was family too. That was nice. And that was enough.

She'd just gotten everything cleared off from the worktable and put away when she heard a knock on the door, and there was Jim, loaded down with coffee and donuts and today's paper. "You're a gem, Jim."

He laughed as he set things down on the worktable. "You're a witty girl, Katy McDowell." He opened the newspaper, pointing to her sketch of a stylish woman in a fur-trimmed winter coat. "There it is—your first column."

"Oh my." She leaned over to read it. "This actually feels pretty special. I didn't expect to be this excited about it."

"I remember the first time I saw my writing in print." He set a mug of coffee in front of her. "I was over the moon."

"Uh-huh." She continued to read.

"I bought several copies of the university newspaper. Some to save and some to send home. I think I still have a copy somewhere." He passed the box of donuts her way.

"Well." She sat down on a work stool and sighed. "I'm a published writer."

"Congratulations." He held up his coffee mug in toast.

"Thank you." She laughed as they clinked

coffee mugs together. "I couldn't have done it without you. Well, my mother and you. Thanks for encouraging me."

"You're on your way, kid."

Katy heard voices. "Sounds like the ladies are arriving."

"Does that mean I need to make myself scarce?"

"No, of course, not. You've been help—"

"Well, look who's here." Ellen came to the worktable, glancing curiously from Katy to Jim. "What's going on?"

As Ellen and Clara hung up their coats, Katy explained Jim's help in unloading the car. "And then he got me today's newspaper."

"We're celebrating Katy's debut fashion column in the paper." Jim held out the box of donuts. "I got enough for everyone."

"How thoughtful." Clara came over to see the newspaper. "I haven't had time to read it yet."

"It's quite good," Jim told her. "I read it while I was waiting for the coffee and donuts."

"I want to see too." Ellen came over and crowded in next to Jim to peer down at the paper. "Why did you use that sketch?" she asked Katy. "We don't have a coat like that in our shop."

"Not yet," Katy told her. "But we might . . . in time. Furs are very popular these days, and Grandmother said they have places in San Francisco that sell nothing but furs. And, next time she goes on a buying trip, I plan to go with her. Hopefully before Christmas. Fur pieces would make lovely gifts."

"But furs are terribly expensive." Ellen made a skeptical frown. "And Christmas is just a few weeks away."

"I know that." Katy took a slow sip of coffee. "But, if our grand opening does as well as we hope, we'll have capital to reinvest. Hopefully in some quality furs in time for the winter season. At the latest, I'd like to have them in the shop by New Year's."

"Sounds like you have a sharp business head," Jim told Katy. "And now that I helped you celebrate your column, I have my own business to attend to."

"But isn't the newspaper office closed today?" Katy asked him.

"Yes, it's not that sort of business." He grinned at her. "I'm looking to buy an automobile today."

"An automobile?" Ellen looked impressed. "You must be coming up in the world, Jim. What sort of car is it?"

He chuckled. "Nothing fancy. Just a used Model T. Eight years old. But it will be handy for chasing news stories."

"Or driving your girl around?" Ellen teased.

"Thank you for the coffee and donuts." Katy walked Jim to the door. "That was very sweet of you."

"A pleasure." He tipped his hat. "Have a good day."

After Jim left, Ellen grew noticeably quiet, and, when Katy attempted small talk, she was met with more silence. It felt like Ellen was angry at her, as if Katy had intentionally done something wrong. Something to do with Jim. Just the same, Katy wasn't ready to touch that powder keg just yet. Besides, there was much to be done in the shop today.

"Well, we all have work to do," Katy announced. "I'm going to finish the window display in front." Then, without saying another word, she hurried out of the workroom.

When Lucille came a couple hours later, Katy was just finishing up the window display. It had been awkward trying to get everything properly in place in such a tight space. Besides that, with the windows still covered with brown paper, it was impossible to really see the effect her arrangements would have from the outside. And the artist in Katy wanted it all perfect. The plan was to reveal the shop windows the afternoon before the grand opening. They would keep the drapes behind the window display closed to prohibit anyone from seeing into the shop, but the display would be attractively lit so that passersby would be enchanted. At least, that was their hope.

"It's looking lovely in there," Lucille told Katy. "I don't know how you manage it. I would feel like a bull in a china shop in that narrow space."

"I'm just glad no one could watch me crawling around in here." Katy climbed down the short stepladder in her stocking feet. "I think it's nearly done."

"Well, everything looks beautiful, and I just read your column in today's newspaper. It's delightful."

"Thank you."

"Can we talk privately for a moment?" She pointed to the seating area. "Over there?"

Katy nodded, following her grandmother, and sat down. "Is something wrong?"

"I'm not sure." Lucille lowered her voice. "First of all, I'm curious if you know anything about Clara and that policeman—Clint Collins?"

Katy shook her head. "I'm not sure what you mean."

"Well, I overheard them talking yesterday. Out in front of the shop."

"Yes?"

"Lieutenant Collins was expressing concern for Clara's safety. And Ellen's too."

"Do you think it's related to Albert Krauss's murder?" Katy felt alarmed as she slipped on her shoes. "Are they in danger?"

"I don't know. But Lieutenant Collins seemed to think so. He offered to walk them home. And then, Clara told me, he stayed for a while, looking around their property as if he thought

311

something was wrong. After that, he walked them to my house, and they spent the night there last night. And this morning I heard Clara mention that Lieutenant Collins was going to escort them home again tonight—and that she'd invited him to dinner."

"This is mysterious." Katy picked lint from her skirt.

"I was just curious if Ellen had mentioned anything to you."

Katy made a face. "Ellen is barely speaking to me."

"I noticed she seemed a bit out of sorts just now. I wondered if it was related to Lieutenant Collins. Perhaps she's worried that he has romantic intentions toward her mother."

"I don't know about his intentions, but I don't think that's what's troubling Ellen. I think she's angry at me. Ellen is smitten with Jim Stafford," she whispered. "It's been going on for a short while now."

"Yes . . . and . . . ?" Lucille's eyes widened.

"I'm sure she thinks I'm trying to steal him from her."

"Are you?"

"No." Katy shrugged. "Not on purpose anyway."

Her grandmother's brows arched. "What does that mean?"

"*I mean,* Jim is my friend. My mother is his

boss. He's good friends with my grandfather. In other words, he's like a member of the family."

Lucille looked relieved. "Yes, but if Ellen is attracted to him, well, it would stand to reason that she might feel jealous of you. Especially if she thought Jim was looking in your direction."

"Even if that were so, what can I do about it?" Katy asked with impatience.

"You can keep on being her friend, Katy. If she's a true friend, she won't hold it against you for being on good terms with Jim."

Katy agreed to do this but wondered if it would make any difference. If Ellen was this determined to cast Katy as the enemy in her imaginary love triangle, what could Katy do about it?

CHAPTER 25

By Monday afternoon, Jim had news for Anna. "I've been doing some real sleuthing, and I think I've got some real evidence."

"Tell me more." She pointed to the chair in her office, leaning forward with interest.

Jim closed the door and took a seat. "First of all, I talked to the owner of the hardware store in Walberg—the town on the other side of the county jail—and he told me he recalled Tom Gardner's coming in for rat poison several weeks ago."

"That's a pretty good memory."

"The reason he remembered was because he was concerned that Tom was having real problems with rats, thinking there was going to be an infestation, and planning to stock up on traps and whatnot. Anyway, the point is, he remembered Tom Gardner."

"Did you let on as to why you were asking?"

"I kept it really casual, Anna. I acted like I'd had some rat trouble of my own." He chuckled. "Guess that's not completely untrue. We are trying to catch some big rats. And speaking of big rats, I followed Clint Collins a bit on Saturday night."

"And?"

Jim scratched his head. "Well, it was interesting. For starters, he was hanging around outside of your daughter's new dress shop."

Anna felt alarmed. "Yes?"

"Seems he was waiting for Clara and Ellen."

"What?"

Jim nodded. "Yep. And they didn't seem the least bit surprised to see him out there."

"That's odd."

"It gets odder. Clint gave Clara a box of chocolates, then took her arm and walked her home. I followed at a discreet distance. But I saw Clint go into the house with the two of them. And he didn't come out."

"Goodness. I know they're all right, because I saw Clara at church yesterday. And she seemed fine."

"I think Lieutenant Collins is attempting to romance Clara."

"Oh, Jim, that's hard to believe. She's only been widowed a few months. Surely she's not interested in him."

"If she's not, she sure put on a good act."

Anna pursed her lips. Perhaps it was time to have a heart-to-heart talk with her old friend. "Anything else I should know?" she asked grimly.

He nodded with a somber expression. "Later on—on Saturday night—I was keeping an eye on Charlie's place. I could tell there was some activity there. At about ten o'clock, Clint Collins went in through the back door."

"Interesting." Anna drummed her fingers on her desk pad. "Don't you think it's about time for the chief to run another raid on that place? Seems like Calvin and his buddies are getting awfully comfortable again."

"You want to know what I think, Anna? The honest truth?"

"Of course."

"I'm starting to wonder if the chief is sold out too. It's as if he's turning a blind eye to the whole thing. How well do you know him anyway?"

Anna blinked. "Oh, I can't believe that. Mac and the chief have been friends for so long and—"

"Mac believed in Wesley too. But Wesley disappointed him. It happens."

"I know . . . but I just can't imagine the chief's being underhanded or dishonest."

"Well, I just don't understand it."

"I think I'll have a little talk with him today." Anna reached for the telephone receiver, then replaced it. "Better yet, I'll do it in person."

"Yes." He nodded eagerly. "We don't need the whole town hearing about it."

By the time Anna was seated in the chief's office, she knew how she planned to go about this. She wouldn't tip her hand regarding their knowledge that Clint was visiting at Charlie's but simply say enough to let the chief know there'd been talk around town.

"I hate to say it," she said finally, "but some people are getting the impression that prohibition is not being enforced by the local police. I suppose if word of this gets to the state police, they will want to intervene. And I'm thinking that might be a good thing."

"People think I'm not doing my job?" The chief frowned. "Don't they know I've run several raids—one just a week ago?"

"I didn't know that."

He shrugged. "Well, it's not common knowledge. It was late at night, and the raid turned out to be unfruitful, so it wasn't like I wanted everyone to hear about it."

"Unfruitful?"

"The only things Calvin was serving up there were coffee and soft beverages like sarsaparilla. The whole thing was embarrassing. And it's happened too often. Calvin keeps threatening to sue the force, Anna. I have to walk carefully."

"I see." She frowned. "Is it possible that someone is tipping Calvin off? Could he know when the place is going to be raided and be prepared for it?"

"I don't know how. I never tell anyone. Not even my wife."

"What about your officers? Surely you must let some of them know."

"Well, of course. Can't run a raid without my men. But I only tell a couple. Just to make sure we have enough on duty to do it properly."

"I'm assuming you tell Lieutenant Collins, and—"

"I can't reveal all the inner workings of our police operations to you. You know that."

"It's just that I care about all this," she told him. "As much as you do. You've got unsolved murders that have hit pretty close to home. I lost a reporter, and my best friend lost her husband."

"Her husband was a criminal." The chief narrowed his eyes.

"I know that, but that doesn't excuse his murder, does it? And what about AJ Krauss—I know you moved him to a safer location, but can you guarantee he won't be hurt?"

He glumly shook his head. "You know I can't."

Anna wanted to ask him what he *could* do but knew that sounded disrespectful. And he looked frustrated . . . and tired. "I'll bet you're looking forward to retirement," she said as she stood.

"That's no secret." He stood too. "But I'd like to resolve as much of this as possible before I turn in my badge."

She locked eyes with him. "Then you need to know who you *can* and *cannot* trust, Chief. And, I give you my word, you can trust me. And Jim

Stafford as well. And you can trust that Randall Douglas is getting an honest affidavit from AJ. We're trying to help with this investigation, but there are people out there—perhaps closer than you think—who are trying to thwart it. So I hope you are keeping your eyes wide open."

He looked surprised, but, before he could respond, Lieutenant Collins poked his head into the office. "Sorry to interrupt." He politely tipped his head to Anna. "There's something that needs your attention right now, Chief."

"Excuse me." The chief reached for his hat. "I'll talk to you later, Anna."

As she watched them hurry off, it took all her self-control not to follow and find out what was going on. But she suspected her company wouldn't be welcomed. At least, not with the lieutenant. She walked slowly back to the office, looking up and down each street as she went, hoping to spy something out of the ordinary . . . something to give her an excuse to find out what it was Collins had needed the chief to look into. But it looked like a typical Monday afternoon in Sunset Cove. And perhaps she should be glad for that.

But then she noticed a small crowd gathered across the street from the hotel. Realizing that it was right in front of the new dress shop, Anna felt alarmed. Was something wrong there? She hurried down Main Street and nudged her way through the fringe of the crowd to see what was going on. To her surprise, they were simply gazing upon the dress shop's windows, which now had the brown paper removed. The area was lit up, and the display was attractive, but to gather such a good-sized crowd? Anna didn't understand.

"Isn't that beautiful?" an older woman gushed. "My daughter would look perfectly lovely in that gown."

"I can't wait until they open tomorrow." A young woman with a baby in her arms sighed.

"I don't see what all the fuss is about," a man grumbled. "Just a bunch of ladies' clothes. I thought maybe there was a fire or something interesting."

Anna smiled to herself. She'd been thinking the exact same thing. And, without saying a word, she hurried back to the newspaper office, where there was work to be done.

The grand opening of Kathleen's went better than anyone had hoped. The foot traffic was so heavy that they had to post Ellen by the front door to regulate the crowd. But, to Katy's pleased surprise, the guests weren't just there to look around. The sales continued to mount as Clara busily wrote up purchases. Meanwhile, Katy and Lucille attended to the customers.

By the end of the day, all four women were worn out. "Oh my!" Lucille flopped down onto a velvet chair as Ellen locked the front door. "That was quite a grand opening. My oh my!"

"I'm just starting to add up the sales," Clara called from the register. "I should have a total soon."

"And then we'll deposit it in the bank," Lucille declared, "and call it a day."

"Wait until you see how my appointment book's filled up." Katy sat on the divan. "I expect new orders will be coming in fast during the next week. A lot of women wanted dresses in time for Christmas."

"We're going to be very, very busy," Lucille said. "I hope we haven't bit off more than we can chew."

"Christmas break begins next week." Ellen sat down next to Katy. "I'll be able to work more hours then."

Katy smiled at Ellen. "It'll be nice spend more time together." Katy had been trying hard to win her friend back the last couple of days, finally convincing Ellen that she had no romantic interest in Jim Stafford—that they were only family friends. "He's like a brother," she'd assured Ellen. "Nothing more."

When Clara announced their grand total, they all let out a happy cheer. It was far better than anyone had expected.

"And this is just the beginning," Katy said as she pulled on her coat.

Lucille picked up the cash bag and gave it a victorious shake. "Now it's off to the bank before it closes. Then, I'm going straight home to soak my feet in Epsom salts."

"Everyone ready?" Clara reached for the light switch, and soon they were all outside on the sidewalk.

"Good evening, ladies." Lieutenant Collins tipped his hat. "I'm here to escort Clara and Ellen safely home."

Katy stifled her suspicions as she forced a smile. She didn't trust the police officer but wasn't sure why.

"Since you're here, why not see Lucille and Katy to the bank?" Clara smiled at Lieutenant Collins. "We've got today's earnings to deposit."

"Glad to be of service." He held out his arm to Clara.

Katy and Ellen exchanged glances behind the lieutenant's back but said nothing as they followed the procession to the bank. Katy was aware that Ellen was not completely comfortable with all the attention Lieutenant Collins had been giving her mother. Like Katy, Ellen was suspicious. But no one could deny that Clara was enjoying it. And, considering the sort of attention she'd received from her previous no-good husband, it wasn't surprising that the lieutenant's chocolates and flowers were being well received by her. Still, it seemed odd.

After the cash was deposited, Katy and Lucille parted ways with the others. "What do you think of Clara's suitor?" Katy asked her grandmother.

"I'm not sure what to think . . . although it is interesting."

"Do you think his intentions are honorable?"

Lucille chuckled. "Well, I certainly hope so."

"Do you know what Ellen told me?"

"No, but I am glad you two girls are talking again."

"Ellen thinks Lieutenant Collins is after her mother for her money."

"Her money? But Clara has no money. Not really."

"Well, her property, then. You know that she's had it for sale. But Lieutenant Collins is encouraging her to hold on to it. He says it's very valuable."

"Is that so?" Lucille sounded slightly concerned now.

"And Clara had planned to use that money to invest in our dress shop—to become a partner and live in the apartment above. How can she do that if she doesn't sell her property?"

"That's a good question. But perhaps she has changed her mind."

"Or Lieutenant Collins has changed her mind. Do you know what else Ellen told me? She said that Lieutenant Collins keeps acting as if they're in some kind of danger. I think he's just using it as an excuse to eat dinner with them every night. That's what he's been doing. And Clara just treats him like he's an invited guest."

"I suppose she's lonely."

"But she's got Ellen."

"Yes, dear. But she might be lonely for a man. From what I heard, her first husband was not a great catch."

"That's for sure."

"Well, Clara is a sensible woman, Katy. I'm sure she knows what she's doing."

"I suppose." Still, Katy was not so sure. From what she could see, Clara was being taken in. Sure, Katy was no expert when it came to relationships with men, but it stood to reason that if Clara had chosen unwisely with Albert Krauss, it could happen again.

CHAPTER 26

After one failed attempt to warn Clara about Lieutenant Collins, Anna had backed off. She wasn't willing to put her friendship with Clara at risk simply because she was suspicious of Clint Collins. After all, they still didn't know anything for sure. As she pointed out to Jim more than once, it was possible that Clint was working incognito on the same investigation as they were. It would be a fiasco if the newspaper's efforts undermined the police force's. And it was not something Anna wanted to be responsible for.

"You're wise to tread carefully there," Randall advised Anna as they were winding up a lunch meeting at the hotel. She'd gone to him for legal counsel, and he had encouraged her to sit on the information she and Jim had collected until they had something really solid. "Like AJ's affidavit in front of the judge," he said. "That's the time to bring this whole thing into the light."

"As long as no one gets hurt in the meantime."

"I suppose if you think that's possible, you have to reevaluate."

"When will AJ's case go before the judge?" she asked.

"Right now, it's scheduled for early January."

"Oh, that's good. The sooner that happens, the better for everyone." She set down her coffee cup. "Well, except for the criminals that will be exposed."

"Hopefully, the authorities won't waste any time in rounding them up."

"Which is just one more reason we need to keep this all under wraps." Anna smiled at Clara as she came into the restaurant. Not surprisingly, Lieutenant Collins was right behind her. It seemed they were making their relationship public now.

"Well, that's interesting." Randall tipped his head toward them. "I haven't heard anything about those two."

"It's a relatively new development," Anna said quietly. "And disturbing."

"Clara has certainly been looking well of late. Being freed from Albert's grasp seems to agree with her. That, and working at your daughter's dress shop. Who knew Clara was so stylish?"

"Yes," Anna agreed. "I've never seen her looking better. But being with Clint Collins . . . Well, I just hope she's not jumping from the frying pan into the fire."

"I'm surprised she'd be interested in Lieutenant Collins. Especially considering AJ."

"Meaning what?" Anna studied him closely.

"Well, it's no secret that AJ is not particularly fond of Collins."

"Is that because he's a lawman . . . or something else?"

"I'm not at liberty to say."

"Yes, of course." Anna set her napkin by her plate.

"But you're welcome to go question AJ yourself, Anna. I go up weekly to meet with him."

"Do you think I should go too?"

"Well, you are a good friend to the family. If you had reason to suspect that Lieutenant Collins was not a good match for Clara, you would be in a good position to intervene."

"So you believe someone should intervene?"

"I didn't say that." Randall had on his lawyer face now.

"When do you plan to go visit him again?"

"Next Tuesday."

Anna considered this. Tuesday was a busy day at the newspaper. Plus, it was the day Katy and Lucille would get back from their quick buying trip in San Francisco, and Anna had hoped to be home. "Let me think about it, Randall." But, even as she said this, Anna knew she had to go. It would be an all-day commitment, but it was important. Not only for Clara's sake—although that was enough—but for Ellen's and AJ's as well. If Clint Collins was who Jim and she suspected he might be, it would be a huge disaster for Clara to continue this relationship with him. Especially since Katy had confided to Anna that Clara was hoping to receive a marriage proposal by Christmas.

After two busy weeks at the dress shop, Katy was excited over the prospect of a buying trip to San Francisco. And the truth was they needed more inventory. Sales and orders had exceeded expectations, and, if this continued up until Christmas, their shelves and racks would be bare. Granted, this would be a quick trip. On Sunday, they would travel south by train, followed by a packed day of shopping on Monday. Then, on Tuesday, they would come home.

"I haven't been out of Sunset Cove in six months," Katy declared as they boarded the train early Sunday morning. "I'm so excited, I feel like dancing."

Lucille just laughed. "Well, I feel like sleeping. So don't mind me if I snooze a bit."

And Katy didn't mind. She amused herself by sketching and visiting with passengers and simply watching out the window. By the time they reached San Francisco that evening, she was not the least bit tired. As the taxi drove them to the hotel, Katy watched out the window with wide eyes. "Oh, I wish we were staying here for a week," she told her grandmother. "There's so much to see and do."

"Next time, we'll stay longer." Lucille pointed to an enormous building up ahead. "That's where we're staying, Katy. The Fairmont Hotel."

"It's beautiful."

"The building was started before the earthquake," Lucille explained. "And, at first, it seemed to have survived just fine, compared to many other structures that crumbled or burned. But, unfortunately, it had sustained damage. They hired a woman architect to work on it, and then it opened the following year."

As the bellhop carried their bags into the lobby, Katy looked around with open admiration. "It's so beautiful, Grandmother. I wish I could live here."

Lucille laughed. "Well, you'd have to become quite rich to do that, dear. But, for two nights, we can live like queens."

And they did live like queens, enjoying an elegant and delicious dinner and retiring to a very grand suite. "Tomorrow will be a long day, Katy. I made lots of appointments. So I suggest we get ourselves to bed."

Katy reluctantly agreed, but, unable to sleep, she imagined what it would be like to live amongst such luxury on a daily basis. Perhaps someday she would be a famous dress designer and places like the Fairmont would be simply an everyday thing. At least she could dream about it.

They got up early the next day, ate breakfast in

their suite, and then, after dressing for the city, got into a hired car and went to the shopping district. There, Grandmother met with various merchants, introducing Katy as her partner and a talented dress designer, and they selected multitudes of items to take back to Sunset Cove. Some would go with them on the train, and some would be shipped later.

"This is the icing on the cake," Lucille proclaimed as they entered a chilly warehouse. "The Bouchard furriers are renowned in this city."

"Lucille!" a short, bald man exclaimed. "I've been looking forward to your visit."

Lucille introduced Katy to Mr. Bouchard, explaining how her deceased husband and he had been good friends and business partners.

"That was long ago," Mr. Bouchard told Katy. "We came out to California hoping to get rich in the gold fields, but we quickly discovered we could get richer by selling merchandise to the miners."

Lucille told him a bit about their little dress shop. "Our grand opening was very successful." She ran her hand over a silvery fur pelt. "So we made this quick buying trip in order to restock our shelves."

"And I want to incorporate some fur into my designs," Katy said, "before winter is over."

"Well, you're a bit late in the season." He chuckled. "But that means some better deals for you." He led them to a showroom, where he talked about the various furs, what they were best for, and gave Katy a general idea of the pricing. She was just wrapping a soft strip of mink around her neck when a handsome young man stepped up.

"And this is my grandson, Lawrence." Mr. Bouchard motioned toward the young man with a smile. "Lawrence, this pretty, young entrepreneur is the granddaughter of a good friend. Meet Katy McDowell, a talented designer and co-owner of a dress boutique in Oregon."

"Pleased to meet you." Lawrence gently grasped her hand, looking deeply into her eyes. "Very pleased."

Katy smiled and returned the mink to its place.

"Lawrence, why don't you take Katy to the cold storage and show her some pieces that might tempt her pocketbook?" He winked at his grandson. "But remember, these ladies are on a budget, and they are our dear friends."

"I understand, Grandfather." Lawrence waved to a side door. "Right this way, Miss McDowell."

"Please, call me Katy," she said.

He nodded. "All right, Katy. Come along. I hope you'll be warm enough in that."

She looked down at her outfit. It was a two-piece, ocean-blue dress—a satin twill weave with dyed-to-match lace trim. Very pretty but not exactly warm. "I think I'll be fine." She smiled.

"Although, I had expected California to be warmer."

"San Francisco can be quite chilly at times. The wind and the fog. And it doesn't even matter what time of year." He waited for her to go inside.

"It feels similar to where we live in Sunset Cove. Though we have some lovely warm days too."

He closed the door. "We keep the furs chilled like this to keep them in good shape." He began to show her various pieces, explaining where they were from and how they were best used.

"I'm learning so much," she said after she'd made some selections. "Thank you for being so helpful." She shivered.

"Let's get you out of here." He opened the door and led her out. "We have a warm showroom— and hot tea."

"That sounds lovely." She followed him up a stairway and gratefully went into the heated room, rubbing her gloved hands together. Before long, she was nicely warmed up and sipping tea in the pretty room that was filled with all sorts of beautiful fur creations.

Lawrence was just starting to show her some of the coats and cloaks, which Katy knew were far too expensive for their dress shop, when Mr. Bouchard and Grandmother came in. They all visited for a bit, comparing notes, and then Mr. Bouchard insisted on taking them to dinner.

"Only if we can return to our hotel to change," Lucille insisted. "And we'll have to make it an early evening since we're catching an early train tomorrow morning."

"We'll dine at your hotel," he told them. "You pick the time."

So it was settled, and Lucille and Katy rode back to the hotel just in time to dress for dinner. "I wish I'd brought a more festive wardrobe," Katy said as she donned the same dress she'd worn the previous night. "I didn't realize we'd be socializing."

"You look beautiful in that sapphire-blue silk, Katy. It's perfect with your eyes." She patted Katy's cheek. "And I think young Lawrence was quite taken by you."

Katy waved a dismissive hand. "He was simply being polite, Grandmother."

Lawrence continued to be polite throughout dinner. With his focusing most of his attention on Katy, she began to wonder if her grandmother was right. Perhaps he was taken with her. After they finished dessert, he invited her to go admire the view. "This hotel, being situated on Nob Hill, affords a lovely view of the city. Especially beautiful at night."

Katy let out a happy gasp as she looked out over San Francisco. "Oh my, it really is beautiful." She slowly shook her head. "It must be so romantic to live here."

He shrugged. "I suppose it's okay. But some-times I wonder what the rest of the world is like."

"Don't you ever travel to get more furs?"

"I haven't been included in that part of the business yet." He adjusted his tie. "I'm not even certain I want to remain in the fur business."

"Oh?"

"My father sent me to business college, with the assumption I'd take over the bookkeeping. But I don't fancy the idea of being locked in a small office day in and day out."

"I can understand that." Now she shared her dream of going to Paris with her grandmother. "Naturally, we can't do that until the war over there is over. And, at the rate it's going, that might take forever."

"I'd like to see Paris too." He sighed wistfully. "But hopefully not as a foot soldier, although a buddy just signed up. He thinks we'll all be going over there before long."

"Yes, my mother is of that opinion too." She told him a bit about the family newspaper and how they'd moved from Portland last summer.

"Your life sounds like it's been exciting."

"Exciting?" Katy frowned. "Not exactly." She noticed Grandmother waving to them. "I think that's my cue to call it a night."

"I wish you didn't have to, Katy. It's been wonderful getting to know you."

"We'll come back," she assured him. "Grandmother says we can stay longer next time. Maybe by early spring."

"That sounds so far away. Maybe I'll just have to make a trip to Oregon in the meantime and see Sunset Cove for myself."

She laughed. "Yes, that's a great idea. Any time." She waved to Lucille, mouthing *I'm coming*. Then she thanked Lawrence for a memorable evening and told him good night. But, as she rejoined her grandmother, she wondered . . . was he serious? Would he really come up to Sunset Cove to visit her? Or was that just something city fellows said? She really didn't know.

CHAPTER 27

Anna wasn't sure if her visit with AJ had been beneficial or not. But one thing she was certain of was that AJ did not like the news of his mother's involvement with Lieutenant Collins. "Tell her to steer clear of that man," AJ had warned Anna. But, when she asked him to explain why, AJ had been evasive. Finally, he said that Randall had instructed him not to talk to anyone about any of the people his father had been associated with. Naturally, she'd asked if that meant Albert had been associated with Clint Collins. But AJ was sticking to his guns. So all she could do was guess.

She continued to guess on the long ride home. But Randall, like AJ, was being very tight-lipped. "This case is delicate, Anna," he said after a while. "I'd like to be an open book, but I don't want to do anything to jeopardize AJ's case. I'm sure I've already told you too much. From here on out, mum's the word."

"I understand, Randall. I'll try to control myself from questioning you."

"I'm sure that goes against the grain with a newspaperwoman."

"Yes, I suppose I come by it naturally. I was raised to be curious."

"I'm curious about how things are going with Clara and Clint Collins. I saw them together again this past weekend. Looked to me like it could be getting serious. Did you have a chance to talk to AJ about it?"

"Am I allowed to tell you what he said?"

"I'm his attorney."

"Yes, well, it seemed to upset him."

"Uh-huh."

"And he wants me to warn Clara to avoid him." She sighed. "That won't be easy."

"I wonder what she sees in him?"

"He's acting like her protector. Katy told me he shows up at the dress shop every day at closing time. He escorts Clara and Ellen home and then she invites him to stay for dinner."

"So is he just trying to get a free meal? Or something more?"

"Katy told me that Clara is hoping for a ring by Christmas."

"Good night! That's less than two weeks away. You can't be serious."

"I'm just repeating hearsay. Hopefully it's not true."

"I really don't like the sound of that. And you say you've tried to speak to Clara?"

"She doesn't listen. I'm not even sure that she'll listen to what AJ has to say."

"This isn't good."

"And Katy is worried that Collins is only interested in her because of her property—the fish business, the boats, her home . . . Katy says Collins sees Clara as a wealthy widow."

"Well, the Krauss holdings are worth something."

"Especially if you want to go into the rum-running business."

He blew out a low whistle. "That actually makes a lot of sense. But that's assuming Collins really is crooked. We don't know that for sure."

"No, we don't." Anna tugged on the cuff of her leather glove.

"But, if he is crooked, nothing could be worse for Clara than to marry him."

"I know."

"Anna!" he said suddenly. "I have an idea."

"What?" she eagerly asked.

"It's a little crazy . . . and a long shot." He laid out a plan where he could act as Clint Collins's competition. He would become Clara's suitor as well. "And some people—present company excluded—seem to think a handsome attorney is a pretty good catch."

"I never said you weren't a good catch," she pointed out. "Just not the right catch for me, Randall. I much prefer having you for my good friend."

"Yes, well, as I was saying . . . I could pursue

Clara and possibly waylay the engagement plans. If we could just hold them off until AJ has a chance to present his testimony in court—and everyone can find out exactly who is who in Sunset Cove—we might save Clara from making an enormous mistake."

"You'd do that? For Clara?"

"Sure. I'd do it for Clara and for AJ and Ellen. And for justice."

Anna's heart softened toward Randall. Had she been too hasty to dismiss him as a potential suitor? Perhaps there was more to him than she'd realized. But then there was Daniel. When she thought about the doctor, she knew the answer.

"So here's the plan . . . I'll make sure to cross paths with her for the rest of the week," Randall continued. "Maybe I can take her to lunch or coffee. Something to show her Collins isn't the only fish in the sea. But I'll need your help. How about if you host a small dinner party at Mac's house on Friday? Invite Clara and me. That'd give me a chance to be with her without Collins nearby. Maybe I can invite her to do something with me on Saturday? Or offer to drive her and Ellen to church on Sunday."

"Clara will be feeling like the belle of the ball." Anna couldn't help but chuckle. "But it's about time she felt special like that. Her marriage to Albert must've been torturous. And I'm sure if Collins wasn't overwhelming her with all that attention—bringing her flowers and candy and walking her home . . . Well, she wouldn't be interested. I just hope she doesn't think she's in love. That could be a disaster."

It was past midnight by the time Randall dropped her at the house. She thanked him for taking her to visit AJ and promised to do her part in their plan to spare Clara from a big mistake. As she went into the house, she prayed that it would work.

Anna decided to involve her mother in the plan to save Clara from Clint Collins. To Anna's relief, Lucille was already concerned. "I don't know why, but I just don't trust that man," Lucille confided as they met for tea on Wednesday afternoon. "He seems to be filling Clara with fear, acting like her protector and as if there's an assassin around every corner. And poor Ellen is nearly beside herself with another sort of fear. She's worried that Clint Collins is about to become her stepfather."

"So Randall could use our help," Anna explained. "It won't be easy to pry Lieutenant Collins away from Clara. But anything you can do will help. I had considered hosting a small dinner party at Mac's in an effort to connect Clara to Randall. But I wonder if it would be less suspicious to have this sort of gathering at your house."

Lucille was glad to accommodate. "I'll invite Clara, and you can invite Randall."

"And perhaps Katy can keep Ellen occupied at Mac's house. That will keep it small and intimate."

"I'm not sure that's the best plan. What if we make it a dinner for eight? I've always felt that's the perfect number for a small dinner party. Of course, Mac and you will join us. And perhaps you could invite the doctor. That makes six. And we could have Wally and Thelma too. I've been meaning to have them over. That makes eight."

Naturally, Anna was happy to invite Daniel, but she wasn't sure what he'd think about their ulterior motives in regard to Clara's love life. Still, she was determined to tell him. Just in case she needed his help.

Fortunately, the following day Daniel seemed quite understanding when she informed him of the plan to "rescue" Clara. "That's an interesting setup," he told her. "Hopefully it won't backfire on you."

"It's not that we want to be devious or trick Clara, but we're worried that Lieutenant Collins might be a wolf in sheep's clothing. And Clara is so vulnerable right now. I'd hate to see her hurt again."

"What if she winds up being hurt by Randall?"

"Oh, I don't think that will happen. I'm sure Randall will handle the situation very carefully.

When it's all over—and Clara finds out who Clint Collins really is—she'll probably be very grateful."

"That is, if you're right about his true character. What if you're wrong?"

Anna grimaced. "Then it shouldn't matter. If we're wrong, which we should find out by AJ's trial, and if Collins truly loves Clara for the right reasons, he'll probably continue to pursue her. And perhaps he'll appreciate her all the more—a man might enjoy the idea that he's beat out his competition."

Daniel looked amused. "Yes, I suppose you're right about that."

Lucille outdid herself at the dinner party. With a candlelit table, flowers, and even soft music playing on the Victrola, her house was the perfect setting for romance. And Randall, true to his word, did an excellent job of showering Clara with attention. Whether it was a sweet compliment, a warm smile, or a helping hand, he was ready and willing to win her over. By the end of the evening, Clara seemed quite pleased to accept a ride home with him.

But, as Daniel walked Anna home, she grew concerned. "I hope Randall isn't putting himself in harm's way," she said as they went onto the porch.

"How's that?"

"Well, what if Lieutenant Collins is the jealous type? And, if he's as dishonorable as we suspect, as well as determined to get Clara and her property, what if he did something under-handed?"

"That would be unfortunate. Hopefully Randall has taken this into consideration."

"Hopefully." She looked up at Daniel, seeing his face illuminated in the porch light. "Well, however it turns out, thank you for helping tonight."

"My privilege." He smiled. "It was an enjoy-able evening, Anna. Much better than sitting at home alone."

She continued to look into his face . . . won-dering . . . Did he want to kiss her? For a short moment, she thought he was going to, but instead, he reached for her hand and, grasping it, thanked her for inviting him and then turned and walked away. Perhaps Anna needed to concoct a plan like the one they'd cooked up for Clara— find someone to make Daniel feel threatened or jealous. Or perhaps she was being too impatient. Patience had never been her strong suit.

Kathleen's Dress Shop continued to draw cus-tomers, orders for dresses kept rolling in, and merchandise kept rolling out. Finally, just days before Christmas, Katy felt worn out and slightly dismayed. She wasn't sure if it was fatigue . . .

or if she was actually somewhat bored with the daily routine. However, she had no intention of revealing her discontent to anyone. Grandmother would be disappointed in her, and Mother would probably start talking about college again.

When the dress shop first opened, Katy had enjoyed waiting on the local women. Their enthusiasm was invigorating. But, as time passed, Katy came to accept that most of her customers had no real sense of style. And yet many of them assumed they were fashion experts. This often resulted in long, tiresome explanations of why Katy had created a particular design in a particular way, or why a gown that looked lovely on a mannequin might not look so nice on a portly older woman.

And, now that it was the end of the day, the shop was closed and everyone else was gone— and Katy was eager to go home too. But first, she wanted to finish Marjorie Douglas's evening dress. They'd all been pleasantly surprised when the owner of the mercantile entered their shop a week ago. Katy had assumed the savvy business-woman simply wanted to spy on her competition.

As it turned out, Marjorie wanted a new dress for Christmas. It was always a challenge to design gowns for older women, but Katy was determined to create a garment that Marjorie would be completely pleased with, and, for that reason, Katy had insisted on doing the finishing sewing herself. Because of the unexpected demand for dresses, they had hired two more part-time seamstresses. Although the extra hands lightened the work, everyone remained busy, and it was expected this pace would continue even past Christmas. It seemed that almost everyone in town planned to attend the Mayor's Ball on New Year's Eve—and many of the women wanted new gowns for the celebration.

As Katy tacked the draped neckline into place, she wondered what Marjorie Douglas thought of her son's recent interest in Clara Krauss. Of course, Clara was enjoying the attentions of a second suitor. Although, Lieutenant Collins was none too pleased. In fact, there'd been a rather tense moment when both men showed up at the shop simultaneously earlier tonight. It seemed they both wanted to walk Clara home, but Mr. Douglas played the gallant gentleman by stepping aside.

Katy realized that was a very smart move on Mr. Douglas's part. Because Clara's expression strongly suggested she'd have preferred a different escort. Ellen had appeared even more dismayed. Of course, she made no secret of her dislike of Lieutenant Collins. Ellen was certain the cop's interest in her mother was a ploy to get his hands on their fishing business. Naturally, Ellen would prefer her mother to fall in love with the attorney instead. She'd even pointed out more than once that Mr. Douglas was helping AJ . . . and shouldn't that mean something?

Although Katy agreed that Clara would be better off with Mr. Douglas, she'd been caught off guard by the whole romantic triangle. After all, it hadn't been too long ago that Randall Douglas had been showing similar attentions to her mother. But then, Katy's mother assured her that Mr. Douglas was simply a good friend and that was how she wanted to keep it. Not long after that, Katy began to suspect that, if her mother were to select her preferred suitor, which remained to be seen, it would probably be Dr. Daniel Hollister. She'd observed her mother's face light up whenever he was around. And, unless Katy was mistaken, the good doctor felt similarly. However, their relationship seemed to be stuck. Or, at best, it was moving at a snail's pace. Nothing like Clara's situation. She was only recently widowed, yet she practically had men fighting over her.

With straight pins still between her lips, Katy stepped back to examine the hang of the neckline on the adjustable dressmaker's dummy. It was almost right. She made an adjustment on one of the folds, then jumped at the sound of someone pounding on the front door. She opened the work-room door and peered out to the showroom to see that she'd forgotten to turn out the lights. Good grief, did someone assume they were still open at this hour?

Of course, whoever was outside could now plainly see that she was still here, and the pounding on the glass door grew louder. She removed the straight pins from between her lips and called out, "I'm coming!" Then, peering out into the darkness outside, she could see it was the figure of a man—and no one she recognized. She was tempted to run for the phone and call someone for help but stopped at the sound of her name being called.

"Katy McDowell," he yelled. "It's me, Lawrence Bouchard!"

"Lawrence Bouchard?" Remembering her friend from San Francisco, she unlocked the door and stared at him in wonder. "What on earth are you doing here?"

"I came to visit you." He smiled brightly. "May I come in?"

"All the way from California?" As she opened the door wider, a cold ocean breeze blew in. "Come in, come in."

"So this is your little shop?" He removed his bowler and looked around with satisfaction. "Very nice."

"Thank you." After closing the door, she tilted her head to one side. "Did you really come here to see me?"

"I certainly did." He unbuttoned his stylish overcoat. "Do you mind?"

"I'm just a little confused."

"I suppose I should've given you some warning." He looked slightly dismayed. "But I hoped to surprise you."

"Well, you've certainly done that." Katy returned to the dummy, made a final adjustment on the neckline, and tried to get her bearings.

"I hope you're not upset by this unexpected visit."

She looked up and smiled. "Not at all, Lawrence. It's just that I need to finish this up. The woman hopes to get it by tomorrow."

"So you actually do the sewing here yourself?"

"Not all the sewing, of course. But we've had so many orders lately, well, naturally, I want to help out." She put in the last pin, then sighed. "But I suppose I can leave this for the seamstresses to finish in the morning. Let me make them a note first."

As she wrote her note of explanation, Lawrence told her about his last-minute decision to pack his bags and hop aboard a train to Oregon. "I haven't even told my family yet."

She pinned the note to the dummy, then looked at him. "Won't they be worried? And so close to Christmas?"

"I'll send them a wire tomorrow."

Katy got her coat, glad that she'd worn the one

that she'd sewn a fur collar onto, and started to slip it on.

"Let me help." Lawrence stepped right up. "This is a pretty piece. One of your own creations I presume?"

"As a matter of fact, it is." She smiled as she buttoned it.

"Very, very pretty." He reached for his own coat. "So, can I take you to dinner? When I checked into the hotel, I noticed a decent-looking eatery there."

"I'm sorry. My family is expecting me home for dinner."

"Oh yes, I see." He nodded glumly as he put on his bowler.

"But, of course, you must join us." She slipped on her gloves with a coy grin.

"Thank you." He looked relieved.

As they walked through town, Lawrence told her that he'd been feeling more and more unsettled in San Francisco. "I just felt the need for a change. A great, big change. I'm not sure exactly why. But I remembered your invitation to come to Oregon, and I thought, why not?"

"That's interesting. I've been feeling a little discontented myself of late. Oh, *discontent* probably isn't quite right. But I've found myself longing for something more." She laughed. "Or perhaps something less."

"Something less?"

"I don't know. But the dress shop has been so busy. I suppose I might be a bit overwhelmed or overtired. It was all so fun and exciting early on, during the planning stages and getting the shop all set up . . . But lately it's felt more like just plain work." She turned to look at him under the streetlight. "But I must swear you to secrecy on this, Lawrence. My grandmother would probably be hurt, and my mother might ship me off to college." She laughed, hoping to make this sound lighter than it felt.

"Your secret is safe with me, Katy." Lawrence reached for her arm, hooking it around his own. "Now, I've met your grandmother, but tell me about the rest of your family."

As they walked, she explained their somewhat unusual family situation, and, for some reason, Lawrence thought it sounded perfectly charming. "Unconventional, yes, but interesting."

"Here we are." Katy paused in front of the tall, stone house. With a Christmas tree in the big front window and golden light pouring out of the other windows, it looked warm and inviting. And, not for the first time, Katy felt glad to be home.

"Beautiful house." Lawrence nodded approval.

Katy braced herself as she opened the front door. Why hadn't she called ahead to announce her unexpected guest? Not for Bernice so much, because she was used to such things, but Mother and Grandpa would be caught off guard. They'd never even heard of Lawrence Bouchard, and suddenly he was here in their midst. Katy chuckled as she led him inside—hadn't she just been longing for something different to happen? And now she'd gotten it!

Chapter 28

The next morning, Anna and Mac sat down to have breakfast together. According to Bernice, Katy had already left for the dress shop. "And she said not to expect her for dinner." Bernice's brow creased as she set the coffeepot on the table with a clunk. "I suppose that means she plans to dine with that *city boy* tonight."

"Sounds like Bernice didn't like him either." Mac scowled. "How about you, Anna?"

"I don't know what to think." She reached over to fill his coffee cup. "I never had the chance to talk privately with Katy last night."

"I figured the young man would leave once we excused ourselves to bed." He clumsily buttered a piece of toast, causing half of it to crumble. "In my day, that was bad manners."

"Well, Katy is a responsible young woman," Anna defended. "And I trust her."

"Well, I trust her too. It's that young man," Mac growled.

"He does appear to be quite taken with Katy."

"What young man isn't?"

Anna sighed. That was fairly true. For the past couple of years, her daughter had caught the eye of most young men. One reason Anna was glad to move to a small town. Although, Katy had never given Anna much need to worry. She'd always been mature for her age and reliable. But she was also hard to read at times. Like last night. Sometimes she'd appeared rather indifferent to Lawrence . . . and then she would turn on the charm. But what was she really thinking?

"I just don't understand." Mac pounded his fist on the breakfast table, making the coffee cups rattle in their saucers. "Why he shows up like this—right out of the blue?"

"He claims he wants to see Oregon." She tried to seem nonchalant, but she suspected Lawrence had more than sightseeing in mind.

"In winter? At Christmastime?"

"It is odd," she agreed.

"His family deals in furs?" Mac frowned. "Are they trappers?"

"No. They're furriers in San Francisco, Mac. And they're friends of Lucille's." Anna took a sip of coffee.

"Well, I plan to pay Lucille a visit this morning." Mac wiped his mouth with a napkin. "I'll get to the bottom of this."

"Good luck." Anna decided to change the subject. "Did you see Katy's fashion column this morning?"

"It was good." He nodded vigorously. "Someday she'll tire of ruffles and lace . . . and realize she's a newspaperwoman."

Anna chuckled. "She's got to find her own path. And the only way she'll find it is if we let her."

"What if she thinks Lawrence is her path?" Mac looked seriously concerned.

"Oh . . . I don't think so." But Anna knew what he was thinking. What if history was repeating itself? What if Katy followed in the footsteps of her mother . . . and grandmother? They'd both married too hastily, only to regret it later. "Katy is a sensible young woman."

"Don't be too sure. That Lawrence seems a determined young man. To come up here like this. At Christmastime too." He pushed himself up and grabbed for his cane. "I'm going to Lucille's right now!"

"And I think I'll pay Kathleen's a visit this morning." Anna set her coffee cup down. "See if I can make an appointment with my daughter."

Mac wasted no time in getting down to Lucille's house. And, if she was surprised to see him at this early hour, she didn't show it. "Come in, come in," she said warmly. "I was just sitting down to breakfast. Have you eaten?"

"Not really."

"Then come join me." She led him to the dining room and called out to Sally to bring an extra plate.

He was barely in the chair before he spilled out the story of Katy's unexpected visitor. "Completely unannounced," he grumbled. "Acting like he was an invited guest."

"Oh, that's wonderful," she gushed. "Lawrence Bouchard is a delightful young man. Katy must be thrilled."

"Thrilled?"

"Yes. She enjoyed her time with him in San Francisco. She complained that it was cut short when we had to come home. I'm so glad he decided to visit. And I wouldn't call him 'uninvited,' Mac. I'm certain that Katy asked him to come up here. Perhaps I did too." Her eyes lit up. "In fact, I shall call the hotel and insist he come and be my guest here. Oh, it will be so wonderful to have a guest for Christmas."

Mac nearly spit out his coffee. *Really?* Did Lucille honestly think having this Bouchard character sniffing around their seventeen-year-old granddaughter was a good thing?

"I want everyone to come here for Christmas Eve," she said suddenly. "You already asked people to your home for Christmas Day. I am officially claiming Christmas Eve."

"But we—"

"No arguments. This is my first Christmas back in Sunset Cove. My first time in this house. Certainly you can grant me this one little wish." She fluttered her eyelashes. "Please?"

"Fine," he growled. "But only if you promise me one thing."

"What's that, dear?"

"You will not encourage Katy toward this Lawrence Bouchard fellow. Don't push her, Lucille."

"Why would I need to push? If she's attracted to him, nature will take its course. You certainly must understand that."

"What I understand is that Katy barely knows him."

"Sometimes it doesn't take long to know someone's true character."

"And sometimes we are wrong."

She patted his hand. "I wasn't wrong about you."

He frowned.

"Don't worry, Mac. Katy is a sensible girl."

"That's what Anna keeps saying." He shook his head. "But I used to think that of Anna. And she was the same age as Katy. And you know how that turned out."

"Dear, dear Mac." Lucille smiled. "I think you worry too much. Everything will be just fine. Wait, and you'll see."

"But you still plan to invite that boy here?" He looked around the room. "To be your guest?"

"Of course. His grandparents are old friends. It's the least I can do. Besides, it's Christmas. We're supposed to show hospitality."

Mac reached for his cane. He'd had enough of Lucille's infernal hospitality. At least for the time being. "I need to get back," he mumbled.

"But you didn't finish your breakfast."

"I'm not hungry." He slowly stood, wishing he'd never come.

"What is it you don't like about the boy?" she asked gently as she walked him to the front door.

"He's shifty."

"Goodness, you barely met him. How could you possibly know that?"

"I can feel it, Lucille. In my bones. He is not trustworthy."

"Oh, Mac." She shook her head. "You're simply being overly protective of our sweet Katy. And I really can't fault you for that. She's a darling girl, and I would fight tooth and nail against anyone who might hurt her."

He looked into her eyes. "I truly believe you would. And that is a comfort. But are you still going to invite him to stay here?"

"Of course." She laughed. "If you're right, if he is shifty, isn't it better to have him under my nose so I can keep an eye on him?"

Anna timed her visit to the dress shop close to lunchtime, hoping she could invite Katy to have lunch with her, but by the time she got there, Katy was gone.

"Where did she go?" Anna asked Ellen in

the showroom, which was, thankfully, void of customers right now.

"She went off with her handsome beau."

"Beau?" Anna bristled.

"I assume he's her beau." Ellen's smile seemed slightly catty. "He *acts* like he's her beau."

"Had Katy mentioned Lawrence to you before, Ellen? Did she say how they met in San Francisco or any of that?" Anna knew her fishing was obvious, but she didn't care.

"This was the first I've heard of him," Ellen admitted. "But, judging by how well they seemed to be getting on, their meeting in San Francisco must've been pretty special."

"How well did you think they were getting on?" Anna glanced over her shoulder to see a pair of women just coming into the shop.

"They were quite friendly." Ellen smiled as she smoothed her pretty dress and greeted the customers.

"Thank you." Anna turned to go into the back room, hoping to find Clara. Perhaps she knew something more.

"Oh, Anna." Clara came over to meet her. "I'm so glad to see you."

Anna looked to where two young women were busily sewing. "I see you've hired more seamstresses."

Clara quickly introduced them. "We've had so much work, we needed more help."

"Do you have plans for lunch today?"

Clara glanced at the clock on the wall. "Not that I know of."

"Then come have lunch with me." Anna grabbed her by the hand. "Before one of your suitors shows up to steal you away."

Clara's giggle sounded like a schoolgirl's. "A year ago, I never could've dreamed up any of this, Anna. Let me grab my coat, and we'll slip out of here before any of my many suitors come calling."

They went out the back door, and Anna looped her arm around Clara's. "This is like old times." She turned to look at her friend. Her eyes were bright and clear, and her cheeks were rosy. "And you seem more and more like the sweet school chum I remember. It's as if you've gotten younger. Younger and prettier."

"Thank you. I do feel younger . . . and it's nice to have an excuse to wear pretty clothes again. Lucille and Katy insist we keep up our appearances at work."

"And how do you feel about your two suitors?"

"I'm completely amazed." She shook her head. "And, to be honest, I'm not completely comfortable with it. After all, I haven't been a widow for long."

"I don't know, Clara. I think Albert left you a long time ago."

She nodded. "Yes, I suppose that's true."

"So, tell me, old friend, which suitor do you like best?"

"To be honest, I thought I would say yes to Clint . . . if he proposed. And I have every reason to believe he plans to."

"Oh." Anna couldn't keep the disappointment out of her voice.

"But then Randall came along . . . and now I'm confused." She turned to look at Anna. "In fact, I've been hoping to talk to you about all this. But we've both been so busy."

"We're not busy today." Anna paused for the doorman to open the door to the hotel. "And I'd love to talk to you about all of it over lunch. My treat."

After they were seated, Clara confessed that she was more attracted to Randall than to Clint. Although Anna felt relief, she also felt concern. What if Clara wound up getting hurt by all this? "Randall is such a gentleman, Anna. And he's so intelligent. I can't believe he's interested in someone like me."

"Someone like you?" Anna frowned. "Clara, you're a beautiful, intelligent, sensitive woman. And Randall was your friend, just as he was mine, back in school. He never understood why you married Albert. We all thought you could've had your choice of husbands."

Clara waved a hand. "Well, I appreciate that. But I suppose I didn't see it that way. Even more so after a few years of marriage. Albert wore me down . . . a lot."

"I know. I saw it firsthand. It always disturbed me." She considered her next words carefully. "And the truth is, I've had similar concerns about Clint Collins."

"Really?" Clara seemed genuinely surprised. "But he's been so protective of me. He goes out of his way to walk me home every night. And he's brought me candy and flowers. If Randall hadn't stepped in, I might've been engaged to Clint by now."

"You say that Clint is protective of you?"

"Yes. Very much so."

"In a way, Albert was protective too."

"What do you mean?" She frowned.

"Albert had a way of acting as if he had your best interests at heart, Clara. But in the end, I think he was simply trying to control you. As if you were a child. Remember how you had to beg him just to go to lunch with me?"

She nodded. "He always treated me like a child . . . or worse."

"I think it's only a fine line between protecting and controlling. And it worries me a little that Clint seems to want to take over for you. What if he turned out to be just like Albert?"

"Oh, that would be a nightmare."

"But someone like Rand . . . Well, I can't imagine him ever being that way."

"No, I can't either."

They paused as the waiter came to take their orders. Then, Anna asked what she knew would be a difficult question. "What about your children? How do they feel about Clint?"

"Ellen doesn't like Clint at all."

"Neither does AJ." Anna had already informed Clara of her son's concern.

She somberly nodded. "Yes, I know. But I assumed it was simply because he's a policeman."

Anna knew there was more to it than that but didn't feel free to say so. Not until the trial was behind them.

"I mentioned it to Clint, that my children are not fully supportive."

"Really?" Anna tried to hide her concern. "How did he react?"

"He said I should disregard their feelings, that they were nearly grown-ups, and it shouldn't matter what they think. They can go their way, and I can go mine."

"Do you agree with that?"

Clara slowly shook her head.

"It sounds to me that you've already made up your mind, Clara."

She brightened. "I suppose I wasn't ready to admit it, but I have made my decision. Not that Randall is asking for my hand . . . not yet anyway."

"Will you cut things off with Clint, then?"

She cringed. "I guess I should, shouldn't I?"

"I think the sooner the better."

"It won't be easy. And I hate to break things off right before Christmas. Clint had hoped to come over for the holidays."

"That's even more reason to cut it off," Anna insisted. "In fact, Ellen and you must join us for Christmas. I thought Katy had already asked you."

"Yes, she did. But I wasn't sure that Clint was invited."

Anna shook her head. "He is not." She held up a finger. "But Randall and his mother will be invited. I'll see to that today. Now, please confirm that you will be coming. And, unless I'm mistaken, I'll bet that Lucille would love to have you and Ellen overnight on Christmas Eve."

"Oh, that would be fun."

"Then it's a—" Anna stopped mid-sentence.

"What is it?"

"Katy and Lawrence," Anna said quietly. "Arm in arm. They're just exiting the hotel."

"Oh, yes, we just met him this morning. He seems like a nice, polite young man. And, according to my daughter, most handsome." She chuckled. "But what's wrong, Anna? You seem upset."

"Not really upset. Just concerned. Katy doesn't know him very well. And he seems, well, rather insistent." Anna explained how he showed up unexpectedly. "I suspect he's here for a specific reason."

"Katy?"

"That's what I'm afraid of. I'm not sure how persuasive Lawrence might be, but I'd hate to see his influencing her in the wrong direction."

"What sort of wrong direction?" Clara looked slightly alarmed.

"Oh, I don't mean anything disrespectful," Anna clarified. "But I suspect he's here to ask her to marry him."

"But Katy is a strong, independent young woman. She has a mind of her own, Anna. She wouldn't agree to marry anyone she didn't love."

"But sometimes, as you well know, a young girl can imagine she's in love . . . only to learn later that it was merely infatuation."

"Yes, I do know about that. But I'm going to stick to my belief that Katy is a fine, sensible girl. She's determined to follow her dreams, and I can't imagine that she'd let anyone persuade her differently."

Anna smiled. "I think you're right, Clara. In fact, I tried to convince Mac of this very thing just this morning. I suppose his worries rubbed off on me. But I agree with you. Katy will be just fine."

"She's probably just showing Lawrence the local sights today. Perhaps he'll get his fill of Sunset

Cove and hop the next southbound train home."

Anna laughed. "Let's hope so."

"Not to change the subject, but did you hear the news?"

"Well, I am in the news business, but I'm not sure what you mean."

"I heard it from Randall's mother. It seems that Dr. Hollister's father arrived by train last night."

"Really?" Anna was caught off guard. "I just spoke to Daniel a few days ago, and he never mentioned it."

"According to Marjorie, he wasn't expecting him. He made a late-night run to the mercantile to get provisions."

"How very interesting." Anna felt suddenly curious. "Well, Daniel agreed to spend Christmas with us. Hopefully nothing has changed there. I'll have to extend the invitation to his father too."

As they continued to visit, Anna was distracted with the news regarding Daniel's father. She wondered what had motivated him to leave his patients behind, travel across the country, and surprise his son with this visit. Perhaps even more curious—what would Daniel's father think of her? And, really, what difference would it make? It wasn't as if she and Daniel had made any progress in their relationship. But she'd hoped that Christmas might've been a turning point. She had a gift all ready for him . . . and she'd hoped he might have one for her as well.

CHAPTER 29

By Christmas Eve, Katy was ready to tell Lawrence Bouchard *adieu*. Unfortunately, that would be tricky since he was her grandmother's house guest. It didn't help matters that Grandmother thought Lawrence was perfectly delightful. And there was no denying the young man was charming and eloquent and attractive. The main problem was that Katy felt no romantic inclinations toward him—and he had made it crystal clear that his intentions were matrimony. Her efforts to politely inform him that she had no interest in marriage only seemed to increase his persistence. As a result, she'd taken to avoiding him, which wasn't easy in a small town—and even more difficult with the family Christmas festivities that Lawrence had been invited to attend.

It did help that Grandmother had invited more than thirty guests to her Christmas Eve celebration. Katy was using the crowd to her advantage, and she managed to slip away from Lawrence again and again. But, as the evening wore on, the evasion grew tiresome, and, finally, she wound up in the kitchen on the pretense of helping Sally with dessert. She was just filling the silver coffee pot when Jim Stafford appeared.

"Katy McDowell." He had a curious expression. "You seem a bit overdressed for kitchen duty."

She shrugged. "It's all right. I'm being careful."

He turned to Sally. "Lucille sent me in here to help carry out things for the dessert buffet."

He was put to work carrying out the heavy coffee service and a couple trays of desserts until there was nothing left to help with. "You go out and enjoy the guests," Sally urged them. "I've got it handled from here on out."

"I just, uh, I want to check on something." Katy ducked into the butler's pantry, where, to her surprise, Jim followed.

"What are you hiding from?" he asked with a mischievous twinkle in his eye.

"Nothing." She fiddled with a box of apples.

"It couldn't be a certain young man from San Francisco?"

She let out a low moan. "Oh, I just wish he'd go away."

Jim laughed. "Then why did you invite him to visit?"

"I did *not* invite him!"

"Oh? That's not what I heard."

"Well, then you heard wrong, Mr. Stafford. He came of his own accord. I may have said something offhanded about visiting the area sometime, but it was just the sort of thing one says to any new acquaintance, not a specific invitation."

"So the other rumor I heard . . . should I assume it's also false?"

"What's that?" she snapped.

"That you're going to become engaged on Christmas Day."

"Oh, *please.*" She couldn't control herself from rolling her eyes. "I've told Lawrence that I do not want to get married."

"Ever?" Jim blinked.

"Maybe." She stood taller. "I'm an independent businesswoman. I don't need a husband to take care of me."

Jim chuckled. "I believe that."

"I don't know why he's so determined."

"Probably because he's in love with you," he said quietly.

"But I've done nothing to encourage him."

"So you say." Jim looked skeptical as he picked up an apple.

"What do you mean by that?"

"I'm not saying you've intentionally done anything, Katy. But you're an intelligent and pretty girl. That alone could encourage him." He took a bite of the apple. "I'm sure Lawrence thinks you're quite a prize and well worth fighting for. And it's possible that your elusiveness is intriguing. Some men love the chase. It brings out the primal hunter in them."

"So what are you suggesting? That I throw myself at him?"

Jim laughed. "No, of course not. But hiding from him is probably not the best plan either. Maybe you should sit down with him—perhaps with your family members present—and clearly tell him that you have no intentions of marrying him. That is, if you're absolutely certain." He took another bite.

"Do you think I'm playing a game here?" she demanded. "I do *not* wish to marry Lawrence Bouchard. And I am *not* going to change my mind."

"*I* believe you." His tone softened. "Now you need to convince *him*."

"I know you're right," she confessed. "The truth is, I hate to hurt him. He's not a bad guy . . . and it's Christmas. Besides that, my grandmother has been enjoying having him here. I thought if I could just bide my time, well, perhaps he'd come to his senses and go home."

"Maybe he will." Jim's smile suggested he didn't think that the case. "You're a smart girl, Katy. I'm sure you'll figure it out."

"Thanks a lot." Katy didn't feel terribly smart at the moment. Perhaps she had done something to encourage Lawrence's attention . . . perhaps she needed to be more cautious about befriending male admirers. Truthfully, she'd enjoyed the attention at first. It had made her life seem more exciting. But it had gotten old fast. And now she just wanted it to end. She wanted to get back to designing dresses and spending time with family and friends . . . instead of playing hide-and-seek.

Anna did not know what to make of the elder Dr. Hollister, and she still hadn't been able to talk privately with Daniel. Of one thing she was certain: Daniel's father was a strong-willed man who was used to having his own way. He'd entered Lucille's home as if he were the guest of honor. And perhaps he was . . . although Anna wasn't sure exactly why. But the way he commanded attention when he told of his long train trip or his accomplishments back in Boston, it was obvious that he was used to being respected. In fact, he seemed to expect it. And, for most of the evening, he had managed to monopolize Lucille's attention. At first, Anna thought her mother was simply trying to be polite, but as the evening wore on, Lucille almost seemed to be under his spell.

"What do you think of Daniel's father?" Mac quietly asked Anna as they visited the dessert buffet set up in the dining room.

"He appears to be enjoying himself." She looked over the selection of pies and cakes.

"And the sound of his own voice," Mac said wryly.

"Mac." Anna glanced around to see if anyone had overheard.

"Lucille is quite taken with him."

"I think she's simply being a good hostess," Anna whispered.

"Humph."

"Sounds like they're starting to sing carols in there." She pointed to the pumpkin pie. "That looks good. Want a piece?"

"I want to go home." His tone grew flat. "I'm not hungry."

She turned to stare at him. "Not even for pumpkin pie? It's your favorite."

"I'm tired." He sighed. "Do you think I'll be missed?"

"Not in this crowd." The noise of singing from the front room was growing louder. "Let me go make our excuses and get our coats. Meet me in the foyer."

He thanked her, and she went to speak to Lucille. "Sorry to interrupt," she told the older doctor, turning back to her mother. "Mac needs to go home," she said quietly. "I think he's worn out from all the activities. Please, excuse us."

"Is he unwell?" Daniel asked with concern.

"I don't think so. But he's not quite himself."

"Let me go with you," Daniel offered. "I'll check him out."

"Oh, that's not—"

"I don't mind." Daniel was already by her side.

"I could use the fresh air." He excused himself, then followed Anna and helped Mac and her with their coats.

"It was feeling awfully close in there," Anna admitted once they were walking.

"And I wanted an excuse to leave," Daniel said with a sigh.

"Too noisy for me." Mac slowly made the way up his porch steps.

"The caroling will probably only get louder as the evening wears on," Anna said as they went inside.

Before long, they were seated in Mac's sitting room, and Daniel was giving him a quick, impromptu examination. "You seem all right to me." Daniel winked. "But, as your physician, I would recommend you get a good night's rest. I know you'll have a long day tomorrow too, Mac."

"Do you want me to get Mickey to help you get ready for bed?" Anna asked.

"I gave Mickey and Bernice the day off," Mac said.

"I'll help you," Daniel offered.

Anna thanked him and slipped out. She went into the front room and turned on a couple of lamps. The fireplace was dark, but logs had already been laid for a fire, so she lit them. Then, she went into the kitchen and put the teakettle on. Remembering the dessert buffet left behind at Lucille's house, Anna decided to check Bernice's pie safe, which was nicely loaded with apple, berry, pecan, and pumpkin pies. And Anna knew that no one's pumpkin pie was as good as Bernice's.

"Hello?" Daniel came into the kitchen. "Mac is in bed, but he'd like a glass of milk."

"Coming right up." Anna opened the icebox and removed the milk bottle. "I'm going to make a pot of tea and have a piece of pumpkin pie. Care to join me?"

"I'd love that."

She filled a glass with milk. "Thanks for helping with Mac. And for checking on him. He really didn't quite seem himself tonight."

"I think I know why." He took the glass. "I'll be back shortly."

By the time Daniel returned, she had tea and two generous slices of pumpkin pie set up on the tea table in the front room, and the fire was crackling nicely.

"This is perfect." Daniel sat down across from her. "Just what the doctor ordered."

"I must agree." She filled the teacups. "Now, tell me why you think Mac was out of sorts tonight." Naturally, she had her own theory, but she wanted to hear Daniel's take on it.

"I'm sure that my father's solicitous attentions toward Lucille didn't sit well with Mac."

She smiled. "I concur with the diagnosis, Doctor."

"I should've warned your family that my father is, well, a bit of a blowhard."

Anna's burst of laughter nearly made her spit out her tea.

"I know that sounds terribly disrespectful, but it's true. My father can be quite pompous and arrogant. He's chief of staff at his hospital, and everyone there treats him like he's royalty."

"Lucille seemed quite taken with him."

"Much to Mac's dismay."

"He'll get over it." Anna set her teacup down. "How long do you expect your father to stay?"

"He hasn't said. You probably heard how he caught me by surprise. I've invited him to visit before, but he always had an excuse. Then, he shows up without a word of notice and acts as if I should be prepared for him. I'm afraid he's not too impressed by my humble abode or bachelor ways."

"Perhaps that will shorten his visit." Anna forked into her pie.

Daniel chuckled. "One can hope."

"But are you enjoying having him here? I know you'd hoped he might visit."

"I'm afraid it was a case of absence making the heart grow fonder. I had begun to imagine my father softening up in his old age. I thought he and I would have some good heart-to-heart conversations . . . that we might mend some old wounds."

"But that's not happening?"

"If anything, he seems harder than I remember." Daniel sighed. "You don't know how fortunate you are to have a father like Mac, Anna."

"He wasn't always like that. I honestly believe his stroke changed his temperament . . . for the better. You probably didn't know him that well before his stroke, but he could be rather stubborn and outspoken. Not unlike your father."

"Well, I can't very well wish a stroke upon my father."

"No, of course not." She reached for her teacup. "Speaking of unexpected guests, have you met Katy's friend from San Francisco?"

"Yes. We had an interesting conversation at Lucille's house. I was quite surprised when he showed me the gift he'd gotten for Katy."

"Oh?"

Daniel frowned. "He asked me not to tell anyone."

"I see."

"But being that you're Katy's mother, perhaps I could give you a hint." He held up his left hand, pointing to his ring finger.

"Oh dear! An engagement ring?"

"So that's not happy news?"

"I honestly don't know how Katy feels. I've barely seen her since the boy arrived a few days ago. Lucille seems to like Lawrence Bouchard well enough, but Mac took an instant dislike to him. And, to be honest, I've got my own mis-givings. I feel he's moving too quickly. He strikes me as rather pushy. And to bring an engagement ring?" She shook her head. "It's not happy news to me."

"Maybe I shouldn't have told you. I didn't want to make you worried."

She sighed. "Well, I'll just have to remind myself of what I keep telling Mac. Katy is a sensible girl. And she's not one to be easily talked into anything."

Daniel chuckled. "Yes, I know." He pointed to the fire. "Want me to put more wood on there?"

"Please do." Anna wanted to change the subject. "So, has your father seen much of Sunset Cove yet? What does he think of our little hamlet?"

Daniel put a couple more logs on the fire, arranged them with the poker, and then turned to look at Anna. "Do you want the unvarnished truth? Or should I pretend he thinks Sunset Cove is lovely?"

"I'm a newspaperwoman, Daniel. The truth is best."

"He's described Sunset Cove as a backwater, backwoods, one-horse town that will probably be attacked by Indians any day now. I'm not joking. He claims that everyone here must be uncivilized, uneducated, and probably on the run from the law." He shook the fire poker for emphasis.

She laughed. "Well, we do have some lawless people in these parts. There's no denying that."

"He keeps comparing the West to the East, acting as if the West is only fit for outlaws, mountain men, and prospectors. He questions why I'd want to be a country doctor when I could work with him in one of the nation's foremost, premier hospitals." He sighed. "The reason he came here was to convince me to return to Boston, where I would eventually replace him as chief of staff."

"Is that what you want?"

"I'll admit that it's flattering to imagine being in such a position." He replaced the poker in its stand.

"That would be like my being offered the editor in chief position at the *New York Times*," she said with realization. "While I can't imagine that happening, I can understand the allure. I doubt I could pass it up, Daniel."

"Medicine is evolving at an astounding pace." He sat down, clasping his hands. "New medicines, new technologies, new treatments . . . I read of these developments in my medical journals. But it's not like that in this part of the country. I can't deny I've felt envious of East Coast doctors and their access to modern improvements and facilities."

"Hello?" Katy called out from the foyer. "Anyone home?"

"In here," Anna called back.

"Is Grandpa all right?" Katy asked with concern.

"Yes, yes, he's fine," Anna assured her. "There was no need for you to come home early."

"He was simply worn out. We put him to bed." Daniel smiled. "Is the caroling still going on over there?"

"Yes." Katy unbuttoned her cloak. "I'm surprised you can't hear them over here."

"Don't you want to go back and enjoy the festivities?" Anna asked. "It's not that late yet. Not for young people anyway."

"No." Katy firmly shook her head. "I'm worn out too." She headed for the stairs. "I'm going straight to bed. And don't wake me up early to say that Santa Claus has come. I plan to sleep in."

"So much for youthful energy," Anna said lightly. "But, to be fair, Katy's been awfully busy these past few weeks. It's no wonder she's exhausted."

"I suppose I should go see if my father is ready to retire for the night." Daniel stood and thanked Anna for the tea and pie.

"And we'll see you and your father tomorrow," she said as she walked him to the front door. "For Christmas dinner?"

"Unless Mac has decided to ban my father from his premises."

Anna laughed. "Well, he might like to do that, but we won't allow it. That's not in the spirit of

Christmas." Still, as Daniel made his exit, Anna wasn't so sure. If Mac had his way, the elder Dr. Hollister might be banished to the kitchen to eat. Whatever the case, she doubted that Christmas Day would be boring at the McDowells'.

CHAPTER 30

By Christmas morning, Anna had made up her mind. The gift she'd gotten for Daniel had been removed from beneath the tree and was now safely stowed in her room. It wasn't that the gold cuff links were overly personal, but they did seem to suggest something more than just a casual friendship. And, if there were a chance that Daniel was returning to Boston to practice medicine with his father, she didn't want him to feel beholden to her in any sort of way.

Despite Katy's claim to be sleeping in this morning, she'd gotten up and was eager to exchange gifts. It was a small, quiet gathering—just the three McDowells, still in their dressing gowns, as well as Mickey and Bernice—but it was perfect. Homey and sweet.

After breakfast, Anna took Katy aside. "I want to talk to you about Lawrence," she said quietly.

Katy looked exasperated. "Do you mind if I get dressed first? Just in case someone decides to pop in on us."

"Like Mr. Bouchard?"

"I'm sure that's a possibility."

"Yes, let's get dressed first," Anna agreed, following Katy up the stairs.

"Will you wear the new dress I gave you for Christmas?" Katy asked eagerly.

"I'd love to."

"And thank you again for the easel and art supplies," Katy said as they stood on the landing. "I'll put them to good use."

As Anna put on the emerald-green, velvet-and-lace dress, she wondered how many occasions she'd have to wear such a fine garment. Still, it was sweet of Katy. And it was certainly festive—and Christmassy. Perhaps she'd wear it again for the Mayor's Ball on New Year's Eve. Unable to fasten the back properly, she went to knock on Katy's door. But, when Katy didn't answer, Anna went in, only to discover Katy was gone.

Anna went downstairs and asked Bernice if she'd seen Katy.

"She just passed through here." Bernice did up the back of Anna's dress. "Said she was going to take a little walk on the beach."

"Oh." Anna peered out the window. "By herself?"

"As far as I know."

Anna was tempted to go change into casual clothes and hunt down her wayward daughter, but she suspected Katy wanted to be alone. Perhaps she needed to think. But that, in itself, was concerning. Did that mean Lawrence had presented her with the ring and proposed to her already? And was she considering her answer right now? And why wasn't she talking to Anna about these things?

"There's the doorbell," Bernice said as she checked on the turkey already roasting in the oven. "And Mickey is peeling potatoes for me out back."

"I'll get it," Anna told her. She hurried to the front door to see Clara outside. "Come in, come in. I'm so glad to see you."

Clara held out a small, soft package. "This is for you."

"And I have a little something for you." Anna went to the tree to remove the package. It was only a book of poetry, but she hoped Clara would appreciate it. They sat down and opened their gifts.

"What a soft, warm scarf." Anna held it to her cheek.

"It's cashmere." Clara opened her book. "This is lovely, Anna, thank you."

"Now, tell me everything."

"Well, it's not been easy. Clint became very upset when I told him I had made other plans for Christmas."

"I wondered about that."

"He asked if I was going to be with Randall, and I told him the truth." Clara grimly shook her head. "That made him even angrier."

"You see, he was showing his true colors."

Clara looked close to tears. "He accused me of betraying him."

"Betraying him? How is that possible? It's not as if you were engaged."

"He said that everyone in town knew he was courting me and that I'd accepted his affection 'under false pretenses.' Those were his exact words."

"Well, that is perfectly ridiculous. It wasn't as if you'd invited his attention."

"Well, I did accept it."

"It sounded more as if he foisted it upon you. I heard he would just show up and assume you and Ellen needed an escort home. And then he acted as if he were protecting you. Protecting you from what?"

"I don't know."

"He's just trying to make you feel guilty, Clara. So that he can have his way."

"He was very angry at Randall too. He called him an interloper."

"I don't think you should give Clint Collins a second thought. He's simply displaying the very things I warned you about. He thought he could control you. And now he sees he can't, and he's angry. I'm glad you broke it off with him."

"I'm not sure if I did break it off."

"How can that possibly be?"

"He told me it wasn't over with yet."

"Well, that makes no sense. If you say it's over, it's over. It takes two people to make a relationship."

"Yes, that's what Randall told me too."

"Was he surprised by any of this?"

"He didn't seem terribly surprised. But perhaps a little concerned." She frowned. "You don't think Clint would hurt Randall, do you?"

"I, uh, I don't know. But I do know that Randall is a smart man. He won't let someone like Clint Collins get the best of him. I'm sure of it." Anna wished she felt as confident as she sounded. But, if Clint was involved with the sort of people she suspected . . . Who could say how he might react? Thankfully, Mac had invited Chief Rollins and his wife to join them today. That, at the very least, should keep a lid on things for the time being.

Katy's elusive disappearing act continued to keep Lawrence Bouchard at a safe distance throughout Christmas Day, but she knew she couldn't keep this up forever. She'd told her grandmother that she needed time away from Lawrence . . . in order to think. She'd explained that his attention had overwhelmed her, and Grandmother had promised to talk to him.

Then, Christmas night, before going to bed, Katy had assured her mother that she had no intention of getting married, begging her not to worry. She admitted that she'd heard about the engagement ring and had managed to avoid that conversation with Lawrence. "I didn't want to hurt him right at Christmas," she'd explained. "But I just need more time to handle this gently. To let him down easily. Grandmother is such good friends with his family, and I don't want to be the one to spoil that. So, please, let me deal with this my way." Fortunately, her mother had agreed. And she'd seemed relieved.

But, as Katy unlocked the dress shop the next day, she wondered if she'd been mistaken to prolong this thing. Wouldn't it be easier to simply tell him, once and for all, that she did not want to marry him? It felt as if a dark, heavy cloud was hanging over her head. How long would she have to put up with it? Still, there was no time to think about that right now. She had three orders for New Year's Eve dresses that needed to be completed by the weekend.

Katy always liked being the first one in the shop. She would go around turning on lights and straightening things, making everything look as pretty as possible. And then she would get the day's sewing organized for the seamstresses. By the time the others arrived, everything was neatly in place and ready to go. Usually, Clara and Ellen were the next ones to arrive, followed by the seamstresses, and, finally, Lucille. But today, it was her grandmother who got there first.

"I want to talk to you about Lawrence," Lucille said as she removed her coat. "I've done as you said, asked him to allow you some time. I told him he'd overwhelmed you, and he felt sorry. He wanted to apologize, but I suggested he wait. And then he decided to go and see a bit more of Oregon." She smiled. "So you'll be relieved to know, he's catching the next westbound train and won't be back until the end of the month."

"He's gone?"

"I thought you'd be glad."

"Oh yes, I'm glad. But I wish I could've set him straight before he left."

"Set him straight?"

"That I can't marry him. I wanted him to accept and understand that."

"Oh?" Lucille looked disappointed.

"I've tried to tell him before, but he wouldn't listen. And so I decided to get through Christmas, then break the news as gently but firmly as possible."

"Oh . . . I see."

Katy shrugged. "Well, I guess I can do that when he comes back. If he comes back."

"He'll be back."

"You know that for sure?"

"He said he plans to live here, Katy. He doesn't want to return to San Francisco."

"Well, I suppose that's his choice." Katy shook her head. She really didn't understand Lawrence.

San Francisco was a beautiful city—why wouldn't he want to live there? It was actually the only thing that had tempted her to consider his proposal. Except that she knew she didn't love him. And that's when she knew it would never work.

During the next week, Anna felt that little had changed in Sunset Cove. Daniel's father remained in their one-horse town, still acting superior to everyone who crossed his path and still trying to convince Daniel to return to Boston with him. Clint Collins was still vexed at Randall for winning over Clara and didn't care who knew about it. Meanwhile, Clara was still hopeful that Randall's intentions were pointed toward matrimony. Anna had been a little concerned about this early on, but, after Randall took Clara to visit AJ shortly after Christmas, she began to wonder. Unless Anna was misreading Randall, he seemed to be developing true romantic feelings for Clara. And he was even taking her to the Mayor's Ball on New Year's Eve.

It was Katy that Anna felt the most concern for. Although she'd been absorbed by working at the dress shop all week, Anna sensed she was on pins and needles—and not the kind she used to sew with. But at least she'd handed in her column today, and, as Anna put the last proofing marks on it, she had to admit it was a good one.

"Hello?" Jim stuck his head into her office. "Are you done with those last few pieces yet? The typesetters are waiting."

"Yes, yes." She held up the stack of papers. "Sorry to be so slow. I guess I was distracted."

"Well, I'm sorry I couldn't do—"

"Never mind, I just want to hear about your investigation. How did it turn out?"

"Let me hand these off to Leroy, and I'll get right back to you."

After he left, Anna straightened her desk. It was quitting time, and the newspaper would be closed until after New Year's. While she looked forward to being home and having the time off, she wanted to hear Jim's report first.

"So, here's what's going on." He closed the door to her office. "I heard there's going to be a New Year's Eve party at Charlie's, and my source, who will remain anonymous, claims the libations will be flowing freely."

"That figures." Anna scowled. "Every respectable citizen, including Chief Rollins, plans to attend the Mayor's Ball. That just leaves the lowlifes to go to Charlie's—and get away with it."

"So I wanted to tip off Chief Rollins, but I hate to do it too soon. Don't want Collins to tell Snyder. I can just imagine the cops showing up full force only to find the good ol' boys sipping on sarsaparilla."

"I wonder if the police would actually raid it on New Year's Eve. And, think about it, Collins will probably be at the Mayor's Ball. Keeping up appearances."

"Good question. Thanks to the ball, the chief might want to turn a blind eye toward the shindig at Charlie's."

"And maybe that would be a good thing . . ." Anna considered this. "Give them the impression no one is looking, and then the police could raid them the next time."

"So what should I do, Anna?"

She shrugged. "I'm not sure, but it seems the chief should know. I like your idea of springing it on him at the last minute, though. Hopefully when Clint is not around."

"How about after the ball is over? Then, he could still pull off a raid if he wants. And I could follow the cops and get the story."

"Not a bad idea."

"Too bad I don't have a pretty gal to take to the ball." He looked hopeful. "How about you?"

She chuckled. "You're too late. Daniel Hollister already invited me to go with him . . . and his father."

"That should be interesting."

"The elder Dr. Hollister wanted to be Lucille's escort, but Mac had already made plans with her." Anna held up a finger. "But I know someone you could take, if you don't mind."

"Who?"

"Well, Katy has looked forward to the ball since the election, but she's not particularly eager to go with us . . . because of Daniel's outspoken father." Anna grimaced. She wasn't looking forward to another evening with the "blowhard" either.

His brows arched. "Are you suggesting I invite Katy?"

"It would probably be a relief to both her and me." She explained about how Lawrence Bouchard was expected back. "Any day now."

"I thought he'd gone for good." Jim frowned.

She explained about the engagement ring and how Lucille had advised Lawrence to give Katy some time. "The problem is, she didn't need time. She was ready to tell him she'd never marry him. But he took off before she got the chance. And now she's worried about his return. Poor Katy. She was so looking forward to the Mayor's Ball."

"Well, I'd be honored to escort Katy. If you think she'll agree."

"I know Katy respects you, Jim. She considers you a good friend. Why don't you go invite her?"

"You don't have to ask me twice." He made a mock salute. "I'm on it, boss."

Anna chuckled as he left. It wasn't as if she wanted to set her daughter up with Jim, but, if it helped Katy to enjoy the ball, it was worth it. Katy had worked hard to help Wally win the election. She had every right to celebrate. And Anna knew she could trust Jim. Even if Lawrence showed up with a ring in hand, Anna knew she could count on Jim to help buffer things. And, hopefully, that would be the end of this dilemma.

CHAPTER 31

Katy felt a sudden rush of anxiety to hear someone knocking on the back door of the dress shop. Was Lawrence back in town, ready to stake his claim to her heart? And, if so, how could she politely send him away again?

"Can you get it, Ellen?" Katy asked. "I need to check on something in front." Before Ellen could answer, Katy rushed out to the showroom. There was nothing to check on there, because the shop had just closed. But Katy walked around the darkened room, trying to gather her nerves . . . silently praying and preparing a polite but firm refusal for Lawrence.

The door to the back room opened, and Ellen called out, "Someone's here to see you, Katy."

Katy took in a deep breath and returned to the back room, where, to her surprise, Jim Stafford was standing with his hat in his hands.

"Sorry to interrupt you at work." He looked slightly uneasy.

"You're not interrupting anything." She smiled warmly, glad it was Jim and not Lawrence. "We're just closing anyway. What can I do for you?"

"Well, I was just talking with your mother.

And I, well, I wanted to invite you to go to the Mayor's Ball with me."

"Really?" Katy felt a rush of relief. "I'd love to go with you."

"What about Lawrence?" Ellen asked from behind Katy. "I thought you were going with him."

"I never agreed to that," Katy said a bit sharply.

Ellen stepped up beside her. "But Lucille said he'll be back by then."

Katy shrugged. "That's not my concern."

Ellen sighed. "Some girls have no one to escort them to the Mayor's Ball . . . while it seems others can take their pick."

Katy glanced at Jim, suddenly feeling sorry for Ellen. "How do you feel about taking two girls to the ball?"

"Sounds like twice as much fun." He grinned.

So it was that on New Year's Eve, Katy and Ellen—both dressed in evening gowns designed by Katy—took turns dancing with Jim Stafford at the Mayor's Ball. And, really, it *was* twice as much fun. And Katy was glad to see Ellen having a good time, even if she *was* shamelessly flirting with Jim. It could've been a perfect evening . . . but then Lawrence Bouchard showed up. He went directly to Katy, acting as if he had every right to claim her.

"Are you okay?" Jim quietly asked her. "Do you need my help?"

"I think I can handle this." She smiled stiffly at Lawrence. "I'm surprised to see you here. I thought perhaps you'd gone home to San Francisco."

"Didn't Lucille tell you I'd be back?"

"Let's go over there." Katy pointed to a quiet corner. "Yes, Lucille thought you'd come back, Lawrence, but I had hoped you'd gone home."

"I want Sunset Cove to be my home, Katy," he said with confidence.

"That's up to you." She looked into his face. "But I hope your decision isn't because of me. I've tried to tell you that I'm not interested in marriage."

"All girls are interested in marriage." He smiled brightly. "Eventually. I just hope I can convince you that sooner is better than later." He reached into his vest pocket.

"Lawrence, *please* hear me out. I will *never* marry you." She made sure her voice rang with authority. "Not this year or next year or ten years from now. You need to accept this."

He frowned. "Do you really mean that?"

She nodded firmly. "I do not love you, Lawrence. I would like to maintain a friendship with you, but it can never be anything more than that."

"You can't mean that." He scowled darkly.

"I do mean it. I'm absolutely certain." She glanced nervously to where Jim was standing nearby and then looked back at Lawrence. "I'm sorry if I've hurt you, but that is how I feel." She stepped away. "Now, if you'll ex—"

"Not so fast!" Lawrence grabbed her wrist. "You can't lead a guy on like that and then—"

"Excuse me." Jim stepped up with a smile. "Katy, I believe this is our dance."

"I suggest you stay out of this." Lawrence narrowed his eyes at Jim.

"You're right," Katy told Jim. "This is our dance. Please excuse me, Lawrence."

"Katy is with me." Lawrence lifted his chin. "If she's going to dance, it'll be with me."

"I'm sorry." Jim kept his tone polite but firm. "I escorted Katy here tonight. She is with me. And this is our dance."

Lawrence's eyes narrowed. "Maybe we should take this outside."

"No, no." Katy cringed to imagine violence. "That's not—"

"Hello, everyone." Ellen stepped up, smiling broadly at Lawrence. "Welcome back to Sunset Cove. Now, if Katy is going to dance with Jim, I suggest that you should dance with me."

Katy wanted to hug Ellen, but instead she turned to Jim. "We better get going before the song ends." And, before Lawrence could stop them, they hurried out to the dance floor."

"That was close," Jim said as they began to dance.

"Thank goodness for Ellen." Katy glanced back to see Ellen bravely leading a scowling Lawrence to the dance floor too—and then they were dancing. As the evening wore on, Ellen stuck to Lawrence like glue, and Katy knew she owed her friend a heap of thanks.

When it was Katy's turn to dance with Wally, Jim went over to speak to Chief Rollins and his wife. After the dance ended, Jim returned with a slightly concerned expression. "I'm going to have to leave early," he whispered. "Something related to the newspaper. Will you be okay here on your own? I'm sure you and Ellen can ride home with someone."

"Where are you going?" Katy asked.

"Covering a story."

"Please take me with you," she said eagerly. "I hate being stuck here with Lawrence still around."

"I suppose I could take you. But only if you promise to stay in the car."

"I promise," she agreed.

"Come on, then."

Anna wasn't overly concerned when Jim came over to tell her he'd informed the chief about the gathering at Charlie's or that he was leaving to cover the story. She watched with interest as the chief and a couple of his officers quietly exited the dance but was curious why Clint

Collins wasn't among them. He'd been here earlier but was nowhere in sight now. And Clara was still dancing with Randall. That was a relief.

As Daniel led Anna to the dance floor again, she noticed Jim and Katy ducking out the back door. At first, she assumed Katy had stepped out to say good-bye to Jim, but, when she didn't return, Anna grew anxious. "Excuse me," she told Daniel. Then, pushing through the crowd, she hurried to the back door and opened it just in time to see Jim's car tearing out of the parking area. "Katy?" Anna yelled, but, realizing she was too late, she rushed back to Daniel. "I need to leave right now."

"What's going on?"

She quickly told him of the police raid about to occur at Charlie's. "Jim left to cover the story, but he took Katy with him!"

"Let me arrange a ride for my father while you grab our wraps," he commanded. "I'll meet you at the back door."

A few minutes later, they were on their way. As he quickly drove down the beach road, Anna gratefully thanked him. "I'm sure Jim wouldn't allow Katy to get in harm's way, but I do wish she hadn't gone with him there. I don't know why on earth she did. I can't imagine Jim would encourage her to go. He knows it could be dangerous."

"Maybe she wanted to get away from Lawrence," Daniel suggested as he pushed his car even faster. "I noticed them having a rather interesting discussion earlier."

"You did?" Anna felt surprised. "I felt sure that Lawrence switched his affections to Ellen tonight. Every time I saw him, he was dancing with her. I must say, I was hugely relieved."

"Well, earlier this evening, I observed Lawrence in conversation with Katy, and it worried me. I was about to intervene, but Jim Stafford beat me to the punch."

"Really? How did I miss all that?"

"You were dancing with the Wally just then. Anyway, it almost looked as if Lawrence and Jim were about to have a skirmish, but then Ellen showed up." He chuckled. "I think she may have quenched the flames. After that, she seemed intent on monopolizing Mr. Bouchard's dance card."

"Bless her heart!"

"So tell me about this raid. How did you know it would happen?"

She explained Jim's discoveries this week. "His plan was to tip off the chief tonight. To ensure that no one tipped off Snyder."

"You mean like Clint Collins?"

She felt relieved that he shared their same suspicions.

"I noticed him leaving the dance earlier tonight.

I thought maybe it was for a smoke, but he never came back."

"How long ago did he leave?" she asked eagerly. "Was anyone with him?"

"Maybe an hour ago. And he was alone."

"That's not good. He could've tipped off Snyder about the raid. Although, I don't see how he could've known, since the chief didn't even know until—"

"Look there." Daniel tapped the windscreen. "Doesn't that look like flames above those pines?"

"You're right. Something is burning up there." She leaned forward to see better as he drove up the rise. "Oh no, Daniel, it's Charlie's!"

A number of cars were parked along the road, and people, including the chief, were scrambling about the inferno. Daniel's car had barely stopped when Anna jumped out and, rushing down the road, finally spotted Jim's Model T.

"Mother!" Katy shrieked, running toward her and nearly falling into her arms.

"What happened?" Anna demanded.

"We got here. Jim got out. He said to stay in the car. Then, there was this big explosion." Katy grabbed Anna's arm. "He's in there, Mother!"

"Oh no." Still holding Katy, Anna stared toward the flaming building.

"Is Katy all right?" Daniel breathlessly asked Anna.

"Yes." Anna turned to Daniel. "But Jim's in there."

"In Charlie's?" He turned toward the inferno. "Oh no . . . no."

Anna stared at the flames in disbelief, feeling the heat on her face. How could anyone survive that? And, with the fire chief and volunteers still at the Mayor's Ball, who could possibly battle it? She heard Chief Rollins and his men shouting out orders and epithets behind her, but she knew it was useless. What could they do?

"Oh, Mother!" Katy sobbed. "Poor Jim."

"Do you really think he went inside?" Daniel asked Katy.

"I—I don't know."

"I'm going to look." Daniel pulled out his handkerchief, held it over his nose and mouth, and took off toward the burning building.

Anna wanted to stop him but knew he wouldn't listen. "Dear God, keep Daniel safe," she prayed aloud. "And, please, please help Jim. And help anyone else in there. Help them all, dear Lord, please help them all!"

"Yes! Please help them all, dear God." Katy sobbed, still clinging to Anna. "Please, please help Jim!"

CHAPTER 32

A lthough it was only minutes, it seemed like hours before Daniel returned, but, when he did, Jim was with him. His face was covered in blood, but at least he was walking.

"Oh, Jim!" Katy ran to meet them. "You're hurt!"

"But he's alive," Anna told her.

"He suffered a blow to the head. Probably from the explosion." Daniel helped Jim over to the Model T and situated him on the passenger side. "Must've knocked him out cold." Daniel removed his cummerbund and wrapped it around Jim's head, then turned to Katy and Anna. "Can you ladies drive him to town? I want to see if anyone else needs my help."

"I'm okay," Jim muttered. "I can drive."

"No, you cannot," Daniel insisted.

"I'll drive him." Katy stepped forward. "How about if I take him to our house? He can rest there until you come."

"Have him lie down and keep him quiet," Daniel instructed her, then paused as someone yelled out his name.

"We've got injured people over here,"

Chief Rollins yelled out. "We need the doctor!"

"I better stick around and see if I can help." Anna took Katy's hand and gave it a squeeze. "Can you get Jim home on your own?"

"Of course." Katy leapt into the driver's seat and pulled on the starter while the doctor gave the car a crank, but her hands shook as she gripped the steering wheel. "Just relax," she said to Jim as she pulled out. "I'll try to drive as smoothly as possible."

Town was strangely quiet as she drove toward home. Of course, everyone was still at the Mayor's Ball, unaware of the goings-on a few miles away. "Here we are," she said as she parked in front. "Let me help you out." She hurried to the other side and put an arm around Jim as he struggled to his feet, then she helped him to walk.

"Take it easy," she said as she guided him into the house. "We're almost there." She settled him on the front room sofa and then ran to get a clean towel for his head. But, unsure of what to do next, she ran to Bernice and Mickey's room, knocked on the door, and—once Bernice had opened it—apologized for disturbing them. "But it's an emergency!" She explained the situation.

Then, with Bernice jumping into action, Katy picked up the telephone and reported to the operator what had happened at Charlie's. "I know most of the town is still up at the grange," she told the woman, "but they're going to need help at Charlie's. Can you let people know? And can you get the word up to the grange too?" The woman promised to do her best. Then, Katy went to check on Jim.

Mickey was just carrying away the blood-soaked towels and wash basin, and Bernice was wrapping a clean bandage around Jim's head.

Bernice glanced up at Katy. "Could you get a blanket from the linen closet?"

Relieved to see Jim cleaned up and looking less frightening, Katy hurried to comply and soon returned with a tartan blanket and a bed pillow. "Here you go." She laid the blanket over him, then gently arranged the pillow beneath his head. "How are you feeling?"

"Like I should get up and—"

"Well, just forget that. The doctor said to keep you still. So close your eyes and keep quiet. And I'll keep watch to make sure you do." She sat in the chair across from him and looked up at the clock. It was close to midnight now. The revelers up at the grange would soon be pulling poppers and throwing confetti. Unless they'd heard the news. In that case, they might be heading toward town. She sighed. What a messy way to end a year. Hopefully 1917 would be better.

As she watched Jim peacefully resting on the sofa, his head wrapped in a bulky, white bandage, she felt her heart stirring. She'd been so frantic over him during that explosion . . . and then to imagine he'd perished in the blaze . . . It was excruciating.

Katy sighed. Perhaps she'd simply been overly dramatic tonight. Although, it had seemed very genuine at the time. And her tears had been real. She'd felt as if she'd lost her soul mate. As if Jim's demise would leave her lonely for life. Oh, she knew she was probably exaggerating the whole thing, but, as she watched him sleeping there . . . she wondered.

Anna had covered some nasty fires in Portland before, but she'd never seen such suffering as the burn victims who'd somehow escaped the explosion and inferno that followed. She did what she could to help Daniel, but she suspected that many of the injured would not survive the night. Before long, more help arrived, including Daniel's father, who insisted on giving medical assistance.

The wounded were soon being transported to Daniel's medical office and various homes, and, knowing Daniel had a long night ahead of him, Anna excused herself to go home with Mac and Lucille, who had come along with the others to see how they could help. Sally's husband was acting as their chauffeur, and Anna sat in front with him. Feeling on the verge of tears and still shocked by everything, she could barely think coherently.

"What a tragedy," Lucille said from the back seat. "So very sad."

"Any idea how many people were at Charlie's tonight, Anna?" Mac asked.

"No." Her voice came out dull.

"Maybe the survivors will know," he said.

"If anyone survives." She shuddered to remember the cries of the victims.

"Do you know what caused it?"

"No." Anna slowly shook her head. Then, knowing Mac would continue to pepper her questions, she told him about Jim's discovery. "He knew illegal alcohol would be present at Charlie's. Perfect chance for a successful raid. He tipped off Chief Rollins at the ball."

"So that's why they left early. Glad they didn't get there any sooner." Mac blew out a loud sigh. "Could've been killed tonight."

Anna then informed them of Jim's close call. "Katy took him home. Daniel was going to check on him later, but I'm sure he's got his hands full."

"It's good the elder Dr. Hollister is here," Lucille said. "I'm sure Daniel will appreciate his help."

"As long as the old windbag doesn't talk them to death."

"Mac," Lucille chided.

"How long ago did the explosion happen?" Mac asked.

"I'm not sure what time it was. We left the

ball before eleven. Shortly after that, I suppose."

Lucille let out a blustery breath. "We got news of it right before midnight."

"Everyone thought it was a joke." Mac shook his head.

"Some of them cheered," Lucille added. "Until they realized it was real."

"And that was the end of the ball."

"Happy New Year," Lucille said glumly.

Sunset Cove seemed to be draped in a dark, thick cloud the following week. And not due to the weather. By Wednesday morning, just in time for the front-page story, the fire investigators released a preliminary statement. The police and fire department chiefs agreed to a total of seventeen fatalities. And, although the cause of the explosion was still uncertain, the fire chief claimed it was most likely the result of an open flame near the highly volatile bathtub gin that appeared to have been in the process of being concocted in Charlie's basement.

Although there was no denying this was big news, Anna derived no pleasure in printing this tragic story. Gossip traveled through town, speculating over who had or had not perished in the fire, but, so far, the investigators were not releasing names. And, despite the rumors, Anna wasn't either. Jim, claiming he was completely recovered from his head injury, insisted that he'd earned the right to act as lead reporter in this case. And Anna was glad to hand it over to him.

She'd reserved the interview with Daniel for herself, though, getting the latest prognosis for the six survivors, some that she'd helped him with on that fateful night. Daniel informed her that the most serious cases had been transported to Portland, but three men still remained in his care and would probably pull through. "My father is actually helping with the patients," he told her. "And it's been surprisingly good to work with him."

Anna was glad to hear that Daniel and his father were getting along so well, but it also worried her. Perhaps this was a warning—maybe Daniel would decide to return to Boston now. And why not? What dedicated physician would pass up such an excellent opportunity to further his career?

By the end of the week, the police investigators managed to identify eleven local men and three local women among the deceased, but the other three remained uncertain. Again, although it was front-page news, Anna didn't look forward to seeing the names in print.

"We are not here to judge them," Anna informed her editorial team shortly after the names had been released on Friday. "They were fellow citizens of Sunset Cove, and, whether you liked them or not, this is a tragedy the whole town should be grieving."

Then Jim assigned each writer a few names. "Find out what you can about each individual. Keep it to just a few sentences and get it to me by four."

"And we'll run a respectful story in tomorrow's edition," Anna finished for him.

Jim pointed to Reginald. "You'll have your hands full with obituaries for Wednesday's edition. Let me know if you need a hand."

Late in the day, the paper was sent to press, and Anna went home thinking she was ready to be finished too . . . for at least a couple of days. It wasn't that the week had been physically grueling, but emotionally, she was drained.

By Monday, Anna felt ready to return to the newspaper and take on the follow-up stories that still needed reporting. First thing in the morning, she called Jim to her office. "It's been more than a week since the fire. Do we still not know the identities of the three other victims?"

"I just talked to Chief Rollins yesterday, and he's pretty sure they were out-of-towners. All were men, ages estimated to be thirty to forty. The state police are conducting their own investigation, but the general consensus seems to be that the unidentified might be some of the rumrunners who were involved with Albert Krauss and his crowd. The chief suspects they'd made a delivery to Charlie's, or they could've been picking something up."

"Well, I suppose that makes sense, but it would be nice to know for sure." She dismally shook her head. "That still doesn't explain Calvin Snyder or Clint Collins. What is the chief saying about them?"

"He still calls them *missing*."

"And no chance they're among those unidentifiable victims?"

"He doesn't seem to think so."

Anna frowned. "Do you think he's being completely forthcoming?"

"Hard to say. I don't think he'd try to protect Snyder, but, if the chief admits his lieutenant was there that night, well, it's a black eye for the force."

"Well, I suppose it's possible that Collins went there on official business." Anna still felt torn over this. "What if he was investigating the same thing we were?"

"I've wondered about that." Jim rubbed his hand over the bandage still on his forehead—a smaller one now. "After all, I could've been killed that night too. People might've speculated about my involvement."

"All right, I understand the chief wanting to protect Collins. But what about Snyder?" she pressed. "What does he say about him? We all know he was there on New Year's Eve, not to mention that he owns the place. Are they absolutely certain he wasn't one of those unidentified victims?"

"Both the fire and police chiefs agree that none of the deceased victims seemed to match up to Snyder."

"But Snyder was there!" She pounded her fist on the desk for emphasis. "The survivors confirmed that they saw him, as well as Clint Collins, there that night! Where are they now? How does the chief explain it?"

"He doesn't." Jim lifted his brows. "He's frustrated too, Anna."

"I know." She sighed.

"Oh yeah, one more thing." Jim shook his head grimly. "Not a very pleasant thing either, although I think the public deserves to hear about it."

"What's that?"

"Well, the fire chief told me that Calvin Snyder had apparently made some recent changes to Charlie's."

"Obviously. He turned it from a respectable chowder house to an illegal tavern."

"Yes, but the fire chief said the front entrance and the windows were all blocked."

"Blocked? Why?"

"Snyder didn't want his patrons to be observed coming and going from his place. So everyone used the back entrance, which went through the kitchen. That was the only way in or out. And the reason more people were unable to escape."

"Oh dear." Anna cringed to imagine the victims trapped inside.

"So Snyder is essentially responsible for their deaths. At the least, I'd think it would be a manslaughter charge."

Anna let out a slow breath. "Do you think that's why Snyder is missing, assuming he's still alive? He's hiding out to avoid being arrested?"

"Makes sense."

"But that doesn't explain Collins." She frowned. "Well, unless he was in cahoots with Snyder. In that case, he probably wouldn't want to show his face in town. And you're still going by their homes every day?"

"Yep, several times a day," he confirmed. "No one's seen either of them."

She thought hard. What was the missing puzzle piece in this? It just didn't add up. "So . . . if they're still alive, that must mean that they left Charlie's *before* the explosion. But why?"

Jim rubbed his chin. "I've wondered about that too."

"Do you think it's possible that they *caused* the explosion?"

"But why, Anna? Why would Snyder blow up his own place?"

She thought hard. "Insurance payoff?"

"With all his drinking buddies inside? That just doesn't make sense."

She nodded. "I know . . . I know. But nothing about those two—Snyder and Collins—has ever made sense to me."

"Besides that, Snyder had seemed pretty thrilled about his *social club*. And I'm guessing it was lucrative. I just don't see why he'd intentionally burn the place down."

"What about those three unidentified men?" Anna said slowly. "What if they *weren't* friends of Snyder's? What if they were there for some bad reason? Like a payoff or something? Maybe Snyder and Collins snuck out of there to get away from them?"

"But, if that were true, if they did survive the fire, wouldn't they be out here claiming their innocence, building their case so that no one could finger them? Otherwise, how would they ever show their faces in town again? And how could Snyder claim insurance money—assuming he had insurance, which I doubt—if he isn't here in Sunset Cove?"

"You're probably right about that." She sighed. "We're like dogs chasing our own tails, Jim. And we've got work to do. You can go ahead and write that follow-up article with the information we have, including the information about the blocked exits, and posing the question of 'Where are they?' Maybe we'll get lucky and some helpful reader will offer some information. In the meantime, I plan to write an editorial to follow up the whole Charlie's ordeal. I want to make it very clear what the price of breaking prohibition laws has cost this town. Whether citizens agree with prohibition or not, people need to be reminded that the law is the law. That's about all we can do for now."

"And I almost forgot." Jim's eyes lit up. "I have another small but important piece to go into Wednesday's edition. I just ran into Randall. Seems AJ has a court date. January fifteenth."

"That's only a week away." Anna felt hopeful.

"Makes me wonder, though . . . Do you think the fire at Charlie's could be related to AJ's trial? What if Snyder got wind that AJ was going to testify against the rumrunners . . . possibly against Snyder himself?"

"Are you suggesting that Snyder set that fire as some sort of smoke screen?" She grimaced. "Excuse the bad pun."

He waved a hand. "Think about it, Anna. What if Snyder knew AJ was going to finger him? And he wanted to get out of town without anyone knowing he'd gone? Could he have purposely started the fire?"

"That's horrible. So diabolical. But it's an interesting theory. Maybe we'll discover some of these missing pieces at the trial. I know I plan to be there."

"You and me both."

"And, unless I'm wrong, about half of the town

too." Anna sighed. For Clara and Ellen's—and even for AJ's—sake, she wished this case wasn't such a conspicuous one. She hoped and prayed that Randall would get it resolved fairly.

CHAPTER 33

By the date of AJ's trial, a couple of significant news events had occurred in Sunset Cove. First of all, the three previously unnamed victims of the New Year's Eve fire had been tentatively identified as men from the north coast area, all wanted by the law. This left Calvin Snyder and Clint Collins as "mysteriously missing." Anna felt relieved when Chief Rollins eventually declared them both "wanted for questioning and as suspects in the cause of a fire that had killed and injured twenty-three people." It had also made for a good headline in Wednesday's paper.

Another story popped up in time for the Saturday edition. It seemed that one of the Krauss fishing boats had been stolen. Unfortunately, thanks to all the goings-on in town, no one had noticed it missing until Friday. But, when Jim questioned various fishermen around the docks, no one recalled having seen it for more than a week. Because it was one of the smaller boats, it might've been easy to overlook. Besides, as Clara pointed out, the fishing business had been closed for months now, and she paid little attention to the smelly, old boats. More than ever, she wanted to sell the whole works . . . hopefully by spring.

Naturally Anna had encouraged Jim to write the stolen-boat story in a way that connected it to the missing men. It seemed highly likely to her that Snyder and Collins were behind that theft. After all, Collins had wanted to get his hands on all the Krauss property. He probably felt it was his right, after being "jilted" by Clara, to simply take one of the boats. Unfortunately, although the Coast Guard had been alerted, the stolen boat could have gotten far away by now.

"Maybe to Mexico," Jim suggested as Anna and he went into the courtroom to hear AJ's trial. "Or sank at sea."

"I just hope, for Sunset Cove's sake, we never see them again." She glanced around the half-full courtroom. "Looks like it'll be a big crowd," she whispered as they took their seats near the front. It wasn't long until the courtroom was filled to overflowing, and, finally, Randall took a seat with AJ. Anna exchanged glances with Clara where she sat in the front row, trying to look hopeful for the outcome but still feeling uneasy. She knew this could go either way.

Jim and Anna took furious notes as AJ was questioned. She was relieved that AJ presented the image of a reformed citizen, ready to come clean about everything. He didn't hesitate to give names and dates and places, including the same suspects that Anna and Jim had been investigating—Calvin Snyder, Clint Collins, Tom Gardner . . . and a number of others.

Jim nudged Anna, nodding victoriously.

"Yes, I'm certain my dad knew who killed Wesley Kempton," AJ answered the prosecutor. "But he never told me."

"Are you saying you don't know the name of Wesley Kempton's murderer?"

"I wrote that in my affidavit," AJ told him. "All I know is that Calvin Snyder wanted my dad to be quiet. My dad said that Wesley Kempton had information that could hurt us."

"Did your dad kill Wesley Kempton?"

"I don't know for sure." AJ looked distraught but sincere. "But I don't believe he did. I wrote this in my affidavit, sir. I believe my dad *knew* who killed Wesley Kempton and that he was murdered because he had that information and someone was worried he would talk. But I don't know that for sure."

The prosecutor continued to question AJ. Sometimes he sounded as if he believed AJ's testimony, but sometimes he challenged his credibility by asking the same questions in different ways. AJ stuck to the same story, and it had the consistent ring of truth to it. Still, it was stressful to see him up there, clearly under duress and occasionally looking close to tears.

Finally, it was Randall's turn to question AJ. He asked him why he got involved with his father as well as his disreputable friends. "You obviously knew they were breaking the law," Randall said. "And yet you went with them. Why was that?"

"I know what I did was wrong *now*," AJ answered. "But I didn't really think it was wrong at the time. At first, it just seemed like fun. Sort of like we were playing a game. I'd take one of the small boats out and pick up or deliver a load and then come back as fast as I could. My dad would say he was proud of me when I made good time. He'd brag about me to his friends. He made me feel like it was all okay. And my dad was really good friends with Mayor Snyder."

"You mean our *previous* mayor," Randall gently corrected.

"Yeah, but he was the mayor then. Plus, my dad was friends with Lieutenant Collins. He would say how these guys were both respectable men. And I'd listen to them talking. They'd get together in our warehouse sometimes for drinks. They'd get to talking, acting like no one had to obey the new law. Like the only reason it got passed was because women got the vote. But they said it would all change the next time it was voted on. In the meantime, they'd make the most of it."

"You mean by selling alcohol?"

"Yeah. They felt it was their right to do that. They'd say that we were free Americans and that we had the right to do what we wanted. I believed them back then. But I've had a lot of time to think about it," AJ's voice cracked with emotion. "Being in jail gives a guy a whole lot of time for that. And I think about those guys who got killed. Including my own dad. And now I realize they were wrong to break the law. I was wrong too." He looked up at the judge. "And I'm sorry."

AJ was excused from the stand, then the two attorneys gave their final statements. Randall's continued to focus on the influence Albert, Calvin, Clint, and several others had wielded over AJ. He held up AJ's sworn affidavit, reminding the court that AJ had fully cooperated with the other ongoing investigations. And then he told of AJ's hope to enlist in the US Army in lieu of prison time.

"Albert Krauss Junior went to jail as a boy, a boy who'd suffered from the bad influences of the men who were supposed to be leaders in our community. Albert Krauss Junior has experienced genuine reform as a result of his incarceration, but now he is a young man with his whole life ahead of him. He deserves a second chance to prove his value to society. And, for that reason, I respectfully request leniency from this court."

Anna wanted to cheer as Randall took his seat next to AJ. Anna couldn't imagine how he could've handled that any better. Hopefully the jury and judge were convinced. The judge announced a short recess and excused the jurors into a private room. A number of people stepped outside as well, but Anna went to sit with Clara, hoping to encourage her. She praised how well AJ had presented his testimony. "I think it will go his way."

Even so, Clara looked close to tears as she nervously twisted her handkerchief between her fingers. "I just don't know . . . just don't know. I sat here wondering how we ever got to such a place. It's all so sad."

"I'm sure it's hard to hear it all coming out." Anna put her arm around Clara's shoulders. "But it's good bringing the truth to light."

"And hopefully the court is sympathetic," Randall said quietly.

Anna glanced around. "Where's Ellen? I thought she was coming today."

"She had planned to come." Clara frowned. "But she changed her mind at the last minute— said it was too stressful."

"Well, that's understandable." Anna gave her a squeeze. "It's enough that you're here, Clara."

"I don't know. I'm afraid I'm barely holding it together," she confided. "But I'm here for my son." She glanced at Randall. "You really think it went well?"

"I do." He sighed. "But you never know . . . not until it's over."

"Let's pray," Anna said suddenly.

"Yes, please, *let's*." Clara eagerly grasped

Anna's hand, and the three of them said a heart-felt prayer for AJ. They were just whispering their amens when the jury returned, and then the judge pounded his gavel, calling the room to order.

Anna held Clara's hand. To her relief, they soon declared that the court wished to exhibit leniency . . . but the rest of the words were lost on Anna, because Clara was hugging her tightly and sobbing. But Anna knew they were tears of joy. And Anna managed to catch the end of the judge's speech. He expected AJ to make good on his promise to enlist in the US Army "as soon as possible."

Although Katy had considered attending AJ's trial, since Clara and Ellen both took the day off, she felt she was needed at the dress shop. She knew she'd hear the whole story later—and she'd promised Clara and Ellen that she'd be praying for AJ during the trial. Clara had been very grateful, but Ellen had seemed almost indifferent. In fact, Katy thought Ellen was more interested in having the day off from school and dressing up in one of their shop's more expensive two-piece dresses. Didn't she understand that AJ might be sentenced to prison for a very long time?

Still, Katy wanted to be understanding. After all, how would it feel to have a brother in trouble with the law? Besides that, she was still grateful to Ellen for the way she'd helped to distract Lawrence Bouchard from his relentless pursuit of Katy. In fact, although she hadn't heard that he'd left town, she hadn't seen Lawrence in days. Neither had her grandmother. Katy really hoped he'd gone home. For his sake as much as for hers.

"Hello?" Clara called from the back door. "I'm back."

"Oh, Clara." Katy laid aside her sewing and hurried to meet her. "How did it go?"

"Perfectly." Clara hugged her. "My son is free. Well, free to enlist in the army. But that's better than prison, isn't it? And Randall is taking care of that right now. We'll put him on the train tomorrow morning."

"Oh, that's wonderful news!"

"And your sweet mother has already been in touch with some army officer friends on the East Coast. Apparently someone pulled some strings to allow AJ to go directly to them." She unbuttoned her coat and looked around. "Where's Ellen? I can't wait to tell her."

"Ellen?" Katy frowned. "She didn't attend the trial?"

"No, she changed her mind. She felt it would be stressful." Clara sighed. "And it was. But I'm glad I went. Isn't Ellen here? I know she was excused from school."

"I haven't seen her since this morning. She borrowed a sample from the shop and left. I assumed she was with you. Do you think she went to school after all?"

Clara laughed. "I hardly think so. Ellen isn't that fond of school." Her smile faded. "I wonder where she could be."

Katy wondered too, but she tried not to show concern. "Well, I'm so happy for AJ. And I'll bet you'll find Ellen at home. Maybe she's fixing dinner."

Clara looked puzzled as she buttoned her coat. "Yes, well, that would be nice."

"A real celebration!" Katy smiled as Clara left, but, as she closed the door, she felt uneasy. If Ellen hadn't attended the trial today, where *was* she?

It was a frantic week. The whole town helped search for Ellen, Anna ran a newspaper story begging people for information or help, and after numerous wild rumors—including speculation that white slavery kidnappers were on the loose—Ellen Krauss reappeared in Sunset Cove on Friday afternoon.

Anna nearly fell out of her chair to see Ellen casually strolling down Main Street—with Lawrence Bouchard by her side! What on earth was going on? Anna leaped to her feet and actually used the secret backdoor exit to pop out on the street, where she proceeded to confront the pair. "Where have you been?"

"On our honeymoon." Ellen held out her left hand to display a sparkling ring. "We got married."

Anna speechlessly stared at the couple. She'd spent most of the week helping and consoling poor Clara. Not only had her son been shipped off to the East Coast to join the army, her daughter had mysteriously disappeared as well! The poor woman was beside herself. And Ellen acted as if nothing was wrong?

"I am now *Mrs. Lawrence Bouchard.*" Ellen's smile was triumphant. "We eloped."

"Why didn't you tell someone?" Anna demanded.

"We didn't want anyone to attempt to prevent us," Ellen answered.

Anna was too angry to respond.

"Aren't you going to congratulate us?" Ellen asked.

"Do you even want to know what happened with your brother?"

Ellen shrugged. "I suppose he got what he deserved."

At the moment, Anna wished Ellen would get what *she* deserved. Instead of saying this, she turned to Lawrence. "I suppose you think that was a respectable way to start off your marriage? To run off like that, without even speaking to Ellen's mother?"

"We're on our way to tell Mama now," Ellen

said casually. "I assume she's at the dress shop."

"Well, you assumed wrong," Anna declared. "She's been too worried and upset to work at all. Your mother is at home. Grieving for the loss of her only daughter."

"Oh, well, I'll just go find her, then." Ellen smiled brightly.

"Good day," Lawrence told Anna in a stony tone.

Anna shook her head with confused frustration. On one hand, she wanted to shake both of them— *really hard.* But, on the other hand, she was grateful. Ellen was unharmed. And, thankfully, it was not *her* daughter married to Lawrence Bouchard. That was something!

Anna paused in front of the newspaper office, wondering how Katy would receive this news. Like everyone else, Katy had been worried sick about Ellen. She'd even bought into the silly rumor that evil criminals roamed the coastline, ready to kidnap pretty American girls to enslave in the Orient. Anna had told her that was preposterous . . . but she'd also made Katy promise to take care coming home from work after dark.

But Anna had another concern as she marched down Main Street bareheaded and coatless. How would Katy feel to hear that Lawrence Bouchard had married her best friend? It had only been a few weeks ago that he'd been smitten with Katy.

Hadn't he purchased that very ring for her? Hopefully Katy wouldn't be hurt or jealous . . . or sorry she'd let him go. Anna certainly wasn't!

She stepped into the showroom of Kathleen's, shivering as she looked around, and finally spied her daughter artfully arranging an outfit on a mannequin in a corner. "Katy." Anna approached her. "I need to tell you something."

"Is something wrong, Mother?"

"Not exactly wrong." She nodded toward the back room. "Let's talk in private." Once they were back there with Lucille—Katy excused the other two seamstresses for a break—Anna told them both the news. "Ellen is back in Sunset Cove."

"Oh, thank goodness she's safe!" Lucille exclaimed. "That's wonderful news."

"Where has she been this whole time?" Katy asked with wide eyes.

"On her honeymoon. She eloped." Anna waited for their reaction.

"Good grief!" Lucille dropped her shears. "Who did she marry?"

"Lawrence Bouchard." Anna watched Katy closely.

"I suppose I'm not terribly surprised." Katy shook her head. "And yet still completely shocked that they'd put Clara through this. And disappointed."

"Why didn't they inform anyone?" Lucille

430

scowled. "Ellen never said a word about this! And that boy was a guest in my home! Why didn't they tell us?"

"Ellen thought someone might try to stop them." Anna turned back to Katy. "Do you mind, dear?"

"Do I *mind?*" Katy sounded indignant. "I can't believe that I thought Ellen was my best friend. And she did *that?*"

"Did you still care for Lawrence Bouchard?" Anna felt sick inside.

"No, of course not! I can't stand Lawrence Bouchard. I had hoped he'd left town for good. But I thought Ellen was my friend. I can't believe she never told me she was going to elope. She never told her mother. I'm furious at her." She turned to Lucille. "I think we should fire her."

"Well . . . It's something we can discuss." Lucille looked uneasy. "But maybe we should talk to her first."

"I don't want to talk to her," Katy declared. "I'm too angry to talk to her. She's a selfish, rude girl—and a little fool to marry Lawrence Bouchard. I really thought she was smarter than that. And she better bring that sample dress back. It was only a loan!"

Anna suddenly hugged Katy. "Oh, how I love you, dear daughter."

"What? What's that all about?" Katy blinked as Anna released her.

"I'm just so glad you're such a sensible girl." Anna patted Katy's cheek. "I don't know why I ever questioned you."

Katy smiled and then sighed. "Well, the truth is, I almost did fall for Lawrence Bouchard myself. When we were in San Francisco, I thought he was something special. But when I got to know him better, I realized it was a delusion. Thankfully, I returned to my senses."

"Well, perhaps he's not a delusion for Ellen," Lucille slowly folded a piece of fabric. "Perhaps he's just what she needed." She shook her head. "We can only hope so."

As Anna walked back to the newspaper office, she wondered how Clara would take this news. Naturally, she'd be thrilled to learn her daughter was alive. But, like the McDowell women, she'd probably be hurt over Ellen's deceit. Still, if Ellen and Lawrence truly loved each other . . . perhaps it would work out. And, as Anna went to her office, she realized that what Ellen had done was not much different than what Anna had when she was the same age. Except that Anna had made no secret of it. And, as she put a piece of paper in her typewriter, she decided she would make no secret of Ellen's elopement either. The town deserved to know the truth.

CHAPTER 34

Life in Sunset Cove settled down considerably in the next couple of months. On a personal level, Anna felt relieved, but as a newspaperwoman, she missed some of the intrigue and excitement that had produced so much gripping copy. However, she was content to see the newspaper devoting more space to everyday stories and local happenings. And, of course, there was always the war in Europe to provide a sensational headline from time to time. Unfortunately, it only seemed to be getting worse over there, and Anna was convinced the United States would soon join the Allied Forces. How could they not?

Clara had recovered from the news that Ellen had eloped with Lawrence Bouchard, but, when her new son-in-law offered to take over the fishing business for her, Clara had the sensibility to decline. Instead, she sold the whole works in early March, then invested her capital in the thriving dress shop and the refurbished apartment above, which she now inhabited. Although Randall was still of interest to her, and the two were often seen together socially, Clara seemed to be enjoying her newfound independence, something she had often thanked Anna for exemplifying.

Oddly enough, Anna felt less and less content with her own independent state of affairs. She didn't particularly like the thought of growing old alone. And, although Daniel Hollister hadn't accompanied his father back to Boston like she'd anticipated he would, Anna doubted that he'd continue practicing medicine in Sunset Cove. Not for long anyway. His father's offer of grooming Daniel to be chief of staff in the prestigious East Coast hospital had to feel like the highlight of his career. How could Daniel resist? And Anna knew there was a time limit on that offer. If Daniel didn't accept before his father's retirement in June, it would be awarded to someone else. Because of that, Anna had been distancing herself from the good doctor this spring. Protecting her heart from the inevitable.

Anna suspected that Lucille had been missing the elder doctor's attentions after he left Sunset Cove in late February. Mac, on the other hand, had been greatly relieved that his competition was gone. But his nose was still a bit out of joint. And even though Mac and Lucille had shared some intimate dinners these past couple of weeks, things hadn't flowed completely smoothly. Anna tried not to be overly amused at her parents' clumsy attempts to recreate a romantic relationship. After all, who was she to judge?

She looked up at the clock. It was only mid-afternoon, but she decided to go home early today. All week long, they'd all been anxiously watching the wire for news of the war. On Monday, President Wilson had asked a special joint session of congress for a declaration against the German Empire, but, so far, it hadn't happened. Anna wondered if it ever would. She was just reaching for her hat when Jim cracked open her door.

"Any news from Washington?" she asked eagerly.

"No, nothing yet. Are you busy?"

"Not particularly." She hung her hat back on the hook. "What do you need?"

"I, uh, I just wanted to talk to you about something else. But, if you need to go, it can wait." Jim looked different, as if he were nervous. Was this bad news? Hopefully he wasn't going to quit. Anna had been relying on him more than ever these past few months. And it had been nice.

Anna sat back down on her chair. "I'm all ears, Jim."

"Okay then." He remained standing. "Now, it's not that I'm asking your permission, Anna, but I would like to inform you that I, uh, I have an interest in your daughter."

Anna concealed her surprise. After all, Jim was a good man, but wasn't he far too old for Katy? Was he saying what she thought he was saying?

"An interest? What sort of interest?" She leaned back in her chair, bracing herself for whatever it was he planned to drop on her.

"But, first of all, I need to come clean on something." Now he sat down.

"What?" Anna sat up straighter, fingers tight around a pencil. She knew that Jim and Katy were friends, but had she missed something?

"I've been deceptive about my age."

"What do you mean?" She rolled the pencil back and forth over the desk pad, waiting.

"You see, when Mac hired me, I presented myself as being older." His smile looked almost sheepish. "I knew he wouldn't think I was old enough to have adequate experience, and I really wanted the job. But I believe I proved myself to him. Proved that you don't have to be old to be a good reporter."

She bristled slightly. Was he insinuating *she* was old? *Was* she old? "I suppose that's true, although you must admit that experience does help with one's ability to write well."

"Yes, of course." He nodded. "But *you* must admit that Katy writes quite well for her young age. And Mac got you started even younger."

"Yes, but she still has room for improvement, and it took me years to truly hone the craft."

"Well, we always have room for improvement."

"Yes, yes. But back to your age, Jim. I assumed you were around my age . . . perhaps a bit younger." She peered curiously at him. "How old *are* you?"

"I'm twenty-four."

"Twenty-four?" She suddenly felt embarrassed to remember how she'd considered him a possible romantic interest at one time—*he was ten years her junior!*

"So the cat's out of the bag," he said. "Hopefully you won't fire me."

She released the pencil. "No, of course not. But I'll bet Mac will be surprised."

"I wonder what he'd say if he knew I was, uh, interested in his granddaughter. I know how protective he is of Katy. At one point, I thought he was going to thrash Lawrence Bouchard with his cane."

"Well, he wasn't overly fond of him. And even less so after Ellen eloped with him, although I suspect he was relieved that it hadn't been Katy. Still, he thinks Lawrence is a deceitful cad."

"I know." Jim frowned. "That's why I want to be on the level with my intentions, Anna."

"So, what exactly are your intentions?"

"Well, I suppose I'd like to court her. And I know it probably sounds presumptuous, but I think I'd like to marry her . . . *someday.*"

"Does Katy know about any of this?"

"She knows that I'm her friend. And she always seems happy to see me."

"But you're *only* friends?"

He nodded vigorously. "I give you my word. And the reason I'm telling you now is because I hope that might change. I'd like it to change." He smiled brightly. "But, for now, we are simply friends."

Anna felt relieved. Perhaps she hadn't missed signals after all. She and Katy had been enjoying a close relationship of late. She didn't want to think her daughter was keeping secrets again. "You do realize that Katy is a very independent young woman? And that she is quite dedicated to her dress shop business?"

"I'm well aware of those things. I find them rather charming."

"And did you know that she hopes to one day go to Paris with Lucille?"

His smile faded. "I do know about that. I don't think it could happen anytime soon, not with the war going on." He brightened. "But, perhaps when the war is over, I could take Katy over there. I mean, if we were married. Perhaps on a honeymoon."

Anna thought that was overly optimistic but kept her opinion to herself. "So you wouldn't be opposed to having an independently-minded wife with her own interests and pursuits, Jim?"

"Not if it was Katy."

Anna smiled to imagine her daughter in a wife's role. "Katy might never be the sort of woman to welcome you home with a lovely dinner on the table, you know. More likely, she'd meet you with a paintbrush in hand or a new idea for a dress design."

He grinned. "I can imagine."

She held up her hands. "Well, what can I say? What are you asking me for? My blessing? Because Katy makes up her own mind. If she—"

"I know all that, Anna. I simply wanted to lay my cards on the table."

"And you have done so." Anna nodded firmly.

"I'm not saying anything will come of it. I realize Katy has the final say and that she's turned down other opportunities. I'm not a fool."

"I know you're not." Anna smiled. "The truth is, I think you'd be a good match for her. You know that she's an independent young woman and yet you understand and respect her."

"I've had some experience in working for an independent woman." He chuckled.

"Speaking of work, don't we have a newspaper to finish up?" She held up the copy she'd just gone over. "Can you give this to Leroy for me? I want to go home early tonight."

"Hopefully not because of what I just said." He looked concerned.

"No. I want to go home because it's a lovely spring day out there, and I'd like to take a walk on the beach before dinner."

"Oh, good." He paused by the door. "And you won't mention any of this to Katy, will you?"

"Not if you don't want me to."

"No, please don't. It's not like I want to rush into this. I just wanted to make sure you were aware . . . in case things ever move more quickly than I expect. But, honestly, in the meantime, I want to just enjoy being around Katy. Without pressure on either side."

"That sounds like a good plan." She reached for her hat again. "And, although you didn't ask for it, I give you my blessing." She smiled as they exited her office. "Have a good weekend, Jim."

As she walked through the newspaper office, she could hear excited voices over by the telegraph machine.

"What's going on?" she asked.

"This just came over the wire." Ed held up a long piece of tape. "Wilson has officially declared war on Germany."

Anna read the announcement without much surprise. "Well, we all knew it was coming. They've been in congress all week." She turned to Jim. "Can you rearrange the front page to accommodate this?"

"Consider it done." He eagerly took the strip of paper from her.

"I can stay to help if you—"

"No." He shook his head. "I've got this. You were going to take a walk on the beach, remember?"

She simply nodded. "Yes, yes . . . I remember."

She recalled her earlier enthusiasm about having a nice beach walk in the sunshine, but, as she walked through town, she felt weary . . . and old. She could pretend it was related to the declaration of war just made, but she'd been expecting that all week. It had been inevitable. As hard as it was to think of the US entering this war, it was also something of a relief. Perhaps it would help lead the rest of the world to peace. At least, that was what many were claiming. And, to be fair, it wasn't the thought of war that made her feel worn out and weary.

As unflattering as it was to admit this—and she'd only admit it to herself—she felt old as a result of Jim's confession regarding his age. It had shocked her to learn he was ten years younger than she . . . and interested in her daughter! Quite naturally, she felt older. She *was* older. And she couldn't blame that on the war.

As Anna walked past the hardware store, she caught her reflection in the gleaming window. The serious winter suit she'd worn to work wasn't helping a bit. She paused on the sidewalk, staring at the dull tan skirt and shapeless jacket. Katy was always quick to point out how much she hated this particular work ensemble and had even offered to donate it to the poor more than once. But Anna had dressed quickly this morning, focused on the day ahead. She'd not cared about her appearance. But now she felt old and drab—

like the bloom was definitely off the rose. And yet, it was springtime, and the April sun was shining with warmth and cheer and hope. Perhaps it was not too late for her. And not too late for a stroll on the beach. That might help her outlook.

Just the same, Anna wasn't eager to be observed on the street looking this forlorn. So she hurried home. After informing Mac about the declaration of war and having a brief discussion over this, she excused herself. "I want to take a little walk on the beach. To sort of clear my head."

"Good for you. And I'll be having dinner at Lucille's tonight," Mac said as she stood. "Katy called home that she has her own plans, so I gave Mickey and Bernice the night off. I hope you don't mind."

"Not at all. Have a fun evening, Mac." Anna went to her room, sat down in the chair by the window, and let out a long sigh. Now she didn't only feel old, she felt lonely as well. Mac had Lucille. Katy had Jim . . . if she liked. Clara had Randall. Even Bernice and Mickey had each other.

But who did Anna have?

Still, she was determined not to give in to such gloomy thoughts. She was going to fight this. She ripped off the overly warm woolen suit, throwing it into an ugly, tan heap on the floor, and then, going through her closet, she selected a dress that

Katy had made for her last summer. Back when Anna had felt so much younger. Not so very long ago.

She pulled the lightweight cotton dress over her head. The soft fabric felt cool against her skin, and, as she fastened the pearly buttons, she knew the aqua-blue shade went well with her eyes. And, when she looked in the mirror, she couldn't deny that she suddenly did feel younger. Perhaps Katy was better at all this than Anna gave her credit for. Maybe it was time to consult with Katy on a regular basis.

Seeing that the severe bun she'd worn to work was now disarranged, Anna unpinned and shook her curls loose over her shoulders, then tied them away from her face with a blue satin ribbon. She smiled at her reflection. She wasn't old! And now she was going to stroll the beach like a carefree young girl. She was going to pray for those American soldiers, including young AJ, who would soon be shipped overseas to fight in this gruesome war. She knew enough about the conflict to understand how inhumane and horrible it already was . . . and likely to get worse before it ended. But, hopefully, that would be sooner now that Americans were involved.

As her bare feet hit the warm sand, she chided herself for her recent self-pity session. Really, what business did she have being so full of woe when other people in the world had such serious and life-threatening problems? And, as far as her friends and family, all who seemed to have the promise of romance in their lives . . . Well, she was genuinely happy for them! After about an hour of walking alongside the edge of the water, Anna felt as if her youth and energy had fully returned to her. In spite of the war news, she felt hopeful. Things were bound to get better.

As she neared the house's beach stairs, she noticed another lone figure walking on the beach toward her. For a moment, she felt concerned, remembering how, not too long ago, they'd all been on their guard against the possibility of rumrunners and criminals along their coastline. But lately, that had all quieted down. Still, she knew it was wise to exercise caution. The man raised a hand to wave . . . probably someone just out to enjoy the spring sunshine like she was doing. But, as she got closer, she recognized the figure. It was Dr. Daniel Hollister. And so she called out a greeting, and he hurried over to meet her.

"Mac told me you were out here." He studied her, shielding his eyes from the sun with his hand to see her even better.

"Just enjoying this gorgeous day." She said lightly. "You never know what it'll be like tomorrow."

He pointed to the horizon, where a band of

clouds were gathered. "Looks like we might have rain in store. But it should make for a pretty sunset this evening."

She nodded. "I'm sure you're right." She tried not to remember that other sunset . . . or the hope it had given her.

"Have I intruded upon your walk?"

"Not at all. I was actually just going in." She continued toward the stairs, and he fell into step.

"Mac told me about the declaration of war. Pretty big news. I'm surprised you're not at the newspaper getting the big story out, working late into the night."

"Jim is covering it." She smiled at him. "After all, I'm not married to my job."

"I'm not either, Anna."

"Oh?" She turned to peer at him. "You mean, you're not married to your job here in Sunset Cove. So, does that mean you've decided to go to Boston for the chief of staff—"

"No, Anna." He shook his head. "I turned that down. Wrote my father a firmly worded letter just this week, in fact."

"You did?" She stared at him in wonder.

"What I meant is that I don't care to be married to my job. Not if it was in Boston . . . or here in Sunset Cove. I don't think it's good for one to be married to a job. Even if he's a physician . . . or she's a newspaper editor."

"You don't?" She continued to look at him,

grasping the handrail and feeling slightly lost in his gaze and pleasantly light-headed.

"I think it's possible to love one's profession . . . and still have time for other pursuits as well. In fact, I think it's rather healthy."

"Is that your professional opinion?" she said with a slight teasing tone.

"Professional and personal."

"Well, the truth is that I feel the same about running the newspaper," she said eagerly. "I'm trying to make some changes too. I'm learning to delegate more, and I've given Jim more responsibilities."

"Good for you." Daniel reached for her hands. "Maybe we can make these changes together, Anna. I can help you . . . and you can help me."

She silently nodded, and, as a breeze rippled in off the ocean, she could tell the weather was about to change . . . and she knew the country was about to change. But she also knew that some changes were for the best.

And then Daniel leaned down to kiss her. And, as she kissed him back, she no longer felt old at all . . . or lonely.